KEEPERS OF A BROKEN LAND
BOOK THREE

EMPIRE BREAKER

MARIE BILODEAU

Cover Art by Simon Carr

Cover Design by Deranged Doctor Design

Map by Kerri Elizabeth Gerow

Proofreading by Erica Ball

ACKNOWLEDGMENTS

While writing this trilogy, a continuation of my first ever published series, *Heirs of a Broken Land,* I couldn't help but think about my writing career and all the people who shored me up through it. Naming them all would double the already great number of pages of this book, but I wanted to at least name a few. Nicole Lavigne, whose constant enthusiasm for my writing, and her own personal strength and creativity, are an endless source of inspiration. Frank Yao, who sprinkles lovely words about my writings just as I need to see them (he always knows). Luis M. Rivas, who sent wonderful letters that inspire me to this day.

And so many others. When I look back at the nearly twenty years of my writing career, I know without a doubt that I'm here because of all the support, cheering on, and kind words along the way. Thank you all so much.

This trilogy, my entire career, would not exist without you.

As always, a big thanks to my family. I am ever amazed that their support has never wavered nor diminished over the years: Suzanne Desjardins, Kerri Elizabeth Gerow, Jessica Torrance, Jean-François Bilodeau, George Bilodeau, Ada Bilodeau, Karen and Dave Henderson, and Kathy and Martin Gallant.

I'd be remised not to thank Lydia M. Hawke, who put up with so much whining as I struggled with this book, rewriting it several times, usually while on writing retreats with her. Her brain and kindness helped make this possible. Thank you, Lydia!

Thanks to my beta readers: Nicole Lavigne, Lina El-Samrout, and Christina Yother.

Thank you all. Seriously. Writing this trilogy was a dream come true and also a terribly intimidating nightmare as I wanted to live up to the first trilogy that led me to meeting so many of you. I'm glad your love of the first trilogy put this pressure on me, because I am so very proud of these books.

Readers make all the difference. Thank you for being an important part of my life.

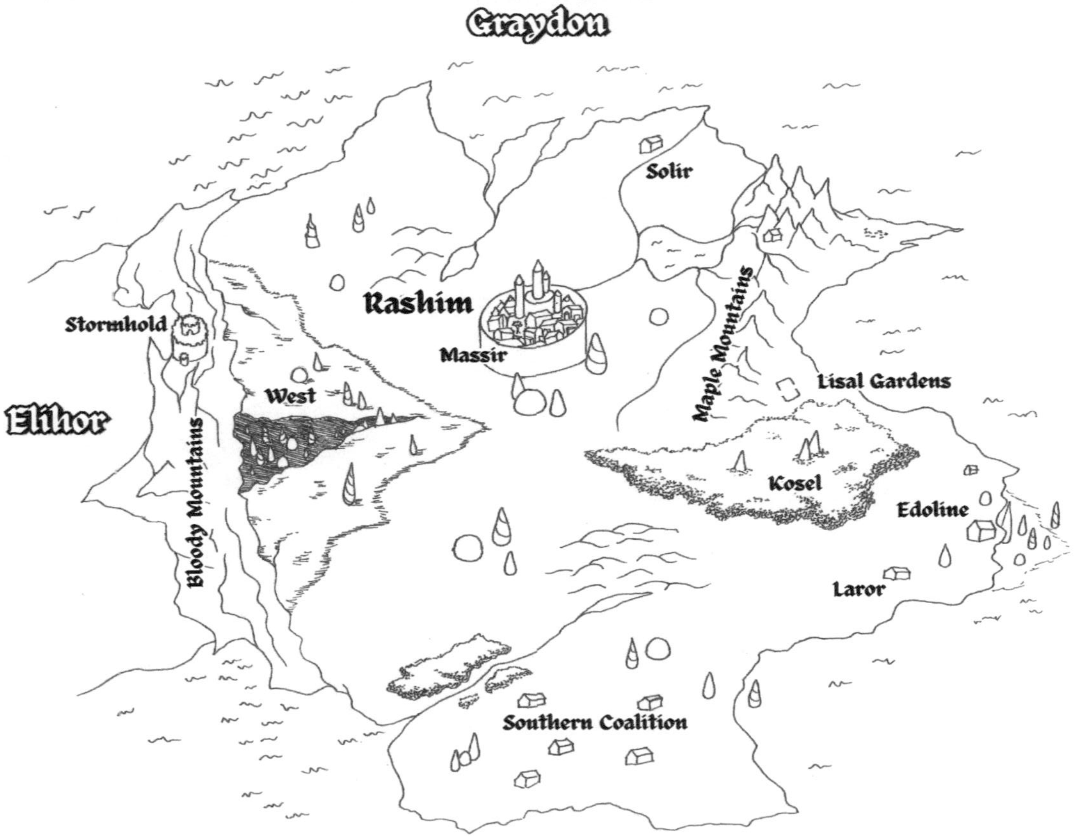

Graydon

Elhor

Rashim

Solir

Massir

Lisal Gardens

Maple Mountains

Kosel

Edoline

Laror

Southern Coalition

West

Bloody Mountains

Stormhold

A ripple in the distant horizon, where water met sky, moonlight and stars dancing on the vast expanse. Crimson Circle Elite Jana stared, not certain anything had actually moved, wondering if her bored mind had simply conjured up something, anything, to make the posting at the Heir of Elihor's home village more interesting.

"Should be some good fishing tomorrow," Dockmaster Haller said beside her, in a bid to start a conversation. She ignored him. She was here in case another monster attacked from beneath the waters, which hadn't happened since Rojon Kolder had left. But she did her duty, waiting for the final fishing boats to make dock, catching the first nightly wave of luminescent shrimp—a delicacy in Elihor.

Behind her, the village was still full of life, people sharing meals and trading stories, fighting against the encroaching darkness with friendship and wine. She had joined them a few times, but not this night, her instincts on high alert for reasons she had yet to determine. She squinted her eyes, tracking the reflected stars to find movement not created by the few scattered fishing boats.

"Good to see things get back to normal," the dockmaster continued, to no reply.

Normal? Boring was his normal. Magic was hers, and there, where the horizon cut the gray sky, she could sense… something. The wind shifted, and tasted wrong. Even the dockmaster seemed to sense it, taking a step back from the water.

Jana focused, took a deep breath, centered herself as best she could. She'd promised the heir she'd protect his village and, despite wishing she was anywhere but here, she intended to keep her word.

The water churned, dragging fishing boats further out to sea as roaring water engulfed screams, beyond the distant island belt.

Dockmaster Haller shouted, face turning red, struggling to be heard over the thundering sea. A bell clanged, sound muffled, followed by another, larger bell as the village's new alert system struggled to be heard. Crimson Circle Elite Jana ignored the shouting people and the bells, walking toward the water, instead.

Toward the churning sea.

The tethered wooden skiffs rocked from side to side, the bottom of her robe and cloak growing heavy, seeped with water as the sea smothered the shore. The docks splintered as something hit them. *No.* As something *pushed them up.*

Jana froze, forgetting her training, watching one of the unoccupied boats jerk up, wood breaking, pierced through. The sea grew more frantic, attacking the shore instead of retreating. Another ship exploded upward, cut through by a long, lean, tall rock.

Jana stepped back, slipping on seaweed gathering at her feet, water lashing at her face. Iron and salt filled her mouth, and she spit as she fought to find her footing again on the treacherous pier as another mountainous stone erupted near her, big and round, pushing thick sediment into Jana, threatening to swallow her.

The earth trembled and she went down again, one leg swallowed by invading sand, unable to pull herself up. Panicking, she tried to intone the familiar spells that might save her, or at least buy her time to escape. Water rushed into her, choking her, mocking her inability to break free.

She struggled up, tangled in her crimson cloak, unable to find life-saving purchase. Then strong arms pulled her to air.

"Come on," the dockmaster screamed, dragging her up the shore as she coughed sand and salt, toward the village, to higher ground away from the sea.

The world felt like it would consume them with water, or stone, or the *growling* that attacked from every corner, sound smothering out logical thought, leaving behind only panic.

The earth cracked, throwing them both to the ground. More villagers pulled them up. Instead of running away, most had run toward the shore. To witness this fresh calamity. To help. To not let more of their people perish, refusing to stand by helplessly this time.

The winds shifted, sucked toward the sea, toward the fresh stones erupting from it, so strong that even Jana's drenched cloak billowed with them, droplets of water turning to sprays.

The ground cracked again, and Jana managed to remain standing. Droplets of cold water mixed with dust spattered the village, swallowing the world and sight... and then, silence.

Jana's lungs burned as she waited for the dust to dissipate, her own uneven breath filling her skull, the silence crushing. A few people coughed on the dust, water trickled, and slowly the dust dissipated... leaving Jana speechless.

Where the shoreline filled with fishing boats had stretched but moments before stood round stone and glass buildings, clung to by seaweed and plankton, stone spires cutting the night sky like silent guardians, the stench of death so powerful a few people retched.

"What is that, Crimson Circle Elite?" someone asked, and she realized people clustered near her, as though expecting her to protect them. She glanced across the once shoreline and summoned the Sight. And saw only red, her beautiful dark strands of magic vanishing into the ground, devoured by the ancient risen stones.

The power of Elihor was vanishing, just like Graydon's powers. Larkhold's magic had been guzzled by the newly risen city, spreading as far up and down the shore as Jana could see, as far away as Graydon itself, past the Bloody Mountains, still hidden by thick dust.

Jana released the Sight, blocked out her magic, and gulped in deep breaths, unsteady on her feet even as the villagers grew silent, understanding that she had no answers to give them.

The shoreline, beautiful gardens leading to jagged cliffs, stretched before King Jayden of Edoline as he strolled away the day's worries. Clothed in greens and browns, the colors of his kingdom, a few Protectors of Edoline trailed him—an annoying, unnecessary act in his small kingdom, and Jayden did his best to ignore them. Behind them, even more annoying, were the two Crimson Circle witches, both currently powerless, but both intent on following their last command received from Shirina.

Protect the heirs of Graydon.

That usually just meant his sister Cassara, the only one who'd wielded Graydon's powers, but Shirina's orders meant all of them, including his visiting young niece and nephew, tucked safely in bed. They'd heard of rebellion in Massir. Of his sister and niece missing.

Then the magic of Graydon had vanished, and all updates had stopped, days ago. And so he walked, in the encroaching dark, trying to shed the day's worries so that he could be rested in the morning to hear the small but still important demands of his court. There was little he could do for his sister, save keep her youngest children safe.

His mind wandered to the scars he could still see on his land, despite years of growth—memories clinging to how it was, eyes forced to see how his land was made to be—the sight impossible to shrug off as the familiar fear for his family clouded his mind. The old hedge that had burned in dark fires, killing his older sister as she fought to save her kingdom. As he failed to save her.

The twenty-year-old purple oak tree growing where he'd planted it, where the Seal that had tethered Siabala to his soul had broken free. Without the hedges which had been destroyed in Siabala's final attack, the once separated courtyards now stood open for all to see and enjoy, though few ever did.

Clasping his hands tightly behind him, Jayden fought against the dizzying spiral of memories and focused on the sound of the sea crashing against the cliffs. Strong, steady, constant.

He took a deep breath, then frowned. The air smelled… tangy?

He turned to his lieutenant. "Darmir, do you—" Before

he could finish, the earth buckled, throwing him to his knees.

Darmir appeared at his side, helping him up, the other Protector looking around, as on edge as the two Crimson Circles.

Jayden ignored them all and turned toward the water. The surf, that crashing background to most of his life, sounded *wrong*. Broken. Angry. He'd lived his entire life with the sound. He knew it as well as he knew the sound of his frightened breaths.

"We must get you to safety, Your Majesty."

"No, wait," Jayden said softly, and the lieutenant let go of him. Captain Orly, once a general in the Southern Coalition who'd supported the young king twenty years ago, arrived with four more Protectors.

"Ensure my niece and nephew are safe," Jayden ordered. Orly nodded, the old face comfortable and familiar to the young king.

"Already done, Your Majesty."

Since his family had been slaughtered in this very mansion, and he'd been kidnapped by Siabala, Jayden had ensured more protections existed within the home, including safe rooms, where his niece and nephew would now wait.

Jayden crossed the Courtyard of Stars, grateful for the clear, bright night even as he ignored the late blooming flowers and evergreens, and headed to the cliffside, coming to a dead stop. His mind struggled to grasp the scene before him. The great weeping willow which had swept over the edge since he was a child was gone. As was most of the final, broken courtyard.

The ground cracked again.

This time, Darmir and Orly didn't wait for their king's permission. They grabbed him and pulled him back, his feet matching their strides as they ran toward the mansion. The sea churned, broiled angrily, spurting out a tangy mist in the air. Jayden could barely breathe as air was sucked back, eyes watering at a sudden warmth. The land buckled, all three thrown to the ground in the shadow of the mansion. Windows shattered, shards of glass showering them. His Protectors covered him, their armor seeing them safe from the dangerous shower. Blood dribbled where a shard cut Jayden's arm.

The sea roared and the ground buttressing the mansion from the water tumbled into the angry mass, taking part of the Courtyard of Travelers with it, the purple oak tree shifting as though something dark pushed it... and then everything grew quiet, eerily different from the constant powerful waves of his childhood.

Too calm. Too quiet.

Jayden turned to examine the new demarcation of his land, and his breath caught in his throat.

The purple oak tree, marking where Siabala had once been tethered, hung on the edge of a new structure, taller than the mansion, at least twenty square meters of his kingdom devoured by it. He examined the ground, felt a familiar ache in his chest turn into numbness which spread across his entire body and soul.

"Get my niece and nephew out of the mansion," Jayden said calmly. The captain barked orders, and Protectors ran to get them out.

Beneath his kingdom, where the sea once stood, spread round structures and spires made of sturdy stone, some with glass reflecting the moonlight. Kilometers of the sea had vanished, leaving the once coastal kingdom stranded on unfamiliar land. Where the courtyard had stood, a tower now rose, its end a loop, its metal partly melted.

The hook that held Siabala. Hidden beneath the ground, chains broken twenty years ago. Now it stood above him, freed from the ground. Freed from his kingdom.

Carefully, Jayden peered over the edge of the cliff.

Captain Orly stayed close, intending to pull him out should he fall. Jayden wasn't sure that mattered as he looked down at the façade of the grand castle that hid just beneath his land, its mighty tower now above it. He recognized the architecture of the risen city. From left to right he looked, and it was as though it surrounded all of Graydon.

"We must get to the village and start evacuating it," he said, voice hollow in his ears, mind and heart unable to grasp how deep the devastation might spread. Avarielle had told him about all the caves she'd found beneath Graydon when she'd hunted Eloms in the East—the same monsters that had hidden in caves beneath his kingdom before they'd attacked twenty years ago. But never once had he imagined that an entire kingdom hid beneath his land.

"Let's go," Jayden said, walking toward his niece and nephew, eyes wide as they looked at the destruction of Edoline. He had to keep them safe. He had no idea what had happened to his sister. Or to Massir. That kingdom lay closer to the Bloody Mountains.

He looked toward it, though he knew he wouldn't be able to see it from here. And his breath caught in his throat again. Over the trees of Kosel, past their swaying tips, smoke drifted upward, clearing to reveal stone structures made of multi-colored glass, casually holding the starlight captive.

Jayden Edoline let the numbness engulf his fear. And he focused on next steps: first, to make sure the village and his people were safe, if such a thing were possible.

In the morning, a new day would rise on this new world, and he feared nowhere would ever be safe again.

The West didn't shake so much as rumble, the moon shifting on the sands like someone sifted flour.

"Move," Trevon shouted, pushing the adepts away from the old city, away from the edge of it. He'd seen this before. Had felt his land shift and fall beneath him. The beautiful sands of his life filtering away, to be replaced by ancient ruins.

"What's happening?" One of Shirina's blue cloaks asked.

"Just move," he repeated, pulling her along.

The ground roared, dust and sand exploding upward, sliced by stone towers, cutting tents to ribbons. His people didn't wait for him to tell them to run, abandoning possessions and homes as the ground quaked and shifted. The ridge at the edge of his beloved land expanded outward, then crumbled. A few people screamed as they toppled over the edge. Trevon dragged the blue cloak, who kept staring back, mouthing spells that would find no fuel.

And then, as quickly as it happened, it ended. Three new towers cast gloomy shadows around them, and more of the ancient city had been revealed. Sand still tumbled down, like a waterfall that threatened to empty the West of sand, though Trevon knew that wasn't possible. Sand was not as fickle as water and did not slither away as easily.

"Is everyone—" Before he could finish, the north cracked, so loudly that it echoed in Trevon's bones. Feeling slow, he turned as parts of the Bloody Mountains, to the north of Stormhold, cracked as though a piece had been sheered clean. The ground trembled as a piece of the mountain range silently collapsed, a hollow at its center. A few people gasped. Thunder slammed the silence away, followed by dust, exploding outward from the roots of the freshly collapsed mountain.

"Sandstorm!" Trevon said, using familiar words to spur

his people into action. They moved quickly to take cover, and Trevon herded several witches into his home, battening it down.

Small rocks and sand slammed into his stone home.

"It sounds like rain," one of the younger witches said, eyes wide.

Rains of blood, Trevon thought, knowing it pointed to Siabala's growing strength.

And my people will once again pay the price. More would lose their lives. More of their land would vanish. And, like Avarielle Grayloft, they would all be killed, one by one, by the destructive reach of Siabala.

Elder Quilsam looked over the city of Massir, capital of the Kingdom of Rashim, the large sprawling city leading to farms and smaller villages. He could hear screams below, but he simply stood and watched, uncertain what to do.

His magic was gone. He couldn't reach his adepts. Beneath him, another section of Massir had collapsed in, this time spires and round structures replacing them. More strange structures had skewered some of the farmlands below. If he squinted, he could see smoke and strange reflected glass throughout the land, as far as his tired eyes could see.

Like a disease spreading over Graydon.

His magic was gone. He couldn't see the threads of

power that impacted the land, but he could imagine the burning red spreading over Graydon. Except in Massir, where the last thing he'd seen with the Sight was it being pulled away from the city.

The land shook, and he turned, slowly, not really wanting to see. The Bloody Mountains had collapsed in the center, a gateway to his beloved Elihor, dust rippling over the West, toward Massir. It didn't overtake Massir, but he could taste it with every breath and covered his mouth with his cloak as a precaution.

And he waited, looking west. Toward Elihor, toward his home, which he could not see, not with the dust and lack of magic.

But he waited, knowing the dust would clear, understanding how terribly he'd miscalculated, and that he could not look away from his beloved Elihor, the sight of her destruction his penance.

When the dust finally cleared, the Elder's hands grew numb as he looked *into* his land, spires and stone structures littering it.

Elihor had not been spared this devastation.

Siabala will destroy all in his path. This time, he hadn't attacked overland. He hadn't turned his people into monsters to attack Graydon. The old god had simply hidden, used his puppets to do his bidding, and destroyed the reputation and power of those who would stand against him.

Cassara Edoline, a rebellion bred to life against her.

Avarielle Grayloft, forced from her home to be more easily killed in this land.

Shirina... *No.*

Elder Quilsam hid his hands in his cloak, bringing them together for warmth and focus.

He hoped he wasn't too late to fix the mistake his pride had helped him commit.

2

Shirina released her staff with shaking hands, struggling to get her breath under control, robes clinging to the layer of sweat covering her body. She'd managed to contain some of Siabala's magic, but it wasn't enough. It would never be enough, the magic flowing across the lands, though now less so from Kosel leading to Massir, the red waves of magic thinned out by her attempts to stop Tally's teleportation spell.

It wasn't enough. It would never be enough, and she'd sacrificed her staff to buy them a day or two. If even that.

She glanced at Cassara, the queen's outline slightly brighter than her surroundings, though it may have been a trick of Shirina's tired eyes. The ground had stopped cracking, they were presumably safe, for now, and Massir glowed in the moonlight, past the farmlands, smoke breaking the shimmering lines of the sprawling city.

Shirina knew exactly what the queen wanted to do.

Her entire stance spoke of resignation, ever since she'd awaited the final blow from the Siabala-possessed Avarielle.

"I would be dishonoring Avarielle," Shirina said softly, evoking the warrior's name like a ward, "if I allowed you to just get yourself killed, Cassara."

Cassara stiffened, glanced at her, then at the staff planted in the forest ground, turned to stone.

"I've managed to capture some of his magic into it," Shirina whispered, not wanting to draw undue attention, though the small forest off the farmlands of Massir seemed deserted of all life. "But I can still see it, from the east, like a slowly approaching wave. We have some time, before…" She trailed off.

"Before Avarielle comes." Cassara finished the thought.

Avarielle.

Siabala.

"Yes," Shirina whispered, the ache of her body almost as cutting as the ache of her soul. The cuts by the silver creature—blood drying on her white robes—and the burns on her hands could not compete with the hollow of her heart.

"We lost, Shirina," Cassara whispered. With effort, Shirina turned to focus on the queen. She was so tired. "We tried our best. We did everything we could. Used all of our magic, all of our strength. And still, it wasn't enough. Tell me that you don't see what I see? Siabala's red magic everywhere, even if you managed to make it thinner here. Elihor's shying away or merging. None of Graydon's light."

"You're using the Sight," Shirina simply said. Another fact to add to her growing understanding of magic, but still, she missed the knowledge necessary to regain it.

"I am," Cassara said. "And it's just enough to show me that there are no strands of magic for me to wield."

Shirina turned back toward the staff. In the final battle with Siabala, Cassara had drawn all of Graydon's magic within her, to separate it from Elihor's and stop Siabala from using the shadow magic.

It had been too much for her, and she'd released it back to recreate the Wall of Loss, without Elihor's magic.

"We're missing something," Shirina mumbled, annoyed with her inability to see what should be so obvious. Annoyed that her usually sharp brain felt so blunted.

"Avarielle," Cassara answered. Shirina's shoulders fell. "We left her, Shirina. She would never have just left us."

Shirina sighed, not out of annoyance, but out of fatigue. Cassara was right. They'd tried everything, and still Siabala had the upper hand. Not with armies, this time, but with coils beneath their very land, traps layered for decades, waiting to ensnare them.

"She wouldn't," Shirina said, turning back to the queen, who stood pale and resolute. "And it would destroy whatever remained of her if she killed you, Cassara." She softened her voice. "And she would have, if not for Kaden."

Cassara's lips grew thinner, her chin fell slightly, tears

refusing to escape. She forced in a shuddering breath, centered herself, and focused back on Shirina, softening.

"Let me see your injuries," the queen whispered.

"I'm fine," Shirina said automatically, but Cassara would not be dissuaded, forcing the sorceress to sit on a tree stump. The world spun and Shirina feared she might pass out, but she managed to recover. Cassara knelt before her and examined her wounds, even if she had nothing to treat them with.

Keeping Cassara busy is good, Shirina's tired mind thought as the dizziness passed. She felt drained, but could at least focus.

"I can't do much for you," Cassara finally admitted. "Just like I can't do much for my people. I don't know what else to do except go to my family and hope I can save them."

"You won't without magic," Shirina said. "You'll just die, and they might have to witness it. That won't help anyone, except you."

"Being dead doesn't sound helpful to me."

Shirina held the queen's eyes and said nothing. A flush slowly crept up Cassara's face, and she doubted it was a hot flash. Cassara was the first to break eye contact.

"If we can figure out how to draw Siabala out of Avarielle," Shirina said, "we may be able to save her."

"We have no magic, as you kindly pointed out."

"No," Shirina said, then she looked toward Massir. "But we know where we might find answers."

Cassara immediately jumped to the same conclusion as Shirina.

"The cave where Tally was?"

Shirina nodded. "The magic of Graydon vanished before they attacked, and we were brought there. Avarielle was also brought there, although indirectly. As was Rojon. It stands to reason that whatever ritual Tally was doing, it began with trapping Graydon's magic, to take down the Wall of Loss."

"And set Siabala free."

"And get him a new body," Shirina said. "Which he couldn't do without Rojon taking an oath with him."

"By killing me," Cassara said. "A descendant of Graydon. They could have taken Altessa, instead." Anger flared across her face. A welcome sight for Shirina—anger was better than resignation.

"Indeed," Shirina said. "We were lucky. In a strange way." She frowned. "A strange conundrum, however. To have a descendant of Elihor kill one of Graydon with the sword forged to kill Elihor herself. The ritual might have been flawed from the start."

"Until Avarielle took the blow," Cassara's eyes widened. "And the magic found her blood?"

"Perhaps," Shirina said, not willing to commit to any one theory, intent on keeping an open mind so she would remain aware of the roads she chose to travel. "Either way, Siabala found his way into Avarielle, instead."

Shirina felt oppressive disappointment in her own abilities, having failed to spot the creeping darkness in the warrior. Some things had been off in hindsight, like Avarielle's healing occurring too quickly, and… Shirina stopped her line of thought. It would help no one to blame herself at this point, least of all Avarielle.

"So we go back there and try to see what Tally would have done?"

Shirina nodded. "It's a long shot. And parts of Massir collapsed, so I'm not sure how useful this will be, or if we'll even get close, but it's honestly all I can think of doing."

Cassara nodded, glanced back toward her city. Her home for the past two decades.

"If we can't figure out anything," she said, "will you let me walk up the winding road to my home?"

"I would be letting you walk to your death, Cassara. You see the magic of Siabala as much as I do. You know he wants your blood. It's safe to say that Avarielle is heading here to claim it."

Shirina hoped she'd pushed Rojon far enough to not be tracked. She assumed, and hoped the assumption wouldn't kill them all, that they'd been tracking Siabala's growing presence in Avarielle and couldn't track Cassara or Rojon. That made sense, at least with what evidence her tired mind conjured.

"I wonder how long," Shirina suddenly asked, "Siabala has had a grip on Avarielle. Did it occur when he returned? When Graysword plunged into her? Or earlier, when she took her oath with him as a child?"

"You mean we might have never known the real

Avarielle?" Cassara's eyes widened, and then her mouth set. "No, that was always her. The kindness and heart. The stubbornness and hope. That was all her, and she wasn't a puppet all this time. Maybe he wanted her to be. Maybe that's why he kept her alive in Siabala's Rage, trying to get his magic into her."

Shirina thought of Avarielle's left arm, and nodded, feeling foolish for having shared such an untested theory with the queen. Cassara noted something on Shirina's face, because she stopped her tirade.

"I know you care for Avarielle, too, and never meant to suggest otherwise," Cassara said. The sarcastic reply about Avarielle being more of a pain than a friend died on the sorceress's lips. It wasn't the same without the warrior to overhear, and grief stabbed her heart at the realization.

This was worse than when she thought she'd died. Then, she'd died fighting. Now… she'd been taken over. If she was still in there, which Shirina desperately hoped and feared, the warrior was helpless. Shirina swallowed hard and shuddered.

"I preferred it when she was dead."

"I know what you mean."

"It might come to that, you know."

Cassara's face twisted with grief, and then her eyes shone more brightly. More resolutely. Ready to do what needed to be done to save her friend. The protected becoming the protector.

"We need magic," Shirina said. "We can't best Avarielle in swordplay, and the chances of sneaking up on her are dim. She'll have Elders with her, and Tally won't let her break free, though I've no doubt that Avarielle is too stubborn to let that witch hold her hostage for too long. But the more blood she claims, the more Siabala will claim her."

"We need magic," Cassara nodded. "You think we can find answers down in the cave?"

"It's the only place I can think of to start. It's not like we can teleport anywhere."

"I'm sorry you had to give up the staff Ravenhold gave you," Cassara said, gripping the sorceress's arm.

"I managed to contain some of Siabala's magic in it," Shirina said, "but it's not enough. We need something bigger, stronger, to contain all of it. And his soul in turn."

"Like the Wall of Loss?"

"No," Shirina shook her head. "Something better, that won't drain you so and rely on your lifespan." Shirina raised an eyebrow at her. "You're not getting any younger, you know."

Cassara scoffed. "I'm almost ten years younger than you!"

"My studies keep me young," Shirina deadpanned.

Cassara smiled what seemed like a real smile, and some stress uncoiled within Shirina.

"Can I say something you'll never repeat to Avarielle?"

Cassara raised an eyebrow, then nodded.

"This is something Shala said," Shirina's voice softened at her mentee's name, "and it stuck with me, though I made her swear never to repeat it." A slight smile, to show

Cassara it was more joke than fact. "She once said that she thought the three of us managed to take down Siabala because of who we are, like the Three Fates. I'm the mind, you, the soul."

"Avarielle the heart," Cassara finished.

"Yes. And it's annoying, because the heart is what keeps everyone together."

"You're afraid we'll break apart," Cassara said, "because Avarielle was closer to each of us than we are to each other."

"I wouldn't quite put it like that."

"Of course you wouldn't."

"If you run off into Massir, and I try to find the magic… we break apart, Cassara. And you're right, Avarielle wouldn't have left either one of us behind, because that's not who she is. She wouldn't have left you fighting Siabala, trapped in the Wall of Loss with him."

It had almost happened. "She's the one who made me go back for you, Cassara. I had given you up for dead. A necessary sacrifice for Graydon."

Cassara's bitter laugh surprised Shirina. She saw the sorceress's surprise and flushed again, then sighed. "I was ready to die, too, Shirina. I was sixteen, away from home, married to a man I barely knew. I'd lost my family, my home, and I had all this magic that was supposed to save Graydon, even though I had no clue how to use any of it." She looked down, then met Shirina's eyes. "I wanted to let go. I was ready. And it would have been so easy."

Shirina shifted, wishing Avarielle were here. She'd know what to say to Cassara.

"And you're right. I haven't been like myself since then," the queen continued. "It's like I'm living a life I wasn't meant to have. Sometimes, when I close my eyes, I imagine a different life, had Siabala not risen. And I love my life," she was quick to add, "and my children, and husband… but, in the dark of night, when the first snow hits, when the weather cools, like the night I gave up my magic and trapped Siabala… I don't think I know who I am, anymore. I never wanted to rule a big kingdom. Or any kingdom at all. I would have been happy as a barmaid."

The queen stopped, grasping for words. When she failed to find them, Shirina filled the void.

"But you're a terrible cook."

Cassara looked at her in shock, then a soft chuckle escaped her. "You're right. Avarielle makes this easier." The queen rallied. "So, how do we get our friend back?"

"I believe, and I may be mistaken, that I've severed the threads of Siabala's magic leading here, meaning they won't be able to teleport to Massir immediately. But it's safe to assume they're on their way."

"To find Altessa," Cassara had never given herself enough credit for her quick spirit, and she would have made a fine sorceress, had she taken one of those other paths available to her.

"We need to get to her, and also to the ritual site."

Cassara nodded and made that face that Shirina had come to associate with bad ideas.

"No," Shirina said. "You're not going after Altessa."

"But—"

"It's a trap, and if they get you, we're no better off. You don't need to do everything yourself, you know."

"I—"

"Avarielle would say something witty that would bring the point home kindly, but I'm not her so I'll just flat out tell you that your actions are near suicidal at times, and Graydon can't afford to lose you, because we'll get your magic back, and you'll need it to save your people. So start making smarter decisions."

Her voice lacked bite, but she meant every word. Cassara stood stiffly before her, and Shirina pushed herself back up and faced her.

"I need you, Cassara. And you're a queen. Surely you can call on someone to help you."

"Did you miss the whole rebellion against me?"

"I really miss Avarielle," Shirina muttered. "Okay, let's think on that. Tally instigated a rebellion against you to grow mages."

"From people I'd failed, Shirina."

"And you'll have to learn to find a way to fix it, or if that's impossible, find a way to live with it. You're a queen, and your actions and decisions affect a lot of people. You can throw it all in and rush to get killed in some sort of misplaced, desperately noble gesture to save your people, which will fail. Or you can decide to use your brain and actually come up with a solution that'll save them. Without getting yourself killed."

Shirina sighed. "I don't know how to tell you that you don't have to sacrifice yourself to fix this problem, and that it'll quite frankly make things a lot harder for me and all of Graydon if you do. So, would you please just start thinking of solutions instead of suicidal ideations?"

She wished she had her staff to grip, or that her body felt stronger.

"I'm sorry," she told Cassara. "I meant all those words, but wish I had softer ones to share with you. I need you. That's all I know. And I need to not worry about your judgment."

Cassara's arms were crossed. She cocked her head sideways.

"That wasn't half bad," Cassara said. "Avarielle snapped me out of my own head a few times. I just… I do want to live. It's just," her voice softened. "It's hard."

"It is," Shirina conceded. "I hate this, too. I hate that my Circle was broken so easily. That we were taken so unaware." She scowled. "I hate that Tally got the better of us so easily."

"*Siabala* got the better of you," Cassara said. "You don't trust Tally to be that smart."

"I don't," Shirina said, then looked down, mind spinning. Siabala must have been in contact with Tally since the fall. Meaning that Tally had something from him that allowed him to communicate with her. Or maybe even a piece of him.

How had he broken free of the Wall of Loss?

"What are you thinking?" Cassara asked.

"I'm not sure," Shirina answered, shaking her head. "Like I'm missing a simple piece of knowledge to make all of this make sense."

"You need to become an Elder," Cassara said, then added more kindly, "and you need some rest."

Dawn would creep across the horizon within a few hours. They needed to move, were they to take advantage of the darkness.

"Ravenhold didn't see me fit to become an Elder. And we have precious little time. We should go," Shirina said.

"You need a few hours of sleep. We can still make it to Massir before dawn if you give yourself some time to sleep."

"We're running out of time," Shirina said. Mumbled, even. Was the ground spinning?

"We rest first," Cassara said, practically dragging her to a small hunting hut south of them, currently unused. Too tired to fight her, exhaustion turning her limbs to stone, Shirina let the queen drag her to the small cot, room spinning as she drew in deep breaths to still her mind enough to find sleep.

"Shirina," Cassara whispered. "You asked me to consider that maybe my people didn't uprise because of my actions, so I ask that you consider this in turn: maybe Ravenhold hasn't said no to you becoming an Elder. Maybe it's still deciding, and that road isn't closed to you yet."

Shirina wanted to tell the queen off, her annoyance at having failed the test she should have easily passed bubbling inside her.

But fatigue claimed her before she could, and she let herself be swept away, understanding sleep would become a more and more precious commodity, as Siabala's tendrils of magic rekindled across the land, forging a promise of fire and death.

3

Altessa stared out the window at her beautiful city, from the palace she'd once felt was her prison. Now that it had turned into an actual prison, she knew better. She knew what it felt like to be kept safe, instead of imprisoned.

Craning her neck, she tried to see if she could spot her father again. She'd seen him, earlier, walking oddly, that broken gait that told her he needed to take care of his legs. He had a blank look on his face, a smile frozen on it, nodding along as Elder Tally walked with him and chatted.

She wanted her father to come find her, laugh, tell her everything was going to be okay. To be his usual loving and supportive self. Or stern! To tell her she shouldn't be so foolhardy, even. Anything, for some semblance of normalcy. For some semblance of *him.*

She tried not to grieve him. Nor her mother. She had

to believe her family could still be saved. That her people could still be saved. If hope was all she had left, she would deploy it to its fullest, as long as her heart allowed her to.

The door to her room was locked and guarded, for her "safety." Guards patrolled the courtyard, too, keeping an eye on the window, making sure she didn't try to climb down.

Her father had been the one to order it, for her safety. Always for her safety.

He hadn't spoken with her since she'd been locked in here. Neither had Elder Quilsam. Nor that Elder, Tally.

A knock at the door, and Altessa hesitated.

"Your Highness, it's Carla." The cook's familiar voice led Altessa to bounce off her window seat in anticipation

Finally, a friendly voice.

"Come in," she said, and the cook stepped in. The guards were ones that Altessa knew, a few who'd survived the rebel attacks. They seemed embarrassed, and closed the door to give them privacy. The newer guards, the ones brought in to "shore up their defenses," would not have been so kind.

"How are you faring, Your Highness?" the cook asked in a soft voice as she placed a tray on a small table, filled with the princess's favorite soft cheese, pickled vegetables, and fresh meats. Altessa's room wasn't that large, having once been shared by four servants, unlike the gilded rooms upstairs. She usually preferred this size, having grown up in it. But right now, with nowhere else to pace, she wished she had more space.

"I'm fine," she lied. "How are you? What news of everyone else?"

She'd been trapped here for days and was losing touch with what was happening with her people. And her kingdom. No news of her mother made everything worse, and her father's strange behavior worried her. Plus, the cracking last night, and trembling ground! She'd feared the whole palace would come crashing down, and dust still clung to the windows. Still no one would tell her what had happened.

"Another part of the city collapsed last night, Your Highness," Carla said. "The Heartfield sector."

Altessa closed her eyes. The Heartfield sector held a Builders Guild and several markets. Plus thousands of souls…

"We aren't many left," Carla said, forcing Altessa to focus back on her. "A lot of the staff left to be with their families, and so many of the guards were killed, and others are said to have defected. Your father…" She glanced at Altessa, worry flickering across her eyes.

"Go ahead, Carla," Altessa kindly said as she braced herself.

"Your father has ordered that they be found and executed. For the traitors they are."

A few weeks ago, Altessa wouldn't have believed her kind father able of issuing such an order. She would have staked her life on it.

Now? Now, she just felt broken. Helpless, and useless.

Before she could ask more questions, the door opened.

Carla bowed to Altessa and quickly left, sidestepping and bowing again as Elder Quilsam walked in. He didn't seem to notice her.

"You are not welcome here," Altessa said. The guards looked inward, as though debating if protecting their princess was even possible at this point.

"Please, Princess Altessa," he said, bowing his head. "I come to discuss important matters with you."

Something about the worry in his eyes stilled her words, and she nodded to the guards, who closed the door.

"You did not listen to me when I came begging for your help," Altessa said, feeling petty and not caring.

"I did not," the Elder said, "and I admit I am perhaps not best suited to understand matters of Graydon. But I understand matters of magic."

Altessa tipped her chin up. "I have been trained by the Circle."

"By Shirina." He waved her off, as though that didn't matter. He continued, pacing slowly, hands behind his back, bunching the dark cloak against his black robes. If he noticed her annoyance, he didn't speak of it. "Something has happened to the magic." He turned to looked at her. "Elder Morik doesn't want us to talk about it."

Elder Morik was an Elder from Ravenhold's new coven. Altessa had only met him once, and she'd disliked him immediately, partly because he followed Tally, and partly because he wore the same robes as Shirina without respecting her.

"What happened to the magic?"

"It's…" He rolled his shoulders back, clasped his hands before him and, for the first time since entering, focused directly on her. She found his fully dark eyes unsettling, with none of the warmth in Rojon's, but she met his gaze regardless. "It's gone, Princess Altessa. The magic of Elihor seems to have vanished, just like Graydon's."

Altessa drew herself up. Her mother, a born diplomat, would have found a generous way to speak to him. But Altessa wasn't interested in being generous to him. Not while he stood by and watched calamity befall her kingdom.

Her family.

"And I take it Siabala's magic is everywhere?" She knew the answer, could smell its tang in the air, turning her stomach.

He nodded, observing her more closely.

"And yet you still insist on mistrusting Shirina?"

He didn't lower his gaze, which disappointed Altessa. She wanted to watch him squirm for his complicity.

"The Circles are built on a very important principle of magic," he started, a teacher's lilt in his voice. "Magic is only revealed when the wielder is worthy, and ranks assigned by it."

"And yet—" Altessa interrupted him. She knew this already and refused to be schooled by him. "—Magic hasn't been doing the choosing of late, has it? Not

Larkhold and Ravenhold themselves, but rather the Elders choosing who is worthy?"

A slight shift of his right foot, and Altessa knew she'd struck a chord. She pressed on.

"So the Circles are basically teetering by the poor choices of the past, and chances are that any past weaknesses or inclinations have only spread roots at their core, Elders choosing new Elders who would simply follow the path into which they'd already steered the coven, no matter how wrong it may be?"

His mouth opened to protest, but Altessa's hand shot up, and he held his peace, though anger or embarrassment flushed his face. She wasn't sure which, and she didn't care.

"*Shirina—*" Altessa used her name like a talisman, "—taught me about all of that, because she thinks about that, instead of just assuming everything that came before her was just and right. She understood the rot at Ravenhold's core had been spread down from its higher echelons, and that this rot had been the crack that Siabala used to conquer the Circle and see to its eventual downfall. She may not be an Elder, but she is more than worthy of it."

Altessa stood proudly, certain she had dealt the decisive blow.

He spoke in a gentle whisper. "Then why hasn't Ravenhold made her an Elder?"

"Because it's no longer there," she answered confidently, though she could sense him coming in for a greater point—one that she did not have the knowledge or finesse to stop from landing, and so she braced herself for it.

"The Keep is a concept, Princess Altessa. A construct. Its stone structure is not what made Ravenhold hold its magic. It is no longer there, no, but what it was, and represented, still is. That never left. And it never gave Shirina the black cloak."

Altessa felt her cheeks flush. "That's not true," she said weakly. "Shirina is worthy."

"I only tell you this to stop you from falling prey to her trap, Princess." The Elder bowed slightly, not to her title as royalty, but to her status as a descendant of Graydon, she was certain. Yet neither her title nor her bloodline proved of any use to her right now.

"Did Shirina know?" Altessa asked, trying, and failing, to modulate her voice.

"That Ravenhold's spirit still lingered in Graydon, somewhere?"

She nodded curtly.

"It is not my concern what she did or did not know. Her knowledge of this would not have changed the outcome."

Altessa's cheeks flushed with anger. "You could have told her and chose not to," she fumed.

"It would not have changed anything," he insisted.

"It would have changed everything," Altessa hissed, shaking. "How dare you suggest that she would not have become Elder without her even knowing it was a possibility? How was she supposed to believe in it and pursue it if she thought the road had been closed?"

"If she'd truly wanted it—"

"She wanted to strengthen her Circle! To tighten the ties with Graydon. To win their trust again. To grow her numbers, and make sure they could stand against Siabala! And she did all those things, *without* an Elder cloak. And now you—" The words tumbled out of her now, angry for Shirina. Angry for herself, who'd never been encouraged to pull on her magic, and who now never would. Just like Shirina. Lied to, pointed elsewhere, and then told it was *her* fault. "—You dare come here and try to undo all she's done because she wasn't *worthy*? Of your judgment, or the Keep's? If she'd known she could have pursued that path, don't you think she would have, to become Elder?"

"You misunderstand me," the Elder said, holding up his hands in a signal of peace. "Surely she knew, or suspected. But the path to Elder is riddled with study and years of contemplation."

"I understand quite well," Altessa said, not letting him dismiss her, or his part in this. "If she *did* know, she chose instead to focus her efforts on helping the Circle grow and building strong foundations, something that might not be fully compatible with quiet years of contemplation. If she *didn't* know, then it's because you chose not to help Ravenhold grow, no doubt hoping to grow your own Circle's power, instead."

He looked taken aback by her outpouring.

"Either way," she kept her voice crisp, "she is more worthy than you will ever be."

The blow didn't quite land as she'd hoped, though at least he had the wisdom to remain silent.

"Now the question is," Altessa said, "and I'm certain my parents would find a more graceful way to ask this, but they are both indisposed, and so I will ask as I would: who will you choose to trust and help? The Elders who claim to still serve Ravenhold and yet can use magic despite it being gone, or the woman who still fights for Graydon despite having lost that magic?"

Before he could answer, if he'd ever truly intended to, the door flew open. A white-robed Elder stood there, looking at Quilsam, not even acknowledging Altessa.

"Elder Vangle, may I introdu—" the so-called Ravenhold Elder cut off Elder Quilsam.

"Elder, you're needed."

For a moment, the room lay thick with expectations. Altessa, willing Elder Quilsam to stand up for her family. Elder Vangle, eyeing the Larkhold Elder, his barked order sitting between them. The echo of Altessa's question growing dimmer, until Elder Quilsam nodded, took his leave of Altessa, and followed Elder Vangle from her room.

The door closed and Altessa stared at it, waiting, terrified of what might happen next, wondering how long it would be before Siabala caught up to her, too. With Elder Quilsam's silence as his crushing answer, Altessa now knew that Larkhold would not stand for her family, or her people, or any of Graydon.

With her mother and Shirina silent this long, she had to start accepting the fact that they were probably gone, and no one would stand to stop Siabala from claiming the two lands as his own.

4

Cassara knew her city well. She'd made sure to review every plan and blueprint, every architectural detail, every proposed renovation and demolition. Builder Gramire had been instrumental in helping her understand how to interpret marks on paper into something usable in her mind. Even then, she'd often left the castle in disguise to visit these places, often with only Avarielle, at the warrior's insistence. These outings helped Cassara understand the entrances and exits available to her people.

Not to mention the city's defenses.

"This way," she whispered to Shirina. Parts of her city had collapsed onto the ancient city lurking below, stone crushing stone. She'd heard the cries of her people as the ceiling collapsed during Tally's ritual, as houses tumbled down. Homes from the southeast, an impoverished section of her city, where people had already suffered so much.

And more so under my rule.

She placed a hand on the large stone wall outlining her city, cold to the touch, the gray flint and mortar not as comforting as she'd hoped it would be. She glanced up, careful to avoid detection by the city guards, though she knew there would be fewer here, focused on helping those within Massir.

Shirina had discovered an access point into the ancient city beneath Massir when she'd followed the escaped rebel, what felt like a lifetime ago. Because Cassara knew her city so well, she could get them there. The predawn shadows robed them in darkness, offering them the concealment they desperately needed. A blanket each, found in the hunting shack, covered Shirina's crimson cloak and Cassara's hair.

Even if Tally could not yet reach Massir, it was safe to assume her Circle had taken over the capital city of Rashim.

The walls of the city almost butted against each other here, with just enough space for one or two houses and guard shacks. Originally no houses had been planned here, but the population needs outweighed fear of an unknown enemy. The close-set walls had been erected to stop monsters or hoards from filing in too quickly. Where larger gaps existed, walls and gates had been built, to force enemies to split apart, and diminish their number in any one place.

They cleared the first two layers, and reached the third, where Cassara knew Shirina's hidden entry lay, because each wall bore different markings and had been built of different stones. Some were harder to climb, others harder to break down. Different markings in each section made it easy to quickly report on where enemies attacked. Not just a city quadrant, but the markings on the walls would allow the army to quickly move toward threats, no matter how small.

Every detail thought of, except the largest one: that Siabala would not attack from outside Massir, but from within.

Only three rows of houses, markets, and buildings existed in this third layer, the area some people colloquially called the Scratch. She hated that name, but she understood why it existed.

And she understood her part in this, now, and why so many rebels hailed from here. There had been so much to focus on to shore up their defenses. Walls, for direct attacks. Allies, for unstoppable foes. An army, for immediate protection, though most of it was stationed outside the West, where Siabala should have attacked. They should have been able to make their way back by now, so they either hadn't been contacted, or they'd been destroyed. Either scenario was just as likely as the other, making Cassara's stomach lurch.

Her army wasn't here. She couldn't easily reach General Akhalon, and she had to focus on what was right in front of her.

She'd tried not to let her people suffer from basic needs—food production had been reestablished, fresh water reinstated thanks to Circle magic, and plumbing had been made available throughout the city. That had all been possible due to the Builders Guild and their growth, adding two more Builders halls and encouraging citizens to join and learn various trades as the city and surrounding countryside and villages continued to rebuild.

But she hadn't been able to rebuild everything here, where the city had suffered the most. The palace still bore signs of the attack, but more had been repaired, especially at first, when tradition deemed it so. When she'd been so focused on healing herself and watching over her husband's healing, and before she'd finally gotten rid of their council which seemed only focused on the royal family and nobility, and not its people.

She intended never again to fall prey to such a trap. She'd broken tradition and angered so many, then she'd worked hard at keeping the peace, while preparing for Siabala's return.

They crossed a few passersby, their quickly assembled disguises passing muster. The blankets were enough to cover Shirina's robes and cloak, and to hide Cassara's hair, though they were both so dirty that she doubted it mattered much. And she wore pants and a simple shirt, which she rarely did while tending to her queenly duties.

She glanced at the sorceress, her words still ringing in her mind, and she tried to focus on them more than on questioning every one of her past choices. That wouldn't help anyone now, except perhaps to convince herself she was above all reproach, when she knew she wasn't. She'd made choices, and people had suffered. On the battlefield, and beyond.

She was a queen, used to have strong magic, and her actions impacted others more than most.

As they would, now, even without her magic.

She let that thought drift into her heart and shore it up. She knew what she would do next, once they'd found the answers Shirina needed.

The city opened up around them, purple trimmings on shops, vendors opening their stalls despite the calamity. People still needed to be fed, and money needed to change hands. Cassara was glad for the clinging darkness, even as the day grew brighter, which at least concealed them somewhat.

"Here," Shirina said, turning down an alley. Cassara followed, her stomach growling at the teasing odor of fresh cooked meat. She pulled out some dried meat found in the hunting shack and bit into it, fighting to chew a piece off. It had been seasoned and retained its smokiness, but it was hardly the fare her stomach called for.

Shirina now took the lead, turning down three alleyways before kneeling at the back of one, searching for seams. She'd seen it accessed with magic, but the sorceress believed it should be accessible without it, as well, considering so many of Tally's followers did not seem to possess magic.

Cassara looked around. The city wall buttressed one side of the alley, the other filled with narrow houses, so close to one another they shared walls. No windows graced the back of the simple homes, too poor for such luxuries. Cassara hammered down her guilt and focused on the wall, the section fairly new, built atop houses that had burned down in Siabala's attack. Sturdy long metal pieces about four feet in height and three inches wide lined the wall, at intervals of about twenty-five feet each. And one was right beside them.

Cassara had studied the wall's design, poured over the plans and concepts, and knew immediately they were out of place.

"This shouldn't be here," Cassara said, placing her hand on one of them. Shirina stood up, wiped the dust on her tattered blanket, and helped Cassara pull one down. It was heavy, but not unwieldy, held up by a simple hook. They would look decorative to the undiscerning, or less knowledgeable, eye.

Shirina slid it across the area where she'd seen the trapdoor. After a few moments, it caught on something. Nothing they could see, almost like a force held it there. Using it like a lever, Shirina pushed down, and the trapdoor opened.

"Interesting," she said, frowning. She placed the key back in place.

Shirina gazed down at the revealed stone stair leading into darkness, as though debating.

"I don't have a light source," she finally admitted.

"Here," Cassara pulled a candle and flint stones out of the well-worn hide bag she carried on her back. She would forever be grateful that the hunting shack had been well supplied, and made a note to repay its owner, should she be given the chance.

Shirina took it from her. Cassara held her eyes. "Do you think we'll find answers down there?"

"It's our best bet," Shirina said, then looked toward the hanging piece of metal. "I wonder who set this trapdoor, however."

"Does it matter?"

"Perhaps not." The sorceress turned to head down.

"Thank you, Shirina," Cassara said. "For everything."

"I haven't exactly been succeeding at much lately," the sorceress deadpanned.

"You keep trying, and never give up hope. That's more than most people."

Shirina cocked her head. "We should get moving, before we draw attention to ourselves."

"We wouldn't want that," Cassara whispered.

She doubted Shirina had heard her, the sorceress focused on next steps, her mind probably already embroiled in theories of what they'd find down below.

She started carefully taking the stairs, indicating for Cassara to follow, and to be quiet.

Cassara waited for her to clear the trapdoor. Then she took a deep breath, and pushed it shut. It closed quietly, only a bit of dust drifting up. Cassara hoped that it would be difficult to open from within.

She knew that Shirina would continue down the stairs if that were the case, knowing time was limited.

If there was one thing that Cassara needed to remember, one thing that she was willing to bet her very life on, and had before, was that her friends would come through.

That Shirina would find the magic again.

That Avarielle would fight off Siabala.

She would stake everything on that, even her very life.

And she just had.

5

---

*S*everal steps down, after the trapdoor had closed shut and she grew reliant on the slight light of the candle, Shirina realized that no one followed her. She looked back, toward the closed trapdoor, her mind racing with possibilities.

Had someone attacked and grabbed the queen? Had they not been as alone as it seemed?

She turned, took a quick step up, then stopped, realizing exactly what had happened. Cassara had decided to go on without her. To go to her home and try to save her daughter and husband. She'd waited long enough, and Shirina hadn't been able to get her the help she desperately needed.

The queen had followed her heart, instead of her mind.

Part of Shirina had known she would. And Cassara would waste no time and head back to the palace. Shirina could follow her and try to help her in her extremely limited capacities, or she could go forward.

You never give up hope, Cassara had said. Her own way of telling her to go on without her. Of thanking her and saying goodbye in the same breath.

Shirina had been so concentrated on the next steps and not getting caught that she hadn't heard what the queen had really been telling her.

With a final glance at the shadows concealing the trapdoor, Shirina turned and continued down the stairs, though more quickly this time. The queen had made her choice, and so had Shirina. She simply hoped she could be quick enough to prove of some help for the royal family before they were all slaughtered by the Elder and her Circle.

Corner after corner she turned, glad she'd memorized the journey beforehand. She had two stops to make. The first, and probably easiest, was Tally's home. The Elder was busy scheming and manipulating others, and hopefully had left information of use behind. The second, and more tricky one, was the site of the ritual where they'd destroyed Cassara's amulet. She hoped she could see what they'd been trying to accomplish, and what had happened to Cassara's magic. And that of Graydon.

She almost turned a corner just as a so-called Circle adept walked by, oblivious to her presence. She stopped, listened carefully. Sneaking around was not her area of expertise, and she wished Avarielle were here.

Beating down the useless thought, she focused back on

her surroundings. The area was entirely busier than the last time she'd been here. Not just adepts, but guards, as well, and what looked like Builders, still pulling bodies out of the collapsed city. She had no idea who was allied with whom, and couldn't risk being seen by anyone, no matter how innocuous they might seem. She blew out her candle as daylight flooded the once dark cavern. At least most of the activity centered where the city had fallen. As she approached Tally's home, everything grew quieter.

A few adepts wandered nearby, but no one else.

Not adepts. Charlatans and pretenders.

The knowledge that those liars and posers had more magic than her stung deep.

Two passed by and kept walking toward another home, and Shirina slipped into the Elder's home. It was empty.

It's nice that one thing is going my way today. She looked around, frown deepening as she discovered nothing. An old, hard crust of bread seemed to be all that had been left behind. No other personal effects, notes, or books.

Of course there wouldn't be, Shirina berated herself. Elder Tally hardly intended to return here when she could inhabit the comfortable palace. She hoped that her little trick with Siabala's magic would throw her off but doubted it would take her long to reestablish the magic over Massir, and use their waves to teleport.

Shirina had to move more quickly.

The ritual site couldn't be far. She oriented herself using the collapsed roof, though everything looked different in the light. Not to mention that she'd been teleported in the first time, making finding her way that much more difficult.

She headed up a slight hill, followed the row of round stone houses, keeping her head down and hoping no one would think of her as anything else but a peasant looking for some food as she pulled the scratchy blanket more tightly around her concealed robes.

"Hold!" She froze at the harsh command, hoping her acting skills, which were nonexistent, would help her.

"I'm just… looking for food," she said, her attempt at a convincing act rather abysmal.

"That's not the way," a man spoke behind her. A young voice.

"Leave me be," she hissed, and started walking again. A hand shot out and grabbed her arm. She turned on him, scowling.

His grip loosened. Not the most courageous, then. He wore an orange cloak and white robe. None of her Orange Circles would prove so easily intimidated, she was certain, because she *was* intimidating, and they could all look her in the eye. The realization inspired her to lean on her strengths.

"I am on a special errand," the lie burned Shirina's throat, "for Elder Tally." A flash of her crimson cloak, gone just as quickly. His eyes widened. "Tell no one you have seen me. I shall tell her how helpful you proved this day."

He hesitated, weighing her lie. She pushed forward.

"I am in a hurry," she said. "As is the Elder."

"Of course," he mumbled, though suspicion creased his eyes. She wouldn't have much time, but she'd have some. He turned around and continued on his way, but he did look back once. Her already minute amount of time had just become smaller.

Shirina hurried up the hill, hoping she hadn't mistaken where to go.

She turned left, opened herself up to the Sight, carefully. A few spells only depended on inside strength, and not on taking in magic, something she wished she'd understood a long time ago. The Sight was one of them, and the only safe one to wield without the support of Graydon. Or so she hoped desperately.

Red strands danced around her, but they were muted and stilled, Siabala's magic thankfully still lessened, showing her spell had proved somewhat effective. She imagined the magic stretching outward, toward the East. And Tally. And Avarielle.

Siabala.

As soon as the strands reconnected, and enough magic linked Massir to where they now stood, they would teleport.

Shirina pushed back her fear and grief, focusing on what once must have been a shrine. Not like the ones they'd discovered twenty years ago beneath the West, but a smaller one, with a cracked altar. Only one of its stone pillars remained standing, but Shirina had no doubt this was where the amulet had melted into the ground.

And, she had to assume, had locked Graydon's magic

somewhere else. The ground still bore signs of their struggle, including the darkened spot where Rojon had run his mother through. Avarielle had stepped before Cassara, so it stood to reason that the amulet had melted in pretty much the same spot, before the queen. Cassara's amulet had ostensibly been Elihor's, given to Graydon for unknown reasons, and wielded by his descendants. It channeled his magic but could, apparently, also draw on Elihor's powers.

That had been the inspiration for her bracers, made of metals of both worlds.

When the amulet had vanished, only Graydon's magic had vanished with it. Elihor's dark strands were now just as gone. The latter complicated her theory of the amulet dragging down Graydon's magic into the ground, but did not completely ruin it.

With her Sight, she looked at the darkened earth.

Avarielle would have died to protect Cassara. And now she might be the one to kill her.

Stop it. You need to focus.

She could see nothing and so closed her eyes, stilled her mind and heart, and cleared her thoughts. With the Sight she looked again, but still, Graydon's magic remained hidden. She touched the bloodied ground, fingertips growing warm where there should have been cool earth.

Her heart beat faster. She began to dig with her hands, having no other tool and no time to find any. The earth was compact, and she soon hit stone. Her hands clawed at the stone, pushing aside the earth, ignoring jagged edges cutting her as she pushed deeper, now on her knees.

The stone shone. She could see it, with the Sight.

Graydon's magic. It sparkled softly, but there was no mistaking it. She touched it, gasped as the power surged through her. For a moment, the walls of Ravenhold closed around her, the dark stone comforting, the smell of books and dust energizing. Just as quickly, it faded away, and she gasped.

Graydon's magic was still here, but trapped in the stone beneath her. How large was this stone? How far did it extend? And how could it be broken, so that she could carry a piece of it with her? Would that be the key to rediscovering her powers?

"What are you doing?" The Orange Circle was back, and she cursed, wishing she had more time. She was so close. She glanced up. He'd brought two other Orange Circles with him. She ignored him, placed her palm on the stone, gently seeing if she could tease some of the magic out. If these false adepts drew from Siabala's magic, they would be limited in powers but could easily kill her. If they had green flames, they would either control them well or not, and could also easily kill her.

If she let them take her prisoner, Elder Tally would make her death anything but easy.

Her options limited, she kept her hand on the stone, felt it tingling at the edges of her fingers, but refused to slip into them. Like her skin was an impenetrable fortress, even though she'd thrown open the front door.

She pushed down harder, imagined the magic slipping into her, feeding her, welcomed into her skin to merge with her as it had with the stone.

Paper. Old books. Incense. She could smell it all. Hear the murmurs of Ravenhold. From the corners of her eyes, she could see its lights dancing, showing her the way.

Down. Go down.

Beyond the stone. Into the rock.

I am not magic's vessel, she realized. *I am simply its guest. I have always simply walked beside it, not carried it.*

The Orange Circle took another step toward her.

"Do you know why your cloaks are orange?" Shirina asked convivially, casually. The tone threw them off and they stopped.

She kept her hand on the rock, making direct contact with it. She'd been trained that magic was meant to be controlled. That an even-paced mind could do so. That thought took precedence over emotions, and steadiness over rashness. But she'd seen time and time again that magic wasn't as understood or controlled as Ravenhold would have everyone believe.

The stone beneath her hands felt like the Keep's, even if it belonged to something deep beneath Massir. She could feel it pulsing with magic. With *life.*

She took a deep breath. Another step toward her. She kept speaking.

"Because it was simply given to you by an Elder, without having to prove where your allegiances stood, and what kind of person you are. And you do not deserve them."

Instead of drawing the magic into her, she gently knocked with her mind. Asked if it would grant her access. Chose to trust the magic she'd always wielded, instead of wielding it. Of commanding it.

The Orange Circles were almost on top of her when a flash of light surrounded her, and Shirina folded into herself as she followed the magic deep, deep down, further than she'd ever been.

To where she could only follow.

6

Cassara walked back to the market. She'd been forming her plan, her return to Massir, since last night. Shirina had been right, in a way. Cassara didn't mind dying. But the sorceress was also wrong. The queen *wanted* to live. Those weren't incompatible thoughts in her mind.

She'd shored up their defenses around the city, and in the West where they'd assumed Siabala would return. She'd made sure the other villages of Rashim had protections, escape routes, hiding places.

But not once did she think she'd have to face him again, the dark god she'd sacrificed all of her magic to contain. And more than her magic. A piece of herself she hadn't even realized had been missing until it was too late to take back.

He shouldn't have returned until her death. But he was here, now. She had no magic. And that piece that she'd lost—her immutable belief that there was always a solution, and that she would always find it. That she would manage to save her people and the world, no matter what. The belief in herself that had brought her to Massir the first time to marry her husband for his army… She was no longer sure if that part of herself had ever truly existed or if maybe she'd enhanced it with time. Increased it in her mind as she felt herself shrinking. Or maybe she'd wanted to shrink, as doubts crept in. As the certainty and brashness of youth were crushed by fatigue and expectations.

But maybe it was still there. Because Cassara had seen in Avarielle's eyes how hard she fought against Siabala. And she knew, without a doubt, that the longer her friend lingered trapped by the dark god, the greater the chances that they'd lose her. And she couldn't live with that. Wouldn't, no matter the risk to herself.

Perhaps it wasn't that she no longer found the solutions, but that no remaining solutions led to a clean victory.

She took off the blanket she'd carefully wrapped over her head, rubbed it against her face to remove some of the dust, and let her hair loose. Straightening her clothing, she then straightened her spine. Walked to the beat of royalty, held her chin up, to show her determination. She would be recognized, she had no doubt.

And that was what she wanted.

Shirina would hunt for magic, something that may or may not prove fruitful. The only thing she could be certain of right now was that Siabala—Avarielle—would come for Graydon's blood, and she had no intention of letting Altessa take the blow.

Part of her didn't believe the blow would come at all. Not by Avarielle's hand. But she knew that her beliefs did not define reality, and had vowed that should that blow come, it would not strike her daughter.

She stepped out from the alleyways, a merchant spotting her, eyes growing wide.

Then again, Maybe Shirina is right. Maybe I am suicidal.

A few merchants bowed, confusing others until they turned and also spotted her, a few gasping in surprise.

Or maybe, just maybe, I'm just determined to see this through, no matter the cost.

The further she walked up the city, the more people came, word spreading like a wave. Most people seemed happy to see her. A few had tears in their eyes.

Either way, I have to follow my own counsel and be prepared to deal with the consequences. In this, and in everything that follows. And everything that came before me.

She kept walking, eyes on the scarred palace before her, her heart growing lighter for being with her people. For being *seen* by them.

"Your Majesty," a nobleman, Count Lensky from the Corallite Canyons to the north of Massir, bowed.

"Count Lensky," Cassara said, her voice finding its familiar crispness, laced with warmth, easily slipping back into being a queen. "What news of the Corallite Canyons?"

He straightened up and answered with a trembling voice. "Most of it has collapsed, much like parts of Massir."

The market, usually a space bustling with laughter, bartering, and shouts, was so quiet she could hear the flags turning on the poles as the wind shifted from the east.

"I am sorry to hear that," Cassara said, placing a hand on his arm. The count had two children much younger than hers, and had been widowed with the birth of his second. He worked hard for his people.

"I had hoped we could get assistance, but…"

"You will," Cassara said firmly. "But not from here."

She looked at those filling the streets, spotting familiar faces. A few Circle witches, which she recognized from Shirina's order. They seemed wary as they stepped out of the shadows. Some guards, whispering. Onlookers, some running off to spread the news of her reappearance. A few noble folk, who kept a wary eye on the queen who'd never made them feel welcome in her court.

Good.

Her eyes settled on a Builder, their emblem, a pickaxe crossing a hammer—tearing down and building up—proudly worn over his heart.

"Where is Builder Gramire? Or Builder Hilar?"

The younger Builder took off his hat, held it between nervous hands. "Builder Hilar is dead, I fear. An attack a few nights ago."

Of course. She swallowed hard. "He was a good man.

My sympathies to all Builders, and the lives he touched." She allowed a moment to pass, held the silence for him. "Does Builder Gramire still live and the Builders Guild still stand?"

"The guild stands, Your Majesty," Builder Gramire said as he stepped into the market. Another younger Builder having run to get him, she assumed, as a girl with the emblem gasped for air near him.

Builder Gramire lowered his head. "I thank you for caring if I lived."

"Of course," she said, and nodded her respect, and he bowed in turn. "Please prepare the city for attack."

The Builder's eyes widened, and he bowed. Then he took off, shouting orders at his two apprentices.

Cassara focused back on Count Lensky.

"Count, I have a favor to ask of you," she said, then turned to three Circle witches. "And of you."

Everyone was too near, and Cassara had to assume that Tally would hear everything.

"Anything, Your Majesty," the count said. He was a veteran of the Days of Blood. He'd fought bravely and had been one of the first to bow to her in court, an act that changed everything for her. How she viewed herself. And how others viewed her, too.

"I need you to find General Akhalon for me."

"He's out west," the count said in a low voice. "Where the king sent the army."

Cassara schooled her features. Dayshon, under Tally's, and Siabala's, holds.

"We have fought many battles side by side, have we not, Count Lensky?" He nodded, though kept his peace. "And now I must ask you for one more battle. Head to the West, with this note for the general. Be quick, and bring the witches with you."

"We have no magic, Queen Cassara," the Orange Circle said.

"But Circle witches may prove of use regardless." *And this will get you out of the city before you're murdered by Tally's rogue witches.*

"Very well, Your Majesty," the Circle adept didn't sound convinced, but they bowed and left.

She wondered if she'd sent them to their doom. Tally might regain her power quickly enough to stop the count from reaching his destination, which might no longer hold her army, or any help. Tally might have seen to that already, too.

But at least she'd have tried. Would her army even be of use? Would Siabala simply kill everyone from within?

She turned to the palace, teetering over the city, at the top of the hill. Despite its collapsed tower, it was still beautiful. A sign of its ruling family.

In Edoline—a small kingdom with just one village— there had always been a separation between Cassara and her people, even if she'd just been their princess. She'd managed to slip in with them, and get to know them, but only to some degree. A wall of class, history, and generational teachings stood between her and her people here, too.

And a veil of secrets.

Secrets that had brought them here, to this moment. She didn't regret holding these secrets. She'd done it for the right reasons.

But that time was gone. She looked around at the merchants, children, ladies, and lords in silks less fine than those worn at court. At Builders. Some soldiers. Citizens curious about the gathering occurring in the streets.

She looked at each in turn, finding her words, giving each a small nod, acknowledging each life here.

"I have failed you," she said, her words soft but easily carrying in the silence of the streets. "I have failed you as queen and protector. The magic, my magic, which kept Siabala imprisoned since last I faced him twenty years ago, is gone." Eyes widened. Some didn't understand. Others frowned. There was so much to say. So little time to explain.

"Siabala has returned," she spoke over gasps, "but you are not defenseless."

As if on cue, the city bells began to ring. The new bells she'd made sure were a part of a network of warning signals. People had been told of them, had heard them being tested. These would ensure every guard was aware of incoming attack, though it wasn't impending. A slow preparation, to shore up defenses and close the gates. More frantic activity would occur once she knew what, exactly, they would face.

"Within a day, maybe sooner," Cassara said, "he will be

here." More gasps. One man cried out. She didn't tell them that Siabala would come in the guise of Avarielle Grayloft. The West had fought hard to be respected and recognized in these lands, and she would not undo all their hard work. Besides, if they faced Avarielle Grayloft, that knowledge would be of little use to them.

"He will come for me," she said confidently, "at the palace, where I will wait. I cannot guarantee your safety."

Questions and shouts poured from the crowd, their silence at their queen's unexpected arrival broken by their fear.

"What are we supposed to do?"

"How will we survive?"

"Why is this happening?"

She held up a hand, and they stopped.

"For now, continue with your day," she instructed them. "Follow the guards' and Builders' instructions, and keep each other safe."

Safe. She had made sure her city could be safe. That her people would never suffer as they had before. That she could provide the protection they so craved. Had so desperately needed.

No one broke or left. More people gathered, and Cassara needed to get to her castle, now. More nobles, too, no doubt eager to see the fall of their queen, to usher in royalty they could support. One not as concerned with "peasants."

Cassara spotted a city guard and motioned for him to join her. A lieutenant, grizzled, uncertain.

"How many of you are left?" Cassara asked softly.

"Not… not many, Your Majesty. The king, your husband, he… he told many to leave. That we'd failed in our duty and were no longer needed." He flushed.

"My husband the king is not himself at the moment," Cassara said softly. "Gather back who you can and who will return, and prepare the walls to sustain attack, as it is your duty to keep the people safe."

"Your Majesty," he bowed deeply. "We will escort you to the palace, first."

"No, thank you." She glanced toward the palace, looming in the distance, over the city. "I believe this is a walk I must do by myself." She looked at each, silencing their protest. "Keep each other, and our people, safe."

With that, she began walking up the hill, toward the palace, where she'd lived more than half her life, and raised three children. The bells of the city chimed around her. Some people were running, looking scared. Others barred themselves in their homes, hoping they could ride out whatever storm hounded them.

Some stopped at the sight of their queen, in regular clothing, walking resolutely up the hill.

Closing in on the castle, she spotted a familiar looking rebel standing on the sidelines. She could have made sure Cassara didn't spot her, but she obviously wanted to be seen. Still, the woman was surprised that Cassara waved her over, the queen equally surprised when she acquiesced.

"I need your help," Cassara told Ramelia.

"Last time we met, I was in your dungeons, Your Majesty," the rebel said, though her voice grew soft.

"And, when we needed help, you stepped up," Cassara answered. "What of my daughter?"

"I helped her escape," Ramelia flushed red, angry. "But she chose to go back to the palace, to try to… I don't know. Die heroically, or something."

The spite in the rebel's voice failed to disguise her true emotions, and Cassara tried to focus on those instead of her own fear.

"I need your help saving her again," Cassara said. "But this might test your resolve."

An eyebrow lifted. "I assure you my resolve is usually fairly solid, *Your Majesty.*" She spoke the title sarcastically, but with little fire.

"Then I trust you to carry through, as you must." The rebel listened to the queen's plans, eyes widening.

"Altessa will hate me," Ramelia said, sounding very much like a young woman afraid of losing a piece of herself.

"Altessa will understand, someday." Cassara placed a hand on the woman's dark, wiry arm.

"She comes from the same ridiculous stock as you," Ramelia said, with a slight smile. "This I will do, but only because you ask as a mother, not as a queen."

Cassara nodded, and the rebel took off. Had anyone seen them? She doubted it would matter. Not now. Ramelia could be quick—Cassara had seen her in action.

The queen walked on, feeling at peace for the first time

in weeks. She'd done all that she could, even if she didn't quite understand what it was that she'd done. The space left empty by her missing magic buzzed in anticipation, and she'd let her instincts guide her.

Her magic.

If it was in her blood, then she had to believe it would return. Or, if it failed to do so, that her death would serve as more than fuel for Siabala's fires.

7

Shirina blinked, then placed a hand on the cold stone wall beside her.

"Ravenhold," she whispered, the lights of the Keep dancing a gentle blue at her feet. She smiled at it, remembering how it had ushered her to safety when the Keep had been crumbling into the sea.

"Show me where I need to be," she asked, and the lights tumbled forward. Shirina followed, fingertips grazing the stone walls, which felt solid and real. Even though she knew that, once more, this couldn't be the actual Keep, but something formed of magic and memories.

The lights stopped at the bottom of the giant petrified oak, then pointed toward a familiar door. Her mentor's study. Light shone beneath it, showing Tanja currently occupied it.

Tanja is dead, she reminded herself. Whatever this was,

it wasn't her mentor. Maybe her own memories had brought her to life before her? Or a magical apparition?

She didn't know, and Ravenhold and its coven had never truly bothered with the afterlife—if such a thing existed—focusing instead on magic in the here and now, and the effects one life could have during its limited time.

Shirina stood before the door, feeling like an adept trying to learn the ways of the Circle again as deep secrets eluded her.

She knocked. The door opened.

A quick glance revealed that the study looked as it always had: Papers scattered on wooden furniture, magical lights dancing along the ceiling, ink circles forming on parchments beneath abandoned quills. The one chair not covered with manuscripts was carved out of wood, without even a pillow, so Shirina stood.

"Elder Tanja," Shirina said, not able to see the woman.

"Crimson Circle Elite Shirina." Shirina turned around, her mentor standing in the doorway in her Elder robes, hands folded before her, cut cheeks and intense eyes shining in the lights of Ravenhold, salt-and-pepper hair pulled back in a twist.

"I have failed the test," Shirina said. "I was offered a staff to wield, and lost it."

"Which test did you fail?" Tanja said. A question. Always a question, when Shirina mostly sought answers.

"The one that would see me become an Elder," Shirina said, voice tense. She took a deep breath. Impatience and anger would not change Tanja's mind. Or the Keep's.

An idea struck her. "Perhaps another one of my Circle adepts would do. Shala is quite advanced in her studies—"

"You would offer the honor to another?"

"If it means stopping Siabala, of course I would." Her despair didn't spread to her rank, though she still hoped to become Elder one day. Her despair was solely focused on stopping Siabala.

"Siabala is coming," Shirina continued. "What do cloaks matter when stopping him must be our priority?"

"If cloaks don't matter, why do you seek to become an Elder?"

Had she always been this infuriating?

"There is knowledge only available to Elders that I require."

"Knowledge is a troubling thing, child," Tanja said softly.

"It can be," Shirina replied warily. "But a lack of knowledge can be worse."

"Do you smell it?"

Before she could ask, Tanja slipped out of her study. Shirina stumbled after her, afraid of losing sight of the woman who tethered her to this realm.

Tanja stood before the large oak tree at the center of the Keep, lit by a gentle green hue.

"Do you know that Ravenhold was built around this tree?"

"I do," Shirina said. This was common knowledge accessible to any Green Circle, and impatience slipped into Shirina's voice.

"Do you know why?"

"Because it's a link to Graydon?" Shirina said, thinking of the tree in the Lisal Gardens, which had shown signs of growth. A promise of life.

"Why do you think that?" Tanja turned around to look at her, backlit by the green hues of the tree.

"Because…" Shirina stopped, giving her mind the space it needed to parse the information. The trees in Elihor grew the memories of those who had passed, drawn from their bodies. Or souls. The afterlife in Elihor was more powerful and celebrated than in Graydon.

The stump of the oak tree in the Lisal Gardens, a brethren to this one, was the most connected thing to the magic of Graydon. Reaching far down below, its trunk long gone but its roots still pulling enough nutrition to survive. Enough magic.

The stone where the amulet had melted. That she had touched. Three keeps made of stone, across the two lands. A prison crafted from the largest mountain, in the stone range that split the lands… a city that spread across the world, beneath them, lifted up from the waters surrounding them. She remembered visiting the city long ago, under the West, and the ancient wild magic bouncing around it.

The magic now gone from the air…

"Because it reached down to the stone where the magic used to live," Shirina said, looking up to the trunk. "The magic is trapped in the rock of the ancient cities. In the stones beneath Graydon and Elihor, where the tree's roots reach."

Tanja smiled and nodded.

"But it's not trapped there, child," Tanja said. "It's returned to where it once belonged. It was in the air that it was trapped, away from its natural home."

Shirina's hands grew cold. Siabala had two brothers, who had slumbered in the ancient city beneath the West. Against cold stone, where the magic of Graydon and Elihor danced within them… it had been their magic, that much she knew. And the Traveler's Song had helped keep Graydon's magic in check.

"Does… did Graydon and Elihor somehow capture the magic and force it out of the ground?"

"Those are secrets only available to Elders," Tanja replied, but her smile told Shirina everything she needed to know.

"How… how do we get the magic back?"

Tanja kept her peace, said nothing, turning to look up at the tree. If the magic had returned to its rightful home, could it be forced back out? Should it be? And what impact would this have on Graydon and Elihor? Possibilities swirled in Shirina's mind, but nothing conclusive. All that she knew was that she couldn't wield the magic this way. Maybe she would get lucky at times and trigger spells like this one, but to fight Siabala, she would need to master her magic.

"I don't know how to fight him," Shirina admitted. "I don't know how to save Graydon."

"Your allegiance is to magic," Tanja said, repeating her words. "You need magic."

"I need magic I can wield in combat. I don't know how to use the knowledge you've given me."

"An Elder would know."

"I don't care!" Shirina's annoyed voice bounced in the Keep, and she took a long, shuddering breath. "I have fought for the Circle, Tanja, and I am not about to stop now, even if you'll never give me the cloak. I'll keep fighting. How do I get magic I can wield? Can I get another staff?"

"You would lose it again," Tanja shrugged, "trying to wield more magic of Siabala."

"The staff protected me."

"It did. But you turned it to stone."

"And bought my friends time."

"Did you?"

Tanja looked beside the tree, and suddenly Shirina stood in the streets of Massir. Cassara walked up the hill, toward the palace, determination plastered on her grim features.

"Oh, Cassara," Shirina whispered, reaching out to touch her friend, but the queen's image shimmered away. Shirina suddenly stood on the edge of a destroyed town, crumbled down below. In the distance, a chunk of the Maple Mountains was gone.

Avarielle stood on the edge, looking toward distant Massir, her features blank. Her eyes blazed with anger, which Shirina could almost sense.

"We're almost ready," elder Tally said. "Whatever that blasted Crimson Circle did is almost done, and your magic has spread once more, my lord."

A nod, barely perceptible. Tally's face turned red with anger.

"Do not fight him, oath breaker. This is the path you were meant to walk." Avarielle didn't reply, or hit. She simply stood there as the Elder gazed at her.

She was locked in a battle of wills, one she would lose without help.

And soon, they would head to Massir.

"Keep fighting, Avarielle," Shirina whispered near her, placed a hand on her arm, felt a slight buzzing in her mind, and stood near Tanja again.

"She will lose the battle," Tanja said. "The soul of Siabala far outpowers her own. A millennia-old god against that of a Westland warrior. She is not his match."

"Do not underestimate Avarielle Grayloft," Shirina said, though her words lacked bite. "If I am not meant to free or wield the magic of Graydon, how can I fight him?"

"There is still one magic that is freely accessible," Tanja said, as red strings of power lit up the room.

Shirina recoiled. "Never," she hissed. "I would take the green flames before I would touch his dangerous magic."

"Only an Elder truly understands where the green flames come from," Tanja said.

Shirina pondered her options, then faced Tanja. "I may not be an Elder, but I'm a willing test subject." Bile splashed the back of her throat. "Can you implant the green flames in me?"

False magic would be better than no magic.

"You would trust the green flames?" Tanja asked.

"No," Shirina admitted. "But I think they're my best option."

"You worship at the altar of magic," Tanja said again and, before Shirina could say anything else, her body grew warm. So warm, she feared it would burn, that her skin would crack and blister.

The warmth spread from her core, and she remembered the stories Carsyn had told Avarielle, of how the green flames had been implanted into him. She fell to her knees, the pain striking every nerve and twisting her veins.

She bit her inner cheek, forced her screams to remain locked within, as the magic snaked beneath her skin, failing to fill the hollow left behind by Graydon's magic.

Rather, it made it deeper, wider, and tarnished it with pain.

Still Shirina did not resist, willing to sacrifice it all to stop Siabala's empire from consuming her world, even if it meant giving it all up: Her body, her mind, her very soul.

8

Layers upon layers had settled on Avarielle's mind, like water crushing her lungs, except it was her thoughts, not air, that threatened to escape and never be found again. So she held them in, kept them close, forced herself to focus on what she could still see, hear, and feel.

Which was precious little.

They'd traveled overnight, Tally sleeping in a cart while Avarielle kept the horses moving. She didn't usually need much sleep, and it seemed that Siabala intended to test her body's limits. He couldn't yet evict her from her body. From the little she understood, she had to kill Cassara and Rojon first.

Please no.

She'd killed Kaden. It would have been Cassara, had he not stepped in front of her. Her arm had moved with a will not her own, intent on striking down its prey.

The old man deserved better than to be struck down by Siabala. She didn't know what had happened to Rojon, except he was gone, and Tally didn't know where, cursing Shirina. She knew Cassara was with the sorceress, the two having teleported away. Shirina had managed to temporarily stop Tally from following, their teleportation spell failing close to Massir.

A muffled sound, a warmth on her arm, and Avarielle rallied to try to push to the surface.

It was like she stood in a tower, her own eyes the windows too high for her to reach. She had to climb the wall, fight up, the see her surroundings for just a few moments before being thrown back down.

Keep fighting, Avarielle, she thought she heard Shirina say, though she wasn't sure, a warmth growing on her arm. Still, it spurred her on, and she pushed up... and couldn't reach the top, like her own mind grew too exhausted to fight.

If Siabala was already this powerful, what would happen to her once her blade cut into the blood of Elihor and Graydon? The warmth from her arm spread and, for a brief moment, she almost felt like herself. She stood beside Tally, empty and limp hands at her side, the Elder berating her for not giving Siabala control of her body.

I'll kill you as many times as needed for you to stay dead, Elder, she wanted to say, but her lips refused to obey her.

You should give up, Siabala's voice danced in her mind. *I'm a god, you're but a mortal. What powers do you have against me?*

Avarielle managed to frown, a look reflected on Tally as she saw the shift in her facial movements. The warrior could see now, more or less. She knew it was only because Siabala had granted her this access, making it possible for her to witness the world around her.

And she hated him even more for it.

No. She had to believe fighting made a difference. That he'd not gifted this to her. That she had power, too. To believe otherwise would be suicide.

"You simply anger Lord Siabala more." The Elder shook her head.

It does not anger me, Siabala said in her mind, kept at bay from speaking the words out loud by her willpower alone. He could control her limbs, mostly, but she would not give him more. Not while she could still fight him.

I made you this powerful. I want to see your strength. I own you already. Eventually you'll come to understand we are stronger together.

Get out of my body! Avarielle wanted to scream, to claw at her own skin, but still she couldn't make herself move.

I've been here all along, warrior, he laughed. *Since you took the oath with me. A piece of me within you, through Graysword.*

Her mind floundered at the possibilities. She'd known this—a part of her had always suspected it. Had felt her power extend from her to Graysword. *His* power.

This is why the oath was needed, Grayloft. To give me access to you, while gifting you powers. Graysword holds some of my powers, but it cannot be triggered without a piece of my soul.

His voice boomed around her, and she forced herself

to remain calm, to remain as grounded as possible while trapped in her own body, wishing he'd just shut up.

Knowing he wouldn't.

How do you think we foresaw all your attacks? All your moves? You told me everything I needed to know about your world and allies. Staying one step ahead of your allies proved the easiest thing in the world when I could see straight into your mind.

She'd betrayed them, without even knowing it. She wanted to feel the thumping of her heart. For its quick movements to serve as the battle call her blood craved. But her heart didn't react to her grief, her anger.

Nor her fear.

I know all of Massir's defenses. All that Graydon's wretched descendant has at her disposal. I know of the Crimson Circle Elite's plans and outposts. I know them all, because they trusted you above all else to keep them safe, and so revealed everything to you. Ironic, isn't it?

Avarielle kept her eyes open, seeing the dimly lit ground around her, even though the sun was freshly risen on the horizon.

The bells of Massir ring. Do you think I don't know all of their defenses? Do you not think I will sacrifice them all, one by one, before their queen, to break her before I have you slice her in two, to join her dead people? Or perhaps I'll just have you cleave her in two, then kill her people with your blade soaked in their queen's blood?

Cassara. She would find a way to stop Avarielle. Wouldn't she? The last time they'd met, she'd just stood before her, telling her it was okay if she struck her down. Did Cassara have enough desire to live to avoid her blade?

She's in Massir, now. Siabala teased. Could he sense her thoughts, or did he simply know her well enough to guess what they were?

Either answer failed to bring her solace.

She'll find a way to stop you, Avarielle said, fury feeding her words.

She'll try, he said, then grew quiet, though his oppressive presence remained. His hatred of Cassara was great, and so was his anger toward Shirina. He wanted them both to suffer.

Her, too, except she wasn't just his enemy. She was his, entirely, to take over.

She would suffer as they suffered, because it would be by her hand.

Let me kill Tally, Avarielle suddenly said. She wanted to buy her friends more time. Killing the Elder would do that.

She has proven loyal to me, unlike you.

She's annoying, and seeks her own power.

True. The silence grew, stifling, pressure against her skull… then it released her, and she blinked. She was back in her body, in full control. In a flash Graysword was freed from its scabbard and she cleaved down toward the Elder, a questioning look in Tally's eyes… and then the blade stopped, barely an inch over the old woman's head.

Avarielle struggled, fought to bring it down, slowly felt herself being pulled back into the depths of her body. She sheathed Graysword, her hands no longer obeying her, but she could still see the world clearly, through her own eyes.

She is still of use to me. But you can witness the fall of Massir, should you desire. And remember your hand in it. The choices you made that led you here. And that I am your master, and you will learn to obey. Or I will crush what remains of your mind, and that would be a waste.

"You really should just listen to him," Tally said, tapping her arm. "It will be much easier on you that way."

Avarielle wanted to answer her. To tell her that it wasn't about the easy road. That some things were worth fighting for. But the words remained trapped, and she was powerless to push them out.

"Let's go," Tally said, squinting as she looked up ahead. "The magic is healing itself. Connecting again. Whatever it is that pest Shirina did, it's almost at an end. Soon, she'll be dead. As will the queen. And it'll be much easier for you." She patted her again, like a grandmother. Anger dimmed Avarielle's vision. "In the meantime, I've sent a message ahead to some awaiting friends of Siabala. To warn them of our arrival."

She helped the Elder onto the horse, abandoning the cart in the hillier terrain, and started walking, feet moving without her accord.

Soon, they would teleport. And Avarielle knew that she couldn't stop the blow from taking her friends.

Even if it came from her own hand.

9

Shirina stood in the middle of a dark room, the lights of Ravenhold still dancing around her, green reflecting on damp rocks. Tilted flat slabs of rock with leather ties formed a circle, covered in dry blood.

"The green flames were created during a desperate time for the Circle," Tanja said. Shirina did not answer. The Circle had given life to the flames of war in the West, starting the Westland Wars with whispers and lies, all in the pursuit of knowledge.

How far would she go for knowledge? She might have understood their tactics once, as a good adept of the Circle. She'd been on her way to becoming an Elder, one of the youngest Crimson Circles ever to make Elite.

I would have understood and supported the tactics. If asked, she knew she would have killed the soldiers tied to these pieces of stones, to fulfill the Circle's will and bidding.

She would have killed Avarielle's mother herself,

driven by the need to succeed and impress those she considered mentors.

Now? Now, as she looked down at the dry blood, and understood the price of power much more clearly... now that she'd seen the downfall of most of the Elders of Ravenhold, and had felt their lives drift out of their bodies.

No. She knew that not all knowledge was power. Sometimes, it was just a distraction. A promise of something that could never be, but still strongly craved. Or knowledge could be just a lie, too, viewed as truth through a lens warped by fears and desires.

"What are the green flames?" Shirina asked Tanja. She knew how they'd been created, more or less, from the point of view of Carsyn. She knew the price had been high, and many had died. And that they'd only led to more deaths on the already blood-soaked sands of the West.

"That is for Elders to know," Tanja said. "But I will allow you to take hold of them, if you so desire."

"It could be as bad as Siabala's magic," Shirina said, slowly walking around the slabs, her feet quiet, heart resonating with the screams that had once echoed here.

"It could be. It could also be your salvation."

Tanja looked at her, a question in her eyes. *How far are you willing to go to save Graydon?*

"Graydon is more than magic," Shirina spoke aloud, musing her ideas, not caring that her mentor, or whatever this was, heard her. "Graydon is a place. A people. It's an ideal, too—to seek peace through diplomacy. And that failed us most during the Westland Wars, when the Circle created the green flames."

"Graydon is about survival, too," Tanja responded. "Before your life, wars tore apart pieces of it, like the Southern Coalition."

"True," Shirina said. "But I live now, and although history can teach us, to base decisions solely on how things were, or how people behaved back then, is akin to hoping for a return to those times so that the decisions based on them make sense. I will not fall prey to that trap. The Graydon I live in now is the one I must base my decisions upon. To do anything less would be foolish."

"Will you take the green flames?" Tanja asked again, offering no input into her logic, which Shirina knew was flawed, as most logic based on human perception tended to be. Perhaps it was more of a philosophy. That Tanja did not correct or demand her to refine her thinking only brought home the fact that this wasn't her.

"Who are you?" Shirina asked, stopping before her mentor. "I watched Elder Tanja die on the fields of the Days of Blood, as she tried to save me."

"And failed."

"Who are you?"

"I am what remains, what's left behind. Tied to you and your mind and heart, for trying to save you from dark magic. I am Tanja. I am Ravenhold. I am magic."

Shirina's mind spun, trying to piece together the woman's words. She wasn't a "who" so much as a "what." Or maybe that didn't matter. Right now, she was all that

Shirina had, the only tenuous connection to Ravenhold. Perhaps this explained the Elder's lack of exploration into life after death. Perhaps they already *had* the answers, and so didn't fear or study it.

"What would you do?" Shirina whispered, a gentle question for a woman who had been harsh to her, forcing her to be the best, pushing her beyond what was reasonable or kind. She'd forged Shirina in fire and magic, and Shirina had reshaped herself into a kinder version of that power. She did not have a Keep to hide within, nor the weight of history backing her. She built with what she had, which at times proved to be very little. And she had needed to gain and maintain the trust of the people of Graydon.

"I would do all that I must to protect Ravenhold."

"You died protecting me, not Ravenhold," Shirina answered, even more softly.

Tanja stood before her, a little too still, waiting for her.

"I am not Ravenhold," Shirina said, touching one of the stone slabs. "Nor do I really represent it, anymore. It's an ideal for another time. Graydon, and Elihor, need something different now."

"Larkhold stands," Tanja said, voice crisp.

"Larkhold was different than Ravenhold," Shirina acquiesced. "But it is not sustainable."

"Who are you to decide it isn't?"

"No one. Just someone who's fought hard to rebuild Graydon's Circle into something better."

"Better defined by whom?"

She sighed. Now *this* sounded like the Tanja she remembered.

"By me. By the people of Graydon. By those who need Ravenhold to be more than just a Keep. To be an ideal of magic, and to share that magic, instead of hoarding it. Like knowledge, it should be accessible."

"You did not tell anyone about the Wall of Loss."

"No," Shirina said, facing her mentor again. "To protect Cassara and buy us time. Which served little purpose, regardless. I am willing to accept that not all my choices were necessarily good. They were simply the best ones I could make at the time, knowing what I knew, feeling what I felt, having seen what I had seen."

"Will you take the green flames?"

Of course it came back down to that—the whole reason they were there. Would she take the green flames? The one magic she might be able to access, which was not dependent on wielding magic from outside herself? It wasn't as sustainable, nor could she wield as much magic if she couldn't pull on Graydon's strands. But it would be better than nothing.

Wouldn't it?

The West's relationship with the Circle was still unstable, and the green flames were known to have killed the wife of their leader, almost forty years ago. The rebels of Massir, the army of Siabala, also wielded green flames. She would get a few spells off before being taken down, but then what? Then she'd shown everyone that the Circle couldn't be trusted. That she'd fallen back on old, bloody ways when the road became too hard. And to little success.

If success was assured, she believed she would be more tempted by it. But it wasn't, and so she wasn't, either.

She glanced at the slabs, built on a pedestal of stone, linking down to the earth. Where magic had been fused into those strapped to it.

While being on stone. She turned away from Tanja, and placed a hand on the stone, ignoring the dry blood flecking under her palm. If the magic of Graydon had been trapped, or returned, to the stone structures beneath the city, was it out of reach? Why had the Circle done these experiments here? She'd first thought they'd been done away from the Keep for deniability, and underground for cover, but what if it was about more than that?

What if… what if some of the magic from the city still existed? And connecting rocks still filled with this ancient power with the magic of the air formed the green flames?

That would mean the Circle had some understanding of the magic in the stones below, and how to channel it into people. Which could mean she could channel it, and not take in any of Siabala's free-floating red magic.

"Will you take the green flames?" Tanja asked, now on the other side of the stone slab. Shirina ignored her, pushing harder on the stone. She closed her eyes, focused her breathing, and reached out with her hand.

And felt the tingle of magic greet her. Her breath caught in her throat and she stilled it, for fear of losing the magic again. She welcomed the power, channeled it through her, careful not to take in anything else. Visualized it traveling her body, to reach her other hand. She muttered a spell, but the magic wasn't in the air, so did nothing.

Of course not. Another deep breath, and she focused inward. This was different magic. Of earth, not air. She'd worked her Circle around the earth. The gardens, plants, how it interconnected them, and all of Graydon. How dependent they were on the physical, and not to get lost in magic.

But now they were the same. Like the trees of Elihor's roots reaching down for their magic.

A deeper breath. She pressed harder against the stone, feeling the magic react to her beckoning. She cleared her mind, forced all thoughts of the past, the present, even the future away, pushed down her worries and anger, and focused on just that magic. Like a seedling needing careful care to survive a drought, she coaxed it further within her. Gently it infiltrated her, like the magic had once done, different but the same. Not green flames. This was the magic of Graydon.

This was *her* magic. Ravenhold's power.

Arm out, fist turned up, she focused on the movements of her body instead of the sounds of her mouth. The slow unfurling of her fingers, revealing her palm where she willed a flame to appear. A deep breath, and she felt it answer her call.

She opened her eyes.

The white magic of Graydon greeted her, pure, steady, unwavering.

Like her resolve.

"I will not take the green flames," Shirina whispered, as though afraid the strength of her voice would frighten the flame, though it held strong, the small ball of magic tinted with blue, adding depth to its beauty. She closed the tether to the stone and slowly removed her palm, the tingle of magic leaving her skin.

But the flame remained, fed by the magic she'd managed to welcome in.

"I will find a way to work with the magic of Graydon, such as it is."

Tanja smiled, really smiled, as she appeared before her, her features glowing in the white flame cupped in Shirina's palm.

"You worship at the altar of Graydon."

Shirina returned the smile. Then she felt herself slip away, focusing only on that flame, on how bright it shone, how steady, and how she would learn not to master it, but to work with it.

10

Cassara walked up the stairs to the large landing, filled with well-kept trees and welcoming flowers. She wore pants and a shirt, loose hair a veil of muted gold, dirtier than anyone at court had ever seen her.

Several people had come to meet her on the grand stairs before her palace. Among them were several Circle Elders from Larkhold and from the false Ravenhold. Those from Elihor looked at her with some concern. Those from Tally's Circle, with greed.

Well, at least it looked like they all agreed on one thing, whether worried or gleeful—her life would easily be forfeit.

A cloak billowed as Cassara faced them, and she saw her daughter, Altessa. The vice around her heart loosened, though it did not let go. Altessa looked older. Her eyes bore dark marks beneath them, grief etched in every fine line.

But she stood tall, and gently acknowledged Cassara's signal to be still, not to interfere. Pride at her eldest's strength and composure bloomed in Cassara's chest. One day, Altessa would make a fine queen.

An Elder stepped forward, and Cassara recognized him as one of Tally's—Elder Rale.

"Queen Cassara," the Elder said, not lowering his head or showing any sign of respect.

"Elder Rale," Cassara answered, "do you speak for Elder Tally?"

Eyes narrowed, followed by a quick nod.

"It seems that we are at an end," the queen said, looking out to the collapsed city, and to the Bloody Mountains.

"I have a proposal for you," Cassara continued.

"Go on," the Elder said, looking suspicious.

"I will stay here and await Tally's arrival, with you. In turn, you let my daughter and everyone who wants to leave go in peace."

"No," Altessa croaked out. Cassara gave her a thin smile and a quick gesture with her hand to stay still. Altessa stayed rooted in place, the winds shifting, playing with her hair.

Cassara hoped the wind would calm down, or her plan might fail her. She'd placed her trust in so many people of late. So many, except herself. She'd trusted Avarielle's and Shirina's judgments above her own, feeling so broken.

But not now. She felt resolve in her actions. This was what she was meant to do. What *needed* to be done.

"I don't see that you have much to bargain with, Your Majesty," the Elder scoffed.

"Siabala wants revenge on me," Cassara said. "For trapping him with my magic all these years. Does he not?"

A moment passed, the bells slowly ringing in the city below, flags turning with the winds fueled by the gray day.

The Elder nodded. She focused on him and him alone. If she looked at Altessa, she feared she would lose all self-control and grab her in her arms, never to let go.

"He does," the Elder said. "Yours will be a painful death, I should imagine."

Cassara nodded slowly. "If you let the others go, I will not rob him of that satisfaction."

The Elder's eyes narrowed. Cassara hoped that Siabala's magic was still weak enough here that the Elder couldn't stop her, even if he wielded Siabala's red strands. She had seen them in action, and knew most of Tally's warlocks and witches focused on attack magics, not on defense.

She held up her hand and an arrow flew by her, piercing a nearby tree. The Elder took a step back.

"They will not target you," Cassara said. "I imagine you have enough magic to protect yourself. But do you think you have enough to stop arrows from piercing me? From multiple places?"

Another arrow flew from the north, from one of the

towers. Guards started running, but it would be too late. By the time they arrived, the rebels would be gone.

"You have ten seconds to make up your mind," Cassara stood before them, fighting the urge to look her daughter in the eye. One of the new guards walked toward the queen, intending to usher her in. An arrow flew through his heart, and he collapsed.

She focused on the lieutenant standing near her daughter. *Lieutenant Garlon.* Trusted by Captain Travin. She knew him. He would keep Altessa safe.

"Order your guards to withdraw, and protect my daughter," she commanded. The lieutenant's eyes softened, and he bowed. Then he took Altessa by the arm.

"No," Altessa said.

"It's okay, Altessa," Cassara said as the lieutenant ushered her daughter down the stairs. The Elders shifted, looking to Rale for guidance. All except the Elder from Larkhold, who looked from Rale to her, as though uncertain what to do. Guards stood before the princess's escape—guards she did not recognize, no doubt under Tally's thumb.

Cassara forced her eyes away from her daughter, back on Rale.

"Let them go," she said, "or you will have but a corpse to offer your master."

The flags of Massir released their tension, draping their poles as the winds died down. The arrows would find their targets.

Elder Rale's gaze flickered east, eyes sparking with

victory. Cassara followed his gaze, at first seeing nothing. She summoned the Sight, and saw the red magic smothering the land, strands lashing out at each other as they reconnected, smoothing the road for spells like teleportation.

"He's coming," Elder Rale said.

Cassara felt the situation slip from her, and tried to regain control.

"And I will be dead before your lord comes," Cassara said, the Larkhold Elder's eyes bulged with glee.

"I will not allow it," he said, taking a step toward her. An arrow pierced the ground before him.

The wind shifted, and she could smell Siabala's magic, sulfur and hatred, come to claim her kingdom. Her stomach turned, but she stood firm. A small sweat broke across her brow as memories of the Days of Blood shook her core. Memories of Siabala's strength and monsters, and how little they knew of how to stop him. Only despair, and hope, though certainly not in equal measure.

How had I done this? She looked to Altessa and strengthened her resolve. She'd done it because she'd had so much to lose. Just as she did now.

She would not fail them.

"Go," Cassara told Altessa. The guards blocking her daughter's path wavered, waiting for Elder Rale to give further instructions. Lieutenant Garlon seemed ready to fight past the other guards, if necessary, though he would be sorely outnumbered. The Elder's face twisted to one of ecstasy as he looked at the incoming wave of red magic.

The world stopped. Even the wind paused, as everyone looked toward the east, even those who couldn't see the red tendrils unifying and reforming, sensing something *wrong* in the air.

The city bells still rang lazily, alerting guards to start preparing the city, but still, it wouldn't be enough. Cassara knew deep within that it just wouldn't be. This was too soon. Too quick. And too unstoppable.

A hand around her arm jerked her back to the now, as Elder Rale grabbed her and yanked her toward him. An arrow scratched Cassara's back, the next one, aimed more faithfully at her heart, stopped by red flames shielding her and the Elder.

"Run, Altessa!" Cassara shouted. The princess hesitated, but Lieutenant Garlon practically dragged her down, shouldering past the guards who still seemed uncertain whose side they were on.

Rale's guards looked at him, but he ignored them, focused on his current prize: Cassara Edoline, Queen of Rashim, descendant of Graydon, jailkeeper of Siabala's soul.

"You would do this?" the Larkhold Elder finally spoke, a tremor in his voice. "You would ally yourself with Siabala?"

"You have no power, Elder Quilsam," Elder Rale said, holding out his hand to cast magic. Cassara struggled, managed to knock him off kilter, but Rale's grip on Cassara's arm tightened. Whatever deal this man had struck with Siabala, it fortified his limbs and made the queen feel annoyingly weak.

He had her, but Altessa was gone. That was all that mattered.

"I have more power than you've ever had," Rale said, his vicelike grip on her arm burning, her skin painful beneath his hand. She bit back a scream, forced herself to remain standing.

Altessa is safe. She found comfort there.

"Let the queen go," Quilsam said, voice shaking, though he drew himself up to his full height.

"Lord Siabala wants an audience with the queen." Rale's eyes glowed a muted red, his powers quickly increasing. Shirina's attempts to stop the magic had reached their end.

Which meant Siabala would be here, soon.

Avarielle.

Cassara's sleeve burned, pain lancing up and down her arm.

"Your Majesty—" Elder Quilsam started to say.

"Go," Cassara said. "Live to fight another day, Elder."

"I don't think that's something that'll happen," Rale said, holding his hand up toward the Elder... but then his eyes flickered, and he laughed.

"The magic restored its connection," Rale said. Quilsam looked to the east, eyes widening. Cassara followed suit, terror and resolve battling for her heart.

"Siabala comes," Rale said, voice trembling.

The air shimmered with tension. Cassara stopped

struggling, standing tall as a teleportation spell coated in red came to a stop on the northern edge of the courtyard. Familiar red hair, face turned away from her.

Cassara took deep breaths as Avarielle turned around, hope turning to ashes in her gut as she met the familiar hazel eyes and saw none of their usual warmth.

Standing before her was no longer Avarielle Grayloft. It was Siabala himself, come to claim her blood.

11

____

ally's magic dissipated, red waves washing over Avarielle as she looked down on Massir. Her feet moved beneath her, though she couldn't feel them move, like Siabala had managed to block her access to them. She tried to shift her arms, watched as one reached for Graysword. Her lips didn't obey her either, and she couldn't even close her eyes as she pivoted, Cassara's light hair swirling in the winds. An Elder held her arm, and Avarielle growled. Low, throaty, and entirely from her, its vibration resonating within her. It felt good to move something in her own body.

Graysword's pommel warmed her palm, its magic licking that of Siabala's. The same magic. The one she'd always wielded without hesitation. Except now the magic danced with the red powers of Siabala, the white flames battling them, or simply accepting them. Maybe both.

"Avarielle," she heard Cassara's voice clearly, Siabala

letting her witness her death. "I know you can fight him, Avarielle." Cassara said it so simply, so matter-of-factly, that it made Avarielle's heart ache.

You can't fight me, Siabala's voice rang hollow, scraping her soul.

Watch me, Avarielle managed to growl again, a simple sound that helped ground her. She felt Siabala's magic on the sword, yes, but also Graysword's magic. *Her* magic. It might have been powered by Siabala, but separated from him for over a thousand years, the magic was its own.

Like me.

Graysword's magic was just different enough, and she was familiar enough with it, that she could pick it out from the other magics. Could sense it beyond Siabala's, and summon it to her.

The blade shone white, magic crawling up her arm, fighting back Siabala. She heard him growl in turn, but not with her throat. Hand shaking, she kept pulling on the magic of Graysword, feeling it both embrace and fight Siabala.

Like her. An oath, now broken. Still linked, fighting to be free.

She just had to fight more strongly than Siabala, and maybe she'd win the day.

Just maybe.

She took a step toward Cassara, the queen meeting her eyes.

"I know you, Avarielle," she said. "You would never do anything to hurt me. Or Rojon."

Rojon. Her steps faltered, Siabala's hold weakening at the thought of her son. She'd tried not to think of him—thinking of him while Siabala's soul held her body would soil her son's soul. Like it would grant access, and maybe an advantage, to Siabala when it came to Rojon. She refused to give him that.

He would never have that satisfaction, if she could stop him.

I will kill him, too. You and I will, together.

Avarielle fought to keep her sword down, but the blade, and her, continued approaching Cassara.

Where in Eli's Dreams was Shirina?

The wind picked up, cold and biting.

I will kill them all, everyone in Rashim, one by one, and make sure they know it's because of their queen.

You're a peach, Avarielle growled. Then, an idea. *So, keep her alive, then. Make her suffer. Make her watch.*

The words stung, and she hated herself for them. Make Cassara suffer so she'd have to watch her die by her own hand? *No.* So they'd still have a chance. If she killed Cassara…

Do you think I'd let my hatred for Graydon's descendant overtake my desire to return? To fully own you?

Avarielle gritted her teeth, pulling on Graysword's magic, the blade shining white and red, reflected in Cassara's blue eyes, which were now so close—*too close*—and still focused solely on Avarielle.

Unless I should have her daughter, and kill her first, letting the mother witness her death? Bathe her in the blood of her firstborn?

Hopelessness and anger engulfed Avarielle. That would be a fate worse than death for Cassara. How could she fight such unrelenting evil when it held all the advantages?

The world began to swirl, the ground glowing white as a teleportation circle appeared between Cassara and Avarielle.

A crimson cloak billowed in the wind, Shirina standing before her, eyes full of that annoying Circle confidence, a staff of dark stone in her hand.

Avarielle had never been happier to see the sorceress, even as Graysword came up for the blow, and she found herself unable to stop it.

1 2

Ravenhold held Shirina in its embrace as magic swirled around her. *No.* Beneath her. Not in the air, but in the ground, solid, an anchor. Instead of going up as usual while teleporting, she went down… and felt a surge of energy from the pure magic dancing around her. She traveled more quickly, lines of magic clearly established, her mind seeing what her eyes no longer could. Cities spreading below. Some crushed by the earth, others still complete.

Round domes, spires, some creatures still maintaining them. Nowhere did animals create burrows—not even rats lingered there. Kept safe, and clean, by the magic that had created it—the same magic that Graydon and Elihor had taken, brought up to the sky, out of its native stone. She followed it, letting her consciousness be her guide.

She needed to be in Massir. And she needed a staff to draw magic.

From the ground.

Rojon had crafted a staff for her. From the sproutling in Lisal Gardens, as it reached up for the sky, for the air. But that wasn't what she needed. She needed its roots. Reaching down, toward the magic's ancient home.

The magic heard her, welcomed her, guided her, brought her beneath the Lisal Gardens. Her fingers wrapped around a root of the tree, the earth solid and fresh around it. She closed her hand and visualized the staff. She couldn't see, sound above her muffled, more like vibrations against the edge of her skin, which wasn't really there either, yet was, an ephemeral shimmering of magic. She held the root with fingers pulsing with magic and, once she could feel the staff as an extension of herself, she pulled away.

To Massir. She focused her mind on the gleaming city of purple and silver, the vibrations shaking the earth around her as she approached, like someone dragged a heavy platter back and forth over a rough table surface.

Massir. Cassara was there… A wave of magic smashed into her, and she forced her mind not to panic at the thought of suffocating under all this earth. She opened her eyes, surrounded by darkness. She needed the Sight. She couldn't see through stone without it, and she needed to know what she returned to.

The ground lit up, Graydon's magic perfect and glowing around her. Not with the strands of the air that she'd always known, but rather with a diffuse, constant glow, like the magic nestled comfortably in the ground.

Because it wasn't fighting this home. It had always been fighting the air above.

Elihor's magic, usually darker strands, also nestled around her, coiling gently around Graydon's, in a way that made her insubstantial body shiver.

She could spend a lifetime observing them and feel peace in a way she never had before, as the magic of both lands supported her, welcomed her, and carried her to her destination.

Reluctantly, because she had little choice, she looked up, to see beyond Graydon and Elihor's magic, to the red strands streaming far above, not surprised when she saw the weaves of Siabala's magic reconnecting. She'd hoped to win them a few days, but hadn't managed to even buy them a full day. Siabala's magic was restored, made whole again, and he'd no doubt already landed in Massir.

The pulse of magic I'd felt earlier.

Avarielle would be in Massir, hunting Cassara.

Quickly, she focused her mind on that one command, and thought of Avarielle. Of the magic of Graysword.

She began teleporting back up, but the movement felt slow, because she hunted the human, whose magic was less powerful. She needed instead magic familiar to the underground threads; she thought of Siabala, of the monster.

And found herself reappearing before Avarielle.

"Shirina!" Cassara cried out behind her. Shirina's cloak billowed, showing the crimson red. She didn't care. Not anymore. She had found the magic by herself. Let them keep their cursed ranks—all she cared about was her ability to defend Graydon, and its people.

Avarielle's features twisted in anger, but her eyes betrayed her joy. She could see the war within her. Siabala's magic ran down her arms, her legs... wait. Not both arms. The arm holding Graysword, its magic active, wasn't fully red.

Avarielle was fighting back. And losing.

"Avarielle," Shirina said, nodding slightly. A silent scowl responded. The sorceress tightened her grip on her staff, took a deep breath, the magic beneath her strong. But it was far below, now, the castle of Massir not part of whatever network of magic connected it to the land. She could at least draw it through her staff, though it would take more effort.

She sighed. "I can't tell if you're still possessed by Siabala. All you ever did was scowl in the first place!"

The warrior moved fast, Avarielle unleashing her anger. Or Siabala, at robbing him of his prize multiple times. She stopped the blow with her staff. Graysword came in sideways, Avarielle holding back the blade as best she could.

Shirina sidestepped, drew the warrior away from Cassara. Avarielle moved quickly, but not as quickly as she could. Shirina had never been at the receiving end of the warrior's blade, but she'd seen her move often enough to know when she was holding back.

Which was just as well, because she was still terrifying.

Shirina summoned the magic through her staff,

sending it into Avarielle, fires losing strength as they hit her. The warrior stumbled, buying her time. Her spell hadn't been powerful enough. She had to try again.

She sent another spell hurtling into the warrior... only to have it snuff out before reaching her.

Shirina's heart raced as Avarielle came in for another blow, the warrior distressingly silent, moving quickly. Several Larkhold and false Ravenhold Elders and adepts moved out of their way, afraid of being impaled. Understandably so.

Another fire spell, and Shirina understood as it left her staff. *Air.* The magic didn't want to be in the air. It had trusted her to understand that, and she'd failed it at the first test. She narrowly avoided a blow from the warrior, the blade biting her arm, red blood dribbling down her not quite so white robe.

She needed to buy herself time.

Shirina knocked the staff against the ground and managed to teleport out just as Graysword swooped into the space she'd occupied, sending Avarielle flying down the stairs. It would buy her, and Cassara, a moment. If they were lucky enough.

She just needed to catch her breath.

She plunged back down, into the ground. She had always relied on fire, and the air that fed it. She'd ridden the breeze riddled with magic and had looked up... but never down.

She let herself be swallowed by the earth. By its beauty. The worms that dug deep within, allowing for life. The fuzzy mammals that burrowed and made it their home. The roots carrying memories and magic up.

Up. But not to the air.

She looked, taking a moment, forcing her heart to steady. The magics of Elihor and Graydon nuzzled in the ground, across both lands. Beneath the Bloody Mountains, a large swath of white stayed there. *The Wall of Loss.*

Cassara's magic, wanting to be unleashed, uncertain how.

Threads of red remained in it, but struggled against the white shimmer, fighting to break free.

The earth contained multitudes. All of life. An entire civilization had fed from it, and been destroyed.

Shirina paused, looking again at the light and dark strands of magic. They traveled the length of the lands. They weren't meant to be separated as they had been by the Wall of Loss.

Magic should always be free. The two lands were really just one, broken to contain Siabala, or perhaps by Siabala himself... she didn't know. Someday, she might. But not today.

Before, when the strands had been free together, in the air, they'd merged. But here, they knew where they belonged. They danced together, able to remain separate. For their power to be whole but individual.

They were of the earth.

They fed both Elihor and Graydon.

The three keeps, made of old stone, keeping them

separate… the Wall of Loss buzzing with Elihor's and Graydon's magics, now only Graydon's…

Free Cassara's magic, send it back in the air, Tanja's voice, now sounding different, more earthy, sounded in her mind.

I can't, Shirina shook her insubstantial head. *It's in her blood, not mine. I can't move it any more than Siabala could.*

Then bring up the magic of Graydon! Force it back into the air.

No, Shirina said, feeling certain as she watched the waves of energy fill the ground. *It is home. It was never meant to be in the air.*

She remembered the feeling of her old magic. How it would drain her, and her witches, probably in a bid to fight back. To be free. How it would dance in the air, and mix with Elihor's, to kill them.

To stop them from hurting it, she was certain.

It's the only way to defeat Siabala.

No, Shirina felt her anger. *It is meant to be here. It feeds Graydon and Elihor. It supports both. It belongs here.*

You would let your friends die.

Hardly, Shirina felt her own certainty. *I trust that I'll find another way. That the magic, as it is now, will support me, as I will try to support it.*

Her body jerked back up, her teleportation spell coming to an end. She felt like she'd been there decades, trapped in the flow of magic, observing the land around her. Mere seconds had passed, Avarielle still twisting on the stairs, planting her feet, preparing to run back toward Cassara.

Shirina twisted around, placed herself before Cassara. As she stepped out of the teleportation spell into fresh, cooling air, she saw her mentor through the magic, her skin like the ancient bricks of Ravenhold.

She smiled.

You serve the land.

Shirina's feet found the ground again.

In the changing winds of Graydon, her crimson cloak billowed, slowly turning black.

Shirina reappeared, the teleportation magic not letting go, instead washing back inside of her. Cassara gasped as Shirina's familiar crimson cloak turned black, the circle at her heart turning equally black.

Her eyes held Cassara's, speaking calmly as though nothing had changed.

"I saw your magic, Cassara, beneath the Bloody Mountains."

The Elder's hand still burned on the queen's arm, but she ignored it. She ignored Avarielle's scowl as the warrior came charging back up the stairs. She ignored the Elders of various Circles looking at Shirina with shock.

She focused only on Shirina's confident look as she pointed toward the Bloody Mountains, where parts of it had collapsed. "It waits for you beneath the range," Shirina said. "We just need to figure out how to unleash it."

Fears and worries assailed Cassara's mind, even though she believed the sorceress. She'd thought she'd never touch the magic again. That she'd be dead by the time it was set free. Part of her had convinced herself she wasn't meant to relive its glory. That she'd burned so bright, so young, that the rest of her life would be spent dwelling in the shadows of her storied youth.

No, she pushed back, seeing Shirina's cloak. Everyone had told her that she couldn't become an Elder. That she never would. But her friend had done it, and so could she.

"Let go of her, Rale," the sorceress said, the Elder screaming as she used some sort of magic against him without chanting a spell. The sorceress turned as Cassara was freed, trying to reach her magic, but focused on the warrior barreling toward Shirina.

Avarielle's sword came up. The bells still rang. The world stilled. Stopped.

Shirina's cloak, fully black now.

Cassara took a deep breath, reached deep within herself. And deep beneath the Bloody Mountains. Beyond the ground, and the city below. Beyond Siabala's Rage, and the stone that contained it. Her hand flew to her chest, where her amulet used to rest, and she imagined its strength. Imagined the magic flowing through it, into her.

She urged her powers to return, feeding her worry not about herself, but about everyone else around her. About Altessa. And Dayshon. Of her children in Edoline. And her brother. Of her friends in the Southern Coalition. And Shirina. And Avarielle, who fought so hard to break free.

Of her people, who would die without her magic.

But still, the magic refused to come, even as Shirina and Avarielle exchanged blows.

1 4

Graydon's magic danced up from the ground, around Shirina, fighting against Siabala.

The warrior held Graysword with two hands, pumping its magic into her. The warrior snarled and struck down. Shirina blocked the blow with her staff, using her magic to hurl a not-insubstantial rock onto the warrior's hand. Avarielle's death grip on the pommel of her sword loosened with the blow, but did not release.

Shirina slammed the same rock back down on the bleeding hand. This time, Graysword clattered to the ground.

"No!" Siabala/Avarielle screamed, red fury sparking in the hazel eyes.

Shirina drew on the powers trapped in the earth. She only drew the white strands, not yet confident in her understanding of her magic to draw both at once.

She wrapped the magic around Avarielle, holding the

warrior in place. Siabala's magic fought back, striking with all its considerable strength.

"I can't unleash my magic," Cassara's voice trembled.

"Stop trying to do everything," Shirina gritted her teeth against the warrior's strength. "Focus on one thing. Help me save Avarielle!"

The queen stepped up, resolute, unwilling to give up. She glanced at the black circle above Shirina's breast, then nodded and took a deep breath.

"Just save Avarielle," Cassara whispered, and placed a hand on Avarielle's cheeks. At first, nothing happened as Shirina watched with the Sight, hoping against hope that magic would explode out from beneath the Bloody Mountains and find haven within the queen again.

Avarielle struggled, grunting against the magic. Shirina could feel her break down her spell, Siabala unwilling to let his prey go.

Then a trickle of magic, not from the ground, but from Cassara herself. A thin strand of white magic, pure white, traveling from the queen's mind toward the warrior, Cassara's eyes forcibly shut, tears of pain streaming down her face.

Cassara's magic found Avarielle and she screamed, then gritted her teeth, features strained.

"Keep trying," Avarielle groaned.

Cassara redoubled her efforts, managing to grab, no, *create* more magic, if Shirina saw the exchange correctly, pumping it into the warrior. Blood dribbled down Avarielle's chin, and Shirina studied the red magic within her. Siabala's magic hooked deep within Avarielle, especially in her left arm.

"Seal him in there like you did with the Wall of Loss," Shirina told Cassara. "In her left arm, here. Use the Sight. See what I see."

Cassara looked at her, then turned toward Avarielle. The queen's movements were slow, magic wrapped around her.

And then she seemed to understand. She took hold of the warrior's arm and used the old fractures and cracks as foundation markers for her magic, forcing Siabala's soul within it. Shirina placed a hand on Avarielle's right shoulder, funneling her magic from the staff into the warrior, solidifying Cassara's spell. Pure magic, which filled the warrior and pushed Siabala toward the queen's forming trap.

Cassara snapped it shut. Avarielle's head crumpled, and slowly came back up. Shirina looked to Cassara, the queen pale and covered in a thin layer of sweat, still pouring pure, blinding magic into the warrior.

"Let go of your magic, Cassara," Shirina told her. Cassara hesitated. "Trust that you will find it again."

"What if I don't?" Cassara said, voice broken and lost. "What if it never comes back?"

"It will," Shirina said, heart aching as she looked at the magic created by the queen. Shirina glanced back, hand still on the warrior's arm, just in case she felt a shift within her. She looked to the Bloody Mountains. No, the queen hadn't created the magic—she'd managed to pull it to her, but only a little bit, like a mostly blocked spout.

"You're connected to it again," Shirina said. "But it's having a hard time filtering through you. You not drawing upon it will not lessen that connection. I don't think it ever did."

Cassara looked at her, eyes shining with fatigue or something else—Shirina couldn't quite tell.

"Will you help me figure out how to use my magic again?"

"I will try," Shirina said, nodding, not promising that which she could not guarantee. The queen seemed satisfied and the bright magic stopped dribbling from her into Avarielle.

"Do you think you can let me go, now—" Avarielle said with a thin smile, "—Elder Shirina?"

Shirina looked at the warrior. She was exhausted. And angry. And relieved.

And very much herself.

Shirina lowered her spell, and all three women faced each other. Shirina picked up Graysword and handed it to Avarielle, who hesitated to take it.

"It helped keep you safe," Shirina said. "The strength of generations of your family taking an oath and then doing everything in their power to stay on the side of good is powerful magic in itself."

Avarielle nodded and gingerly took the blade, sheathing it with a trembling hand. Around them, Circle adepts and guards gathered.

"I wouldn't, if I were you," Cassara said. Shirina turned around. Elder Rale had vanished, as had all of Siabala's adepts. A few of Tally's adepts had been left behind, those who couldn't teleport. The Larkhold adepts… well, they looked angry.

Especially Elder Quilsam.

"She is Siabala," he hissed, gnarled finger pointing at Avarielle. Cassara and Shirina stepped before the warrior, in a reversal of roles.

"I thought you didn't believe Siabala still lived?" Shirina deadpanned, unable to stop herself.

Excellent behavior for a new Elder.

"Crim… Elder Shirina," he said, voice shaking. "We have had our differences in the past, but I have seen for myself what Siabala and his minions can do. And our magic is gone! They must be stopped." He glared at Avarielle. "*She* must be stopped." His eyes grew wide in panic. "And where is Rojon Kolder?"

"Safe," Shirina said, offering no further information. Somewhere deep within Avarielle, Siabala fought to free himself. Cassara had trapped him, but that was temporary, just like the last time. Best the warrior not know where she'd teleported Rojon. He'd be long gone, by now, and hopefully far out of their reach.

"Am I supposed to simply take your word for it?"

"Yes," Shirina said, gripping her staff more tightly. Cassara stepped aside, letting Shirina face the Elder, though she remained before the warrior, making it clear she was under her protection as more guards showed up.

"You should have listened to me from the start," she said, keeping her voice as flat as possible, to give him nothing to fight against. "You should have listened when I warned you of Siabala's return. You should have lent more aid when Graydon's magic vanished. And you should have helped the citizens of Massir when you had the chance."

He didn't reply, stiffly acknowledging with a nod. *Only because I'm an Elder.* Well, let him learn next time to listen to those in other stations. It would be a valuable lesson, if he bothered to learn it.

"You have become Elder," he said. "But… how?"

"I did not make a deal with Tally, if that's what you're implying," Shirina said, voice low, trying not to lose her temper. "You would have let her destroy everything I've built, simply because of the color of her cloak."

"She is an Elder…"

"She is a servant of Siabala," Shirina said, wishing she hadn't brought the conversation back to Avarielle, the warrior distressingly quiet. She quickly weaved words together to redirect him. "And I became an Elder through Ravenhold."

"Ravenhold is gone," the Elder said. Shirina raised an eyebrow.

"Keeps are more than just stone, Elder Quilsam." He looked flushed, as though on uncertain footing.

"I know, but…" He stopped, and she didn't push, not wanting to completely humiliate and undermine him in front of his adepts and peers. She needed him still, which was the only reason she relented.

For now.

"Perhaps we should have a discussion on everything we have learned and know, so that we may be best prepared to face Siabala. And," she added, seeing his eyes dart toward Avarielle, "I believe I can show you how to tap back into the magic of Elihor, if you're willing to learn some new skills."

"I must see to Dayshon," Cassara said. Shirina gave a slight nod, showing she would stay with Avarielle.

"Very well, Your Majesty," Shirina said, and Cassara left, followed by her few remaining loyal guards, the others kept at bay.

"We'll speak more shortly," Shirina informed Elder Quilsam, his face turning red at her casual dismissal. "For now, I must tend to a few things." Shala wasn't here. Nor were any of her adepts. "If any of my adepts return, please send them to me."

"Shirina," Elder Quilsam said, then nodded as she turned toward him. "Elder Shirina," he corrected himself, swallowing hard. "I look forward to our discussion. But is it wise to let Siabala roam free?"

"We're not letting him roam free," Shirina said, placing a hand on Avarielle's arm. The warrior's muscles were so tight Shirina feared she might break. She could sense the magic throbbing within her bones and muscle, beneath the skin. "He is secured with Graydon's magic, from Queen Cassara. And I shall make sure it holds."

She turned from him, keeping a hand on Avarielle's arm and leading her to a study in the southern tower.

Despite being damaged, it still stood. And it was the furthest from the royal family.

She was certain Avarielle knew exactly what she was doing. As certain as she was that she approved.

Then it struck her, and she felt like an idiot. Her racing mind had missed the obvious.

She looked to Avarielle, the warrior tired and subdued. "Where's Tally?"

Avarielle's eyes widened, and the two took off racing down the corridor, toward Cassara.

15

Cassara walked briskly to her home. A few of her loyal guards followed, men and woman she'd known for years, who'd watched over her family, some for as long as she'd been queen.

"Your husband, the king, has not been well, Your Majesty," one of the royal guards said as she kept pace with her, Sergeant Ily.

She walked faster. "What has been done to him?"

"I am not sure," she said, "but he has not been himself. None of us have even seen him in days."

"Captain Tralin?"

"He was gravely injured protecting the king, and then dismissed. He would have died, had we not snuck him out. He would have gladly given his life for your family, Your Majesty."

"I'm glad you both lived, sergeant."

They crossed into her living quarters, still the same,

but so different. Without the familiar faces that usually filled it, the place looked empty. Devoid of life. Tired.

Cassara wanted to ask the sergeant about all of the other loyal guards she didn't see, but focused instead on the task at hand. Secure her husband. Weed out the illicit Circle. Make sure her city was ready for whatever attack would follow.

She felt more ready than she had for a while. She'd managed to touch her magic and use it to save Avarielle, even if it felt like pushing a stone through her brain. Still, she could feel it, even if wielding it proved difficult. It clung to her, a link to her heart and mind, as though as afraid of being separated from her as she was from it.

She cast the thought aside as she approached her bedroom. She could smell it. The rot. The infection. Her stomach lurched up and her heart sideways, and she pushed open the door. Dayshon sat at the edge of the bed, chin on his chest. His legs were still attached, and he obviously hadn't moved or showered, or removed his prosthetics, in days.

"Get Shirina," Cassara ordered, stopping the guards from entering. Dayshon had his pride, even if Tally had done her best to rip it from him.

"Dayshon?" she asked softly as she went around him. His head moved up, a strange, jerky movement. His eyes were completely red, brimming with Siabala's magic.

"Oh, Dayshon," she whispered, voice raw. She reached for him, afraid he would lash out, but he stayed completely still. She traced the contour of his face, his skin riddled with unfamiliar stubble and sweat. His brow was hot, fever coursing through him. She looked to his prosthetics, dry blood clinging to their tops where blisters had formed and released. They were stuck to his legs. Removing them would hurt, badly. Shirina was good at healing magic and could help.

She had to be able to help.

"Dayshon, hang in there," she whispered.

"He can't hear you, you know," Tally said from behind her. Cassara whipped around as threads of magic stumbled over her, holding her in place. But she had her magic, too.

She called it forth, tried to push against Tally's magic, but her strength failed her, her magic unable to pierce the funnel of her heart. Her fear blocked her magic as effectively as festering wounds held Dayshon's prosthetics in place.

"I'll leave the rest of your family alone," Tally practically cooed. "I just need you."

Cassara gritted her teeth and tried to call on her magic again, to focus on just one thing, just as the door burst open. Several guards streamed in, and Avarielle and Shirina. Tally focused on Shirina.

"Elder! I'm impressed, Shirina! No Elder has been granted a black cloak directly from Ravenhold since… I don't even know since when."

Shirina ignored her. "What did you do to Dayshon?"

"Avarielle knows," Tally said, a wicked grin splitting her face as she looked at the warrior. Avarielle looked to

Dayshon, saw his red eyes, and grew even more pale. Then she turned on the Elder, face twisted by rage. "Oh, he knew you'd love this! Can you not feel his joy?"

Avarielle screamed, holding her left arm, falling to one knee. Shirina stepped between Tally and the warrior, hit the ground with her staff and, without uttering a spell, caught Tally in a net of light.

"If only it were so easy, right, *Elder?*" Tally hissed and looked to Avarielle. "You want to save the king? You know where to find me. Where Siabala would like to go."

And she was gone, red flames tearing apart Shirina's magical net.

"Your Majesty," Sergeant Ily helped Cassara back up as the threads released her.

"I'm fine," she said. "Please guard the door, sergeant, and let no one else in."

"Of course," she said, looking to Avarielle.

"Avarielle and Shirina stay."

Muted gray eyes glanced at her, before the guard exited the room.

Shirina didn't hesitate, walking up to Dayshon and examining him.

"I need to remove his prosthetics, but they're infected," Cassara said. "Can you heal him?"

She knelt before her husband. Before Dayshon, the man she'd grown to love as dearly as she'd ever loved anyone. Before the slack features and red eyes.

"Siabala's magic is... he's filled with it, Cassara. I'm afraid my magic might hurt him."

"But there must be…" She remembered Tally's words to Avarielle and turned to the warrior, taken aback by the stony look not directed at Dayshon, but toward the window. Away from them. Away from Dayshon. Away from herself.

"Avarielle?" Cassara asked gently. She stood, Shirina watching carefully though she remained near Dayshon. She hated how wary they both were of their friend. They'd trapped Siabala again, but what had Avarielle been made to do since they'd last seen her? The thought twisted her gut, and Cassara placed a hand on Avarielle's crossed arms. The warrior didn't move.

"It's not your fault, Avarielle. Whatever happened, it's not your fault."

"Kaden's blood is on Graysword," Avarielle whispered, meeting her eyes, which shone with anger. "How many more innocents will I kill before this is over? Before Siabala wins?"

"I need you, Avarielle," Cassara said, clutching the warrior more tightly. "I know it's not fair. I wish things were different. But I need you, to save Dayshon." Despair tumbled out of her, gripping the warrior, not knowing what else to do.

"Cassara…" Avarielle started, the way she did when she wanted to leave.

"No," Cassara said, cutting her off. "Don't do this. Don't distance yourself. Don't go noble sacrificing hero on me. I *need* you."

It had been years since she'd had to plead with anyone. It seemed that she hadn't lost her touch.

"Noble sacrificing hero? Is that a thing I do?" Avarielle said, voice raspy, like she'd been shouting too long, as she tried to make light of things.

"It is, and it's heroic, but not now. I know you're hurt. I know this isn't fair. But I need you. Please. Please help Dayshon. What did Tally mean?"

"It's not that I don't want to tell you," Avarielle said, finally uncrossing her arms. Cassara held them both, feeling the warmth of her left one, and the strength of her magic. "It's that I don't want to talk about it." The warrior sighed, shook her head. Felt Siabala in her, muted, crushed even, by Cassara's magic. But... still there.

"It's just that... Eli's tits, this is weird, but I don't want Siabala to hear me tell the story. Because he *likes* it."

Cassara's eyes slowly closed, as though she couldn't stand to ask her friend to push into such painful territory, but her hands stayed on her arms, a silent plea.

The warrior stayed silent for what felt like an eternity.

And then, softly, she began to speak.

16

When she looked back at her life, Avarielle Grayloft saw two versions, like two books had been written about the same story, by vastly different authors. Like the books she used to read to Rojon, about heroes and legends. Like her parents would have read to her, she was certain, if they hadn't been busy trying to survive a war. And failing.

In one version, she was a powerful warrior who'd worked hard at protecting her people and her friends. Honorable, determined, unstoppable. She liked this version best.

In the other version, the one she tried to keep locked away but that currently outshone the more beloved tale, she was a puppet. Not a real person, but a creation, made to obey a god's will, to follow it no matter what. Even when she truly believed she was making her own decisions, she was being manipulated.

From taking Graysword to fight the demons he'd sent. Sealing an oath to activate its magic, to save her people. To save herself. Killing her beloved dance teacher and others, she should have been a dancer. Instead, she'd traveled a path of blood, whether she'd wanted it or not. Born to it, her first memory of green flames devouring her mother. The stench of burning flesh imprinted on her mind. The Eloms, Siabala's monsters, had smelled differently but similar when she'd cut them. They'd been people once, too. She hadn't known that, at first. Once she did, she'd tried to save some.

To keep the first story alive. But she needed to protect others, too. And so she kept attacking, and destroying. Killing.

While trying to be the hero.

Twice she'd broken at his will, manipulated so greatly a piece of her had fractured. The latest was with Kaden. She would have killed Cassara. She killed him, instead. Neither made her feel better.

Nor had the first time she felt truly lost and without power...

She looked at Cassara and Shirina. And then at Dayshon.

Her world had stopped, when Siabala had crushed her. She could feel him, still, in her.

I always could. She always had. Now, she could just no longer deny it.

Dayshon's eyes glowed red, like Kryde's had, in the end. Her son had seen what she'd done. The sorceress had seen Kryde once, when Avarielle had allowed her a glimpse at her memories. But she'd never talked about it with Cassara and Shirina. Nor with her beloved son. Not really.

It hurt too much, and she hadn't needed to. Kale told Rojon of his father, filling the gap of stories.

Or so she liked to tell herself.

She wasn't sure she'd handled anything well, but she knew Kryde would understand. Just as he would expect her to walk into the burning flames of memory to help her friend.

"Kryde and I met in Rokor, you remember, the one where he was bound in the chicken coop?" Avarielle started softly, gently easing herself into it. Cassara nodded. She hadn't gone to see the man, but the three had been together at the time, trying to find an answer to the Elom infestation.

"We met again in Siabala's Rage. He was heading back to Elihor. He freed me. Gave me a sword so I could go after your brother, Cass. When I couldn't make it back to Graydon safely, I headed to Elihor, instead."

Shirina studied her. Cassara's hand went to her chest, forming a fist.

"We spent months together fighting enemies, trying to survive. Then I had to go back to Graydon, for Jayden, who was being killed by Elihor's magic. We tried crossing the straits, but only Jayden made it." She'd been thrown off the boat, and Kryde had come after her.

She'd worked hard to not fear water. She'd learned to

swim in Elihor, thanks to Laora's help. She hoped her friend was okay. She hoped the village still stood, so that Rojon would always have a home to go back to.

"Then we decided to climb the Bloody Mountains. Go through Stormhold."

The climb had been long and arduous, but also beautiful. She hadn't had Graysword, but she'd had Kryde. They'd kept each other safe.

"Siabala," she swallowed hard, "Siabala wanted, needed, Kryde's powers. He already had your amulet," she spoke softly, looked to Cassara's eyes, found comfort in their openness. "And he needed Graysword. Which you had." Cassara nodded slightly. She'd kept it safe for her. She'd saved her people, too.

A debt that could never be repaid, even if Avarielle lived for a thousand years.

"So, he attacked when we came closer to Stormhold. I was hurt, and Kryde… Kryde's magic exploded. Protected me. But he fell into the hands of Siabala's minions."

She looked at Shirina's dark cloak, remembering a time when such a cloak had vanished, holding Kryde prisoner.

"I went after him, of course. Took days to scale the rest of the mountain. And then… then…"

Her eyes finally found Dayshon and held the sight of his slumped shoulders as she relayed the rest of her tale.

"I found him like this, by Siabala." Cassara sucked in breath and held it prisoner. "He'd been… turned into a puppet, Siabala said. A gift for me."

The red, soulless eyes. Could she have saved him? Had she not been alone, and so hurt?

"I called Graysword to me, then." Tears ran down Cassara's face. Because of memories, or because her heart lurched for the warrior. Or maybe for Dayshon. It didn't matter. Avarielle still felt numb, and she was grateful for the queen's ability to feel. No matter what, or how hard.

"The Wall fell. Siabala left. And…" Could she have done something different? If she'd waited, maybe tried to bring him down with her? Everything had been so desperate back then, so broken.

"You did the only thing you could," Shirina said, soft voice filled with certainty. "He was Siabala's by then."

Avarielle held the sorceress's eyes. What had she gone through to find the black cloak? The warrior always feared it might harden the witch, make her more like she used to be. But it hadn't, or at least not so far.

"I ran him through," Avarielle looked back to Cassara, the queen's fist turning white with strain.

"But—" Avarielle quickly closed the gap between her and Cassara, taking that fist in her hand, "—I didn't have the resources we have now. I didn't know everything we do now."

"And Siabala would not have bated Avarielle if there was no hope of saving him," Shirina concluded, speaking the words that made Avarielle hesitate.

After a time, Cassara whispered, "Is the choice between you and Dayshon?"

"That's a false choice," Shirina immediately said. "He's

trying to control the situation again. We can't let him do that."

"He can hear us, I'm pretty sure," Avarielle said, then added, "I think he's always been with me. Or a part of him, since I took the oath with him."

"That's my theory as well," Shirina nodded. Cassara looked from one to the other, growing stiffer. Avarielle let go of her and took a step back.

"Look, I need to get away from you two," Avarielle said, holding up her hand to stop Cassara's all too slow reply. "I'll go to Stormhold, into Siabala's Rage, and see if I can find something that'll help Dayshon."

"He's luring you there to get you fully under his control," Shirina said matter-of-factly.

"No, for that he needs Cassara and Rojon." She held Shirina's eyes, let her see the plea in them. "I can't be near them, Shirina. I can't live with this. I won't risk it."

"No, you won't," Shirina answered, "but there are other ways to do things than stubbornly throw yourself at them, you know."

"I've never seen you try any other way," Avarielle said, standing straighter. "Tell me you became an Elder through anything else than sheer stubbornness and I'll call you a liar."

A slight smile played on the sorceress's lips, then she grew serious again.

"I'm going to try something," Shirina said. "It might hurt."

If Shirina didn't offer more details, that probably

meant she was going after Siabala and didn't want him bracing for whatever was to come. Avarielle nodded, stood her ground.

"Stand back," she told Cassara, who took a step back. "Maybe give her Graysword, first," Shirina said. Avarielle looked at her incredulously but handed scabbard and blade to the queen. Cassara stood back, before Dayshon, as though intent on protecting him.

"Some secrets of Ravenhold have been made known to me," Shirina said, and Avarielle knew that she spoke to Siabala, not her. "And I am sorry."

Avarielle looked at her with surprise. Shirina ignored her and focused on the ground at her feet, and the staff in her grip.

She placed a hand on Avarielle's arm.

"You may want to sit for this," Shirina said.

"I'll stand."

Unsurprised, the sorceress nodded. Then, without another word of warning, she reached for Cassara's magic. And tightened its weave.

When she was a Green Circle, a new adept with little understanding of what Ravenhold and its mission stood for, Shirina had run away.

She'd been taken a few months prior during the latest Circle Harvest, and didn't know how to get back home. She missed her mother. Her brother. Her cousin.

Her own room, and the drawings she used to work on. The scent of burning logs as she sat with her mother by the fire, learning how to sew all those tiny little stitches to mend the family's clothing. Soft laughter drifting as they told stories and jokes. Meals served around a small table. Not always full of food, but always full of love.

She hadn't had a mission then. Nor new shiny white robes. But she hadn't felt alone, either.

Before she'd been renamed Shirina.

Madeline Monlie.

She still wanted to be called that. For her brother to make fun of her name and use it in random annoying rhymes.

She'd been only eight years old, and she was scared, and lonely, and the halls of Ravenhold frightened and gutted her with their austerity and silence. Their lack of life and smells of home.

She'd never made it back home. Not until Siabala had attacked and, broken and hurt, she'd managed to find her way back to that small hearth. By then, it was too late. Her family was mostly dead. They'd even erected a small grave for her.

Madeline Monlie was gone, a victim of the Circle's Harvest—a practice that Shirina then ended.

But, sometimes, parts of Madeline came back to her. Rarely, but sometimes. Cassara's gentleness reminded her of her mother. Avarielle's teasing, of family meals. Larkhold during cold winter nights smelled like fire in the hearth.

And now, she focused on the magic around Avarielle's bones, keeping Siabala trapped. Cassara had done what she could, but the drips of her magic had just been freed, and didn't want to be trapped again, coursing across Avarielle, red lines in every bone. With time, and unlimited resources and power, maybe Shirina could figure out how to remove Siabala from the warrior's body. His soul was sewn in, but not every stitch complete, pieces of him still frayed at the edges.

This was not something Shirina understood, but

Madeline did, learning under her mother's careful guidance. Sometimes, the fabric was worn, but you worked with it to create something new. Instead of just hemming, you embroidered. Adding a splash of beauty to distract from the frayed bits beneath.

Shirina had seen, *felt*, what Siabala's home had once been. He'd been ripped from his home, too, as she had been. She reserved judgment for now, the threads of history and legends wrapped around her thinking too tightly for her to fully understand what had happened. The truth might never be revealed, but she at least understood that what she knew wasn't the truth, either. Only a part of it. A tale concocted to ease the understanding of a messy history, where good and evil weren't as clear-cut as historians and kings wished.

She couldn't get Siabala out, no, but she could use Cassara's magic, already pumped into Avarielle's body, to stitch Siabala's soul in, to weave him in more tightly. On the scars of the broken bones of her left arm, broken with *his* magic, she embroidered over his soul, to hold him there. A place of comfort, where he might not be likely to escape as quickly.

She hoped that—just as she lingered in the comfort of Cassara's kitchen, fingers wrapped around a warm cup of tea, hearkening back to a long-lost home—his soul, weary from battling Avarielle for control, would accept his surroundings and rest for a while.

It might buy them time. She wove the magic over his

mind, unable to pull all of his threads into the scars, but enough that she felt his thoughts close in.

Avarielle shifted, and Shirina's grip on her arm tightened. She was hurting the warrior, she knew, but the woman was too damn stubborn to admit it. Or maybe it felt good to feel this pain, instead of just being trapped in her own body.

She closed her eyes, focused on that magic, on its threads, stitching the embroidery over him, her own hand shaking with exhaustion, her mouth dry. She ignored her own fatigue, retreated into the magic, focused on the pattern of the homelike prison she created for Siabala. On making it look like what she had seen and felt from traveling the magic of Ravenhold, like the ancient structures below. She didn't know how it had smelled, but she could add some of her own childhood warmth to create a prison for a dark god. For a monster, the thing intent on killing them all.

A prison like a home. Because she knew, and *he* knew, that she couldn't hold him forever. That none of them could.

Trapped by the magic, he conserved his strength, or so Shirina assumed, and nested within the home she created for him. Made of magic, but feeling like stone, the yellow glow of lights around him.

Cassara's magic was the thread, Shirina's pattern the embroidery. To strengthen the weave, she called on power from her staff, reaching deep into Graydon, welcoming the magic to coat the arm. To keep it safe.

She was done, but her hand stayed on the warrior, unable to tell where was up or down, only that Avarielle stood by her. Too much magic. Not to mention her mind had been pounded with the knowledge of Elders. Pieces of information kept forming themselves into place, like an entire library of books was suddenly available to her, but she'd yet to catalogue it to understand what was there, much less read all of it. Yet information kept presenting itself in her mind, like people pulled out tomes and read passages to her loudly, one over the other, of things she should know.

That she now knew. Some that she couldn't grasp, foundation blocks of knowledge eluding her.

"She's done," Cassara's voice cut over the din of the new knowledge fighting for control of her mind.

"In more ways than one," Avarielle said, and she felt herself guided to a seat.

"I just need a minute," she managed to mumble, or thought she did.

Then she repeated it in her mind, more loudly, to ground herself, and quiet all the voices fighting for control. Fighting to be understood, and to share centuries' worth of knowledge. She would understand it all, given time and meditation. She suddenly understood why Elders spent so much time alone in their studies. A luxury she could not afford.

"Can you move your arm?" Cassara asked.

"No," Avarielle answered, "but I don't hear him in the back of my mind anymore, so it's a fair trade off."

That slowly dragged Shirina back, as she forced her eyes to open. The chair she sat in was plump and comfortable, and she allowed herself to lean into it, for her body to receive rare comfort.

"I trapped him further, so he won't be able to hear," Shirina said, words sliding in a tired drawl. When was the last time she'd gotten decent sleep? "It seems I've also damaged your arm."

"No, Siabala did that a long time ago," Avarielle said. "You made sure I had a fighting chance. I appreciate it."

Shirina nodded, took deep breaths. Cassara said something to Shirina and stepped out of the room.

"Are you awake enough for a conversation?"

Avarielle stood before her. Shirina sighed, straightened her back, the fatigue clearing a bit as she stretched her muscles. She chose to remain seated, but looked up at the warrior, whose left arm was in a sling made out of one of Cassara's shawls.

"Purple looks fetching on you."

"I'll take that as a yes," Avarielle said. "I'm going to go to Siabala's Rage."

That snapped Shirina awake.

"You'll be walking right into his trap," Shirina said, meeting hazel eyes.

"He's still inside of me, Shirina. I think I'm already well trapped."

"There's a difference, and you know it."

"I want to save Dayshon," she said softly. "I want to save him, when I couldn't save Kryde."

"I know," Shirina said, the weariness smothering her senses. "But there must be another way."

"Do you know any, now that you don a black cloak?"

"I might," Shirina admitted. "I need time to process it. It's… a lot. All competing for my attention."

"We don't have time," Avarielle said. "Siabala could break free, or Tally will show her ugly mug, or Dayshon could die, or more monsters…"

"I know, I know," Shirina held up her hand to stop the warrior. It wasn't like the usually stoic Avarielle to spew anxiety and worst-case scenarios. Unless, of course, she was worried about her loved ones.

"As soon as I have enough energy," she said softly, "I'll make sure Rojon is safe."

"Thanks," the warrior mumbled, running a hand through her hair, then looked annoyed at her arm. "Just… don't tell me anything. Just in case. I've already betrayed you all enough already."

"You didn't betray us," Shirina said softly. "Siabala used you." She gave her a thin smile. "That'll teach you to make deals with evil gods."

"Lesson learned," Avarielle whispered. "What if you just kill me? Would that destroy Siabala?"

"I've considered that," Shirina admitted, looking up at the warrior.

"I'd expect no less," Avarielle said, with no accusing bite.

"I could kill your body, but not his soul. Then he'd find another vessel, probably your son. And we would have to find him, while still not knowing how to deal with him. Now, at least we know where Siabala is."

Avarielle looked down at her arm, a scowl on her face. "What if I rip this arm off?"

"An interesting idea. But he has hooks all over you, Avarielle. I've contained his mind, but…" she stopped.

"You're not sure you can separate him from me." Avarielle finished the thought.

Shirina nodded. She wanted to comfort Avarielle and tell her that she'd find a way. But the warrior didn't need her hollow reassurances. Nor was she foolish enough to think Shirina would choose Avarielle over all of Graydon.

So instead, she comforted her with the only true words that seemed to fit the situation.

"I promise that I'll do everything I can to stop him, no matter what."

"I have no doubt," Avarielle said, trying to cross her arm then scowling at the useless limb. She placed her right hand on her hip, instead.

"So, how does it feel, being an Elder?" she asked as Cassara opened the door, tray in hand. She handed Shirina a warm cup of tea, Avarielle a mug of sweet-smelling ale, and she dragged chairs over and a small bedside table so they could eat some of the open-faced meat and cheese sandwiches. And the sugar cookies.

"We have to keep our strength up," the queen said, heading to Dayshon with a glass of water to try to make him drink. Shirina and Avarielle watched as water dribbled down his chin, but some seemed to get in.

Shirina took a warm sip of tea, heat revitalizing her. But the comfort of the chair called so deeply, and she desperately wanted to answer it. She took the sandwich Avarielle handed her and tried to at least give her body food, while refusing to give it sleep. Cassara was right. They all needed food, before the next attack.

"Can you save him?" Cassara whispered as she joined the other two women, looking at Dayshon, the glass of water still mostly full despite her efforts.

Avarielle and Shirina shared a quick glance.

"I'll do everything I can," Avarielle said. Shirina kept her peace. If she could, she would. But her focus had to become narrow. She needed to focus on the most necessary and difficult task: stopping Siabala.

Dayshon might become a casualty of war. She used to find the cold calculations of need much easier to conduct before she'd allowed her heart to become entangled with so many lives. But it was still necessary, no matter how much she hated it. Unable to express this to Cassara, she kept quiet. The queen didn't seem to expect anything of her.

"If he'll just suffer, or… or if he's suffering while he's trapped… I can make sure he doesn't…"

Avarielle took Cassara's hand in her good hand. "No. Look, I don't know if he's still in there, but I was, when Siabala took control of my body, so chances are he is, too. And maybe he can hear us. And if he can," she turned to him, "then he'll remember all he's done for his people, and his family, and that he's already won so many battles. The war's not lost until he gives up. So fight, Dayshon, with everything you are, and everything you have. I'll find a way to save you. I couldn't save Kryde, but I *will* save you."

She turned back to Cassara. "You just have to keep him safe and alive, as best you can. He was healthy and strong. He has time yet."

"You're leaving, aren't you?"

Avarielle shifted. "I can't take the chance of staying near you, Cassara. Siabala wants me to kill you, remember? I couldn't live with myself. I don't even want to imagine it. But I can try to find some help for Dayshon, at least."

"Are you going to Siabala's Rage?"

"I'm trying to convince her to go elsewhere," Shirina said, "but I'm not sure where that would be, yet."

"You're going, too," Cassara said.

Shirina nodded. "As soon as I know you're safe, yes. I'll go with Avarielle."

"Of course," Cassara said.

"We need to get you away to safety," Shirina said to the queen. "Somewhere Tally and Siabala's rebels won't find you." Shirina pondered where that could be. If Siabala knew Avarielle's mind, then he knew everywhere they'd set up as a safe space. He slumbered now, or at least hid in the prison she'd crafted for him, but he'd probably informed Tally of those places long ago.

That meant she'd have to rely on places only she was familiar with, which turned out to be surprisingly few places, considering she and Avarielle hadn't really seen each other that much over the past twenty years, having come to an undiscussed agreement that they'd swap off watching over Cassara. A few exchanged greetings here and there. A battle or two. But that had been it.

Shirina knew of old Circle outposts that were hidden and hadn't been used in years, of which the warrior would know nothing. They wouldn't be the most comfortable for Cassara, but they would do.

She needed to find her witches, too. To give them back their powers, so that the Circle she'd created could help fight. Not just warriors, but all of them. The healers. Those worried about food. About the water. All of them were necessary to survive and win this day.

And keep Cassara safe.

"No," Cassara said, so softly that Shirina almost missed it, lost in her ponderings.

"No?" Shirina repeated, to make sure she'd understood correctly. When she looked at Cassara's stubbornly set features, she knew that she had. "Cassara—"

"No," the queen repeated, as though simply refusing a second cup of tea.

"Cassara—" Avarielle stepped up.

"No," she said again, and then sighed. "I know you're trying to protect me, and I appreciate it. But the king... Dayshon cannot rule." She glanced at her husband, then focused back on Shirina and Avarielle. "Altessa is safe, and my brother will be keeping my youngest children safe, I trust in that. I'll call back the guards, see who's still alive. We'll fortify the city and neighboring crops and villages. I will not abandon my people. Not now, when war is coming. I'm sorry, but I'll be safer here than anywhere else." She paused, turned to Avarielle. "Especially if you take Siabala away from me."

"I don't disagree," Avarielle's voice was steady. "But his disciples will try to capture you and get you to him. To *me*."

"I assume as much," Cassara said, holding up her hand. "I can still feel my magic around him, holding him prisoner." She looked at Avarielle's arm. "Shirina, is my magic safe to use, or will it release him?"

"I fortified his prison so it'll hold. He will eventually break free, but you can draw safely on your magic." She paused. "We just don't know how long we have before he escapes."

"Hours or days?" Cassara asked.

"I don't know," she admitted. "Days at most." She looked at the magic. It held, Shirina's weave strong. But already a few threads were weakening. Strong enough to welcome the soul of a god. Too weak to contain it forever.

"Maybe two," she said. "At most." She met the warrior's determined eyes, then turned to the queen. "I need to get Avarielle out of here, in case I'm very wrong."

"Will we be able to count on the Circle?" Cassara whispered.

"As soon as we're somewhere safe, I'll reach out to them and hopefully help them reconnect with their magic."

"What did you mean, when you said it was in the ground below us?" Cassara asked.

"It's… it would take too long to explain," Shirina said, mind swirling with the knowledge not just of how the land was, but also how it used to be. "And I'm still trying to parse it out. But think of it like ground water now. It's no longer droplets in the air. Your magic is hiding under the Bloody Mountains… I think yours wants to be in the air. It's shuddering for it, like it's trapped in turn."

"Mine is different?"

"Yes, and no. It's the same, but it's been trained, if you will, to stay in the air. The rest of it is more comfortable in the ground."

"In the ground," Cassara nodded, "and in that which connects it, like the metal of my amulet or the root of your staff."

"You would have made a fine Circle adept, Your Majesty," Shirina lowered her head. "And now we must go. I can't risk your safety anymore." She hesitated.

"I'll wait outside," Avarielle said.

"Thank you," Shirina whispered as the warrior closed the door behind her.

"Will you be able to save her?" Cassara asked immediately. "To save Dayshon?"

"I honestly don't know," Shirina said. She wanted to lie to the queen, her friend. Tell her that she would do everything in her power to save them. But she found that she couldn't, and doubted Cassara would believe her, anyhow. They'd been through too much together to easily swallow the lies, now.

"I can't promise anything," she said, "and my priority, like yours, must be stopping Siabala and saving as many as we can."

"A numbers game," Cassara said. "That's the game we played twenty years ago when we abandoned the troops to take the fight to Siabala."

Shirina went to protest, but Cassara continued, voice faint.

"And how many more would have died had we not done that? If Siabala had broken free, and his armies destroyed all of Graydon? What remained of it?"

She met Shirina's eyes. "I keep trying to think of how we could have done things differently, but I think we did the best we could under the circumstances. This time though, I won't lie to my people, and I won't sneak away in the dark. I won't abandon them, even if it means my downfall."

Shirina nodded slowly.

"It's not because I don't want to live, Shirina," Cassara said. "It's because I don't want to live knowing I didn't do everything I could. Just as you couldn't just abandon your Circle. Nor will you be able to abandon Avarielle."

"Low blow, Your Majesty." Shirina said with a slight smile. "Avarielle and I are in agreement on one thing: we save *you*."

"When you take her away, you worry about Graydon.

I'll worry about Rashim. And you take care of her, and try to save Dayshon, but…"

Shirina stopped her from having to say the words. "I promise I'll do the best I can, no matter what. It's all I've ever promised, Cassara."

"And it's gotten us this far." The queen stood along with the sorceress, and gathered Shirina in her arms. Shirina held her back. "Be safe, Shirina."

"You, too, Cassara," Shirina said.

And with that, Shirina went to find Elder Quilsam. They were long overdue for a chat.

1 8

Avarielle stood in the kitchen, her left arm useless in its sling, but the loss of her limb had led to regaining her mind. A worthwhile trade-off. She could fight with one arm, even if it would require some new moves and differently honed instincts.

The distraction might prove nice, though she hoped they wouldn't have to scale any cliffs.

She'd give up her arm if it meant keeping Siabala at bay forever. But that wasn't the deal. He was trapped in her, or he would go after her son. She wouldn't let that happen.

No matter the cost.

Shirina entered the kitchen.

"I must confer with Elder Quilsam for a moment. Then we can be off."

"Now that you're an Elder, can you tell him that he's an idiot?"

"I'm still new at this," Shirina said, though a slight smile played on her lips, "but I don't think that's quite Elder protocol."

"Shame," Avarielle said. Then hesitated. Shirina seemed to read her thoughts.

"You're safe, for now. I don't know how long the spells will last, but now they're strong." Shirina looked up from her arm, met the warrior's eyes. "Say your goodbyes to Cassara. Just in case."

Just in case.

Avarielle nodded and turned to head back toward the rooms. Shirina was gone in a flutter of black cloak. The warrior appreciated the sorceress's straightforward approach. Her words might have seemed cruel to some, but they brought comfort to Avarielle.

Because it made clear that Shirina had no intention of letting her get close to Cassara if there was any chance Siabala would claim her blood.

Cassara and Dayshon had never danced, despite their twenty-year marriage. Not a true dance of Rashim, anyhow, quick moving with the crescendo of music, carried by a flurry of fabric and high notes. They'd been married while monsters attacked the lands and had led an army west the morning after their wedding day.

Then, there had been fighting. Funeral pyres. Magic. Trying to get to know one another despite it all.

He'd made it seem easy. Dayshon was meant to rule, caring for his people more than himself. And he was meant to be a husband, putting her needs above his own. He'd easily forgiven her for leaving him in the middle of battle.

She'd come back to find him near death, tended to by healers. His feet had been burned clear off. Magic was back enough for the Circle to help, which Shirina had, to the best of her abilities, but the damage had been done.

Months of healing, then of learning to walk again, of pain, of fears… and then, they'd never danced.

It was a weird thing to think about as she gently pulled off his prosthetic legs, ripping infected skin with it, where blisters had formed and broken. He'd worn them too long, walked too much, and had paid the price.

Now, she needed to make sure more infection wouldn't follow. She should have asked Shirina to use her magic on him and help heal him. But the sorceress had been exhausted, and she needed her magic to teleport Avarielle away.

Cassara dropped one of the prosthetics. She closed her eyes, took a deep breath riddled with the sweet stench of infection, and got water from the commode, and some healing salves that would help against the burning skin.

"This will hurt," Cassara whispered to Dayshon, who said nothing in turn, mouth slack.

She swallowed hard, looked back down to the broken, reddened flesh, and began cleaning it. Dayshon didn't react or move, so she hoped that he couldn't feel what she was doing and went in deeper, cleaning the infection as best she could, careful to move the broken skin and apply salve.

Shivers ran down her back, and she kept her breath steady, blinking away the tears that couldn't help but form, like she felt his pain where he couldn't.

They had never danced. It had all seemed unimportant until now, when she realized they might never dance. That he might not come back. That this might be all that's left of him.

The door opened and gently closed again, but Cassara focused on the wounds, on disinfecting and carefully dressing them, on keeping his body as healthy as his mind allowed. She had gained lots of experience dressing wounds on the battlefield. It was not something she would easily forget.

Avarielle sat on the ground near Cassara, leaning back against the bed, as though trying not to intrude on her and Dayshon.

"I'm glad you're here," Cassara said softly. "I'm glad you're back."

The warrior said nothing, simply staring ahead. Cassara focused back on Dayshon, feeling time slipping through her fingers. Her loved ones slowly leaving, one by one. All the people she'd relied on during the last war to keep her safe, or to fight alongside her, vanishing one by one.

"I don't know if I'm coming back, Cassara," Avarielle

said. "But I'll do everything I can to save Dayshon. I promise you that."

Cassara nodded, absorbing the words, finishing up with Dayshon. She'd be alone, soon. With the husk of her husband, her children gone, Avarielle and Shirina off to dangers unknown.

She felt either at peace, or numb. Her tears stopped, and she sat back, looked at the warrior, committing her features to memory. The strength of her limbs, the casualness she carried herself with, while being ready to pounce. The sharpness of her eyes, the cut of her cheeks, the usual grin on her lips, currently missing. The short hair, hacked more than cut, turning slight gray, the red more muted than when she'd been young. But still just as powerful. Like her.

Unstoppable.

She'd believed the warrior dead not long ago, and there had been a gaping hole in her world. Now that she was back, every moment counted as precious. That hole would never be filled, she knew. Avarielle had been the first person to see her as more than just the princess of a small kingdom. Their lives had become intertwined, and they'd relied on each other. Well, Cassara had relied on her, anyway.

So much.

But she knew she could stand on her own two feet, too. Avarielle had helped her understand that. The warrior had always been there to help catch her if she fell, but those times were gone.

"I don't know what to say," Cassara admitted. "I don't know how to say goodbye, when you're such a big piece of my life. Of my heart."

"We don't have to say goodbye," Avarielle said, finally looking at Cassara and meeting her eyes. "In the West, we sometimes say 'until our tracks cross again.' That's what I'll say to you, Cassara. Because no matter what, we'll meet again, someday. In some form. Besides—" that grin again, which Cassara committed to memory, "—I'm real hard to get rid of."

"That's true," Cassara said, trying to return the grin. Avarielle reached over with her right hand, squeezing her arm. Cassara would miss this, most of all. The warrior wasn't shy about sharing strength through touch, something less common in the Eastlands. The physical connection helped ground Cassara in ways she would forever miss.

"Listen," Avarielle said, with that urgency she used to have on the battlefield. Cassara found herself listening more closely, leaning in to capture every word, which could save her life. Which had, so often. "You need to find your allies, and find them quickly. There are more of them than you give yourself credit for. Stop wailing about what you don't have, and start focusing on what you do have, because that's what will save your life."

Cassara bristled at the harsh words, but kept leaning in, listening, as Avarielle continued. "Tally let me go to face you alone, meaning she either knew this would happen, or trusted that Siabala had full control. Maybe

Shirina becoming an Elder was a surprise her witchy pride hadn't foreseen. Either way, she'll want to finish the ritual. She'll want you, and me, in the same room again."

"Better me than one of my children," Cassara said.

"Agreed, but on multiple levels you're not going to like. Siabala wants you to suffer, Cassara. All of us, but you particularly. Now that you've escaped his grasp, I know he'll want you to watch your husband vanish. Your people die. Your city collapse. And then, to have me kill you, slowly, so you're well aware, and I'm well aware, of what's happening. Your chances for an easy death, or as easy as Siabala would allow, are gone."

Cassara swallowed hard. Nodded.

"I think Shirina is our wild card," Avarielle said, "and Tally will soon realize it if she hasn't already. They wanted to crush her, but she defied their expectations. She thought differently and found a way to tap back into the magic and become stronger. Probably because she has the head of a bull and is too stubborn to quit."

Avarielle shifted, as though still getting comfortable with her arm in a sling.

"And I think that's the trick. We expect each other to act in certain ways because, well, because certain ways have worked for us. Now that Siabala won't have access to me, and in turn you—" a deep breath, "—the trick will be to do the unexpected. That's what they won't be ready for."

Cassara nodded, the warrior's desperate energy washing over her. To do something different was all great and good, but the breadth of options overwhelmed Cassara.

"And," Avarielle said, lowering her voice. "Make sure it's not something I would easily predict. He might not have full access to or control over my mind at the moment, but he will, Cassara. Assume that he will. And assume that he'll know what I've just told you."

"You know me better than most," Cassara said. "And you've fought in wars more than I have. You're a warrior through and through. How am I supposed to outthink you?"

"By drawing on your own unique experiences, Cassara. Eli, do it in whatever way you can, and do it fast." Avarielle's features grew even more serious, her grip on Cassara tightening. "You have instincts. Some of your magic is back. And," she pressed on, stopping the protest forming on Cassara's lips, "you just have to trust yourself enough to know you'll find your way. That's most of what you used to do, you know. Just trusted yourself enough to tell Shirina and I off and force our hands."

"I don't seem to recall things quite that way," Cassara said, though a smile played on her lips.

"I know there's more to consider, now. And we've all had failures, or lived long enough to witness the consequences of some actions we wish we'd never seen. And that tempers us in different ways. It can slow us down. It's not a bad thing, to hesitate to ensure we're doing the right thing instead of rushing in with the certainty of youth. All you need is to be sure of what you're trying to accomplish, in all its complexity, and then trust your instincts, as you once did, to make it happen."

"So many of my instincts lead to failures," Cassara admitted. Something she rarely said as a queen.

"And so many lead to successes," Avarielle said. "You're just focusing on the failures, because you've defined failure clearly in your mind, but you're still unclear of what success looks like."

"I know what success looks like," Cassara said. "We stop Siabala."

"Sure," Avarielle shrugged. "And failure is easy then. Siabala wins."

"Exactly," Cassara lifted her chin.

"So if we stop Siabala but sacrifice Shirina, we still win."

"Yes, but—"

"Or Dayshon."

"Well."

"Altessa?"

"No."

"What about your people?"

"Stop."

The warrior did, though she watched her with sharp eyes.

"This is exactly like it was back then, Cassara," Avarielle said more kindly. "You decided Edoline wouldn't suffer. Your brother would be saved. My people would be supported. And then you decided to take the battle to Siabala. To finish him."

"And I failed," she whispered, looking up at Dayshon's half-closed red eyes.

"No," Avarielle said. "Edoline survived. Your brother rules it. My people were hurt but are still fighting. And, when you couldn't kill Siabala, you imprisoned him, which was the best option at the time."

"It all feels like failure."

"Just because it isn't a complete success doesn't mean it's a failure. You're being unfair to your own accomplishments by thinking that way, and you're slowing your decisions down. That'll get you killed fast, Cassara. Probably by my sword."

Avarielle held her eyes. "Please don't let me do that, Cassara. I trust you. I trust your judgment, and your instincts. They've saved me in battle time and time again. Saved us all. I need you to trust them, too, because I trust you to stop me from hurting you, okay? Because that will break me, and Rojon will be next. And I can't..."

The warrior's voice broke, and it was Cassara's turn to take the warrior's hand in hers.

"Okay," Cassara said, feeling the strength of that hand. Its warmth. "I will. I'll find a way to stop this."

"Promise me you'll trust your instincts, Cassara. Promise me you'll trust yourself, like I'm trusting you right now." The warrior's jaw clenched shut.

"I promise," she whispered.

"Good," Avarielle seemed relieved, as though the matter was resolved and Cassara wouldn't be left with the crushing weight of her own hesitation and mind. She stood up, glanced at Dayshon. Then back to Cassara.

"In that case, may our tracks cross again, one day soon."

Before Cassara could reply, or hug her, or thank her, or think of something, anything to say that would somehow encapsulate decades of friendship and trust, the door closed shut, and the warrior was gone.

19

Shirina clutched her staff as she walked swiftly down the hall, heading toward Elder Quilsam's adopted study, guards and a few Elihor adepts scrambling out of her way.

Wise. She wasn't in a playful, nor an overly kind, mood. For years she'd fought to gain their respect and her Elder cloak. Now that she had it, she found it solved very few of her problems.

In fact, she had simply become aware of more of them. It had allowed her to help Avarielle, which was great, but it also showed her just how much trouble her friend was in, highlighting the depths of Siabala's clutches. It had helped her find Cassara's magic, but now she understood at least pieces of how that magic had come to be, how dark its journey. And the magic remained trapped, save for the drips Cassara had managed to pull through, spurred on by Avarielle's needs.

Shirina hated most of all that she understood why the old Circle had trained adepts the way they had, forcing them to choose logic over emotions. Because most of Cassara's current problems connecting with her magic stemmed from her emotions. The fact that she both understood the Elders of old and felt like she was made to find fault with the very thing that had always made Cassara strongest angered her to her core.

Her face turned even more sour and a guard jumped back as she turned into the study, slamming the door behind her.

"You knew," Shirina said. "You knew where the magic came from, and where it had gone."

"Elder Shirina," Quilsam said, eyes calculating, riddled with mistrust.

"Don't look at me like I'm the one who can't be trusted," Shirina said, voice laced with a threat. She was done with him. Done with them all. "You're the one who kept all these secrets. You're the one who stood by as they almost killed me. As they killed my adepts!"

He ignored her later accusations, focusing on the first. "It would have been inappropriate of me to tell you anything. You were not an Elder."

"Nor would I have ever been, if left up to you."

He wisely didn't answer, though that was answer enough.

"Anyhow," he said, as though she'd simply stated to him that the day proved beautiful, "you have much to read, still, to become aware of all the lore. It would be wise of you to stop stomping about and take the time you need to learn the true secrets of Ravenhold."

"I find stomping about necessary," her voice was dry, "when there are so many that annoy me. Including Siabala."

"He is within the Grayloft. It would be wise to dispose of her."

"Dispose of her?" Shirina scoffed. "So that he could simply hop into her son's body, the next in the Grayloft line?"

He grew visibly pale. Apparently the Elder had not put much thought into what this meant for Rojon. Anger fluttered across his features, and she imagined he intended to go on about his "soiled bloodline." One look at her face, and he wisely changed tactics.

"She must be contained, then. And Siabala with her. To stop him."

The ground shook. Shirina connected her staff with the stone floor, followed its shivers through the city, toward the north. And the south. More holes, more parts of the kingdom collapsing.

"He attacks, still." Quilsam's voice trembled.

"What he has set in motion will not end with him," Shirina said. "His empire will rise, with or without him. And his followers are ready to fall in line."

"We hold him prisoner, and tell them to stop or we'll…"

"We'll what?" Shirina asked. "We cannot kill his soul.

Avarielle Grayloft holds him within her for now. That is our best bet."

"We take her far, then," he went to go around her, but Shirina stood before the door.

"I will take her away from here, yes, to ensure she cannot harm Cassara. But his followers will come. And they will try to capture her, and gift her to their master."

"You must take her to safety—"

"Queen Cassara intends to stand with her people. Little that I or you say will change her mind."

"And Elihor's heir?" he asked after a pause, as though he feared the answer.

"Free, last I saw him. And safe."

"Where?" His voice trembled with fear. Shirina shook her head.

"I do not know, and I think it wise that we not let anyone else know. For his own safety."

"Don't assume to know what is best for the Heir of Elihor." The Elder crossed his arms, hands tucked in his sleeves. Shirina studied him. She didn't like him but, if she was honest, he was her best chance of protecting Cassara right now.

"Will you stay and protect the Heir of Graydon?" Shirina asked him, ignoring his statement.

"I have no magic."

"You don't, for now," Shirina acquiesced, "but I will work at freeing it, so that you can access it."

"*You* will free Elihor's magic?"

"No," Shirina shook her head. "That magic will never

be free again, save in the heirs of Elihor's blood. Much like Graydon's. You know as well as I do why."

"But magic in the air is necessary—"

"It isn't. It never was. And we'll find a way to work with what we have."

"Siabala will undo us."

"Perhaps," Shirina pondered. "But I don't think so. We can work with the magic as it is, Elder. It is our duty to help adepts understand it. I will teach mine, but you must be honest with yours."

"Give them the secrets of Elders?" he scoffed.

Shirina met his eyes. "Empower them to better understand what they choose, Elder."

He held her eyes for a few moments, as though weighing the strength of her character and of her words. Her determination. Then he sighed and looked down.

"Where will you go?"

"You will know once I've freed it, Elder. You know where to look for it." *Just as you knew Ravenhold was not truly gone.* She bit back the words, though she wanted to fling her anger in his face. "Until next we meet."

She turned to leave, but stopped when he called her name.

"I... I just want to know. What was it like? To bask in the magic of a Keep?" His eyes were wide, his hand held toward her. He'd become Elder by being appointed by another Elder. He'd not known the trials of the Keep. He'd not burned in memory and time. In magic that was, that should be, and that still could be.

Shirina had no words to describe it. Even if she did, she doubted she would share them.

"Until next time," she repeated, and exited the chamber.

The warrior waited for her near the old teleportation circle, the plants burnt and seared, stones from the collapsed towers sprinkled on the ground. The day was already spent, between trying to heal Dayshon, gathering supplies, and forming their plan. Shirina hated the feeling of time slipping through her fingers, impossible to grasp, more like water than the sands of the West.

"Ready?" Shirina asked. The warrior nodded.

Cassara stood by the castle door, fingers interlaced tightly before her, knuckles turning white. Shirina caught her eye and nodded.

The queen returned the gesture.

Without waiting, she struck the ground with her staff, willed the magic to dance up to her, and take her and the warrior away from here. Far away from the broken city, leaving it to fend for itself.

Far away from Cassara, leaving her to mend her people, or die trying.

20

The trees of Kosel stood like silent guardians, casting long shadows that smothered Rojon. That, and the silence.

Rolly, Pakana's giant lizard friend, walked carefully, avoiding fresh holes and stone structures which had erupted last night, shortly after his mother…

"Look at those trees," Pakana said, breaking him free of his spiral. Again. It had been like that all day. His travel companion had yet to grieve for her father, but he gave her the distance she needed, trapped in his own snare of emotions.

Besides, his mother had killed her father. She'd been controlled by Siabala, but it had still been her… Graysword…

"Rojon," Pakana's crisp voice pulled him back again. This spiral was difficult to escape.

"I'm sorry?" He focused on her, on the shadows falling

across her face, the cut of her cheeks, the hardness of her eyes that failed to hide the grief threatening to erupt, in anger or tears.

"The trees," she pointed. "There's something wrong with them."

Rojon focused on the tall pines, cushioned in the dense forest, always in shadows despite it still being day. Where was he supposed to go now? What would be most helpful for Cassara and Shirina? And for his mother? He was lost in Graydon, and didn't even understand its forests. How could he be of use to anyone?

"I don't see anything," he admitted under her piercing gaze.

"There, near the trunk," she said, then added. "The trunk, too, I think. Actually, it might come from that." She walked carefully into the tree, navigating around the large branches and pine needles. Rojon followed, finding solace in this forest. The trees were the biggest he'd ever seen, always swaying in the breeze, the carpet of pines beneath his feet filled with interesting mushrooms and pieces of bark.

He loved it here, and imagined all the things he would accomplish in Elihor once trees reached this seemingly impossible height.

Close to the trunk, the needles prickling him, the sweet piercing scent enrobing him, Rojon could see what Pakana referred to. Where the branches met the trunk, the needles didn't move. He reached, and pulled back immediately at the pain. The needles were ungiving stone. As was the bark.

He reached in to make sure, careful not to impale his arm on the stone needles.

"What is this?" Strangled words from Pakana.

"It looks like they're turning to stone," Rojon said, placing his palm on the pine, surprised to find it warm, despite being stone.

"What could be causing this?" she asked, breathless. Rojon recognized in her what he'd felt when his village had been under attack. The fear of losing his home.

"I don't know," he said, "but I'm guessing it has something to do with those spires and stone buildings. Maybe something leached up the trees, like a disease?"

A breeze caught the top of the tree and danced its way down, and Rojon could see that the top branches swayed more easily. He looked up, then down.

"The bottom branches are turning to stone faster, so I'm going to guess it's definitely coming through the roots."

"But… why?" The question was so soft, so broken, that it tore at Rojon.

Why had any of it happened? Why had her father died, why had Siabala taken over his mother, why had Shirina thrown them deeper into Kosel, why was the world crumbling around them, and why did he feel like he couldn't do anything about it?

They both withdrew from the tree, back to Rolly who

seemed antsy. Rojon looked around, seeing the same strange stony rot climbing the trees slowly.

"Do you think this is spread across Kosel?" Pakana asked, looking at the stone creep up a pine. The tree they'd looked at more closely was now almost fully stone. Without the movement of the branches, the entire forest felt more claustrophobic.

Rojon looked left and right, spotting the same phenomenon in every tree. "I don't know," he said, walking further in the thick forest to see if he could spot the same stone rot elsewhere.

Pakana and Rolly stayed near him. Everywhere they went, the trees turned to stone.

"Rojon," Pakana grabbed his arm, forced him to look at her, her eyes wide with fear. "What if it's everywhere? What about the towns?"

"I'm sure they'll be fine," Rojon frowned. "The houses won't turn to stone—they don't have roots."

"Rojon, the trees *are* the houses!"

Before he could say any words of comfort or wrap his mind around what that settlement might look like, Pakana had jumped on Rolly.

"Wait," he shouted, "I'll come with you!"

"You have other things to do but worry about us," she said, but he grabbed hold of Rolly's harness and pulled himself behind her. Without further argument, Rolly headed off, deeper into the forest, away from the edges of Kosel they'd been traveling toward.

"You don't have to do this," Pakana said.

"I do," he said, not knowing how to explain to her that he owed her. That she was giving him a purpose. And, just maybe, that in helping to discover the cause of this rot, he would be helping his mother break free of Siabala.

Chances were low, but they still existed. Right now, he was willing to pursue this thin trail of hope.

Once again, Ramelia dragged the princess down the city, using alleyways and secret passages, staying away from marketplaces and thoroughfares. The city brimmed with a different energy, as the bells alerting of incoming, though not imminent, attack rang in the day. Altessa had tried to stop a few times, but Lieutenant Garlon and Ramelia made it clear that she should keep going.

They reached the edge of the city, fields sprawling around them, cut by copses of trees and roads, by spires and round structures, and a few sinkholes large enough to swallow entire farm fields had vanished.

The bells stopped. And so did Altessa.

"Enough." She'd tried to sound regal, but just sounded frustrated. "I need to know what happened at the palace." Her eyes threw darts at both her companions, daring them to contradict her.

Ramelia was unphased. "We know your mother wants you out of here, and there are crazy people up there who want to kill you."

"Crazy people *you* belonged to not that long ago," the lieutenant raised a gray eyebrow, dark face lined with a question.

"Ya, well, I didn't like their methods," she mumbled.

"I wonder what your parents would think of you running in their circle at all," the lieutenant said, and Ramelia grew pale.

"You know my parents?"

He nodded. "From the Days of Blood. We still share a pint now and then, too."

Ramelia looked at him defiantly.

"I'm not about to go tell on you," the lieutenant grinned. "But, trust me, they'd be proud of you standing up to help the princess."

"I need to go back home," Altessa said. "You probably do as well." Her heart flip-flopped at the thought of being left alone, but Ramelia had a family, too. Altessa had seen their home. They deserved to be together.

"My parents are city guards and really busy right now, and you need to get far away from here." Ramelia threw up her arms in frustration. "Why is it always the same argument with you? You're supposed to run away from people trying to kill you, not toward them!"

"I can do more good if I'm at the palace than hiding in some hole somewhere," Altessa snapped back.

"You're of no use to anyone dead."

"I don't intend to get killed." Altessa gritted her teeth. "I just need to help! I'm the heir to the throne. I can't run away every time an attack is imminent."

"When you're queen, save us all, you can stay like an idiot on the throne."

"Oh, I'm the problem here?" Altessa scoffed in a very non-royal manner. "You're the one who keeps coming back. I didn't ask to be rescued!"

"Your mom asked me to!"

"I thought you didn't like the queen?" Altessa said sweetly. Ramelia scowled.

The lieutenant looked from princess to rebel, apparently deciding he didn't need to get between them.

Wise.

"Look, all I'm saying is that we have no plan and no clear idea of where we're going," Altessa said, trying to appeal to their reason, though she really wanted to just storm back to the castle. She sighed, swept her arm up to indicate the land of Rashim, battered and beaten. "I don't think anywhere will be safe, no matter how far we run."

"Your mother wanted you to be safe from Siabala." Ramelia's voice grew muted as they took in the destruction surrounding them.

"Where would you take me to keep me safe?" Altessa held the rebel's dark eyes captive.

"Anywhere but here," Ramelia said, but there was no fire in her voice.

Altessa placed a hand on Ramelia's arm, then let it drop.

"I'm going back," she said, pressed on before they could interrupt her, "but I could use your help."

Ramelia crossed her arms but kept silent.

"Lieutenant, do you think you can find Captain Travin and the missing royal guards? Whoever you can find who is loyal, and who *wants* to return, bring back to the palace. We'll need them in the days to come."

"And deserters?" The lieutenant's voice turned the word into a hiss.

"Let them run," Altessa said. "Nowhere will be safe regardless. Give them a chance to stand up and fight, instead of being killed while running."

"Ramelia." She gave Ramelia a pointed look, bringing her point home, but the rebel still looked toward the fields of Rashim. "If you could use your magic to scout ahead, carefully… and if it's safe, then I'll return to it."

"And if it's not safe?" Ramelia asked softly, turning to face the princess.

"Then I promise I'll follow you to whatever safety we can find, for however long we're allowed to know it."

Ramelia studied her, to make sure she wasn't lying, something Altessa wasn't even sure herself. If Siabala was already there, if her parents were dead, the throne was hers. But, despite her bold words and high actions, Altessa did not want to die. She was eighteen, and not ready to let go of this life yet.

She'd live to find a way to help her people, and dedicate her life to creating safe havens for them, if even possible.

Neither of her two companions argued with her, and Altessa found herself very much missing the life she hadn't wanted just a few weeks ago, now impossibly out of reach, torn to shreds by Siabala as effortlessly as he'd shredded Rashim's once beautiful fields.

22

Shirina followed the ground where magic led her, missing the sights she used to see from the sky, the land stretching around her. Now, darkness mostly surrounded them. She wasn't used to navigating this way, and focused on going west.

Toward Siabala's Rage.

Avarielle's eyes darted around, the warrior snapping to attention as the teleportation bubble took them through the earth. A few times the spell dove deeply enough to glimpse a city, lit by magic, or too dark to see save for the impression of something looming around them, like they traveled through air instead of stone.

The magic kept them whole, and they could even see each other, the earth offering them safe and even comfortable passage. Perhaps it was an illusion she conjured in their minds to keep them sane. She wasn't certain, but she was well aware of the warrior beside her, close enough to reach out and touch if necessary.

"This isn't better," a growl left Avarielle, which Shirina knew to be fed by fear.

"We're almost there," Shirina said. "I think," she added, unable, or perhaps unwilling, to stop herself from teasing the warrior. It was nice that this magic, not requiring her chants, allowed her to pull Avarielle's strings.

"You think?" Avarielle bit, perhaps to distract herself from the earth around her. The magic pulled on Shirina. Unexpectedly, traveling in the ground felt much easier than the air, as though she followed old conduits of power long created for this purpose. Roads created for travelers, sturdy, defying the tests of time and ignorance.

"I'm new to this," Shirina said.

"Let's just get this over with," Avarielle whispered. "Just get me to Siabala's Rage."

The magic twinged around her, and Shirina realized it moved to the beat of her heart, which beat faster due to the warrior's words. No, it was Avarielle's tone that bothered her. The defeat in it. She wanted to finish what needed to be done, and then... who knew what the warrior was planning.

"I'm not heading directly there," Shirina said, the warrior tensing beside her. "Relax, I'm not going to drag you anywhere else. I'm just not teleporting us directly in. I'm not even sure I can, if its magic is currently active. We might be blocked, and killed before I even end this spell."

"What's your plan?" Avarielle said.

Shirina sensed around her, willing magic to guide her where her eyes could not. She knew where she wanted to be. Close enough, a place known and, just maybe, a people that would remind Avarielle of who she was. Maybe that would help the warrior, who was too stubborn to listen to her, anyway.

Shirina followed the magic, sensing the draw of people she knew, of a place she'd been in... and felt the familiar guidance of her adepts. The tension wound around her heart released, and she smiled, letting the magic bring her where Avarielle needed to be, and where Shirina also needed to be.

The sorceress recognized the ancient underground city as it sprawled around her, the sky visible above, day already turned to dusk. *The West.* Avarielle's home. Her trusted pupil and friend, Shala, was here, too, in the shadows of the Bloody Mountains.

Shirina guided the magic to bring them near the camp, where no one currently dwelt, behind one of the sand dunes. The spell gently released them, feet touching warm sand, sunset cooling the air already.

"What in the falling star of Elihor are we doing here?" the warrior spat, but kept her voice down.

"Shala is here," she said, speaking the name lightly, with hope and joy, "as is the research affected in the city below. Now that I'm an Elder, I need to glance at a few things I think I may understand."

"That's not a good enough reason to delay this."

Delay this. Shirina narrowed her eyes.

"Delay what? Going after a cure for Dayshon? That's not why you want to go to Siabala's Rage, is it?"

"I can walk from here," Avarielle said. "It'll be simpler that way, and you can find the knowledge you need. That's more important."

"No it isn't," Shirina said. "I'll come with you. Teleport us the rest of the way. Just let me rest a bit."

In truth, Shirina wasn't tired, teleporting while being supported by the ground being a much less tiring endeavor. She certainly wasn't as tired as ensnaring Siabala had made her. The warrior saw it, so remained unconvinced.

"I need to get away from you, and you've got things to do here."

"I can strengthen the ties that hold him as needed, Avarielle. Siabala set a trap for you. Dayshon is the bait. Or, at least, curing him is. Just like—"

"Don't, Shirina," the warrior growled, stood over Shirina. "I'm warning you."

"Fine." She let steel overtake her voice. "The question now is: will you fall in his trap again?"

"I don't have much of a choice, do I?"

"You do," Shirina said. "You trust *me* to do it instead."

"You'll head into his trap?"

"I have more magic than you."

"Yes, and you'll get annihilated!"

"If need be, so be it."

"That's ridiculous. You've just received your black cloak. So now you'll just cast it all aside and get yourself killed? To save one man when you could save so many instead?"

Shirina didn't feel any victory flash in her eyes, though the warrior had walked right into her trap. Avarielle knew it as soon as she spoke the words and scowled at her.

"This isn't the same thing," Avarielle said, though some of her anger dissipated.

"It very much is," Shirina said. "If you lose this battle, Avarielle, we lose the war. Siabala runs free. He's imprisoned for now, and we need all the time we can get to plan our defenses."

"Well what am I supposed to do, Shirina, just wait until he breaks out?" A hint of despair courted the warrior's voice, and Shirina sighed. Of course. The warrior wanted to do something of use. She wanted to save her friend.

No. She wanted to find salvation for having lost Kryde, by saving Dayshon.

"This is infuriating," Shirina mumbled. "I know you want to save Dayshon, and I want to, as well. But we don't have the resources. We'll have to trust that Cassara will find a way."

"She'll be busy getting her kingdom ready for invasion."

"She can multitask," Shirina said.

"How do you do it? Be so blasé about saving a man's life? A *friend's* life?"

"I'm not," Shirina said, focusing fully on the warrior's eyes. "One person's life is all it takes to change the world. Elihor dying, and Graydon erecting the Wall of Loss out of grief. Siabala destroying so many for reasons that are nebulous, but I'm sure are linked to some form of heartache. And you…" Her voice grew so soft that she barely heard it over the gentle desert wind. "You, bringing down the Wall of Loss to avenge one man." Avarielle didn't react, but held the sorceress's eyes. "So no, Avarielle, I don't underestimate the impact one life can have on history. On our world. But I also know that I'm here, and I can only affect so much. My powers are best served reactivating the Circle. Yours are best served keeping Siabala at bay. And, if along the way, we can save Dayshon without falling into Siabala's trap, so be it."

"He'll get free, you know," Avarielle said. "What if there's something in Siabala's Rage that can be used against him, still?"

"There's nothing left." Shirina said. "I had my adepts inventory every room, every fiery chasm, and we found nothing. No sign of how his body was trapped there. Remember, his soul was in the Wall of Loss, while his body was trapped in the prison. Now, he's only a soul."

Avarielle looked at her bandaged arm. "I know that."

"So, the only thing we might find in Siabala's Rage is how to trap his body, not his soul."

At the victory lighting the warrior's eyes, Shirina stopped. It seemed that Avarielle was laying traps of her own, and the sorceress had just as easily walked right into one.

"No," she said. "We won't trap you in there."

"If it trapped his body once, it stands to reason it can do so again."

"It's not the same thing," she said. "The soul is there, too."

"So trap the soul as well. Trap both. It might buy you time."

"No," she repeated. "There must be something here that can help us come up with a better plan."

"Shirina," Avarielle said.

"No," the sorceress repeated. "We tried trapping him before, remember? And now he's free."

"And we tried killing him before, Shirina," Avarielle sounded exasperated. "And that didn't work either, remember? So, throw me in there. If he wants a body, then let that body be trapped."

"He'll just break free again."

"Yes," Avarielle said. "And you'll be able to stop me then."

"How?" Shirina said, facing off with the warrior. "I've had twenty years, and I don't have a clue how to stop him still, or has that not been made clear to you yet?"

"Shirina," Avarielle said, placing her damned hand on her shoulder, trying to ground her. Shirina felt herself tremble beneath the steady grip and hated the warrior for it. "You're an Elder now. You just need time to find the right knowledge, or magic, or whatever it is bloody Elders do, and you'll know how to beat him. But you need time."

"Avarielle—"

"I've made up my mind." An eyebrow raised. "Unless you have another cunning plan."

Shirina opened her mouth and closed it again. She had no other ideas. Nothing that remotely made sense.

"I'm not sure I can get the Rage active again," she said, though the argument was weak. There were documents in Stormhold, the keepers of the Rage. Elder Quilsam would have ideas, if she ran out. He'd be more than happy to lock Avarielle in and throw away the key.

Avarielle waited her out, and Shirina looked up to meet her eyes. Warm, and resolute, and determined, and so unapologetically stubborn. Avarielle Grayloft had decided that she would give up her freedom, her life, her soul, to save the lands. And once a Grayloft made up their mind, you were hard pressed to change it.

"I should have become an Elder before now," Shirina said, not sure why she was telling Avarielle this. "I could have, maybe. I just needed to reach out to Ravenhold. I should have known, realized, some of the old Circle tricks were at play…"

"You followed the path you were meant to follow, Shirina," Avarielle said. "You're an Elder now, and you'll make the best of it. You're too pig-headed not to press on at this point. Besides—" A grin. *That* grin. The one that told Shirina the warrior wanted to stop talking before things got too real. "—You'll finally get to throw me in a prison. Isn't that how we met, twenty years ago?"

Shirina smiled. "My first real mission, which I failed at."

"Well, now's your time to shine."

The attempt at humor felt leaden in both their stomachs. Shirina leaned forward, and Avarielle folded her good arm around the sorceress, who returned the gesture. They'd never hugged. She wasn't a hugger, but she'd hugged Rojon often enough. And Cassara. But never Avarielle. The warrior was all muscle, and she could feel the magic pulsing in her arm. But she was soft, too, a gentle hand on her back, chin leaning on her hair.

And then, just as quickly as it had happened, it ended.

"I'll bring you myself, once I've rested a bit," Shirina said, giving in to the warrior's terrible plan, finding no better one.

Avarielle nodded and stepped back out into the darkness. Shirina watched her go, took a deep breath of dry air and burnt hopes, and started slowly, very slowly, wrapping her mind around the steps that would seal Avarielle Grayloft into Siabala's Rage.

She hated how calm she felt. How accepting.

Like she'd given up, and the warrior would pay the price.

23

Shala pushed scrolls across the large stone surface she'd been using as a desk, straightened her aching back and sighed. The translations were so close, but so much was still missing. Libraries filled with knowledge they couldn't necessarily interpret or decipher.

"Eat." The old Westland warrior, Trevon, brought her a bowl filled with some kind of stew, which smelled of thyme and fennel, if she wasn't mistaken. The sun was low on the horizon and robbed her of much needed light, so she took the offered food.

"Thanks," she said, and sat down on the sand, imminently more comfortable than the rocks, and ate in silence. The meat was gamey, and the vegetables, some carrots and some kind of cabbage, she guessed, were positively delicious.

"It'll be night, soon," he said. "We should head back in."

Shala nodded. Creatures had been invading the

Westland, and new spires and a few round structures had broken through the ground, sand shifting around them as they erupted—structures like those in the city that spread beneath more of the lands than they'd thought possible. Perhaps beneath *all* of the Westland, and all of Graydon. Not to mention Elihor. The thought elated her as a scholar, and terrified her as a resident of those lands.

"Were there more creatures spotted?" Shala hated not having the means with which to defend herself, or help others. The last time she'd fought monsters, it had been on the ridge above, with the forces from Massir and the Southern Coalition, and the Westlanders, twenty years ago.

She hadn't had magic then, either.

"Coming in from the north," he said. "Not from the west."

His gaze turned toward the Bloody Mountains, a silent monster beside them. Trevon had grown up in the shadows of the mountain, and they didn't seem to bother him as much as they did Shala. She'd grown up in a small quaint village, until the Circle's Harvest had taken her to Ravenhold. And then, after pondering her options—offered by Shirina after the Days of Blood—Shala had decided to return to Shirina's side in the Lisal Gardens.

She'd never regretted that decision. Not even now, stuck trying to decipher an ancient language in the Westland, clothes dirty and hands chapped. She smiled as stars winked into existence. The skies above the West were the most beautiful, the dark shadow of the Bloody

Mountains cutting the sky up to the twinkling stars, like an unfinished section of a canvas. She kept her gaze away from the collapsed portion of mountain in the distance.

Westland warriors skulked on the perimeter, keeping an eye out for potential attack. Their camp was on the periphery of the one easy way down to the city, where quite a few Westlanders had relocated. The Circle, who'd basically waged war on the West forty years ago, wasn't welcome below. Shirina had managed to gain them access to the archives and scrolls, under supervision, only thanks to Avarielle Grayloft's support.

But when Shala had brought the adepts she'd managed to save from Massir, knowing that Shirina needed answers on their magic and she wouldn't find them in the city, it was Trevon who'd championed their work.

Once done eating in silence, Trevon stood and escorted her to her hut, in the small village cropped up beside the old city. She shared it with four other adepts, the least occupied of the three huts that had been lent them for their stay.

They were eighteen all together. So few. So many left behind, probably to their deaths.

A howling in the distance and she looked toward it, drawing her crimson cloak closer.

"Just scavengers," Trevon told her. "A good sign. If they're here, that means no monsters are near."

She nodded, then gave him a thin smile. "I'm just not used to not having my magic to defend myself with. It makes me jumpy."

He gripped the pommel of the broadsword at his hip, nodded, his once red hair completely white now, and tied at the nape of his neck in a ponytail. Wrinkles mixed with scars surrounded eyes that had seen wars yet refused to give up their warmth.

"I imagine I'd feel much the same if I didn't have my sword." A smile lit up his eyes. "But, as I recall, you were excellent at throwing a punch, too."

She laughed, the sound scattering on the open sands.

"Desperate times," she said seriously, though she couldn't hide her smile. She'd met the Westland warrior during the Days of Blood. He'd been everywhere trying to help everyone, and she'd been trying to save what she thought was Ravenhold, at the time.

Except it hadn't been Ravenhold. Simply pretenders who'd linked up with Siabala. Allies to Tally.

Shirina had been the true path to Ravenhold, the Crimson Circle Elite's open-mindedness and steadfastness, once annoying traits, had saved the Circle as far as Shala, and hundreds of adepts, were concerned.

But now she had no idea where Shirina was, nor what had happened to her. She might be dead, for all she knew. Siabala had obviously been toying with her, having targeted her and Rashim's queen, and the Grayloft.

"Where did you just go?" Trevon asked softly. She realized that every emotion had settled on her face. *I would have never succeeded in the old Circle,* she thought. Although she'd really wanted to. Her ambition had blinded her to a lot, back then.

Just like it did now.

"I'm just… I'm thinking of Shirina, and the Circle." *There's where else I would have failed. The old Circle didn't share, especially not with Westlanders.*

"You're worried for your mentor," he said. She nodded, then immediately caught herself.

"I'm so sorry, Trevon. You're still grieving the loss of Avarielle, and you've been so kind to keep us safe. I've no right to impose my concerns on you."

"Your worries won't change my grief," he said, "but helping you with them will distract me from it." He looked toward the dark distance, toward Siabala's Rage. "Life is a series of losses and grieving, Shala. And not just with death. The people we love change. Are hurt. Broken. And we can't fix them. And we grieve what we'd once had, and wished we still did."

His eyes shone as he turned back to her. "You and I have not crossed paths often, but I see in you a kindred spirit." A rough laugh. "Had you not decided to continue your work with the Circle, I might have taught you the ways of the sword, with your spirit."

Shala smiled. "I would have liked that." She meant it. Even though a sword felt foreign in her hands, she enjoyed testing the strength of her body.

"It's never too late," Trevon smiled. He was in his sixties, by her estimates, and she in her late thirties. She could easily learn to love him like a father, seeing the same kindred spirit in him as he did in her.

"If this Circle thing doesn't work out," she jested, "I might take you up on that."

"I sincerely hope not," the familiar voice sounded, and Shala turned, slowly.

Stepping out of the shadows near a tent, looking exhausted, stood Shirina. In the darkness, it took Shala a moment to realize what was different.

A black cloak.

"Shirina?" Shala asked, but did not go to her friend. Trevon's smile lessened at Shala's reservations. Shala wanted to be happy, but how had she become an Elder? That could be faked. Reports from Massir were that Elders ran amok, Tally apparently having no problem with passing on the honor. But would Shirina…?

Shirina saw her hesitate, her lips tugging into a smile. "I found Ravenhold," Shirina said. "Or, rather, it found me."

"How?" Shala asked. She wanted to be excited. Happy for her mentor. Her friend. If Shirina was an Elder, that opened up worlds of possibilities for her, too.

"Honestly? I was thrown into frigid water and think I got swept up in its magic."

Shala frowned. She had no idea how Elders were created, really. They were gifted the honor by another Elder, usually.

"Either that," Shirina said, voice crisp, "or I've decided to join Tally and put up with her inane conversation for decades, working closely at her side, while doing the bidding of her master, the very demon I've spent decades preparing to stop."

Shala flushed slightly at the ridiculousness of her obvious thinking.

"But caution is always warranted and wise," Shirina said. "I found the magic of Graydon again, Shala. We must get prepared for our counterattack. Things are moving quickly."

"I don't mean to distrust you," Shala said. "But you said yourself that you couldn't become an Elder."

"True," Shirina said. "But I also said that I did not have all the answers. I have found some answers, and it seems I was mistaken."

Shala ached to feel the magic again and to see her mentor, but she feared allying herself with the enemy accidentally more than she'd thought. Shirina seemed to understand.

"Even if by chance I am allied with Tally," Shirina said softly. "There is nothing I can do to turn you to him. You know this, Shala. If you refused, you'd simply get killed. And, quite frankly, without your magic, that would be a rather easy feat at this time."

"I can throw a good punch," Shala said, holding up her chin.

Shirina showed her hand, the knuckles scraped. "I recall, and I'm afraid I've been doing entirely too much of that myself, of late."

The sounds of their voices drew out the other adepts, who stepped out of their tents. Some gasped, some smiled. Others looked wide-eyed at Shirina's cloak. None had any idea what was happening, or what to make of it.

Shirina nodded to each in turn, then turned to Shala.

"You got so many out," she whispered.

"I left so many behind," Shala said, grief blooming at her core, remembering the only choice given her—run, or die.

"But you saved so many," Shirina said, holding Shala's gaze, forcing her to acknowledge her words. "Without you, they would all be gone. Focus on what we have, not what was taken from us. Thank you, Shala, for fighting for the Circle."

In Shirina's eyes, in that casual moment of gratitude and recognition, Shala knew that this was *her* Shirina. Because no Elder in the old Circle, nor in Tally's, would ever behave in such a way.

"Elder Shirina," Shala said, acknowledging her title. "What would you have us do?"

Shirina examined her, a slight smile on her lips. Then she turned to Trevon.

"Trevon." The warrior stood with arms crossed, waiting for the Circle witches to finish their debate. "I've brought a mutual friend to see you. She's waiting in your hut. Or nearby. I can't keep track of her."

Trevon's eyes widened, and he looked down at Shala. She gave him a wide smile. Avarielle Grayloft, despite all beliefs to the contrary, had lived. Of course she had. The woman seemed unkillable.

Trevon crossed to Shirina and gave the Elder a large hug.

"I've always liked you, the pretty singer." And he took off with a wink, wide strides carrying him into the darkness, toward the Grayloft.

There was no doubt in Shala's mind that it was Avarielle. Shirina could be stern, but she was not cruel. Something else that set her apart from the old Circle. Shala found herself standing straighter, proud of the Circle she belonged to. Proud of everything they'd accomplished. And everything they could, now that they had an Elder.

Should, of course, they survive Siabala's return.

"Now," Shirina turned to them all, every Circle witch standing straighter. "I've always said that I would offer you the choice to stay or go." There were only witches around them, now. The Westland warriors who patrolled the area seemed to be staying clear, probably unwilling to get embroiled in Circle matters.

"Siabala has returned," Shirina said. A few of the adepts shuffled uncomfortably. "I have seen him, and he is contained for now. But his Circle, under Tally and other Elders, grows strong. They are targeting Massir, where Queen Cassara intends to make a final stand. And he intends to see her dead."

"You left her there?" Shala asked, surprised. Shirina gave her a nod.

"She is queen, Shala, and needs to make the best decisions she can. Right now, our job is to figure out how best we can assist her. Have you uncovered more in the translations?"

Shala shook her head, frustrated. "Not much. Some words, a sentence here and there, but nothing truly comprehensible."

Shirina nodded. "I believe I may be able to help with that, now that I have access to Elder knowledge. Shala, will you step forth?" The words were spoken softly, with pride and humility all at once. Shala stepped to Shirina.

From this close, she could see several nicks and scars on the new Elder's face. How more white streaked her hair. The fatigue under her eyes. But those eyes were as sharp as ever, if not more so.

"I haven't had the time or space to truly understand all of my powers yet," she said. Shala nodded, understanding. *I came for you as soon as I could.* "But I know that having you near me will only help me be better, and more powerful."

"I will always step up beside you, Elder," Shala said, and meant it.

"I will never hold you to that, Crimson Circle." Shala knew Shirina meant that, too. "I find myself torn." Everyone listened more intently. Shirina had worked hard on sharing some of her thought processes, and not just the final decisions, so that her adepts could learn from the journey, and not see the destination as so obvious that none other had been considered. "We are at a grave disadvantage. They have many more Elders, fully connected to Siabala's magic, and they will hunt us down to kill us, or to force us to join them." She didn't mince words. She never did. Still, they all stayed. "I could skip over Crimson Circle Elite and make you an Elder." Shirina looked to Shala. "I have that knowledge, and know you are worthy. It is the way Elders have been chosen, since before the Westland Wars."

She stopped and waited. Shala's ambitions danced with her fears, tempting her to join them. To become an Elder would make her stronger. It *had* been done before.

"Tally was made an Elder during the Westland Wars," Shala said, "as were many others who fell to Siabala."

Shirina waited passively.

"No," Shala said, hands turning to fists. "I will find my way to being an Elder as you did, Shirina. By proving my worth to Ravenhold, wherever it may be. I will not sacrifice all we have built to only become weaker within decades. But I will gladly accept the title of Elite, should you see me fit to wear its cloak."

"You have always been worthy," Shirina said, pride flashing in her eyes. "Our magic is changing," she told Shala, the others forming a circle around them, listening, watching. "And so must we." Shirina tapped her staff, which looked to be made out of stone but much lighter, and whispered a few words. There was no pomp. No circumstance.

But Shala felt the weight of magic, and closed her eyes... and saw all of Graydon's magic dancing beneath her, through the ground at her feet, the city, its stones and crevasses, the chisel marks, the strange yellow lights that still bathed the city some nights.

It was still there. The magic was still there, all around her.

Do you see it? Shirina asked in her mind, arm on her shoulder.

I can, Shala said. *But I don't know how to touch it.*

You will, in time. I will show you.

Shala opened her eyes, realized tears streamed down her cheeks. She looked down, the circle above her breast now silver instead of black, the color of the full moon on calm nights.

"Welcome home, Crimson Circle Elite Shala," Shirina said, smiling at her. And then, in a move not at all like her mentor, she hugged her. Not a quick hug, but one that she leaned into, as though offering support while asking for it.

Shala returned the hug, glad she'd come back to the Circle, that she'd followed Shirina and, even though this journey might lead to her doom, that it would be while wearing the white robes of Ravenhold.

And, above all, Shala was glad that she'd made this Circle her home.

2 4

varielle ran her hand down the side of the thick adobe hut. The home wasn't big, but it was enough for Trevon. He'd made it his, after the Days of Blood. To stay here, near the city of the dead below, just in case.

Just in case you get bored and might want to settle into a quiet life? She'd joked.

He'd visited her often, her village in Elihor barely a week's walk from here… if you went through Siabala's Rage. Otherwise, you had to cross the Bloody Mountains. He always said he did, but Avarielle had no doubt Shirina facilitated his travels to and from Elihor.

She could hear others speaking in the dark, not too far from here, because everything was so quiet within her.

For now.

A large tower had burst out of the sands near the

camp, darker than the dark night, and she hated how it marred her beautiful home. Her arm itched under the splint, which annoyed but also heartened her, the sensation so ridiculously human. She leaned against the hut and waited. She didn't want to go in without asking his permission, though he would allow it. He always had, since she was a child. Until he'd moved into her family's ancestral home, a larger home fit for the once leaders of the West.

A title that had died with her father. She'd given it up, since. How could she lead her people, knowing she belonged to Siabala? Although that hadn't seemed to bother her family, recent or ancestral, it did her.

But, then again, how many had actually taken the oath with him? Her father would have, when the Eloms started streaming through, and when the war began. But before that, before the Eloms… it might have been since the time of Graydon and Elihor themselves.

Her brother had taken the oath, too. She didn't know what happened, or how, though she'd heard rumors of him murdering his childhood friends—rumors squelched by those fighting to preserve Westland hope in their rulers.

By the time she took it, well, she'd killed everyone who could have started a rumor, so there was nothing to squash.

She hadn't even remembered herself until Siabala reminded her, unlocking the truth from deep within her mind. She might have blocked the bloody event because she couldn't face it, but she didn't think so. This felt like Siabala trapped in her arm now. Like magic had squashed a piece of her and kept it prisoner so the rest of her could function.

A truth too impossible to bear—a truth that would slow her steps and make her useless to Siabala.

She pushed off the wall, focused on the air around her instead. It had been years since she'd stepped into the land of her ancestors, and of her youth. A canvas for so many tragedies, but so many joys, too. She took a deep breath of dry air, cool with the falling sun. The land where her family had been born and died, for generations.

No more. Rojon would never stay here, his home being in Elihor. And she… she doubted she would die here, for her body to be abandoned under the expansive sky, to return to nature. Who would even mourn her, if Siabala managed to win her soul and destroy all that she loved?

She glanced at the moon, its silver glow a comfort, cutting the darkness before clouds swallowed it again, and turned as she sensed someone approaching in the darkness.

"Trevon, old friend," she whispered, turned toward him.

"Avarielle Grayloft," Trevon said, swallowing hard, taking in her appearance. She looked like hell, she knew, and had a hard time meeting his eyes. Before she could force herself to, Trevon was holding her gently, avoiding her injured arm as he gathered her in his. Like he'd done when she was just a young girl, her parents dead. When her brother had died, killed by his own people.

When she'd had to say goodbye, so often, to so many things.

But never to him.

"I thought you dead." His voice trembled. "I should have known better."

Avarielle leaned into him.

"You know I'm harder to kill than that," she chided, though her heart wasn't in it. He sensed it, knowing her better than she knew herself most days, and pushed her away to examine her, holding her shoulders. Grounding her.

He led her into his home, settled her on one of the two chairs near the fire, set up very much like the ones in her home in Elihor had been set up. Like her childhood home had been set up, too. He prepared a pot of dark root tea, handed her a cup and took one for himself, settled in a chair, and finally spoke.

"Tell me everything."

And she did. She told him of Siabala. Of her oath with him. She told him of killing Kaden, and knowing she would have killed Cassara. Of Shirina trying to save her, but the sorceress knowing time was running out, and bringing her here to say her goodbyes.

A kindness not reflected in Avarielle's voice as she told the man who was like her father all the terrible things she'd done and would yet do. He listened, didn't interrupt, her voice soft, his silent. Only his eyes spoke volumes, and so once she was done, Trevon didn't meet her eyes, looking into the flames of the fire instead. Its flickers were reflected in the lines of his face, some created by time, others by battle. His hair, more white than red, was as wild as hers if perhaps a little bit thinner than he wanted it to be.

Avarielle didn't really remember her father. He died in the Westland Wars when she was just a child. She remembered the sword more than his hands, had learned of steel from him, not tenderness. But she liked to think that he'd known his failings and had wanted his children to know the tenderness that their mother no longer lived to give them. His best friend, Trevon, had been able to give them that.

Trevon had never had children of his own and offered them the kindness that their father could not, or would not, give them. When Avarielle looked at Trevon, she knew that she looked at the man who was more like a father to her than her own father had ever had the chance of becoming. Not his fault, in the midst of war and grief and survival.

But her father had made sure they were taken care of. And for that, she would always love him and remember him fondly, despite the fact that she mostly remembered the warrior and not the father.

Trevon absentmindedly took a sip of tea, kept staring at the fire. He sat close but still felt far away as the fire failed to dispel the chill at her core, where Siabala slumbered.

Her son hadn't known his father either, much less so than she'd known hers. But he'd also known Trevon. And not just as a warrior, but as someone who made him laugh, taught him how to work with wood, how to fight. How to handle the sword, of course, but also how to show affection, how to be a man and not just a warrior.

He had been her son's grandfather in everything but family name, and he, along with Kale, had been exactly what her son needed. And exactly what she needed, too. She trusted Trevon to watch over Cassara when she couldn't, when she kept an eye on her son, trying to split herself between warrior and maternal instincts.

"Did I ever tell you how I first met your father?" Trevon suddenly said. Avarielle raised an eyebrow.

"I believe it involved something with hunting a beast, falling into a pit, and angering every single elder in the village."

A slow rumble, as close to a laugh as she expected she would get from him for some time.

"I guess I did tell you, though I'm not sure I quite captured how incensed the Elders were." A grin. That grin, the one that she'd always loved seeing, that she'd emulated without meaning to. The grin that everyone assumed meant he was her father. Something that hadn't happened until they went to Cassara's home, because everyone in the West knew who she was. Avarielle Grayloft. Daughter of the leader of the West, warrior, fighter, dancer… deserter.

Here, she was known. And so was Trevon.

"That's how I met your father, sure, but how I really got to know him was when he was about to propose to your mother. I didn't think he stood a chance, she was much too good for him." A smile, though it didn't reach his eyes. "Your father had always been a bit of a showoff. You come by it honestly." He looked at her then, just a bit, then focused back on the fire, as though he couldn't stand the sight of her. Or the sight of what she would become. It might have been kinder not to let him know what exactly was in store for her. Perhaps she was already forgetting the value of kindness, or perhaps she simply had none left to spare.

"Except he didn't do anything rash, for a change. He took her somewhere romantic, I assume—those details, he never shared. Everybody expected him to do something stupid to show off, but she once told me he took her to a calm and beautiful place, and they'd simply talked. That's it. That surprised me because he showed me, and he showed her, that he was more than what people expected of him. Something that he showed us time and time again, even during the Westland Wars." A pause. "Losing your mother killed him. But that doesn't matter now. I guess I'm just a rambling old man now." This time he did turn toward her, straightening.

"But when you tell me that you have no choice, that you're trapped, all I can think of is your father winning your mother's heart despite everyone saying he couldn't. I think of you surviving the Westland Wars, of your friends uniting with you to fight the greatest enemy despite no one believing it possible to ally the forces of this land. I think of how you gave up leadership in the West to save your people, and I think of fires raging down the Bloody Mountains before a young princess stopped them with nothing but her powers, after coming here because of her friendship with you. I've seen a lot of things, Avarielle, and so have you."

He clasped his hands on his lap, the cup secured between his palms. "And if there's one thing I know for sure, it's that Graylofts will *always* surprise you."

She'd expected him to react this way. It wasn't like him to give up. But he hadn't felt, or seen, what she had. He hadn't heard the voice of a devil god ring in his skull.

But Trevon was good at hope, and hope was good for Trevon.

"Promise me," Trevon said, holding her eyes. "Promise me you'll do everything you can to survive this, Avarielle. Survive, and come home to me. I outlived your mother, your father, and your brother." His voice cracked. "I don't want to outlive you, too."

Avarielle met his eyes, felt a crackling along the bones of her arm, a rippling in her muscles. Despite her best attempt to hide the pain, Trevon saw it.

A scream from outside. The pain intensified, and both jumped up. Trevon grabbed his large crossbow, his broadsword comfortably slung on his back.

Avarielle pulled Graysword free. Trevon nodded, and she followed him out, sure-footed but careful, leading toward the strange tower near their camp. Avarielle clenched her jaw at the war drums beating in her arm, Graysword's warm pommel like a ward against the dark magic pushing to escape the cracks of her bones.

She needed to find Shirina. And she needed to find her now.

A second before a cracking sound shattered the night, the magic somersaulted beneath Shirina. A warning, or so she chose to interpret it, and she opened the Sight to see beneath Shala's feet a gathering of magic, forming a perfect line from north to south, splitting the ground deep below.

Shirina didn't shout a warning or use her magic—she reacted by sheer instinct and grabbed Shala out of the way, sending both crashing to the sand as the ground cracked. Dust, sand, and stones exploded up and showered them, and it was Shala's turn to pull Shirina to her feet as both started to run toward Westlanders and adepts who did the same, leading toward the edge of the city beneath the West.

"Behind me!" Shirina held up her staff, struck the stones at her feet—strong, centuries-old, unwavering— held out her other hand and pulled power from below, weaving it around them but leaving it tethered to the stones that were its home. It protected witches and warriors as the sand and dust settled, clearing the air around them so they could breathe.

The night grew darker as dust blocked starlight, and the ground stopped shaking. Dust clung to the air like an unsettling fog. Westlanders drew weapons, and her adepts looked to the ground, as though trying to will the magic to come within them. Only Shala looked up at the magic woven by Shirina, analyzing its strong connection to the ground.

She looked to Shirina, dark skin reflecting the blue glow of her magic, dark eyes sharp.

"You're using the same strands of magic as before," she said, "and something else."

"I am," Shirina said, not bothering to hide the pride from her face. "And something else. The old magic from the cities below."

"Is that good, or bad?" Shala asked. Shirina did not answer, focusing back on possible attack as the fog of sand began to thin.

A few figures ran toward them. A Westland warrior, looking like he'd rolled around in the sand, coughing wildly, sand sticking to a nasty wound on his head. He was tended to quickly by Orange Circle Olaram, an elderly woman who'd raised five children and had joined the Circle to do something for herself. She was skilled in healing, and no-nonsense.

Her hands began to clean and bandage the wound, practiced fingers tending to his needs. Shirina watched as the magic answered her bidding, Olaram's lips moving in familiar incantations. The magic crawled up her knees and arms, into her fingers, and began to heal the wound. Olaram didn't pause or stop, either expecting the outcome, or not willing to risk diminishing it with her interference.

Shirina kept her shield up, blue sparkling around her. It didn't drain her as magic once had. Her mind insisted she should be exhausted, but she ignored it in favor of what her body told her. She'd need to figure out the limitations of her magic quickly, so that her mind and body could get realigned.

Or she could simply not question the magic as Olaram did, but Shirina knew that was not her way. She needed to understand. She *yearned* to understand.

"Shirina!" Avarielle cried out, to Shirina's relief.

"Here!" the sorceress answered, and soon Trevon and Avarielle stepped out of the dust, both covered in sand, cloths covering their mouths and noses. She looked at the blue flicker, the magic reflected in her eyes, the pupil disturbingly large. Then she looked to Shirina with a question.

"Just step in," she said. And they did, the magic easily granting them access.

"A second tower just burst out of the ground," Avarielle said casually, though Shirina could tell she was anything but relaxed, taking in every detail around her, including

Olaram's healing of the man, who began to stand on his own.

"I think the magic responds to our movements," Shirina said, to Avarielle, and Shala, and her adepts. "Like it responded to our words, now it responds to… movement. But not just any movement. Like the staff helps me focus mine, it responds to practiced movements trying to accomplish something. Like helping a plant grow, or healing someone."

"How do we access our fire magic?" A Yellow Circle asked.

"I'm not sure I can tell you," Shirina said. "Not in any certain terms. At least, not yet. I think it's individual and will draw on whatever you need to happen. Whatever you're willing to ground yourself with."

Keening swallowed her last word. Shirina turned to where Avarielle said a tower had risen, though she couldn't see it for the darkness and sand fog. She held her staff and tried to send blue flames into the sky to light the way, but the magic wouldn't take flight.

It wanted to stay tethered to the ground.

Shirina stomped her foot, a very un-Elder-like movement, and struck the ground with her staff, willing the magic to brim to the surface. The ground cracked, blue lines dancing just beneath the sand. Shirina twisted her staff, magic rippling in it, as though sensing her intention. She held it up, grasped it in both hands as another keen broke the sky, warriors stepping forward, swords and bows at the ready.

"Follow the sand up," she whispered, uncertain how to clarify her need with movement, and then she struck the ground again. Grains of sand beneath her staff flew up, forming balls of light. Shirina's chest tightened at their sight, so familiar.

Another keen, followed by a shout from the east, cut short too quickly.

"They're going to kill everyone!" someone hissed.

"Wait," Avarielle ordered. "We need to know what we're facing, first."

Shirina nodded, and willed the blue lights out, to find their enemies and reveal them. The blue balls skimmed the sand, sending trails of sparking sand flying as they raced out. They found a silhouette, something with glassy eyes… *a head.* A Westlander head, red hair glowing purple in the blue light. Shirina moved her foot to the right, encouraging the balls of light to find the attacker, and not the prey.

They shifted, moved, dancing over one another. She couldn't tell how many there were as they merged in and out of each other. Could she get enough of them free to illuminate the entire area? She forgot about the idea as the blue lights illuminated something else. Six sleek legs, long and piercing, silver-like blades, each leading to a round silver ball, which connected like joints to a light oval body that looked to be made of some kind of stone. There was no head, just dark orbs, perhaps eyes, forming a circle around it.

"What in the two lands…" Trevon began to whisper,

and the creature locked in on his voice. Its legs shot out straight and started spinning, flying toward him at ridiculous speed, sand rippling away. Avarielle shouted his name as Shirina reinforced her shield. The creature struck, the entire shield buckled, turned dark blue, and magic slammed back into Shirina. The sorceress managed to brace for the blow, losing only a little ground as she clutched her staff. But the shield wavered. Without missing a beat, the creature shifted sideways and went for Shirina.

The blue lights flickered up into the creature's eyes as Shirina gasped back at the giant silver legs striking her shield as they spun. The shield collapsed and Shirina twisted back but her cheek burned, blood trickling down a fresh cut. The magical balls struck it back, protecting her. The creature keened—no, Shirina realized—it wasn't keening. The noise came from the creature shifting its legs in midair for another attack. Her blue lights clicked on its edges but were unable to slow it as the razor disk targeted her again with merciless speed.

Avarielle stepped before her, Graysword lit with magic. Before it could connect, the creature shifted sideways to the left. And fell back.

It stayed near them, moving slowly as it observed Avarielle.

"It fears Graysword!" one of the Westlanders declared, to cheers and battle cries. Avarielle and Shirina doubted that was what kept them at bay. Pulling on the Sight, she glanced at Avarielle, the red magic slowly seeping out of her.

The blue lights whipped apart, highlighting at least a dozen more attackers of various sizes and number of legs. Some hovered, others skittered on the ground, like a pack of wolves waiting to attack. Deadly, sharp, silver wolves.

Shirina turned to Shala and her adepts. "The magic is still with you," she said, "just not in the air. You know how to work with it. You know how to work with the land, too. They're united, now. Find a way to connect to it and use it. From the ground," she said. "It wants to connect with you. You simply have to allow it, and respect its choice to stay grounded."

A few of her adepts fell to the earth right away, placing their hands in the sand as though water to save their parched bodies. It wasn't graceful, but it was effective, the magic finding their hands and connecting with them. The witches didn't seem to know what to do with it once they'd found it, tears running down their cheeks at feeling the power again.

Shala's eyes narrowed as she concentrated on something. Olaram healed another Westlander, the old witch's connection to the magic of healing undeniable.

They need a purpose. Once they understood what they needed the magic for, exactly, they'd be able to draw it into them. *Like Cassara.* Right now, some waffled with indecision, the magic not certain how to react to the lack of clarity, simply dancing near their extremities.

Clarity will come soon enough.

Shirina focused back on the enemy. Her shield hadn't withstood an attack from a single creature—it certainly wouldn't take an attack from all of them. A quick glance at Avarielle and she saw the red strands held at bay by Graysword's magic grow, as though the creatures fed its fires.

"We need to get rid of them, now," Shirina said to the warrior. Avarielle nodded, not needing to be told what was happening, sweat streaking down her face. She was losing the battle already, and she knew it.

The creatures crept closer while Shirina's blue lights moved with growing intensity, as though warning her. Avarielle's hand on Graysword began to tremble ever so slightly with pain.

There was no more time for hesitation.

Shirina held out her fist, her other hand grasping the staff. Out of habit and familiarity, she sang a quick incantation, then whipped her fist around and opened it, palm up toward the sky while her staff connected with the ground. The magic reacted, waves of blue flames exploding outward from the sand, destroying about half the attackers in a single, powerful arch of light.

Then the battlefield turned to chaos.

Shala stared at Shirina, her mentor's movements assured and pointed, the magic reacting as decisively. Shirina had never been very expressive physically unless you knew her. Then, the smallest of movements meant approval or disapproval, spoken or otherwise.

But Shala had given up long ago on containing her physical nature. She was hotheaded, quick to move, quick to punch. Once Shirina had made it clear she did not expect her to pull back on her emotions or on expressing them—unlike the old ways of Ravenhold—Shala had decided to embrace them.

She'd thought they'd grown tame with time. Now she realized that they'd just become more focused.

The creatures, flying whirls of death, flew toward them, and Shala grounded her feet and punched. Not actually touching the creature—she'd lose her arm long before she'd made contact, but she willed the punch to connect, for the magic to follow her movement.

And it did, the creature erupting into blue light and crashing to the ground, broken.

Ulya, an Orange Circle Shala quite liked, did a similar movement, but with a shake of her hips that made Shala's mouth open and cheeks grow warm. A creature melted in blue flames before it reached Westlanders. Ulya caught Shala's face and winked.

We all have a past, Shala thought, focusing back on the battle.

Three creatures still lived. They seemed to retreat and a few Westlanders shouted in victory. Shirina focused on them, keeping her blue lights near them. The three creatures stopped, stacked on top of each other, and merged to form a column of whirling death. Without pause or giving them the time to form a plan, the three-story-tall monstrosity cut toward them, quickly dicing the bodies of two Westlanders and an adobe hut, as though they hadn't even been there.

Shirina sent two more stone lances at its base, but they barely wounded it as it eviscerated the warrior Olaram had just healed. Shala and Ulya stepped forward, as did two other adepts, pulling on what magic they could to try to stop it—sand, stones, and blue flames striking the column of death.

Still, the creatures came.

Shirina took another step forward, held up three fingers with a quick flick of the wrist, and a stone lance erupted from the ground, striking the creature's base, impaling it. A few people shouted in victory, but it quickly broke free and kept coming. The bottom row of sharp metal no longer twirled, as though the bottom creature had been killed, its body dragged by its other two brethren, pointed legs moving as quickly and sharply as ever.

Shirina took a step back, and Shala realized that the Elder was falling, not retreating. With a quick movement she managed to catch her, the woman crumpling to her knees.

Shirina looked stunned, like she'd had a bad blow to the head, and couldn't even open her eyes, though she struggled to.

"Shala," she whispered.

"I'm here."

"Avarielle. Don't let them…"

And she collapsed, her skin so deathly pale it practically glowed in the blue flames as the small orbs gathered back toward Shirina. *Why weren't they extinguishing?*

Spells usually ended when their caster passed out.

A mystery for later.

"Take her," Shala ordered Olaram and Ulya. Olaram had already started checking over Shirina, shooing away the blue lights who stayed close, like they worried about the Elder.

Shirina had ordered her to, to… *something* to do with Avarielle. Shala stood up, standing by the warrior, who'd taken a protective position before the fallen Shirina.

"Is she alright?" Avarielle whispered. Trevon came to stand on the other side of Shala, and she felt safer for having the old warrior there. Avarielle's sword glowed with magic, sure, but Trevon had always been the one there when she most needed a hand.

"I don't know," Shala answered honestly. "But she won't be if they get through us."

Avarielle nodded, a scowl on her face. Shala noticed the slight trembling of Graysword. She was forced to wield it one-handed with her other arm in a sling. Maybe if Olaram could help heal the arm, the warrior wouldn't be so disadvantaged.

But Shirina could draw on her magic, and would have healed a broken bone, so this was probably something else. Frowning, Shala focused on Avarielle's arm and shoulder, to see if she could help at all... and saw red whisps of magic reaching for the creature.

No. Not reaching for it. Summoning it. And the creature seemed to be deciding how best to approach the warrior, which probably meant it didn't intend to kill her. If it meant to do that, it would have cut through her. That would be simple enough.

Shirina wanted to keep Avarielle out of their clutches, and she could venture a strong guess why, considering the red magic trapped within the warrior.

The only way to do that was to stop it.

Shala punched, slamming it with magic. But the blue flames were broken by the twirling blades, and the creature moved forward, focusing on her instead of the Grayloft.

Shala tried to hit it with her magic, using a punch, which amused Avarielle, though the mirth hardly bubbled out of her. The thing, whatever in Elihor's dark pits it was, just dissipated her magic.

And turned toward Shirina's second.

Not to mention Trevon.

Avarielle moved quickly, without thinking, throwing herself into Shala, which knocked her and Trevon down. Before either could recover, Avarielle threw herself up, wishing she could use both arms as she pivoted, silver arms connecting with Graysword, the strike reverberating through her entire body as she planted her feet and refused to give it quarter.

For a moment, she feared Graysword had met its match. But its magic held true, severing two metal arms. She could end this, except for the magic in her left arm, writhing around her bones, threatening to erupt. The closer that thing came, the more she could feel Siabala's magic, whispers starting to ignite in her mind.

If she attacked the creature, she feared she would only feed the monster within her. As though sensing her hesitation, the creature moved right and headed toward the two adepts tending to Shirina.

Avarielle didn't think, only acted, throwing Graysword into the creature, cutting its center, the blade's magic holding long enough to cut it in two. The screeching flew over the two adepts and crashed into the ground just beyond Shirina, Graysword's hilt sticking out of it, the blade muted, away from her.

The pain in her shoulder grew more intense, the red magic tracing her bones, scraping every scar, like Siabala intended to shove himself out of her arm and back into the world.

Slowly she fell to her knees, grinding her teeth and trying to will the power back into her. But there was nothing she could do. No more than there had been when she'd run Kaden through with her blade.

He was too powerful.

"Avarielle," Trevon threw himself to the ground beside her, cradling her.

Get away from me, she wanted to scream. *I don't want to kill you!*

The world narrowed, and she couldn't sense him anymore, her vision turning inward, to Siabala and his powers, to his hatred of her and all that she held dear.

Then something grounded her, and she felt the familiar metal and magic of Graysword in her hand. It fought back Siabala, crashed into his might, pushed back his powers into her left arm. Didn't push him back completely, the cracks along her bones like a window for him. But at least it contained him.

She gulped in air, hand trembling on the hilt of her sword. Slowly, she opened her eyes, to find Shala looking into hers.

"Is he contained?" she asked softly.

"For now," Avarielle said, wincing. Trevon didn't say anything, staying near her. "How's Shirina?" she asked, partly to stop the witch from staring at her so intently.

"Exhausted," an Orange Circle said, kneeling before Avarielle. "Instead of how the magic used to work," the older woman continued, "where we would get tired and then collapse if we pushed too far, it seems that this form of exertion is more like hitting a wall, with little warning of it approaching."

"That'll make it hard to gauge how much magic we can use," Shala said, nodding.

"Indeed, Crimson Circle Elite," the woman seemed as pleased at using the title as Shala was at hearing it. "Do you require healing?" she asked of Avarielle, wise enough not to simply heal her.

"No," Avarielle said. Then added, "Thank you for asking." She didn't even want to think what might happen to the Orange Circle if she used her magic on her.

The Orange Circle didn't seem convinced, but nodded and stood up.

"What can I do to help?" Shala asked. Avarielle's first instinct was to tell her to leave her alone, but she bit it back.

"Help Shirina," Avarielle said, "so that she can get back on her feet faster. We need her knowledge."

Shala nodded and headed to her mentor. Avarielle turned to Trevon.

"We need to find out what exactly came out of the ground."

He nodded, stood up, and offered her a hand. She clasped it, still as strong as ever, and he pulled her up.

"I'll take a scouting party," he said. "We'll go fast, quiet, and slow. You stay here."

"I'm not—"

"Yes you are," he cut her off, then lowered his voice. "Those things wanted you, Avarielle. Or whatever's in you. It pains me to say it, and I certainly never thought I would, but we'll be safer going without you."

Avarielle bit back her automatic response to that, too.

"Be safe," she said in a whisper. Trevon nodded and went to find his scouting party.

Avarielle looked at the broken creatures. She sheathed

Graysword, but kept her hand on its pommel, trying to ignore the pounding on her shoulder, like a knocking at the door.

One that intended to, no matter what, eventually break through.

In the week Tally had taken over Massir, she'd gutted Cassara's supporters. More might come, of course, but it was clear to Cassara that Siabala's intent was to leave her and her people without defenses to withstand his final attack.

Dayshon was with a trusted healer, and Altessa was gone, hopefully heading out of the city.

Siabala would not claim her daughter's blood, though if he rose again, there might be nowhere safe to hide… she stopped the line of thinking and focused on what she could affect as she made herself a cup of tea, alone in the small kitchen she'd made a home.

Avarielle knew all of her city's defenses, and most had been torn down by Tally, or would be useless. Her city guards had been decimated, and her royal guards killed and hunted, save for a few.

Elder Quilsam was still here, but mostly because he

and his Larkhold adepts had no magic with which to leave. She didn't count on him sticking around. Shirina's adepts were also still here, the few who had been posted in the city instead of the castle, but they were equally powerless. Cassara had confidence that Shirina would find a way to unlock the magic for them, but didn't count on it being done in time to save them.

Rashim's army had been sent to the West, orders issued by her husband while he still had a voice, though she doubted a mind. She'd sent for them, but she knew they would not be back for at least three days, depending on where in the West they'd been stationed, something that her husband could not tell her.

Enough time for Tally to get her attack underway.

She couldn't send for help to the other city-states or the coalition, or any of the allied kingdoms and countries. Monsters had started to stalk the lands just outside the gates, and a few farmers had managed to make it in. She couldn't help her villages, either, nor those outside the walls.

The walls. Where the line was always drawn. Those within them, and those outside of them.

Those who had, and those who had not.

Some of the bigger villages had walls and cellars for hiding. But it wouldn't be enough. Not while their land seemed to be vanishing to an ancient city beneath them.

The ancient city. That was something she didn't use to have access to, or even knowledge of its existence.

Avarielle would expect her to do something with it, probably. But she wouldn't know what.

She wished she could discuss her plans with the warrior, which she really couldn't, or with Dayshon, which she also couldn't. How was she supposed to be unpredictable to the person who'd taught her most of what she knew, and had suggested most of the defenses?

She needed different input, and not from the people she'd always leaned on, though she'd already called for Builder Gramire, to get a full state of the remaining defenses.

Who else should she call for advice? Who would be unexpected?

Cassara warmed her palms on her teacup, an old chipped artifact from the Days of Blood she simply couldn't part with, and walked out of the kitchen, in their small sitting room, toward the window. The city stretched beneath her, seemingly peaceful. People moved about, despite the impending attack, though many had taken refuge in the safe zones—all of which Avarielle had helped design. The guards worked to get the citizens safe or at least to prepare for other countermeasures. But she still had to issue orders of what exactly those would look like. The guards had reported that a few monsters had been dispatched near the walls, and their numbers were growing.

Some people were trying to leave, though the gates had been shut due to wandering monsters. Outside her city, the land appeared peaceful, vast fields stretching around the lowest walls. She forced her gaze back on the city proper. Over fifty thousand people called Massir their home. Merchants usually funneled in and out, as did traders. And all those people would be doomed unless she came up with a plan. She knew this view by heart, always looking out this window. A window built for the servants.

She needed a different point of view. One she'd tried hard to avoid, as she quite hated it. But one she needed—the point of view of kings and queens long gone. From the ramparts, where Dayshon's parents had watched the city being invaded, dooming their lower quarters in a failed attempt to save the rest of Massir.

She used to go see the city from there, to view the progress on the walls, and see how defended her people were. Over the years, she'd stopped, the progress too slow, her mind on other matters of trade and community. The Days of Blood seemed further and further away, and the urgency vanished for more pressing matters, like poor crops, neighborly kingdoms requiring help, villages in need of better trade.

So many details. Too many, perhaps. Dayshon had handled some, and she did her part. Despite all efforts, the giant puzzle of her kingdom still had too many missing pieces to glimpse the picture she desperately tried to assemble.

She climbed the stairs to the gilded home of ancient rulers, to the roof, then up the final stair made of simple pragmatic stone, leading to the castle's ancient ramparts, beneath the adorned towers, one of which still lay abandoned and broken.

She stood above her kingdom, the few guards giving her a wide berth as she gazed down, able to see the entire city from here.

Her gaze swept across it, from fallen sections and markets still selling needed goods for people to eat—she had made sure they wouldn't hike prices to take advantage of the current lack of trade—to the guilds and then her usually avoided section of the city, the noble's quarters. She focused on the ancient stone mansions built in the highest parts of the city, near the palace. She'd blocked the view with gardens when possible, focused on those who needed her more. The nobles did not have the run of the court as they used to and resented her for it. She'd made powerful enemies, some slowing the progress of the queen's "pet" projects, including walls in the lower city. A lost shipment, redirected to another project. The Builder's Guild choosing a different part of the city than one she'd championed. Dozens of different ways they'd whittled at her authority and effectiveness over the past decades. Dayshon had said this was simply the ways of the court, ways which would prove impossible to change, at least not in her lifetime. Then again, Siabala hadn't been supposed to reemerge in her lifetime, either.

She didn't regret sidelining them. But their hobby of gathering gossip in court had been replaced with creating gossip *about* the court, and slowing its progress. Trying to trip the young foreign queen, unwelcome here.

She'd shown them all she could rule, and did so with

patience and grace. And now? She looked down at their homes, highly defended and guarded. They'd done nothing to help, of course. Simply hidden in their homes. Cassara's hand gripped the edge of the wall, knuckles turning white with rage. She truly despised their way of thinking.

And that was why Avarielle would never expect her to call on them for aid.

Reluctantly, with extremely leaded feet, Cassara headed back down the stairs. She would call on them and ask for help and, if they refused to give it, she would force their hand.

The time for putting up with their haughtiness in the name of diplomacy had come to an end with Siabala's shadow looming over her kingdom.

2 7

Stone wrapped around the trees of the small settlement. No, not wrapped around. The bark had *turned* to stone, the hollow crevices bleeding sap. Pakana banged her fist on stone, which had once been a door, its edges barely noticeable. She pounded with the side of her hand, flesh raw, shouting for whoever was inside.

Rojon had stopped trying to dissuade her as she pounded on every door sealed with stone. He looked at the sap, slowly leaking through the bark before hardening and turning to stone. He picked up a twig from the ground, still very much wood, and fetched a sample of partially liquid sap.

"Rojon, I can hear people trapped inside!" Pakana's panicked voice distracted him.

"Is there no other way out?" he asked, joining her before a sealed door.

"No," she said. "The whole point of Kosel was to stay hidden! I mean, visible but hidden is kind of the whole unofficial moto."

"Okay," Rojon simply said, but she continued.

"If there's sign of danger, people hide in the trees. It's always been the way, and it kept lots of people safe when Eloms roamed the lands. With all the rumbles and sprouting buildings, they would have hidden inside. Like my fathers' inn…" Her hands hung limply at her sides. "Rojon, what do we do? Can we stop this?"

Rojon examined the twig with the sap that had been turning to stone, to study it and maybe determine how it interacted with the tree. Except the sap was perfectly clear, no longer showing any signs of turning to stone. Rojon frowned, held it up to what light was being allowed through the canopy of leaves and pines, to make sure the specks of stone weren't just diffused in the light.

He twisted it, then touched it with a fingertip, sticking slightly to it. He walked back to where he'd collected the sample—the remaining sap had turned to solid stone.

"What is it?" Pakana asked from right beside him, and he jumped. He'd been so concentrated on the sap that he'd forgotten he wasn't alone.

"I was looking at the sap," he said, showing her his twig. "It was turning to stone on the tree, but stopped when I pulled it away."

"Rojon, people will suffocate in there," Pakana said. "Focus!"

"I am, I just don't think that we can break through stone, not without the right tools, anyway."

The screams of those imprisoned within drifted in the air and crawled in his blood, making the hairs on every limb stand on end.

Pakana's fists trembled at her sides, and he saw in her the same helplessness he'd felt when his village had been under attack, and his grandfather had perished.

"If it stops being stone once it's removed from the tree," he mused out loud, trying to get *her* to focus on solutions, "that means that the roots are more than likely the feeding system."

"How do we get the roots to stop bringing up whatever is leeching into them?"

"I'm not sure," he admitted. The screams grew more quiet.

"They're suffocating," Pakana said, Rolly nuzzling her, the giant lizard surprisingly gentle.

Rojon studied the tree near them. He knew trees. Knew how they worked. Understood how they fed, why they reached for the light. The trees were different in Graydon, sure, the two lands having had no cross-pollination for over a thousand years, but they were also very similar. Roots to feed from below, leaves from above. What fed the tree forged it.

In Elihor, the roots didn't just feed on the earth. They fed on magic, too. On the memories of those buried below...

"The ground kept shifting last night," he said, looking

down at the ground beneath him, and the spire he could see through the trees. The root systems in Kosel had to be ridiculously strong. Probably the strongest in Elihor and Graydon. "Shirina said that she thought the magic was in the earth, that's how it fed the sapling she asked that I turn into a staff."

"So the magic is going up the roots?" Pakana asked, distractedly looking around.

"It is. Or seems to be. Actually, I think it always has been. In Elihor, anyway, to some degree."

The magic was in the ground. Working up the roots, into the trees. Maybe a lot of magic was trapped here? What if the trees of Kosel were absorbing too much of it, too quickly, through their vast root systems?

"We need to slow down the absorption of magic," he said.

"How do we do that?" Pakana vibrated with impatience. "Rojon, we need to do something now!"

"I…" How had he done that? He'd worked to create Shirina's staff. He'd studied it, cut it, forged it from the oldest tree in Graydon. He had respected the rivulets the tree had created itself, trusting it to understand the flow of magic that crawled into it effortlessly.

He didn't know if it had worked or not, since Shirina had never wielded it, whisked away before she could… but he'd *felt* the tree's desire to carry the magic. To help hone it, and hold it.

He'd specialized in working with trees and architecture—to understand and respect the flow of nature, and simply nudge it in a way that would marry well with human needs. He'd built aqueducts from encouraging trees to grow within one another. His mentor had at times wondered if his connection with Elihor gave him greater understanding of how magic flowed in trees. Rojon had balked at that—he'd worked hard to learn everything that he had.

Tired of waiting for him to finish his sentence, Pakana had gone back to trying to smash down part of a stone tree, screaming in frustration.

Shirina thought the magic had gone underground, somehow. His own powers were different from anyone else's before him. Part Grayloft bloodline, part Elihor, he was a child of two worlds.

Siabala is in my mother.

His mother also straddled two worlds—that of daughter of the West, and slave to Siabala. She'd been trapped most of her life, accomplishing feats few believed possible.

Siabala took her over.

Pakana's voice grew hoarse from shouting, her screams growing as silent as the trees.

His mother would find a way to become free. He had to believe that. Just like she'd believe he'd find a way to free these people.

He'd been helpless in Raklar. Torbolem had died at sea. His grandfather had perished saving him. But his magic wasn't like his father's and his grandfather's. It didn't just protect his loved ones. It protected him, too.

And he truly believed he could use it to protect others.

He realized that the world seemed muted—the pine branches had stopped dancing, turned to stone. Kosel had grown deathly quiet, the shadows no longer dancing, stilled in the breeze.

Pakana had collapsed to her knees before a stone tree, weeping at the lives she couldn't save, at her home, her forest, betraying its people so.

"My village was by the sea," he said softly to a tree, placing his hands on its rough, cold bark. "But its people were not all that different. Strong, brave, and willing to stand up for each other."

He did not close his eyes. His hands touched stone, but he saw the tree for what it had once been, had its roots not betrayed it.

"Rojon?" Pakana asked, voice faint as he let himself drift toward the stone, focusing on the sap beneath the bark. On the roots below the tree. On the network of ancient roots supporting Kosel. He respected trees, and forests, and all that nature did to support the people who called it home.

Release the magic, he felt toward the tree, using words only to visualize something that the tree might be able to interpret. A breath, and two. He pushed his hand harder on the coarse trunk, but the tree pushed back, or so he sensed. He imagined the magic flowing up, from the pine needles and leaves, into the air…

Nothing.

Frowning, he removed his hand, pondering other alternatives. If he couldn't push the magic through the tree, Rojon decided his next best plan would be to push it out by filling it with *his* magic, instead. He sorely wished Shirina were here to counsel him. This time, he slowly fell to his knees and closed his eyes, imagining the root system beneath the forest, and the life teeming around it. Like trees released precious air, Rojon imagined the roots letting go of the magic. Releasing it instead of absorbing it.

Elihor's magic danced beneath him, and within him. He could sense it, though the magic in the ground differed from his own. Like they came from the same family, but were distant cousins. But he knew it, and it knew him, and he focused all of his energy on saving the trees of Kosel.

Protect them. His magic danced within him, responding to his need. The magic twirled and somersaulted in his stomach, but refused to leave him for the tree. He tried again and again, but none of his efforts were any more fruitful.

He exhaled, frustrated.

"Are you alright?" Pakana asked, leaning against the tree, observing him closely.

"I'm trying to figure out how to get the magic out of the tree," he said. "It's not as easy as I hoped it would be."

"Magic is causing this?" Pakana sat down, folded in on herself, making herself small in the silence of the forest, the birds and animals as quiet as the stone trees.

"It's going up the roots," Rojon said, "but it won't come out anywhere else, so its petrifying the trees."

"Why would the trees absorb the magic?"

"Good question," Rojon mumbled, parsing the new information in his mind. "In Elihor, the trees automatically absorb some magic. Maybe they do the same in Graydon?"

"I have no idea." She sounded resigned, and Rojon hated that as much as he hated not being able to help.

A deep breath, the scent of pine stilled, and inspiration struck.

"What if it used to, and just hasn't of late because there was no magic in the ground? Or so little we didn't notice?"

"Where would the magic go?"

"You're really good at asking the right questions." Rojon offered her a weak grin. "I wish I was half as good at offering answers."

"You're pretty good." Pakana shrugged, then looked back at the trees. "What happens to the magic in Elihor? Once the trees absorb it?"

"Well, it's not a lot of magic," Rojon said, thinking of the memories absorbed in the fruit. "It goes into fruit, basically."

He looked up at the pine trees, ideas gelling into his mind, from his early learnings in Elihor to Shirina's mentions of the magic being *in the ground*.

"What if it usually escaped through the pine needles, but now the magic doesn't want to go back to the air?"

"I'm not following," Pakana frowned, but Rojon's mind spun so fast he couldn't distract it by trying to explain to her. Nor did she seem to expect it, standing as he did, feeling the shift in energy as thoughts coalesced into his mind.

"It's like when a tree has too much water," he said. "It has to get rid of it, or it'll rot. I mean, it always gets rid of some water through leaves, but when there's just too much, it can expel some from its roots."

"Okay," Pakana said, obviously waiting for the euphoric answer Rojon was slowly attaining.

"So, say the trees are absorbing all this magic because it's in the ground for the first time in a millennia. And not just Graydon's, which at least it knows from the air. But Elihor's magic, which is used to climbing up trees, and would find comfort in the network of roots that sustains Kosel."

He could see it, now, feeling his own magic reacting enthusiastically.

"Elihor's magic goes up the roots. Graydon's follows. Neither magic can, or maybe *wants* to be expelled by the pine needles, fearing it'll get trapped in the air again. The tree becomes overwhelmed. The magic turns it to stone, trapping magic inside."

"And people," Pakana added.

"And people," Rojon repeated, then immediately wished he'd added more gravitas, but his idea robbed him of focusing on much else as his course became clear. He placed a hand on the trunk. "If it could understand that it must release the magic…"

He closed his eyes, took a deep breath, his magic settling within him. His love of plants had sprouted long before memories locked in his mind. He'd grown up with the new forests of Elihor, after Siabala had burned them all to the ground. His mother planted joyful flowers before their house, and always smiled at them when she came home to them, to him. He'd unlocked some of their secrets with his apprenticeship, understanding their strength and willingness to aid in a way few had.

Maybe it was because of his hard work, or maybe because the magic of Elihor danced in plants, much like it danced in him.

It could fill him, too, and Shirina had helped him learn to trust it, and himself, to wield it.

Let it go down your roots, he visualized, and felt his magic trickle from his hand into the bark, travel the length of the tree, guiding the magic back down to the roots.

"I can get them out!" Pakana screamed, and Rojon's eyes flew open.

Beneath his hand was rough bark, not stone, and pine needles sang their thanks in the gentle breeze.

One tree. He'd changed one tree back.

And he would change them all, one by one, heart lurching at the thought of those trapped within running out of air before he could save them.

2 8

The throne room bore the scars of the attack: Scorch marks on the floor, missing long purple banners burnt to a crisp, the feeling that it still held its breath.

Cassara settled on her throne. She wore her favorite blue dress, hair fully up in the traditional way of the queens of Rashim, crown firmly placed upon it. She kept her hands relaxed, her back straight.

The nobles filed in, curiosity compelling most of them to answer a summons from the throne after so many years of silence. Of course, she'd seen them at events and formal occasions, and had been friendly with them. But they'd obviously only spoken to her out of cordial necessity, in case the power games that had ruled Massir so long still mattered.

They did, and they didn't. Cassara had tried to do away with them and, given another two decades, might have crumpled more of the aristocracy. But she was out of time, and she needed them. And they, for now, needed her.

Countess Trilliam filed in, a pleasant woman Cassara actually got along with. She bowed before the throne, stepped aside, and stood, no chairs having been provided. Her keen eyes weighed Cassara, and the queen thought she spotted approval and interest in them.

Lord Rushil, who Cassara disliked, bowed, but not as deeply, simply keeping things formal enough not to draw the ire of the throne.

Cassara never relied on the ceremonies of the throne this way. But, today, she made them file in, follow the dark purple carpet down, stop at its edge, as proper, and bow.

All of them.

It would anger them, she knew. But it would remind them of the power they assigned this throne. And, right now, she needed to remind them that she was their queen. That she could do things differently, but could simply fall back on tradition, too.

Others filed in, of her long list of invitees. Builders, architects, veterans, soldiers, guards, representatives from every guild and noble house, from every community house and official institution. Farmers, citizens... everyone was welcome.

The nobles had been welcome again, but not at the price of everyone else's voice. That was the difference, which slowly dawned on their faces as those wearing regular attire joined them, the throne room filling up.

She would listen to them all and, should the noble houses choose to refuse to help her, they could do so before the citizens of Massir. They would all be accountable to one another.

And to her.

Once everyone had entered and bowed, the doors to the room closed, guards standing before them. She wished she had more allies here. She'd never once held court over so many people, especially the nobles. And certainly would have never dreamt of doing so without Dayshon. None of her children were here. Nor her usual allies.

It was just her, and her people.

She held up a hand, silence blanketing the room. She'd worked the words in her mind all day, but they deserted her as all eyes fell on her. She took a deep breath, gave her stomach a moment to settle. Dayshon had always advised her that silence could be wielded as effectively as words. All she had to do was look as though she was in control.

She wasn't sure she was pulling off the look, but she did go from set of eyes to set of eyes. Some looked away, others locked eyes with her. She broke down the crowd into people. Into sets of eyes. The seconds slipped by with the weight of hours, and she found her words again.

"Siabala has returned, and he intends to destroy this city." A visible wave of worry trembled throughout the crowd. Cassara continued before anyone could voice their questions.

"King Dayshon has been injured by the fake Circle led by Elder Tally. She follows Siabala."

At this, she paid attention to the assembled, as did the guards. Some had associated with her closely during her stay, and anyone who seemed ready to follow Tally again would get well acquainted with the dungeons.

"Any who continue to deal with her, considering what they now know, will be charged with treason and dealt with harshly."

She'd wanted to say executed, but knew that was a slippery slope. Executions had not been a part of Massir's Code of Law during her and Dayshon's reign. Now was not the time to institute it. She wasn't dismissing it out of hand, but she wasn't willing to travel down this road.

Enough people had already died.

"Will the king live?" a tentative voice asked. Cassara found the speaker. Guild Leader Aline, a healer who'd helped perfect Dayshon's prosthetics, and revolutionized their use in Massir, and all of Graydon, even all the way to Elihor.

Before she could answer, the doors opened at the back, Altessa and the rebel Ramelia slipping in. The rebel looked uncomfortable, but Altessa walked the length of the room in its center, following the carpet to the throne, its people parting to let her through as soon as they realized the heir to the throne had joined them.

Cassara fought against rising emotions. She had not wanted her daughter to come back. She'd ordered the rebel to take her far away—the same rebel who now leaned against the back wall, arms crossed, looking as annoyed as Cassara that Altessa walked toward the throne.

Altessa reached the edge of the carpet, executed a perfect curtsy, and walked up the stairs to stand by her mother's throne. A show of strength, and a united family, that the court would not miss. Pride in her daughter's wits and control tempered Cassara's annoyance. At least partly.

She squeezed her daughter's hand, let it go, and answered the question.

"That is uncertain at the moment," she said, to another ripple. She swallowed hard, softened her features. "He is in the greatest of care, and is a fighter, as we all know." She realized she gripped the throne and forced her hands to relax. She knew speaking of Dayshon would be difficult, but the people needed to understand exactly what ailed their kingdom.

"How is Siabala free?" A voice from the front. Nobleman Axlex. He'd courted Tally, but might not have known of Siabala. Regardless, he didn't respect her and didn't hesitate to tell anyone who would listen.

"The Wall of Loss was taken down," she said, still uncertain how that had happened. "And he prepares his attack against us, as does Tally."

Murmurs. Cassara could almost taste their fear.

"Why will he attack us?" Laswella asked. A strength in the wards, Cassara needed her support.

Which she would not gain unless she told them the truth. She stood. Slowly. Her daughter stayed back, letting her mother address the people. Altessa held herself with grace and strength, and Cassara wished she'd had half that poise when she'd been eighteen.

The questions stopped, silence blanketing the room, leaving space for the queen's voice.

"Twenty years ago, I left the battlefields of the West to take the battle to Siabala," she said. She spoke softly, but her voice traveled across the entire room, its acoustics legendary in Graydon. "I had powerful magic, and so went to stop him, protected by Avarielle Grayloft and Crimson Circle Elite, now Elder, Shirina." She invoked their names like a shield. And let them know that Shirina was now an Elder.

"We found Siabala and managed to kill his body, but we couldn't destroy his soul, which proved too powerful. And so we trapped it in the Wall of Loss." They knew most of this, though they'd never heard her speak of it directly. These stories were part of history books already, a strange thing when you yourself were still alive.

"But the magic of Graydon and Elihor was spent and corrupted. All we had was my magic, as a descendant of Graydon. And so I spent all of it to erect the Wall of Loss again." Her stomach rang a gong of guilt. "You should have been safe until I died, of old age, one assumes in these peaceful times." She was still young. She could have easily enjoyed another forty, maybe fifty years.

"But he somehow found a way, thanks to Elder Tally, to bring it down."

She hesitated here. To tell them the full truth, or leave them hope. She stood straighter.

"Twenty years ago, I left the battlefield without informing anyone, not even my new husband, because I feared knowing that our magic was gone would rob the troops of hope."

She looked across the room, to the veterans scattered across the room, those who had fought alongside her during the Days of Blood. "It was unfair of me to think that the brave soldiers of Rashim would so easily lose hope. For that, I apologize. But today, I trust in you. Although Siabala took down the Wall of Loss and my magic should have returned, it did not. And Avarielle Grayloft and Elder Shirina had little choice but to go fight on another front."

The throne room held its breath. Every person, every drapery, every strand of hair. There they had it. They were alone, without magic, and no allies. Their king was ill, possibly dying.

And their queen was powerless. Well, without magic, anyway.

"So we are it. We are all that remain. And Siabala knows every defense we built into this place." She looked to Builder Gramire. "He will use our tactics to his advantage. We must think of new ways to utilize them."

"We will prepare to defend," Builder Gramire said, eyes shining. "We watched Massir crumple once. Never again."

"Thank you," Cassara said. "There will be monsters, no doubt." She looked to the nobles. It was time to test them, and their willingness to support their countryfolk. "I am certain that we can count on the noble houses to support the defenses of Massir, with your security and protection."

Part question. Part command.

She met Lord Rushil's eyes. If she won him over, she had the others. He disliked her, this foreign queen, but he loved his city. And he loved getting the chance to be the hero.

"We will aid in whatever way we can." A bow, not full, but nearly.

"Thank you." She lowered her chin in acknowledgement. "All of you are here because you have a role of leadership in the city, and can help to rally and calm the people." She looked up. "We will work with the guards to send down orders, and to protect the citizens, but we need your help to make this happen. The guild houses were built in different quarters of the city, partly to support the economic structure of each neighborhood, but also to give each a point of contact and leadership, if needed.

"This was not unforeseen, and we are more ready than we were twenty years ago. Your guild houses are reinforced to take more attack, and the walls, well, the Builders will send you the plans." She nodded to Builder Gramire. "But remember that the enemy has them, too, and that they wish to kill everyone here."

"To claim revenge on you," Lord Rushil said. Of course he'd figured it out. Cassara did not bristle, nor looked annoyed. She simply nodded.

"To make me suffer," she said, "by having to watch my

people die before he destroys me. That's the plan he has for you, and I'm sorry. If I could stop him by giving myself up to him, I would. But it would not help."

"How are you so sure?" Rushil asked. Cassara kept her features smooth. She didn't like that man. Never had. Probably never would.

She met his eyes. "Because I already tried."

His eyes widened. A few chuckles in the back, and the energy picked up in the room. A subtle shift, but one that Cassara easily picked up on. He'd tried to show them she was weak, and she'd shown them all she was committed to their safety. She hoped his embarrassment wouldn't cost her.

"Siabala thinks he has the upper hand," she increased her voice, calling them all to attention. "He has studied me and my plans for twenty years to figure out my weaknesses and how to best destroy me," she left Shirina and Avarielle out of this, "but he did not take into account my greatest strength."

Lord Rushil bristled, ready to scoff. Cassara ignored him and swept the room with her eyes.

"You. Massir. Rashim. The bonds that unite us, the blood that runs in your veins. You are smart, quick, and prepared to protect your own, and others. Siabala may think he knows me, and he might, but he does not understand the strength of Massir. We will *make* him understand."

The room erupted into cheers, mostly from the back, the nobles more contained. But Cassara had driven her point across, and given them something to believe in and cling to.

"City leaders will work with each ward and the guards will coordinate defenses. I know it was a long day, but we must prepare for the attack now, and get people to safety." She nodded to her awaiting staff, who started handing out city plans, all carefully copied this afternoon by as many scribes as they could find.

"Each of your wards have strengths and weaknesses. A few are marked with a crossed out circle on the map—those will be evacuated to the noble houses immediately." She did not confirm with Lord Rushil. A small show of force, but an important reminder that she was his queen.

"Bright roads to us all," Cassara ended with the traditional saying. The people bowed and filtered out, their terror and need for action palpable, a current in the air like lightning about to strike.

It would either become a source of power, or decay into chaos.

The second the throne room emptied, Cassara turned to her daughter and hugged her fiercely. Altessa leaned into her mother, holding her back just as tightly.

"You were supposed to go somewhere safe," her mother whispered in her ear. "I wanted you to be safe, away from here."

"I couldn't leave my family, and my people, any more than you," Altessa said, breaking free and looking her mother in the eye. "I am your daughter, after all."

Pride and annoyance competed for attention on her mother's face. Ramelia stood on the stairs by the throne, uncertain what to do, and Cassara focused on her.

"You were supposed to keep her safe."

"She's too stubborn to listen to anything I have to say," Ramelia shrugged.

"I believe that," Cassara said, tone softening. "My

apologies for giving you the most impossible task in the kingdom: keeping my daughter in check."

Cassara turned to Altessa, and sighed. "This will not be easy," she said. "The upcoming hours, maybe days, will see you witness the best and worst this world has to offer. And the best and worst the people of Rashim have to offer, too."

Altessa shrugged. "I've already seen so much of it, Mom. But you're here, after I thought I'd lost you, and I don't want to be anywhere else."

"There is much I must tell you," Cassara said, eyes shifting toward Ramelia, asking the question: *do you trust her?*

"She came back for me, twice," Altessa said. "I trust her."

Cassara examined her daughter a few more moments, then nodded. Surprise at her mother's easy trusting in her judgment and pride at being taken into confidence made her stand taller.

"You are welcome to join us as a guest," Cassara told Ramelia. The rebel looked surprised and Altessa feared she would refuse, but instead she nodded stiffly.

"Come," Cassara said, walking back toward the section of the palace they called home. The guards, ones she recognized, escorted them from a respectful distance.

Altessa trailed her mother, Ramelia at her side. Cassara's speed made it clear she didn't want to speak about anything until they were safely within their home.

Once past their doors, the guards closed them, keeping vigil while Cassara guided everyone to the small kitchen.

"Would you like tea?" she asked Altessa and Ramelia. Altessa knew her mom. She was buying time, gathering her thoughts.

"Please," Altessa said, waving at Ramelia to take a seat.

"I don't need to be here for this," Ramelia said. "If this is private family time—"

"I'd like it if you stayed," Altessa said, not fully certain why. No, she knew. Because Ramelia saw her not as a daughter, like her mom, but as a person. As someone who did right, sometimes wrong, and who tried her best. And she wanted Ramelia to see her mom for who she was, too: Very human, and trying hard to do her best.

Besides, she felt she owed Ramelia—the rebel had tried to get her out of the city, but Altessa had once again headed back to the palace. This time, Ramelia had come with her.

"Then you stay," Cassara said, surprising Altessa again. Cassara caught the look, and smiled as she placed three teacups and a tea pot on the small table.

"I had allies, too, and friends I trusted. You'll need them in the days to come, and throughout your reign. If Ramelia is that for you, then she stays."

Ramelia looked from mother to daughter, looking bewildered. "I probably shouldn't remind you of this, but I was in your dungeons not that long ago."

Cassara poured some tea. "And you could have easily killed me with your arrow, but didn't."

Altessa blinked in surprise at Ramelia. "You were the one shooting arrows at my mother?"

"I asked her to, Altessa." Cassara said.

"You didn't know we were friends!" Altessa couldn't wrap her thoughts around her mother's thinking. "You just knew her from the dungeons!"

"I knew she'd tried to help when Tally attacked, Altessa. And I needed someone I knew loved Rashim enough to risk death." She looked at Ramelia. "I'm sorry for putting you in that position, but I thank you for saving my daughter."

Ramelia stammered a "you're welcome" and drank some tea, burning her lips on the hot brew.

"Can I see Dad?" Altessa asked, partly to draw attention away from Ramelia. She held her breath, fearing the answer.

Her mother looked down at her cup, long fingers wrapping around it.

"Siabala did something to him… he's not himself."

Altessa's heart sank, looking at her mother's profile, at the steam rising from her cup, at the slump of her shoulders. Then she saw her shift back into the queen— back straightening, eyes blazing as she turned to look at her daughter.

"But Shirina has reconnected with magic, and is an Elder, and she will try her best to save him."

"Shirina is back?" Altessa allowed herself to hope. "Does she know how to help him?"

"She's still growing used to her new powers and

knowledge as an Elder, and there are no guarantees she'll manage to. Especially given the lack of time."

"Is she with Dad now?" Altessa's breath caught in her throat, fanned too powerfully by hope and despair.

"She had to go," Cassara said gently. Then turned to Ramelia. "I would ask that you not share the next piece of information, if you would."

"The people deserve to know," the practiced words tumbled from Ramelia's lips.

Altessa held her breath as Cassara and Ramelia faced off.

"I'll let you decide once you know, then," Cassara said, surprising Altessa once again. The queen focused back on her mug, as though strengthening herself.

"Siabala is in Avarielle," she whispered, words slapping Altessa's grieving heart.

"Avarielle… Avarielle is dead."

Cassara's face softened as she focused on her daughter. "She's not, because she's still of use to him. Just like I am, Altessa. He's trapped in her for now, but he'll find a way to escape. Shirina will try to contain them, I'm sure of it, but chances are that it's Avarielle who'll walk the armies into Massir. Or she'll walk over the bodies of our people to reach me."

The image was so powerful in Altessa's mind that she reeled back, physically. The warrior with the quick grin and kind words, showing her how to defend herself, would come for her mother's blood. For her best friend's blood—the friend she'd vowed to protect.

"Avarielle would never—"

"No. She wouldn't. But Siabala would, and he's more powerful than her. She's trying to stop him, Altessa, but she knows she won't be able to. She told me so when she left." Her mother's voice cracked. "I need to give Massir the best chance of survival, which is why we need help. But I also need you gone, Altessa. Because she might use you to get to me. She knows where your brother and sister are, but they're out of the way. But you… you're right here. Avarielle knows you're in the city. And she knows that I would do anything to save you."

"You're sending Dad and me away, then?"

Altessa had never seen pain flicker across her mother's face like that. Intense, cruel, grinding, and gone as quickly as it had come.

"Your father would slow you down. He's not himself."

Then it struck Altessa. Her mother would do anything to save her. But her father…

"You'll find a way to save him, won't you?" Her voice was so soft, so childish, yet Altessa couldn't help it. Ramelia looked down at her cup, probably wishing she were anywhere but here, witnessing the princess crumple.

"I promise I'll try, Altessa, and I'm sorry for all the hard truths. But here's another: your father would never want me to sacrifice our people for him. And so I won't, even if it shreds my heart to pieces."

Our people. They were her people, too.

"I won't go," Altessa said. "I can't. No more than you would."

Ramelia looked up slowly, speaking before the queen.

"Altessa, your mother doesn't want to see you die," she said softly. "She just wants you safe."

Cassara looked at Altessa, her face fractured by grief, and fear, and hope.

"I know," Altessa responded gently. "And I don't want to die. But you need me here, Mom. You need me to help rally people. I can hide when Siabala comes."

"Avarielle knew all of our plans," Cassara's voice stiffened. "And so does Siabala. There is nowhere to hide that he won't know."

"Ramelia will know," Altessa countered, despair speeding up her thoughts. "She's a rebel. She knows things about our city even we don't know, and neither does Avarielle."

"It's true," Ramelia immediately backed her up, as Altessa had known she would. "I understand why you want her gone, but she'll be useful here, and I promise I'll keep her safe."

Cassara looked from one young woman to the next. A thousand objections flickered across her face, then she just sighed and shook her head. "I'm sure my parents being gone by the time I got embroiled in war made things much easier for everyone." She rallied. "Alright, we don't know how long it'll be before Siabala comes, but Shirina will do her best to detain him."

Him. Avarielle. Tears threatened to engulf Altessa, thinking of the woman who'd made her laugh, taught her how to fight, and just generally filled this place with light whenever she graced this home.

"Where's Rojon?" Altessa asked. Her son would be heartbroken all over again. Worse, even. Grieving his mother's death seemed easier than grieving her enslavement.

"Safe," Cassara said. "Somewhere in Kosel, I think. I'm not sure. Shirina sent him away when Avarielle, when..." Cassara let her voice drift, unable to say the words.

"He saw?" Altessa asked in a strangled voice.

Cassara didn't answer.

"I can't imagine what went through his mind Mom, I can't..."

"If you stay here, you'll see things that will scar you, Altessa. Siabala will burn Massir to bring me out. He wants me to watch my world burn." Cassara's voice grew steady as she looked at her daughter. "He'll then start hunting those I love, including you. I will stay here, and help lead the attack to protect the city. I will keep your father safe, and try to heal him. And, Altessa," her voice grew intense, pleading Altessa to listen carefully, "I promise I will not let myself be easily captured and sacrificed. Not at the blade of my friend. I will do everything in my power to stop that from happening. But, if he doesn't get me, if I manage to rob him of his revenge, you'll be the one he'll come after next. And your brother and sister. I will not allow that to happen."

"You'll let him get you?" Altessa barely managed to voice the words.

"To save you, yes. Every time. And, if you come to save me, you'll witness my death, or I'll witness yours."

Altessa tried to swallow, her throat dry.

"So I'm willing to respect you wanting to stay and stand with your people," Cassara said. "But you have to respect my choice to face Siabala alone. Without you. To hide when he gets too close. I've faced him once before and will do so again. But I won't be able to fight if I'm crushed with the grief of losing you. I know I won't be able to, Altessa."

A deep, shuddering breath, and Cassara continued. "And he knows it, so he may hunt you." She turned to Ramelia. "You'll have to be faster and smarter than him. Don't assume you're safe. Find Shirina, if she lives. And, if you find Rojon, keep him safe. He wants him, too, to crush Avarielle. To bind her to him forever. Keep him safe, too, if you can."

"Avarielle was supposed to be dead," Altessa mumbled. "I'm just…"

"I know," Cassara reached across the table and took her hand in hers, running her fingers over hers, as though memorizing every bit of them. "You will learn quickly how to keep moving despite the pain, because you'll have to. If you give up, if either one of us gives up, so will the people. So, no matter what, if you stay in Massir, you fight."

Altessa met her mother's eyes, felt the strength running from her hand, and nodded.

"I promise I'll fight. And, when the time comes, I promise I'll run."

"And then you'll have to survive in a world conquered by Siabala," Cassara's voice cracked. "I never wanted that for you."

Altessa squeezed her mother's hand. "Remember, we don't give up."

Cassara smiled and squeezed back. "If you're too stubborn to listen to me," Cassara regained her motherly composure, "then join me for the battle plans. Ramelia, you're also invited. You'll bring a much-needed different perspective. Now, if you'll excuse me," her mother stood, "I must take my hair down or I'm going to rip it out."

Altessa couldn't help but laugh. It felt good to know that, even heading into the end of times, her mother was still very much herself.

Cassara had just enough time to change into something more casual and take stock of her home's defenses, remaining staff, and guards, and to make arrangements for the families of those who had not made it, while grieving for them, before standing in her home's dining room, maps of the city littering the table.

The nobles seemed thrown off by the royal family's humble abode. The citizens seemed at home. Cassara wondered if there could have been a better middle ground so that everyone could be comfortable, but she doubted it. Some gaps were too wide for any dining room to unite. Plates of cheese, both fine and common, were ignored as they all focused on the city. At this rate, Siabala would attack before they'd reached consensus on anything.

"We cannot sacrifice the Tranak Quarters," Builder Gramire said, his strong build dwarfing the noble. "It's barely repaired, and those people have suffered enough."

"But it's the logical entry point," Lord Rushil countered, silver hair as perfectly coiffed as the folds of his coat were crisp. "Because it's at its weakest. The enemy will know to attack there first. So, we let them in there. Funnel them through."

"Funneling isn't a bad idea," Cassara mused. The two stopped bickering, and all faces turned toward her. She'd been mostly listening, intent on letting them come up with different ideas. But a referee was needed, and she was the only one they would all listen to.

"We did it in Rockor," Cassara said, her voice soft as she pondered possibilities. "We funneled the Eloms through town, with archers on both sides to whittle down their numbers. Then, at the end of the funnel, Avarielle struck the remaining ones with Graysword, and I used my magic on the rest." She'd saved them with her magic. It had taken everything she had to keep the spell going for a long time, almost losing herself completely in it.

They all looked at her with a variety of emotions. Some looked with wonder at the fact that their queen had fought such monsters so often. Others, veterans of the Days of Blood, looked with pride or pain. Then, of course, some looked annoyed.

"They would expect a move like that, unless..." she stopped, pondering what to say next.

"Unless, what?" Lord Rushil said, in a huff. Ideas began to congeal in her mind. A sleight of hand might be enough to win them some time, and by the time the plan became clear, it would be too late to change course.

"The enemy we faced could jump over our walls," Cassara said, giving Builder Gramire an apologetic look. "But they will hold back other enemies. They would not expect me to sacrifice the lower city," Cassara said softly. "They would expect me to protect it at the cost of winning the day."

Avarielle and she had argued against it often. The warrior had been right, of course. The edges of the city were difficult to defend, the walls longer and would suffer first contact. Avarielle had told her to think differently, and she would never expect her to sacrifice them.

"Why would you do that?" Lord Rushil said. "It's not a defensible position."

"Because they were sacrificed once," Cassara bit his words, silencing him, "and will not be again."

"We've put extra places for people to seek protection, and the walls are twice the thickness there, with three back-to-back. But they're not complete," Builder Gramire sounded sorry again.

"We all thought we would have more time," Cassara said softly.

"What of the army?" Lord Rushil asked. "I assume you sent for them?"

"I have," Cassara said. "But they are a few days hard ride away. We cannot assume they will make it in time to save us." She paused, held his eyes. "Siabala is the one who sent them away, so it's safe to assume they won't make it back in time, in fact. He would have done all these calculations already."

Cassara turned to a silent party in the room, one that she'd considered not inviting at all.

"Elder Quilsam, will you share wisdom with us? Perhaps Elihor has different protective tactics than us?"

"I'm afraid not, Your Majesty," the Elder approached, looking down at the map. "We do not build our cities likes yours. Yours are built looking to the sky," he pointed the height of the palace, overlooking the city. "Ours are built to stay grounded. To hug the earth, not escape it."

"The earth," Cassara looked to Altessa, who looked out of her depth. She'd learn quickly enough. Cassara had, and her daughter was definitely no less than she was. "Does the old city spread below all of Massir?"

"I think so?" Altessa turned to Ramelia. Where Altessa looked out of her depth, the rebel looked like she wanted to run out of there.

"They do, as far as I can tell," Ramelia said, annoyed at being called upon.

"Can you estimate where the earth separating the ancient city from Massir is thinnest? Those would be probable access points to Massir."

Ramelia looked down at the map. She pointed at the one access Cassara already knew of, where Shirina had vanished. And another under the east wing of the palace.

"That's how I came back to the palace," Altessa said.

"The old escape tunnels?"

"No, older than that," Ramelia said. "Something you weren't aware of."

Cassara ignored the pride in the rebel's voice and

focused on the map. Slowly the plan formed in her mind. It had twists. Turns. Depended on everyone working together. And on their timing being impeccable.

Trust your instincts, Avarielle had told her. Instincts forged in experience and molded by magic.

She could feel in her gut just how much this plan was right, and hoped beyond hope that it would keep Avarielle off footing, and that she'd manage to surprise the warrior. Her city's survival depended on fooling the one woman who knew her better than she knew herself.

She looked at each person in turn. They sensed the shift in their queen and leaned in, even Lord Rushil, to hear what she would say.

And none of them left, even as a few gasped as she laid out the plan.

Her people would be safe.

They would hate her. But they would survive.

The day had been long and, despite her fatigue, sleep eluded Altessa. She didn't want to be in her room. Not right now. Sweet moments talking with her mother or Rojon were blanketed with being imprisoned here, trapped against her will and unable to get out.

She slipped on a robe and slippers and stepped outside of her room. A few guards wandered the palace, but none currently here. Altessa walked quickly down two rooms and knocked on the door of a guest room. The one in the home, not in the royal palace proper, symbolism that had not been lost on Altessa.

The door opened a crack, Ramelia's eyes widening at the sight of Altessa. In her robe.

What in Eli's world was she doing here? What had she been thinking?

"Hi, um, I just... I wanted to see if you needed anything?" Altessa managed to sputter out.

The corridor was narrow, created with servants in mind, and the rooms fairly small. Ramelia stepped aside to let Altessa in before she was spotted. She shut the door and spoke as softly as Altessa.

"The crown princess of Rashim is worried whether or not I have enough towels?"

Altessa flushed. Ramelia wore only a loose nightshirt, the candle lit by her bedside making it slightly see-through, and her legs were exposed... She flushed deeper and focused on Ramelia's amused eyes.

"No, I just..."

"I was lonely, too," Ramelia said, placing a hand on Altessa's hand and sparing her more stuttering.

"I was just a prisoner in my room," Altessa said, relieved. "It just feels odd being in there, that's all."

"Well," Ramelia shrugged, "I have a smaller bed here, but you're welcome to take part of it."

"Oh," Altessa said. She hadn't really considered... or had she?

"For sleeping," Ramelia said, a grin tugging at her lips, though she'd obviously read Altessa's mind. "You need your sleep, and so do I."

"That's what I... anyway, it doesn't matter. Thank you." Altessa felt exhausted. Just the thought of not being alone, and not being locked in her room... it robbed her of any awkwardness or fatigue. She slipped off her robe and crawled into the back of the bed, against the wall.

Ramelia climbed in after her, blowing out the candle and settling in.

∼

The princess was quiet for a few minutes, and Ramelia wondered if she'd already fallen asleep. Altessa hadn't slept much of late, and that took a toll—one that Ramelia was all too familiar with.

Altessa shifted, her leg touching Ramelia's.

"Sorry," the princess mumbled. *I really don't mind,* Ramelia almost said, but chose another approach, in case she hadn't read Altessa correctly.

"Your mother could have offered me a bigger room," Ramelia said. "Then you'd have more space."

"She offered you a room in our home," Altessa said, voice thick with sleep. She wanted her to just drift off and get much needed sleep. But she also wanted to whisper to her all night long and get to know everything about her. "That's telling you she trusts you, Ramelia. Not many get to stay in this room."

Ramelia stayed on her back, looking up at the ceiling, trying to be quiet as Altessa's breath grew longer. The rebel was damaged goods, and she knew it. She wanted to tell Altessa to leave her, to go away, to find someone more sane and more stable who could comfort her. Instead, she focused on being quiet. Her heart hurt, at the trust of the queen. At Altessa's innocence. At her own indecision, and fears, and loyalties splintered long ago.

"Would you have done it?" Altessa asked, a whisper in the dark, apparently unaware of the turmoil ignited in Ramelia's breast.

"Done what?" Ramelia asked, keeping her voice too low for her to detect the pain in it.

"Killed my mother?"

It struck Ramelia as rather ironic that the one time she'd agreed to follow her queen's orders seemed to be the one time it would cost her more than she was willing to pay. A thought that surprised her as much as it made her feel ill.

"I think so," Ramelia said honestly. "But I wouldn't have known until I let loose the arrow aimed at her heart."

Altessa stayed silent beside her. Then, to Ramelia's surprise, she turned, placed her head in the crook of Ramelia's arm, and draped her arm around her, holding her. They stayed silent until Altessa drifted to sleep.

Ramelia stayed awake longer, trying to control her breathing as tears ran down the side of her face, onto the perfect hair of the princess.

3 2

a boulder had surely landed on Shirina's head. Her skull throbbed, her mouth was dry, and lead had been poured into her entire body. Or she was made of stone. As simple as that.

"I'm healing you gently," she heard Olaram's voice. "Please don't use your magic, and trust me."

"I trust you," Shirina said. Or tried to, her words garbled. A practiced grandmother, Olaram made soothing noises that reassured her she'd been heard. Shirina basked in the glow of the healing magic, strengthened by its provenance from the ground, and by the adept's steady hand on her forehead and abdomen.

Her mind wandered, remembering the first time she'd met the adept. About to become a grandmother, she'd wanted something for herself.

"It's time for me to follow my own interests," she'd simply said. She'd always wanted to be a healer and had spent one year in Laror helping in sick camps. Shirina and her adepts had come when summoned to help the out-of-control disease rampant in the capital, fed by infected well water. They'd healed the sick, had found the sewage spilling into their water, and fixed that, too. They'd used some of the same magic to help Graydon's new water supply issues, especially in Massir.

"I want to not just heal symptoms," Olaram had told her. "I want to heal the root cause."

"If you're willing to learn, I'm willing to teach you," Shirina had simply said. When they'd left, she had followed them back to the Lisal Gardens, and had become a strong adept over the past five years.

Her grandchildren had even visited her a few times, and she'd gone to see them. It was rare for families to visit the Circle, though Shirina didn't discourage it. Most people came to the Circle looking for something different, and their families often took that the wrong way.

She slit her eyes open, wanting to see the grandmotherly features of the Orange Circle. The face came into view, but her cloak caught her attention, a blur of orange. *Orange hair...*

Avarielle. Siabala had been breaking free.

Shirina croaked out the name and struggled to rise, Olaram holding her down. The older woman certainly wasn't lacking in strength.

"I'm here, Shirina," Avarielle said, from somewhere near her head.

Shirina forced her eyes open.

"Please rest," Olaram said.

"I'm okay," Avarielle whispered. Shirina blinked, turned her neck to see her, and gently summoned the Sight, a sweat breaking across her brow at the simple spell.

"Stop using your magic," Olaram said, sounding exasperated. "You have worse impulse control than my five-year-old grandson."

Shirina frowned but pushed through, and saw the red rippling across Avarielle. Graysword was in her hand, the magic fighting it back. It wasn't perfect, but it held.

She dropped the Sight, nausea slamming into her as the room spun. A cold compress found her forehead immediately, relieving some of the symptoms.

"Sleep," Olaram whispered, and Shirina had too little strength left to fight back.

She drifted, in the land filled with Olaram's magic, fed from the ground. The strands tugged at her, pulling her down. Not threateningly, but invitingly.

She stepped into the ancient city below the West. Not as it was, but as it had been. She'd seen it come to life, once, its yellow and multicolored magic dancing. Where Avarielle had killed both of Siabala's brothers, despite her protests.

Could they have helped prevent what was happening now, had she been able to prevent their deaths?

Individuals with large hats and strange clothing walked by. They looked like her, but didn't. Larger eyes, wider faces, shorter limbs, longer torsos. They danced more than walked, and joy spread in the atmosphere.

Shirina smiled, looked up. Her mentor, Tanja sat at what looked like a café, laughing with three inhabitants of the city. Tanja saw her and waved her over.

"Shirina," she said, laughing in a way she'd never done while she lived, as far as Shirina knew. "Come join us." Her three hat-wearing companions—perhaps that was their hair?—nodded enthusiastically.

"Thank you," Shirina said. But there was no chair for her. There was no chair anywhere.

Tanja didn't seem to notice as she continued talking. The sun shone, refracted by stained glass windows portraying plants and animals, and into the multiple fountains of the city which sprinkled water up and created a multitude of rainbows.

She turned back to Tanja and they were all gone, including the table. Shirina whipped around. Tanja and the three sat beside the fountain, where rainbows danced wildly. The sight of them looked odd on the Elder's white robe and black cloak.

Like mine.

She walked toward them.

"They were just telling me," Tanja continued, as though nothing had changed, "how we'd killed their people."

Shirina looked from her mentor's smiling face to the other three. But they were gone. The sunlight stopped hitting the ground, the rainbows and fractured light vanished. The ground turned to frost, and blood ran in the water. Then froze.

"Tanja, what—"

"Shirina," a voice called to her, but it wasn't her mentor's. It was Shala's, dragging her back to the present, to the now, and to her aching body. Less aching, now.

The threads of her dream began to fade, and she took a moment to recount them to herself, but could feel them vanishing, leaving only horror behind.

"You were having a dream," Shala said. "Calling for Tanja in your sleep."

Shirina pushed herself up. Shala helped her sit up and handed her a cup of water, her throat feeling like it had been scraped by sand. Which it probably had, considering where they were.

The water splashed down her throat like a soothing salve, and she closed her eyes, seeing rainbows and ice blood. Her eyes flew open.

"I don't think it was a dream," Shirina said. "Maybe a vision. Or something. I'm not sure, and it's fading quickly."

"What do you remember?" Shala asked, ready to help her retain whatever remained of it.

"Not much," Shirina admitted. "But there were rainbows. Something with the sun. And blood in the water." She paused. "In the ice."

"That sounds… ominous."

"Then again," Shirina said, "it might have just been a dream."

"I doubt that," Shala said.

Shirina looked around, seeing they were alone.

"Avarielle has gone to see what Trevon and the others found while scouting the tower," Shala said. It was still dark, so she couldn't have been out that long. Sensing the question, Shala answered it. "You were only knocked out for a couple of hours."

"Good," Shirina said. She felt like she'd slept for a full night, more than likely thanks to Olaram's magic. "We should go hear what they have to say." Shirina went to stand up, then thought better of it. "Actually, perhaps you and I should talk first, while we're alone."

Shala nodded and sat on the bed beside Shirina, looking eager to chat with her mentor. As Shirina had once been with Tanja, though she'd never felt as close and welcome as she hoped she made Shala feel.

"I know Siabala is in Avarielle," Shala said. "I saw his magic in her left arm, though she seems to have it in check. For now."

Shirina nodded. "Siabala is using her to gain a body. We managed, Queen Cassara and I, to trap him in her."

I'm sorry. She'd said she was sorry for trapping Siabala in a vision of his home. Her dream teased the edges of her memory. Siabala's old home, which had been beautiful. Had it not?

"But he's not staying put."

"No," Shirina said. "He seems rather determined to be uncooperative."

"Strange," Shala said with a grin. Then her mood sobered. "I know Avarielle is a good friend."

"She's a pain, much like Siabala," Shirina deadpanned. "And also rather uncooperative."

"And one of your oldest friends," Shala repeated, to bring home her point. "I know you don't want to hurt her."

But. The unspoken words hung in the air between them. Shirina was proud of Shala, more so than ever. She was willing to do the extra work everyone avoided. To make the hard decisions, no matter the cost. And to pay the price. To save Graydon. And Elihor. And all they held dear.

We destroyed their world. The words drifted in and out of her mind, difficult to grasp.

"I don't mind hurting her," Shirina said. "The problem is, that won't stop Siabala. Right now, he's contained in her. If he escapes, we won't know where he is, and Rojon is still out there. That's his next target."

Shala nodded slowly. Very slowly, a realization dawned on her.

"You're not staying, are you?"

"I'm not," Shirina said. "Are the other adepts learning to connect with their magic again?"

"They are, some more easily than others," Shala said. "But they're using your words as guidance, and it is helping. How did you know?"

"Being Elder comes with strange flashes of insight, Shala." Shirina herself hadn't known that, because Elders had never spoken of what it meant to *be* an Elder. Adepts had to accept that Elder magic was as absolute as their word. But that was not the Circle Shirina had built.

"If I focus on something enough, I at times find the right information. Like an entire library lives in my head, but I'm unfamiliar with its classification system. But this… this was fairly easy to pull up. Maybe because it was of such importance that past Elders had thought of it, too."

"Or maybe because it meant so much to you." Grief flickered across Shala's face.

"Maybe," Shirina softly agreed. Shala gathered her in a hug. Shirina leaned into it, and returned it lightly, grateful for the kindness of her adepts.

Then Shala pulled away, clearing her throat.

"So, what would you have us do?"

"Siabala's empire erupts around us, and I'm afraid nowhere is safe. Not anymore. Help the adepts here find their magic. If you can, head back to Massir. Help Cassara survive whatever comes next. Bring Westland Warriors, if they're willing."

"They would be if Avarielle asked."

"Which is precisely why she won't."

Shala studied her.

"Because Siabala controls her?" she spoke the words so softly that Shirina barely heard.

"No, because she feels she owes them, and they owe her nothing." Because she'd left them, when Eloms attacked. Because she'd killed some to unlock Graysword's magic. Because she didn't think she belonged anymore, even though the wild sands of the West still ran in her veins. "But the West's memory is long, and the Days of Blood not that long ago. Cassara once saved them in the name of Avarielle. Now, her city needs help. Hopefully they will agree to honor that, though if they choose not to, it's understandable. Their lands are under attack, too."

"I'll speak with Trevon," Shala said. "Or will you?" she asked, hopeful.

"You can handle this," Shirina said. She had to get Avarielle out of here as soon as possible, and it would be easier to ask the West to leave once their unofficial leader was gone. Shala would draw the same conclusions, Shirina had no doubt, and so did not bother telling her. She stood up, feeling the strength of her body, of the magic beneath her feet. The blue lights flickered to life around her, gently circling her feet as though pleased to see her.

"Didn't my spell end when I passed out?" Shirina asked.

"It did not," Shala said. "Which raises many interesting questions."

"And worrisome ones, too." A shield spell might stay active. But so might an attack spell.

"Will you be able to contact the other adepts and tell them how to unlock the magic?"

"I'll send a ripple through the ground to all adepts,

from Ravenhold and Larkhold, as soon as I've dealt with this, to make sure we're not overheard."

Shala nodded, grim determination on her face. The blue lights drifted up near Shirina's face.

"They remind me of Ravenhold's lights," Shala breathed out. Shirina agreed, though she couldn't quite parse the information yet. Was this a reflection of the magic dwelling within Ravenhold?

She used to speak to those lights. Encourage them to dance away from her, or stay near. It had been just a habit of loneliness. Though she'd loved them, the walls of Ravenhold could prove crushing. And she could have sworn a few times that the lights understood her, especially as the Keep had collapsed around her.

"We still have much to learn about this new magic. Once the lines of communication are reopened, let's make sure to share what we know, and to tell them to be careful." She held out her hand, palm up, and a blue light jumped into it. She looked at it, could swear it looked back at her. Using the Sight, she saw it was connected to her. Tethered, even, as were all the others, who jumped into her palm to create a single blue ball of light, slightly smaller than her fist.

Not sure what to do with it, she placed it on the end of her staff, where it happily stayed.

"I think we should treat this magic with respect, Shala, like an ally instead of a tool. Olaram seems to have connected easily with it. Speak with her and see what wisdom she has garnered. As soon as I can, I will contact you. I promise."

"I know," Shala said.

"Siabala's empire is rising, Shala, and even without its emperor, enough momentum might have been gained to sow destruction."

She looked at her second. Her friend. Her trusted adept.

"Be safe, Shala."

"Until next time, Shirina, may your thoughts be heavy." The old Circle saying.

May your steps be steady.

"May your heart be steady," Shirina replied instead.

The words washed over Shala and her eyes shone. Shirina squeezed her arm and they stepped outside into the night air, toward the gathered Westland warriors.

Shirina tested her strength. She had to use her magic, and hoped she wouldn't hit the wall again.

Her heart skipped a beat, and the blue light intensified, as though soothing her.

She looked at it, visions of rainbows and blood water dancing in her mind, and focused on the task at hand: ensuring that Siabala didn't escape Avarielle, no matter how much Shirina's heart might break.

Avarielle stood with her hand on the pommel of Graysword, trying to get her left arm comfortable. An impossible feat as it was locked in place by magic. Her muscles grew tense and painful, throbbing from lack of movement. She'd tried massaging it, but to no avail, and the Orange Circle healer looked like she was about to throw healing magic into her if she looked more uncomfortable.

Shirina's timing couldn't have been better. Her waking up had distracted the adept. The Orange Circle had healed her, and then had gone to lie down, more fatigued than exhausted, according to her.

Avarielle had left shortly after Shala had arrived to inform her that the scouting party had returned. And said nothing of Siabala.

There was no doubt in Avarielle's mind that Shala knew. Instead of annoying her, as she hated her secrets to be known, it made her feel better. Twenty years ago, Shirina had vowed she would do everything within her power and abilities to regrow the Circle in a way that would help stop Siabala.

Seeing Shala's quick thinking, seeing how they'd all stood up in battle, how they'd found ways to connect with the magic with only a few directions from Shirina… Avarielle had no doubt that Shirina had succeeded.

Shirina had just been waking up when she'd left, to give them time alone. They would need it to discuss Circle things, she was certain. And to give Shirina the space to talk about the warrior without her being there, overhearing.

"It's a tower at least as tall as Beck's ego," a Westland warrior said, referring to the leader of the West. They all laughed. Avarielle shook her head, grinning. She'd stepped back, letting Beck take position as leader. She was better liked than he was, but Beck was here, and his only calling was to take care of the West, which he did to the best of his abilities, always.

That was something Avarielle simply couldn't do, her attention too split to be of use in the West.

"It looks empty enough, now. Not sure those things came from there, anyway," Trevon said. "We couldn't find a way in, and there were other holes near the tower, where they might have crawled out."

"Did more of the West fall?" Avarielle asked. Trevon met her eyes.

"I don't know. We'll know in the morning, and we can

send scouts out running. Right now, in the darkness, with those things out there… it doesn't seem wise."

"Let's rest up for the night, and keep watch," Avarielle said, and the others nodded. "And tomorrow, well, let's see what the morning brings."

They all agreed and headed off to the gathered Westlanders and adepts, to divvy watches and duties, and plan for what they would do in the morning.

"Let's see what the morning brings?" Trevon said. Shirina and Shala walked toward them, Shirina's cloak darker than the dark night. The adepts waited at a respectable distance.

"I trust you," Avarielle told Trevon, meeting his eyes. "No matter what you choose, or decide to do, I trust your judgment."

He examined her, understood her words, and sighed.

"And I yours, Avarielle Grayloft. Just make sure I won't have to bury another Grayloft in my lifetime. This old heart can only take so much."

"That old heart," she said softly, placing a hand on his chest, "is the strongest I've ever known. It is a beating heart of the West, and never forget it, Trevon."

"Never forget yours, Avarielle Grayloft."

It struck her then how old Trevon actually was. In his sixties, but to her, he would always be Trevon, trapped as his younger self, raising her, laughing with her, teaching her the ways of the sword.

She hoped she would see him again. If not, she hoped

he would have warm memories to keep him going. And that Rojon and he would reunite.

"May our paths meet again, old friend," Avarielle said.

Trevon tried to repeat it but choked on the words. Before she lost all willpower, she turned away from him and walked toward the awaiting adepts.

"Time to go?" Avarielle said, examining Shirina's determined features, the deathly pallor gone. "Are you well enough to do this?"

"I am," Shirina said. The blue glow stayed on her staff, like a whisp of legend. So many things she never thought she'd see come to pass.

"Be well, Shala," Shirina said. The Crimson Circle Elite took a step back and nodded, crossing her arms as though to ward off a chill.

"Take care of Trevon," Avarielle told her. The adept seemed surprised at the request, the two never having spoken much. Avarielle gave her a grin. "The old goat's practically adopted you already. I think that makes us sisters."

Shala laughed, a bright, earthy sound, and Avarielle joined her. They clasped hands, and she nodded. She would do everything she could, and that was all Avarielle could ask.

The warrior stepped beside Shirina and looked around her. Not at the marred landscape of her youth or the scar on the ground that revealed a broken city, nor at the tower that loomed over them. Not to the Bloody

Mountains, a dark shadow in the background of her entire life. Instead, she looked at the people.

To the Westlanders, trading food and jokes around campfires, enlivened by the fight, wary for the next one, ready for battle. At the adepts who mingled among them, while others worked at connecting with their magic.

She'd grown up when the Circle was hated, having fabricated the Westland Wars that had cost the West so much, including Avarielle's family. Now, the two worked together to keep the West, and all of Graydon, safe.

She paused over Trevon, the warrior standing tall and proud, looking at her as though he memorized everything about her, or of this moment.

Shala stood beside him, a silent, supporting presence.

Shirina waited patiently. This was her gift to Avarielle. She wasn't sure what the sorceress planned, but she knew they weren't going to find a cure for Dayshon. Not with Siabala already escaping.

She suspected Shirina had always known the wards wouldn't hold for long, which was why she'd brought Avarielle here. For knowledge, yes, but mostly to give Avarielle a chance to say goodbye. Because during their next stop, Shirina would do everything she could to keep Siabala trapped. Even if that meant trapping Avarielle, too.

The wind blew across the sands, the fires flickered. Once, that would have made her think of battle and death only. Now, it smelled of life, and hope, and peace, and shored up her heart as she removed her hand from Graysword for the journey ahead.

"I'm ready," she whispered.

Shirina unfurled her spell, the blue whisp glowing more brightly. Avarielle closed her eyes so she wouldn't see the ground beneath them.

To stay in the West, with her people, for just a moment longer.

3 4

ltessa slipped into the kitchen as dawn warmed the sky. She hadn't meant to stay all night in Ramelia's room, but she'd fallen into a deep, dreamless sleep, waking up refreshed for the first time since the attack on the castle.

She knew her mother would be awake, as well, and desperately wanted some time with her. Planning an attack took a lot of time and meetings, and without her father to help, her mother had been busy nonstop. And Altessa doubted that would soon end.

But, when growing up, even during busy times, her parents had instituted a ritual that they maintained to this day, and Altessa assumed still would. At dawn, the family gathered in the kitchen. Just them, and the cook's delivery of food, unless her mother decided she would cook.

It was usually better if the cooks did it, but Altessa always loved when her mom cooked.

She entered the kitchen, found it empty, and almost deflated until the door at the other end opened and her mother walked in, wearing practical clothing for the busy day ahead, carrying a bowl of some kind of mix. She smiled at seeing Altessa.

"Good morning," Altessa said, taking the bowl from her. Sometimes, not often, Altessa realized that she was taller than her mother. She'd been for years, but Cassara held herself so regally that she seemed taller for it. Now, as Cassara handed her the mix, Altessa noticed that her mother looked tired. A bit crushed by everything.

"How's Dad?"

"Same," Cassara said, pulling out a pan to make pancakes from the cook's mix. The queen added some blueberries and soft cheese rind to the mix while Altessa busied herself preparing the tea.

It was strange, just the two of them. A few weeks ago, her brother and sister would have been here, as well, taking a lot of space. Alex would tell them random history facts he'd picked up, and Traina would make them all laugh with whatever joke she'd dreamed up. Their father would laugh, and maybe tell a story or two about growing up.

They'd talk about how their days would go, and what they hoped to accomplish. Cassara would smile and listen, and interject when Dayshon told stories of their romance, making them all laugh. Sometimes, she'd tell stories of Edoline and her family, who were all dead save for her brother.

She loved those stories so much, getting to know the woman her mother used to be. Her father would interject in those stories, too, and often her mother would end up on his lap, the two laughing.

When Avarielle was here, they peppered her with questions about her adventures and her people. About Elihor and Rojon. The Westland warrior was more than happy to oblige, her presence filling the small kitchen with enthusiastic stories. Sometimes, she told stories that included their mother, but she always seemed to cut those short, after several looks from the queen that made the warrior grin.

When Shirina was there, the sorceress did not always join them, busy with Circle business. But at least once during her visits her mother would convince her to come, and the sorceress would share stories of the history of Graydon, or of magic. A few times she ended with a dry joke, always taking them by surprise.

She whipped out her jokes the times her mother was particularly quiet, often when fall turned to winter. Shirina would come to the end of an interesting but serious tale. She'd pause. Then with her usual crisp tones, would say a non sequitur or something completely unexpected like, "and that's why all cats are gray in Elihor."

Cassara would look at her puzzled for half a second, then laugh. A rare sound, during those days, and a welcome one. It had taken Altessa years to figure out that Shirina did that to reach Cassara. Once she'd figured it out, Altessa's respect for the sorceress grew tenfold.

But now, it was just the two of them. Neither Altessa nor Cassara were the talkers in the family, and so they worked in companionable silence. Once the pancakes were cooked and mostly unburned, the two sat down. Altessa poured some tea, preparing both cups with honey and milk.

Altessa's stomach growled and she dug in, noticing that her mother barely touched her plate.

"You need to eat, Mom," Altessa said between bites. "Keep your strength up."

Cassara's perfectly shaped eyebrow rose slowly. "I'm sorry, did you say something amidst all that chewing?"

Altessa flushed, then laughed as Cassara did.

"I'm glad you made a friend in Ramelia," Cassara said, "but perhaps you should let your manners influence her, instead of the other way around."

Altessa grinned, then flushed. Her mother must know Altessa had spent the night in Ramelia's room. The guards wouldn't have missed that, and they surely would have reported back to their queen.

"I, um, Ramelia…" Cassara held up her hand, stopping her in a surprising regal gesture. She usually kept those for the throne room. As though catching herself, Cassara lowered her hand and reached across the table to take hold of Altessa's hand.

"It's your business," Cassara said softly. "I vowed that I would never force my child into a marriage, and I meant it. Just make sure to choose someone who treats you like the beautiful soul you are, and you'll always have my support."

Altessa met her mother's eyes, seeing no lie in them, and nodded her gratitude.

"Would you have married Dad if you hadn't had to?" Altessa asked. She'd always wanted to ask her mother. First, Cassara had been sent to Massir to marry Dayshon after he'd proposed, right at the beginning of the Days of Blood. Nobody had cared who he married, and he'd liked Cassara's "spunk" and "quirkiness," two words that her mother always gave her Dad a look when he used them to describe their first meeting in the gardens of Edoline.

The then king of Edoline, Cassara's father and Altessa's grandfather, had given her the choice to join the Circle instead, an offer made by Shirina that very day.

Before Cassara could choose, Edoline was attacked, her father was dead, and she was shipped off to marry the prince of Rashim. And then, she was attacked en route, rescued by Avarielle, and had only continued her journey to Massir after Avarielle had been taken by Siabala. Cassara had hoped to secure an army to help Avarielle's people.

The then king and queen of Rashim would give her an army to fight back Siabala's monsters under one condition: that she first marry their son.

And so she had. And ridden to war on the dawn after her small wedding, one that was still talked about to this day because Queen Cassara had defied expectations.

But Altessa had always wondered and now, with time slipping away from them, she desperately wanted to know.

Cassara squeezed her hand and let it go.

"Honestly? I don't know, Altessa. I was sixteen." Altessa grimaced. She was eighteen and couldn't imagine getting married now. "I don't regret it though." A slight smile played on her mother's lips, eyes faraway. "So I'm glad I did. I don't regret that."

Something was left unsaid, and Altessa prodded.

"But you regret something else?"

Cassara blinked in surprise, then her smile deepened. She looked at Altessa with such pride that it made the princess's heart swell. "Sometimes I forget you're not my little girl anymore, Altessa." The smile lost some of its luster. "I regret having to leave Edoline. If I'm honest, I regret living in Massir. I wish I could have lived somewhere else. These walls, this palace… it never felt like home, even though I have so many wonderful memories here."

Altessa swallowed hard, trying not to take her mother's feelings personally. A difficult thing to do when all your life had been spent in the one place your mother regretted living in.

Cassara leaned back in her chair and studied Altessa. "I don't regret my family, however. I never will."

Altessa nodded, took another bite. Found her appetite was gone.

"There will be a lot of unpleasant truths over the next

little while," Cassara said softly. "I wish I could make things different for you, Altessa. I wish Siabala hadn't returned now, and you'd have had more time…"

"Siabala was supposed to escape when you died," Altessa said. "That means I would have been a new queen, with war on the threshold, while burying my mother."

Cassara's eyes widened. "No, of course not. Your father and I never intended to stay on the throne to our deaths. We would have stepped down at our fortieth year of coronation, and given you the throne."

It was Altessa's turn to blink. Usually rulers in Rashim and Edoline stayed on the throne until their dying breaths.

Cassara smiled softly. "It was something your father offered to me, even though he didn't know about my magic holding up the Wall of Loss. He offered that we could spend our twilight years in Edoline, listening to the surf against the rocks, the wind in the orchards, and enjoy a quiet life. With regular visits to Rashim, of course."

"I didn't know that," Altessa said. "It feels like I know so very little."

"I know," Cassara said. "And I'm sorry for that. I've kept too many things from you, though not because I don't trust you."

"Your Majesty," Lieutenant Garlon knocked on the door. "The Builders are ready to see you. As are the nobles."

Altessa looked up, senses at attention, hands numb.

"Thank you, Lieutenant," Cassara stood up. "Did you find Captain Travin?"

"I did, Your Majesty." He shook his head, unwilling or unable to say more.

"Thank you, Lieutenant," Cassara said, then took a deep breath. The door closed again. "I will appoint him as new captain later today," the queen said, then turned to Altessa. "You head to work with the Builders. Take Ramelia with you. I'll deal with the nobles."

"Mom, I don't—"

"You listened to the plans last night, did you not?"

"Yes, but—"

"And you understood them?"

"Yes. But I don't know how to enact them."

A slight smile from her mother. "Here's the trick: you don't have to know how to enact them. Your job is to make sure they feel they are doing what they should. What we've asked of them… they'll need to have responsibility removed from their shoulders, by a royal decree. That's what you'll do. They're experts and know how to enact the work. Your job is letting them know they are doing what must be done."

"Right," Altessa said, straightening herself. "You make it look so easy," Altessa mumbled, "being in charge."

"Don't mumble. That'll help." Cassara said. "And it's not easy, and I'm mostly uncomfortable with the throne, Altessa. But I've watched others, and emulated behavior I thought worked for me. And I don't let others see my doubt, unless it serves me in some way."

"You made that sound easy, too."

"It'll get easier," Cassara cupped her daughter's cheek. "Or, you'll find your own way. Give yourself grace, Altessa. But don't allow yourself to retreat from your duties. I have no doubt you can do anything you set your stubborn mind to."

She kissed her daughter. "Don't tarry. Get Ramelia and get going. We're all on a very tight schedule."

Without another word, her mother stepped out of the room, and Altessa walked toward Ramelia's room. She didn't want to, afraid things would be awkward. Not that anything had happened, and yet…

"Altessa," Ramelia said, bouncing down the stairs. "I was looking for you."

"Upstairs?"

She shrugged. "I was also curious about the fancy part of the house."

"The Builders are waiting for me," Altessa said, "and my mom thought you could help advise."

As soon as she said it, she knew what Ramelia heard. *My mother wants you to keep me safe, and pull me to safety, should the attack come sooner rather than later.*

"Let's go," Ramelia said, throwing on her simple brown jacket as she trailed the princess toward the awaiting coach that would take them down into the city, where they were about to do the unthinkable.

35

*E*very tree turned into a blur, every community a dream he could almost touch, but not quite.

Rojon slumped against a healed tree, taking in water and a bit of food, as Pakana helped a family escape their home.

"Where's the next community?" he asked, and she nodded to the left. Rolly had also rested, and was ready to whisk them there, the giant lizard on edge at the strangeness of the forest.

"Let's go," he said, but Pakana helped him up. She didn't suggest he rest, nor did he demand it. People were suffocating.

My mother ran her father through with Graysword.

He held on to her waist as Rolly moved quickly, the slight movements of her knees offering him directions, and they were soon dismounting.

My mother ran my father through with Graysword, too.

The parallel of stories struck his exhausted mind as funny, and he started laughing so hard tears streamed down his face.

"What's so funny?" Pakana asked, and Rojon shook his head, but managed to stop the laughter from rippling out of him.

"I'm just tired," he offered as an explanation, not sure she would find the parallel funny, because he certainly no longer did. His body just translated grief into laughter, exhausted by magic, emotions, and just life at this point.

He should have been in Elihor, learning more about tree-crafting and architecture. Not about how trees can suffocate people by turning to stone.

"This is a home," Pakana said, not prodding any further. She'd grown more and more quiet with each rescued home. He should have asked her more questions, but doubted it was his place.

Because his mother had killed her father. This time, the thought sobered him.

He placed his hand on the smaller tree, felt his magic slip out of his fingers, into the bark, showing the magics of Graydon and Elihor how to escape back through those roots, and felt it return to him. His magic was warm, cozying within him, increasing his fatigue. He leaned against the tree, closed his eyes... he must have fallen asleep, blinking awake when Pakana approached, trembling.

"What's—"

"They're all dead," she said. "Blue in the face. Nothing to be done."

A hardness lined her features, but her lower lip trembled, hands helpless at her side.

"There's no point going further," she whispered. "All the remaining people are dead."

"But we haven't made it back to your village yet..." Rojon didn't know how to finish. Pakana slipped down the tree, wrapped her hands around her knees, and collapsed into them, shaking with sobs.

Slowly, in case she wanted no comfort from him, he placed a hand on her back, and kept it there when she didn't shrug it off.

When she was done, they sat in silence, listening to the tree's dancing needles.

"I don't know what to do," Pakana whispered, finally looking up, eyes glassy and face blotchy. "My fathers would know. They'd lived through wars. But me? I've never done anything."

Rojon looked to Rolly, practically one with the ground as he made himself as small as he could, staying near her.

"Rolly doesn't think so," Rojon said, then flushed. "I'm sorry, that might have been a stupid thing to say in Graydon."

Pakana looked to Rolly, and held out her hand. The giant lizard pressed its dark purple snout into her palm, making a sound akin to purring.

"He was an orphan, too, you know," she said. "I had Kaden and Carsyn, and he had me."

"He *has* you," Rojon said softly. "I'm sorry about your fathers."

"Me, too," she said, then laughed. "Then again, they would have balked at having to fight another war. Carsyn would just want to nap, and Kaden, well, Kaden would have dragged them both off to battle…" She paused, took a deep breath, shook her head. "You know, I don't even know where they would have gone to fight. Would they have stayed in Kosel where they'd planted new roots, or would they have headed back to Cassara's side?"

"New roots," Rojon repeated slowly. Pakana, sensing his distraction, looked sideways at him. "Do trees in Graydon form new roots united with those of nearby trees?"

"I really don't know." She shrugged. Rojon placed a hand on the ground, directly onto a patch of earth. In Elihor, some trees strengthened their roots by growing into each other. Even decades-old trees could intertwine their roots and grow entirely new ones, even deeper, if they managed to reach others of their kind.

He closed his eyes, sensing Pakana shift beside him. If the trees were willing to learn something from him, perhaps they would learn this trick. Maybe the magic could help them reach for one another, roots connecting beneath the earth, and creating not just a system of magic for one tree, but one big enough for all of Kosel.

That way, the trees would teach each other how to circulate magic and maybe, just maybe, more people could be saved.

A deep breath riddled with old, secret-filled earth, and he encouraged his magic to slip out of him and into the earth. He sent it with the intention of joining roots, reassured them that they would become stronger for it. And he bade them hurry.

The ground shook under him. Not a lot, but enough for Rolly to jump up and Pakana to make a startled noise.

"It's okay," Rojon said, to her, to the magic, to the trees. To himself.

He hoped he wouldn't damage the beautiful forest by encouraging it to shift its roots. Two branches rubbing for years could lead to rot and kill a tree. Forcing one to change its root system could do much worse, but most of Kosel's trees had already turned to stone.

The trees would want a chance to fight, too. He renewed his efforts, sensing his magic expanding beneath him. The ground shook more strongly, pine needles raining around them as Pakana gasped.

From tree to tree, root to root, Rojon let his magic loose and wild, encouraging trees to join roots and to let go of the magic, teaching one another through centuries of familiarity and shared ground. His magic rippled out, trees shifting back to their normal selves as they shed the magic and stone, each pine sharing its secret with nearby brethren, the entire forest turning into a circulatory system of magic.

Rojon smiled, no longer feeling the strain of magic, but rather euphoria as his power traveled from root to root, across much of Kosel, skipping and dancing. Then, realizing it was no longer necessary to teach the roots what the forest now knew, it headed back into Rojon, like a warm blanket on his cold and tired body.

Pakana helped people out of their homes, a few had survived in bigger habitations. All was not lost, and he was certain he'd saved others by saving the trees.

Save the trees, save the world.

He opened his eyes, mouth parched. Before him, a silver thread. His mind worked too slowly, his body even more so as it wrapped around him, not cutting, simply binding.

The silver thing from the stables of the Lisal Gardens appeared before him, grinning.

"I do like it better when the pines can sing," she said, then held a finger to her lips like she shared a secret. He could see through parts of her, the body not forming as well as it had before, fewer strings tied together.

"Your mother hurt me," she said, looking annoyed. "She took pieces of me. But that's okay. I heard the master is taking much bigger pieces out of her!"

An arrow struck the woman, who ignored it, focused on Rojon, who struggled against the silver bindings.

"Pakana, run!" Rojon said, having seen what the woman could do, and her ruthlessness.

"Eli's tits I will!" she answered, another arrow striking the woman's face. Rojon couldn't see Pakana but heard her cry of pain.

"Leave her alone," Rojon hissed. The woman smiled, tilted her hair sideways. Rojon growled, like his mother would have done, a battle call to his magic, so close to the surface still. The silver woman's eyes widened, more curious than afraid, as his magic exploded out of him.

She yelped, and his magic, having learned a new trick, separated the woman's silver strands and forged new roots with her, silver bands across huge trunks, on rocks, homes… splattered in the clearing, and no longer moving.

"Pakana." Rojon tried to stand, but found he was too dizzy.

"I'm alright," she said, kneeling near him. Her arm bled, but the cut was fairly shallow. After a few moments, she added, "Thank you."

The pines of Kosel sang in the breeze above him, the cracking in the distance speaking of magic being released back into the earth, of roots being united, of his magic protecting an entire forest nation.

He smiled, took a deep breath of earth and, for a few moments, managed to focus solely on life instead of death.

36

Shirina let the magic guide her through the earth, the warrior silent beside her, as the sorceress focused on the veins of power around her, letting her instincts guide her where her knowledge proved difficult to grasp, her black cloak not making itself as quick to master as she'd hoped. But she now understood that the Elders had known of the magic trapped below. And that they'd chosen to pervert it, break it, and force it to be something it wasn't.

That magic leached into some of the old stones, deeper beneath the earth, which had been turned into underground chambers. Like tombs, never meant to be disturbed. In them they created slabs of stone built of the same rock, onto which they strapped test subjects and forced the old magic into them. Those who survived received the green flames. It was a blessing that so few had survived, or the Westland Wars would have seen all of the West perish under the perverted flames.

Once done with the chambers, afraid of their deception being discovered, Ravenhold Elders had sealed them, then denied all involvement in the wars.

Old secrets. Old lies.

And old prisons and traps.

Shirina saw it, a dark patch ahead, like the magic feared courting the place where it was desecrated. The blue flame trembled beside her, crawling up her shoulder as though afraid.

"It'll be okay," Shirina told it.

"You're not the type to give false reassurances, Shirina," Avarielle said. "Don't start now."

"I wasn't reassuring you. I was reassuring the blue whisp, which is entirely more sensible than you."

Avarielle didn't respond, waves of tension flowing from the warrior. Shirina focused ahead, on the stones magic feared to enter. This was what she needed. Her heart tumbled in her chest, hope and anger beating a sporadic rhythm.

Hope that it would hold Siabala.

Anger that it would also hold Avarielle.

I have no choice. Avarielle wanted her to trap her in Siabala's Rage, but that was too obvious, playing straight into the enemy's trap. This... this would have to do.

Unable to penetrate the stone with her magic, Shirina brought them back to the surface and stopped her spell outside the entrance to the underground Circle lair, hidden by sand, in the shadows of the Bloody Mountains. The terrain was quiet, a lone wolf howling somewhere in the distance. A good sign that no monsters currently roamed.

"Where are we?" Avarielle asked.

Shirina planted her staff gently, and the dark sand shifted to reveal the ancient door. Glyphs marked it, worn away badly by time and sandstorms. She couldn't make them out, but ran a hand on them, finding the familiar triggers left behind to unlock it.

A door slid inward.

She stepped aside, looked at Avarielle. She didn't have to say anything. She didn't know what to say, which words to use that would make this somehow okay. Somehow acceptable.

So she said nothing. The warrior could decide if she trusted her enough to step within.

The wind picked up, but the sand seemed content to stay in place. The sun broke the horizon, to the east, beyond Edoline. When Shirina looked that way, over the sands of the West, she imagined the horizon and landscape, where towers and ancient structures had broken through the surface of Graydon, and Elihor, on the other side of the Bloody Mountains.

A land forever changed.

She looked back to Avarielle as the warrior crossed her and stepped into the stone shrine. Shirina took a deep breath and followed, into the cool darkness.

The blue light flickered nervously.

"We won't stay long," Shirina reassured it, and it seemed to understand, settling down. She followed Avarielle, the warrior's footing assured on the cold steps, the blue of Shirina's independent spell glowing purple on Avarielle's hair.

They had gone down at least five stories before reaching a cool, dark cavern. The ground was stained, the walls and ceilings uneven, like they'd been chiseled too quickly. In the center of the chamber reclined six stone slabs, two of them cracked in the middle, all of them stained dark brown. At the back, another door, silent even with the Sight, blocking all magic below. This is where she intended to leave Avarielle. If her magic couldn't penetrate, chances were that Siabala's couldn't escape, either.

He would not be able to call for aid. Nor strengthen his power by calling on his magic, trapped beyond the thick stone dungeon further below.

Shirina handed her pouch to Avarielle. She'd asked Olaram for it—a pouch that held strong healing spells, stored in stones. If the magic stayed in the ground and spells could live beyond a caster's intended purpose, it stood to reason that spells could be stored in stones. So far, the experiment has worked. The dark, terrible experiment.

The warrior would go hungry, and be thirsty, but she wouldn't die. Weakening Siabala's chosen vessel seemed wise, though Shirina hated that she'd even devised the plan. To wrack Avarielle with hunger pains that would never end. Thirst that couldn't be quenched, but also wouldn't kill her. Her body would beg for air, but the stones would keep her alive enough to hold Siabala, and too weak for him to do anything.

Cruel, but necessary, for a chance to stop Siabala once he'd taken control of her body.

Which, at the rate his magic fought, wouldn't be long.

"Place these around the chamber below," Shirina said, standing by the door. "Stay in their center. They will keep you alive so that Siabala's soul stays trapped in you."

Avarielle took the pouch, looked to the stains on the ground and slabs, old blood from slaughtered adepts, her body perfectly still. Then she turned to Shirina, eyes blazing.

"I'm ready."

Shirina nodded, mind spinning, looking for another option. And again, finding none.

"Hang in there," she said, her words feeling weak. "I'll find a way to get you out soon. To contain him for good."

The warrior simply nodded. Shirina pressed her hand against her shoulder, pumped it full of her magic, every bit that she'd stored in her staff, tightening the wards laid by Cassara as much as she could, sensing how far they'd already deteriorated. She'd made a cozy home for Siabala, but Siabala wasn't seeking comfort. He was seeking revenge.

And he was so close he could taste it.

Blood in the water. Rainbows in the sky. She took a deep breath, mind spinning.

"Graysword will help keep him at bay," Shirina said. "I don't yet know quite how, but—"

"Shirina," Avarielle softly said.

The sorceress stopped, looked to the warrior one more time. Avarielle's eyes blazed with certainty. With determination. She might not know Shirina's plan completely, but she trusted her enough to follow it.

And that hurt Shirina more than she'd expected it would. She would learn to hate her, soon enough.

The sorceress placed her hand on the seal holding the door shut, and all magic out. She spoke the ancient words in the air, let the vibration fall to the ground, activating the magic.

The door opened, to a place where the failed adepts, rendered insane with the green flames but refusing to die, were sent to their deaths, for their magic to be contained while they were studied. She could see some of it, in her Elder mind, but didn't want to know it all.

She was sending Avarielle into the dark, with the bones of the failed troops created to slaughter her people.

"Thank you, Shirina," Avarielle whispered. Shirina swallowed hard, said nothing.

What could she say? Warn the warrior of where she'd taken her? Avarielle had heard Carsyn's stories. She knew, and still, she walked into the darkness beyond, not once looking back, stepping down those treacherous steps as Shirina watched, paralyzed by uncertainty. No, by loathing of her own plan. Of her *ability* to come up with it, and execute it, and not think of herself as a monster.

Is this what being an Elder was like?

She survived Siabala's Rage. She can survive this.

She's survived. She would again.

Shirina waited until the warrior vanished around the corner, and then, a few moments later, spoke the closing incantation, an ancient dialect even her Elder understanding couldn't translate. The doors shut with a thud, a crunch that reverberated across the underground crypt.

And then all was quiet, save for a faint echo in the air of what was, and a stain on the ground of what should never have been.

Avarielle laid out the stones, careful to feel her way around the round chamber, ignoring the cracking of dry bones beneath her boots. Her eyes could find no saving grace, here, and so her mind conjured up ghosts and monsters, dark imaginings that would keep her company.

Once the stones settled around her, Avarielle kicked aside bones and sat cross-legged in the center, Graysword across her lap, both hands on the blade, touching its magic. The white flames did not activate without a monster, but she could feel it coursing into her, strengthening the wards.

This will not hold me, Siabala whispered in her mind.

"I know," Avarielle said. "But it'll slow you down."

Siabala did not respond, and Avarielle focused on her breaths, knowing air would run out eventually, understanding what the sorceress had chosen to do to weaken Siabala. She wished she would have taken the time to let the sorceress know she was forgiven.

Admired, even.

In the dark foot of the Bloody Mountains, Avarielle Grayloft, trapped by Siabala and stone, still found the strength for her lip to curl up at imagining Shirina's undoubtedly dry reply at the thought that Avarielle admired her cunning.

On the closed and sealed door, Shirina's hand shook. She was angry, an anger she hadn't felt in years. She'd pushed down her anger, learned to work around it, to spend it working the earth, curb it for other people's emotions, to make room for theirs but never her own.

But now, she was angry. And she didn't know how to stop it. No, she knew. She could take deep breaths, focus on something else, go for a walk, look at the sky… but she didn't *want* to stop the anger. She wanted to embrace it. She'd ignored it for so long, and now she found that she didn't care to refuse its hold on her.

Siabala had already won so much. They'd lost too much ground, and no matter what victories they gained, he found a way to strike back.

She removed her hand from the door, formed a fist, grief and anger sweeping over her. She cried out, unleashed her anger, punching the door, knuckles cracking, the pain jolting her back to her senses.

She fumbled back, suddenly embarrassed, glad that no one had witnessed it. The only person who would have understood was locked away. Her anger bubbled up again, and Shirina clutched her staff, knuckles screaming in agony as her hands trembled with unspent grief.

She looked at the bloodstains on the floor.

Was that what would happen to them all? Would all their souls be lost to Siabala? Avarielle's first?

"No," the word slipped out of her mouth, followed by a growl so deep she surprised herself. And then she hit the ground with the end of her staff, into that dry blood.

The ground beneath her flashed, the stone rumbled, and the blue whisp glowed brighter.

Shirina took a slow breath. The magic reacted to her anger, understood her fury.

Curiosity tempered her, but she looked to the blood. To the door. Remembered the beauty of the Lisal Gardens before they had been attacked. Thought of all the humiliation she'd suffered. Of how she could have been an Elder before now… and she struck the ground again with her staff.

And light exploded in her mind, magic trickling into her, riding her emotions to her mind. Just like when she'd used magic to find her friends. Like when she'd fought

Avarielle, trying to save Cassara. And now, hoping to save the warrior.

The blue whisp danced on her staff, splitting back into smaller balls who drifted on the air around her. She closed her eyes, walked into the light, trusted her gut. She did not resist the magic, welcoming it, willing to learn from it if it would save all that she loved.

37

*B*elow Graydon, lines of power laid down millennia ago, long before the names Graydon and Elihor were known, thrummed with magic, tapped into by the sorceress known as Shirina.

The lines were old, worn, and bled into the ground around them, mixing with potent magics it should never have, though the Lost One had always hoped they would.

Siabala.

The magic shivered with the name of the one who would save them. Who would destroy them.

Whisps of power ignited, responding to the simple wish of the one called Shirina: to stop Siabala. She had been willing to sacrifice her own heart to stop him, as had Elihor and Graydon, long ago.

But a thousand years ago, the two lovers had tapped into the magic at once to erect the Wall of Loss, forcing the magic up, into the sky, separating it.

Trapping so many souls above, unable to return to the ground, to the conduits of power, to what fed and nurtured them. The magic had fought them, stealing their energy every time they called upon it, burning them when pushed too far.

Still, they persisted.

In Elihor, magic was more respected, more understood to reside in the ground, where memories and souls came to rest. But not in Graydon.

Given the chance to escape by Siabala and his followers, the magic had retreated back down, where it was safe. Familiar.

Except for some, who wanted to fly still. To be with the bloodlines they knew.

And now, the witch known as Shirina called upon the powers of magic. Not of Elihor, nor Graydon. Not of the land, nor the air.

Just of magic. And she understood, felt the ripples, the knowledge coalescing as she drew knowledge from the same powers that had gifted her a black cloak, a symbol long before any Circle existed.

The magic needed to respect her to answer. Needed to understand her. It prodded at her mind. Her heart. Knocked and asked permission to enter.

And she opened herself to them.

Let them see her soul. Her heart. Her mind. Her determination. Her fears.

Her childhood, her anger. Her shame, her pride.

All of her. It was messy, as all humans were. But it was

beautiful, too. Because she no longer shied away from who she was, and who she'd become. She no longer excused the past, nor forsook the future. She embraced it all, accepted it, made peace with it.

And still stood up to undo the injustices around her. To help those who needed her. Hands for war. Hands for healing. Hands to tend to the people. To tend the earth.

The magic had not understood the old Circle. It had fought it, hated it. But this sorceress was willing to learn. She knew that she knew just enough to know that she knew almost nothing at all. To see the cracks in her learning and knowledge. To be willing to embrace them, and change them. To be more than she had ever been, while not afraid of being less.

To be.

The magic responded to her pain. To the choices she'd been forced to make, but that she *had* made, because she needed to. To the hand she'd been dealt. To her worries for her adepts, for the lands.

For the eventual release of Siabala.

Siabala.

She had trapped him away from the magic, where he could not tap into it. They understood her need for quick movement, for the Lost One would escape again. He who once tended to them, but could not let them go once the world had changed.

The magic understood her need, her fear, and responded to it, rippled across Graydon, and Elihor, across the vast landmass that existed beneath them, the layers of ruins, of those who had lived before Graydon and Elihor.

The need spread wide and far, and the magic opened up to the sorceress, willing to trust her, at least for now. Her life was a flash in time, and one that could change everything for them. For the better. For the worse.

For her people. For the magic.

For them all.

Shirina followed the magic beneath her, around her, supporting her and willing to be her ally. The whisp's blue light glowed beyond her closed eyes, dancing, inviting her to follow.

And she did, traveling the veins of the earth, the vast network of caverns, and she sought her adepts, to introduce the magic to them, one by one, in an instant, a lifetime, a thought across all of magic all at once.

Not just her adepts, but those from Larkhold as well. Anyone who had known magic, who had wielded it, who had spent time to learn how to tame it. They would now learn to befriend it, or the magic would desert them.

The choice is yours, she told the magic as her spirit expanded, covering all of Graydon and Elihor. She found Ollir, who felt the magic ripple up her feet, her body, her arms. Her cloak billowed as it changed from orange to pure crimson. Shirina's words echoed in the veins of power, *When your cloak takes on its true color, you will know that the magic of Graydon will have been freed. Use your instincts then, follow the magic, and find me.*

She reached for them all, those who had vowed their lives to the magic, from green to black cloak, and she spoke in their hearts and minds, *The magic is beneath you. Reach for it. Do not force it—befriend it. Welcome it in you. It awaits your invitation. Battle is coming. Armies march on Massir. Siabala has returned.*

She could see the troops marching, red with Siabala's powers, creatures rising from his broken empire. The magic reached for the surface as her witches connected, or failed to connect, with the power brimming beneath them, several adepts on their knees, crying as they felt whole again.

As simple as that, as complicated as that, Shirina had raised an army.

The day she'd asked them all to prepare for was finally here. With a heart both heavy and light, Shirina allowed the magic to take her where she was most needed, away from the prison of Avarielle Grayloft, to fight the monsters already unleashed.

If Siabala were to break free, which he undoubtedly would, there would be little she could do here, alone. But with her Circle? With both Circles?

Hope could prove treacherous, but it was a chance Shirina was willing to take.

Shala forced herself to look from the snaking blue lines in the ground to the black tower casting dark shadows. The blue magic didn't lance up it, though she could see it dancing in the city nested in the large seam scissoring the lands of the West.

The creatures who had been attacking moments earlier retreated into the tower, the Westland warriors shouting.

Before she could try to figure out what exactly she was seeing, she heard Shirina's message.

And she knew she would head to Massir.

Shala had seen Shirina teleport. She'd looked at how it was done, and how much easier it seemed to be. It was contradictory. Air should be easier to travel than rock. But it wasn't through the rocks they traveled, as far as she could tell. Ancient magical conduits, now shining strong beneath her, filled with Graydon's magic, awaited to bring her safely to her destination. The mists and threads that used to cling to the air seemed a weak web compared to the strength of the land.

"What's happening?" Trevon asked, as he joined her.

"Shirina is telling us to head to Massir. That Siabala is coming."

"Does that mean…" Trevon didn't speak the words. Shala didn't know how much the Westland warrior knew. Avarielle could have told him everything, or she might have told him nothing, and he'd simply figured some of it out.

It wasn't her place to tell, but she knew the old warrior enough to know that he wouldn't back down from a fight.

"I assume so," she simply said. If he meant that Avarielle would eventually be heading to Massir, then she hadn't lied. If instead he'd asked if Shala intended to head to Massir herself, well, she would be hard-pressed to be anywhere else but where the Circle would make its stand.

Hopefully not its last stand.

She was desperate to speak to Shirina. To ask her what exactly she'd done, and what she'd seen. She would get the chance soon enough in Massir.

"I'm coming with you," he said, stepping up right beside her, as though he had no intention of letting her get away without him.

"I should hope so," she said. "But first, let's make sure this place is secure."

He grinned and ran off, trusting her not to leave him behind. And she wouldn't. She'd need time to speak to the adepts, and to make sure she was secure enough in the magic to teleport two people to Massir.

She'd have to leave some adepts behind. Many couldn't yet teleport. But they would be useful in other ways. Siabala's battle would erupt everywhere, just as his empire had, and so the Circle would need to stand everywhere.

Those who couldn't fight would heal. Those who could do neither would record for history.

There was a role for each of them to play, and Shirina had never asked them to do anything but their best, no matter what that might be.

A fighter, Shala would go to the battle, and hope to live to tell the tale.

∼

The bells around Massir quickened their cadence as armies approached from the north and south, twisted looking creatures and monsters from the deepest nightmares.

Massir had no army. No magic.

Elder Quilsam remembered the twisted creatures of Siabala from the last war. The monsters created from his people, his brethren. He could only imagine who or what he'd now twisted for his means, his hands shaking at his sides at the memories.

Queen Cassara prepared for the final attack, a piecemeal approach that kept people busy with preparations. The Elder did not trust that her plan would work. It would buy time, but that was it.

There was no end game. No final victory for her. Only time.

Time for what? the Elder had questioned.

She'd looked at him, as though at peace, as she'd answered, *Just time, Elder. We can't win the war. All we can do is win time, and hope.*

Yet his question remained: time for what? For salvation to come from an unexpected ally? The whole world was more than likely busy fighting Siabala's monsters and risen structures. No one would have time to save Massir, as they desperately fought to save themselves.

No, Elder Quilsam did not believe in false hope. He'd hidden, once before, to save his Circle. He would do so again if he could, but Shirina's vague instructions did not exactly help him access his magic, nor teleport away to safety.

Queen Cassara had advised him to find refuge in a noble home, in the protected area of the city, near the palace, known as the Tapestry. Riddled with large mansions, manicured lawns, and sturdy walls, it would be beautiful if more light could reach it, instead of the shadows cast by the palace and its walls.

Elder Quilsam had chosen to stay in the palace, intent on finding a way to tap into the magic before everything crumbled down.

If Shirina had done it, he had no doubt he could.

The ground trembled and he looked down with the Sight, blue sparks dancing in the earth. Far below, around Massir, like lines of power erupting and then dissipating, to reappear again, like a throbbing heart. Had it been there all along? Yes, but deeper, he realized. It bubbled to the surface, as though seeking something, crawling up even Massir's walls, houses, the palace grounds… and then he heard it. Shirina's voice.

If he was honest, he hated her. He'd hoped he could take over Ravenhold and append it to Larkhold. To make one strong Circle.

And now, here she was, speaking directly into his

mind, through the strands of Larkhold and Ravenhold. She had found the magic, or it had found her, and had gifted her a black cloak.

He hated her, but admired her, too, even as he knew that she would fall, eventually. Siabala would kill her, or her own pride would. One did not wield so much power without attracting enemies.

He listened to her message. She would come here.

As would Siabala.

Elder Quilsam took a deep breath and headed back to his study. Shirina may have found knowledge in the earth, but he still believed in the written word above all else.

He had precious time left, and he would need to be ready for battle.

This time, there would be no hiding.

Elder Tally of Ravenhold saw the blue lines of magic, even if they did not seek her out. Shirina had grown impressively strong and learned much in her short tenure as Elder, but she'd not yet realized how the rippling magic could be traced back to its caster.

Or to what they desperately tried to keep from them.

Tally had championed the green flames during the Westland Wars, and she knew everything about their chambers. Where they were. And how to breach them.

The time for her master to finally rise again was at hand.

Across Graydon and Elihor, the blue magic rippled under the ground, raced up trees, avoided the traitor's power, and danced as it tapped into adepts, and then into others. So many new voices, new souls, new hands and feet. New hearts, new minds.

Across the two lands, the words of Shirina traveled, and the magic carried them, happily flitting freely, understanding that freedom was worth fighting for, and choosing its best ally to do so.

It traveled up the Bloody Mountains, avoided Siabala's Rage, and crossed into Elihor. Found Larkhold.

Then it sped into the sea, found the remnants of Ravenhold.

Then traveled up Stormhold, curious about the keep located atop a single stone spire in the middle of the Bloody Mountains.

But Stormhold was more than just a keep, and the trap that had been set millennia ago sprang.

The magic shrieked, pulsed like electricity, fought against its oppressors.

And then it snapped.

3 8

Partway through her teleportation spell, Shirina felt the magic crumple, the blue whisp on her staff shrieking in her mind as though in pain. Instinctively she pulled herself up, the spell ending as she threw herself into the air, landing hard on her side, scraping the side of her face.

She scrambled to her knees, the magic ball writhing on the ground as though wounded.

She placed her hands on the ground near it, feeling the blue whisp's pain as it began to dissipate, steam of blue magic evaporating into the air, as though dragged back where it didn't want to go.

"Stay," Shirina whispered, cupping her palm over it as though she could stop it from leaving the ground it craved.

She felt helpless. For one glorious moment, she had connected with every adept from both Circles, and then the magic just… broke. Had it been because too many had attempted to connect at once? She doubted that, somehow. Had she forced too much of it near the surface, to connect with witches just above the ground? She doubted that as well—the magic had certainly not fought her. It had welcomed her, danced with her, allowed her to become one with it and stretch beneath both lands.

The blue whisp rolled against her palm, warm, patting her as though it wanted to be held. Shirina gently picked it up, smoke curling up at its edges.

"I don't know how to help you," she whispered, her mind and heart trying to parse the information as her elation turned to dread. With little recourse or understanding, she fell back on old habits and sang a healing song, uncertain what else to do.

The whisp seemed to calm, and Shirina doubled her song, turning it into an incantation. If the magic was being pulled back into the air, perhaps her old ways of connecting with it would help it stay whole.

She mixed lullabies with spells and, after a few moments, the blue whisp grew calmer, no longer losing pieces of itself. She could feel it pressing against her, as though trying to hug her. Gently, she ran a finger over it. It felt… substantial. Soft. Warm. Vibrated from within, as though purring.

"You're not a spell at all, are you?" Shirina said, and gently she reached with her mind, Elder knowledge forming like a web of ice over her.

They had known all along where the magic came from.

Images formed in her mind. Rainbows in the sky. *The Circle, the first one, her people with their cloaks, above the underground cities.* Bloody water. *The people below, ripped apart, blood in the underground waters.*

The death of a civilization, as magic was ripped from the ground which tried to protect its people, hiding entrances to their underground cities. But it was too late. The attack from the invaders above had been assured and swift, and merciless.

The whisp deflated in her palm.

"You were there," she said, heart dropping. This wasn't a spell. What they called magic was more than that.

They were using the souls of those who had come before. Those who used to live in the great cities beneath theirs.

A shiver ran in the whisp, warming her. Magic used to run in conduits across the lands. Siabala... he'd tried something to save his people. Dark magic that covered the cities. But it had been too late, and his people had perished.

A dark king. A dark god.

Magic coerced. Just like Elihor and Graydon had done, trying to stop him. No, before them, even, though the details lacked in her mind. To save *their* people. Those who had come after. Drawing magic up into the air, not paying attention to what had been, what deserved respect and understanding. Using what they needed, instead of respecting those who had been here long before them.

They'd forced magic into their hands—magic created by the souls of a people. And those souls had fought them for a thousand years, becoming spells when summoned but draining the caster's energy.

This is why the Wall of Loss existed. Not just to trap Siabala, but to keep the magic separate, because when the strands united, they could attack their jailers, the very witches who could wield spells.

But now, this, the blue whisp waiting expectantly... this was different. They were being dragged back into the air, which would ruin magic for her witches and, more importantly, hurt the souls even more.

"Show me," she whispered, and she saw Stormhold, the first of the keeps to be erected, before even Elihor and Graydon. The one that maintained the Wall of Loss to trap Siabala's soul, along with his red strands of magic. The spire of stone upon which it rested glowed with fractured light, dragging magic from below and into it, back into the air. Once, it would have fortified the Wall of Loss and the magic of both lands, ripping apart the two strands of magic and throwing them on different sides of the Wall.

Now... now it simply took the unwilling powers, turned them to gas, and the strands of dark and light connected to become shadows—the one magic her adepts could not wield.

Had she done this? By pushing the magic to find every adept, had they tripped ancient traps within Stormhold?

The whisp glowed, then puffed out. She gasped, palms still held out, and looked with the Sight. The blue magic evaporated up, turning back into shades of white and black—into *both* strands of magic.

They'd split the souls in two, making them helpless to attack. The gray strands had been united souls.

Shirina felt sick to her stomach, at all the actions she'd taken which had hurt so many. But this wasn't about her, and so she focused on finding a way to help. The whisp fought, blue light reemerging in the vapor of its soul.

There was time.

But not a lot.

"Tell me what I must do," she said, realizing she didn't care about using the magic as much as she did about helping it. She'd grown up wanting to master it. It turned out that, all along, she should have focused on befriending it.

The whisp came to her forehead, and she did not back away as it lifted a veil in her mind, showing her the location of the knowledge she couldn't quite access yet. Because the Elders had known the functions of Stormhold all along, ripping the magic, separating souls for their means.

Shirina's angry gaze turned toward the Bloody Mountains.

Toward Stormhold.

"I need help getting there," she said.

The blue creature danced, grew, as though inviting

more magic to join it, until the sphere was large enough to ensnare her.

She shot up into the sky, toward Stormhold, toward the keep at the heart of the land, the great engine that ensured magic stayed active, and enslaved.

*A*varielle knelt in the middle of the chamber, the darkness so thick she imagined cutting it with Graysword. But she stayed in the center, seated, hands resting on her blade.

She was hungry. Thirsty. Tired.

She had no idea how long she'd been here. It could have been days, or hours. She focused on the knocking at her shoulder, the war drums of Siabala. She could not look away from this enemy, nor ignore his presence.

She could only confront him, find a way to fight him. To keep him at bay, despite all odds.

She gripped Graysword, her ancestral blade's magic dancing up her arm, her entire body.

How long do you think you can stop me?

Long enough.

My armies will destroy your friends. Your family.

They would find a way to win the day. They had to. But she knew that their battle wasn't hers.

No more than hers was theirs. She had but one enemy standing before her.

Within you.

And so that's all she focused her energy on.

The ground cracked. She opened her eyes as the door opened above the stairs. For a second, she hoped to see Shirina, the sorceress perhaps having had an Elder epiphany on how to contain Siabala.

Then she was washed in the red glow of magic. Slowly she stood, Graysword in her hand, pumping its magic up her arm, knowing she'd already lost.

That's no reason not to fight.

"Did you really think it would be so simple to hide from me?" Tally said, stepping through, bowing before her. "My dear, I've been following you this whole time, through the very strings of power Shirina is desperately, and foolishly, trying to save."

Avarielle wanted to jump her and try to behead her again, cut across the stone covering her neck, but she realized that she'd stopped moving. In the glow of the red magic, she could only watch as her right hand sheathed Graysword. She then removed the wrapping around her left arm, which felt stiff but fine.

Siabala's prison had collapsed.

Did you really think you could stop me?

"Now come. We have someone who misses you very much."

Avarielle had been ready to suffer for months, years, even. She would have gladly wasted away while Shirina sought answers. Anything to stop Siabala. Instead, she followed Tally up the stairs, and stepped into the awaiting teleportation portal, a trick of Siabala's magic she hadn't seen since going into his Rage.

She fully expected to reappear near the towers of Massir.

Instead, she heard the dancing of pine, smelled their freshness. And she knew, without a doubt, that Rojon was still somewhere in Kosel.

She gritted her teeth and fought with all that she was, knowing it wasn't enough.

Shirina stood atop the wide, large keep nested within the Bloody Mountains, upon a perch of stone defying architectural feasibility.

Stormhold.

The tallest keep in the lands, erected straight in the middle of them. From here, she could see the land stretching. The magic dancing. The structures and towers that surrounded and defaced the two lands.

And, using the Sight, she could see the magic being dragged up to Stormhold, released from its highest tower once burned and turned to smoke.

The blue whisp shrunk again, and she gently placed it on her staff, where it stayed, shivering. The souls were being churned back into the magic she'd always known. She'd expected them to immediately turn gray, but realized from up close that she'd seen gray simply because of the superimposed strands.

They remained separate, instead, perhaps not yet having regained the wherewithal to reunite.

Below, she could feel Siabala's Rage rumble with power.

"I don't know how this will impact Siabala," she said. The whisp grew still. She could let this continue—let the magic go back to the way it was. Find a way to keep it separate that didn't involve the Wall of Loss. They'd be more prepared to fight with their old, known magic.

But now she knew, she *knew* what magic was made from. She'd be complicit in the destruction, the shredding, the enslavement of souls, of a people which had perished long ago.

She wasn't sure what even encompassed a soul. The people of Elihor believed memories stayed in the land. What if it was more than that? What if the souls themselves, as long as they remained tethered to their bodies, fed their sweet nectar into the apples? Was that why she saw Tanja? Why Siabala had turned the Circle witches into undead monsters? To stop their souls, or use their power?

Too many questions. Too few answers, even for an Elder.

But one thing was clear to her, above all else. No matter what she did today, she would impact the success of the battle below, and the future of the two lands. She gazed across them both, then looked down at the magic being dragged toward Stormhold, slowly, like it dug its claws in the ground trying to fight back.

"Forgive me," she whispered, then struck the stones of the keep with her staff and forced her will into Stormhold. The fortress had been crafted for one purpose—to trap the magic from the ground, separate it, and send it into the two separate lands.

Release the magic, Shirina thought, willing the keep to follow her bidding. Millenia-old stone buckled but did not crack, set with magical mortar that refused to obey Shirina.

"I'm not done yet," she whispered to the blue whisp, which vibrated with pain.

Shirina placed her staff on the mortar instead of the stone, and closed her eyes. Old habits were hard to break, but they could also support current needs. She began to chant a spell, voice confident and strong, following not a preset spell, but rather the vibrations of her staff, from stone to bone. She closed her eyes, focused on those vibrations, and how they might impact the magical mortar.

The blue whisp screeched and her eyes snapped open, just in time to see a shower of green flames tumbling toward her. She shifted her staff, tried to call on the magic, but even as she reached for it, she could see it dragged away from her and into Stormhold, the keep greedily holding it prisoner.

Shirina threw herself back, knowing she couldn't stop the green flames from consuming her, but unwilling to go down without trying. The blue whisp erupted before her, grew wider, and absorbed the blow. Or as much as it could, flames still slamming into her, sending her flying to her knees, staff clattering away. At least the flames' power failed and left her unharmed.

The whisp floated down, barely lit. Shirina caught it in her palm, cupping it gently, as its essence began to vanish.

"Hold on," she whispered, and it flickered in answer before growing muted again.

"So, you managed to become an Elder?" Vangle stepped forward, a grin on his face that Shirina very much wanted to wipe off. She picked up her staff, placed the whisp carefully on it, where it latched on, resting.

"And you're still an idiot." She stood back up to face him.

"You've been a problem," Vangle said. "Elder Tally would now like you to stop being a part of the fabric of this world."

"If she really wanted that done, she should have sent someone competent. Although I suppose I should thank you for helping me reconnect with Ravenhold."

His smile turned into a scowl, making her feel entirely better.

"I will personally kill you and every single one of your witches, *Elder* Shirina."

Shirina grasped her staff, gifted to her from the roots of the ancient oak of Lisal Gardens, by magic which yearned to be free. The magic knew her. Understood her.

Trusted her.

The whisp flickered again, as though agreeing with her.

You can hear me? she thought toward it, and it glowed a bit more brightly.

You're here to help me? Another glow, and she couldn't make out words, but she could understand its intent. It was here to guide her. To show her how the ancient magic worked, and how to safely reach it.

Vangle was blathering on about something power-wise, and she ignored most of it until he mentioned Tally.

He saw her focus on him, and that grin returned.

"Tally knows where she is, you know. Did you really think that you could contain our lord and master in such a feeble body?"

"It's your mind that's feeble, not Avarielle Grayloft's body," Shirina snapped back. "Why are you here, Vangle? I assure you I don't care for your company."

Of course Tally knew where Avarielle was. She wasn't surprised by that—just annoyed, heartbroken, and angry.

"You found the useless underground magic," Vangle sneered, "and so Tally thought it would be nice to send it back into the air, as the mixed magic that will kill your adepts."

Blood in the water. Rainbows in the air.

Stormhold stood above the Bloody Mountains, below the division of the Wall of Loss. Shirina looked down, the mortar between stones coated with something sleek looking. With the Sight, she could see the magic trapped in it, quivering with panic.

Blood in the water.

She looked up, toward the sky. She'd fought Siabala

here, once, with Cassara and the others. Rainbows had exploded upward when she'd used all of her magic.

Rainbows in the air.

"Do you know why Stormhold was created?" she asked convivially, making Vangle even more suspicious. Why he didn't just kill her was beyond her. No, perhaps not. Tally more than likely wanted her alive, to bore her to near death before having Avarielle finish her off.

She continued, placing the tip of her staff over the mortar, where conduits of power grew. Like the magic was trapped there. *No.* Conduits of power like a jail.

"It was to separate that ancient magic, send it into the air, and force it to remain. A way to keep forces living beneath our feet from destroying us. Forces and creatures who had been here long before us."

The whisp glowed gently.

"Power makes right," Vangle said. Shirina slowly raised an eyebrow. No wonder she'd not accepted him into her Circle. "And your power is at an end, *Elder.*"

Shirina pushed down through her staff, ignoring Vangle's hurled spell, pushing against the mortar with all of her magic. The ground cracked, Vangle's spell missing her by a hair as he lost balance.

He looked at her with concern as he regained his balance.

"What are you doing?" he asked as the Keep cracked again. She couldn't force the Keep to follow her will. But she could undo the bars keeping the magic trapped.

"I'm trusting the magic," she said, and struck down,

hard. The Keep rumbled, from deep within. She broke one bar, a line of mortar, magic escaping into stones, glowing with ecstasy. She slammed the adjoining mortar, which crumbled and released old stone, waves of power crackling away from the ancient prison... the entire keep was coming down.

Vangle started teleporting, but the ground magic attacked, snaring him down as he screamed, that portion of Stormhold vanishing deep below. Shirina trusted the magic as it had trusted her, letting it sweep her down, away from the Bloody Mountains as Stormhold was swallowed by it, finally unleashing the mechanism that had trapped magic for so long.

The magic followed her heart, bringing her to Avarielle's confinement. She solidified, feet planted on earth, the blue whisp dancing around her, to find a broken door and an empty prison.

Avarielle was already free.

She held out her hand, the whisp settling into it.

You don't need to come with me, Shirina said. *You can be free if you so wish.*

Feelings of agreement and understanding washed over her, and Shirina interpreted them as a thank you, but the creature chose to stay with her.

The spell.

The soul.

Her guide, freed from a thousand years of imprisonment.

Avarielle was gone, but finding her would be easy.

There was only one place the warrior would go.

Don't assume.

She felt the tug at her mind, the whisp floating just before her face.

"I can follow her trail," she whispered. The magic of Siabala was everywhere, but she might be able to follow Siabala's trail, just like Tally had managed to follow hers.

"Bring me to her," Shirina said. "Bring me to Avarielle Grayloft."

The magic answered, not to her words but to her despair, hurling her across the land, the cities below now more lit, the released magic bringing them back to life. Or so she surmised from the little she saw, a kaleidoscope of colors and stones.

She realized she grew hot, red light dancing around her, interfering with the teleportation spell. Without overthinking it, relying on well-honed instincts, Shirina called the magic to bring her to safety. She found herself on the ground, collapsed, bruised. Had she been teleporting over Graydon, she would have fallen. She hated to think what would have happened if her spell had failed while deep in the earth.

Shirina tried to find her bearings. The night was still dark, day still a few hours away, she thought. Silent sentinels stood before her, tall, reaching for the sky. She summoned the Sight, revealing threads of red magic forming the trap that had almost dissected her spell. Never before had she seen magic used this way, and left to its own devices. She made note of it, studied it, thought she could replicate it.

Then, she focused beyond the webbed shield, and her breath caught in her throat. The tall sentinels were pine trees, reaching for the sky. Magic danced in them, both strands, strongest among them the magic of Elihor.

Rojon's magic.

She was in Kosel, where she'd last seen Rojon. Where he'd found a way to tap into his magic, making it easy for Tally to track him.

Her heart fractured.

Tally had brought Avarielle to him, to claim his blood.

Shirina hurled magic into the shield, which danced over it and dissipated. With her staff, she pulled all that she could through the ground, trying to destroy the shield from beneath, but the red threads had deep roots. She cast spell after spell until, exhausted, she fell to her knees, the great trees of Kosel swaying as though mocking her.

The little blue whisp threw itself at the shield, but its powers also proved useless.

"We need another way," Shirina said, breath catching in her throat. Time slipped away, like water streaming through her fingers. The whisp bounced before her, and then gently settled on the ground, making a little "eee" sound which vibrated in the air around them.

"Communication. I can talk to anyone in there using the ground's vibrations?" The whisp jumped up.

Black cloak wrapped around her, Shirina placed both hands on the ground, the whisp settling between her hands, as though ready to listen. To help. She spoke to it, toward the ground, into Kosel and anyone tuned in to magic who might listen.

"Hear me, Circles of Larkhold and Ravenhold in Kosel," her voice softened, grief curling within her. "Avarielle Grayloft is within it and Rojon Kolder is in grave danger. Siabala is controlling the Grayloft." The words pierced her heart. For the boy she considered family. For his mother whose soul would be claimed. "Stop her, at all costs. Keep Rojon safe," she ended, sitting back on her heels, trying to think of her next steps. Of something, anything she hadn't tried, so she could save Rojon, instead of waiting to see if anyone had heard her plea. Who but her could even stand against Avarielle?

Could even *she* stand against her? Uncertainty rattled her core, and grief, and fear, and helplessness shredded her belief that she could keep anyone safe, especially those she loved.

The blue whisp sat quietly beside her as the Ravenhold Elder, for once in her life, did not bother to stop her tears from streaming down onto the Circle above her heart. Then, having done all she could, including grieve for what she could not do, she did the only thing left to do—head for Massir, where Siabala would next strike. She would need to prepare.

With one final glance at the red shields, Shirina struck the ground gently with her staff, knowing that she left a piece of her heart behind, and that she would never recover it.

41

"Now, now, let's not make this any harder than it has to be," Tally said, the old woman tapping her arm in a grandmotherly fashion. Avarielle wanted to hit her, rip out her eyeballs and stomp them, cut her in a thousand pieces so even she could never rise again. To leave her body burning in Siabala's remaining fires.

If you do as I ask, I may gift her to you. Siabala rumbled, sounding cozy, like he reclined in her body. Which was what this felt like. She wasn't imprisoned below like before, able to see, hear, maybe even talk, though she certainly had nothing worthwhile to tell that old witch—that would just encourage her to talk and make her more insufferable—but she couldn't control her body.

I don't want any of your gifts, Avarielle scowled the thought loudly, to be rewarded by a laugh.

Tally had wanted to gift Avarielle to Siabala. Now

Siabala wanted to gift Tally to her. The whole thing grated on her, but also struck her as amusing.

That's it. I'm losing my mind.

To me, Siabala replied. *But I don't want you to lose it. I want to own it, that's all. You'll make this so much easier on yourself if you just... give in.*

She kept her silence, the moment of mirth she'd temporarily found evaporated.

"You can blame your sorceress friend for this," Tally said. "That bothersome Shirina should have perished years ago, when Lord Siabala first emerged. Your suffering now is her fault."

"Shirina is a hundred times the witch you'll ever be," Avarielle hissed out, glad she could tell her off.

"If she were," Tally responded, "she wouldn't have so easily fallen into my trap. I hope she's well and dead."

"What did you do to her, old woman?"

"Lured her to the edge of the world, and then shredded her in a thousand pieces." Tally tsked. Actually tsked. "She forced our hand, you know. Her and your little blonde friend. If they'd have just let you go... ah well. Thankfully someone is cooperating with us."

A pit formed in Avarielle's stomach, threatening to swallow her. She wished it would—just take her away from this plain, taking Siabala with her. That's what she and Shirina had tried to do. She preferred dying to *this*.

No, please. She heard herself say as they cleared the pines of Kosel, a familiar settlement coming into view. She'd been here, before, to find an old man with hopefully answers that would help her win the war. Before she'd killed him in his home.

Do you want me to make this easier for you? Instead of fighting me, just let me take control. You can stay safe, below, and not witness the death of your own son. By your hand.

For a second, Avarielle considered it. To hide, away from where they were bringing her, away from seeing her son's face, away from feeling her blade cut him. From seeing life escape him.

For a second, she considered it. Then, she growled. Deep, throaty, reverberating in her entire body, helping to ground her. Siabala *wanted* her to feel helpless. But maybe she could still speak, could still see, because he wasn't yet strong enough to escape Shirina's prison. She had to believe that he needed her to give up, so that he could stake his claim.

I will always fight you with all that I am, all that I have, Siabala.

He laughed, practically purred inside her, pleased with her reaction.

I would expect no less, oath breaker.

Avarielle gritted her teeth as they walked to a door.

"This is it," Tally said. "It was nice of your son to leave us such a lovely trail."

"I will rip your head from your body first chance I have," Avarielle hissed.

"Of course you will," Tally patted her arm.

Something pierced Avarielle's back and she grunted, familiar with the pain of arrows slipping between ribs.

The shot was true, and Avarielle crumpled to one knee.

Tally turned and erected red flaming shields as Avarielle slowly twisted around to see. Pakana, Kaden and Carsyn's daughter, stood by Rolly, firing shot after shot, all bouncing uselessly off Tally's magic.

"Run!" Avarielle screamed, tasting blood.

"Not until this is done," Pakana screamed back. "Rojon doesn't want to lose you, but he already has, so I'll do the thing he won't be able to do." She fired another arrow, and gave a sharp whistle. Rolly thundered forward, the ground trembling as he charged them.

"Run, Pakana!" Avarielle screamed again, wishing she could move, stop the Elder from casting her spell... with an easy flick of the wrist, Tally threw Rolly back. The lizard cried out, bouncing backward into Pakana, the two vanishing into the dense forest with a crash.

"No!" Avarielle said. "Leave her be!"

"People make terrible choices when they're grieving," Tally turned to her, leaving her shielding spell up, "especially with the person who killed a loved one."

"You—" Avarielle was ready to unleash a string of expletives, but Tally reached down and pulled the arrow out with a strength Avarielle would not have believed the old woman to have. The arrow ripped organ, muscle, and flesh, scraping ribs.

Avarielle threw up blood, gasping with the pain, trying to grit her teeth against it, unable to shift to make it less.

"I'd heal you," Tally said, "but your powers will take

care of it. If you're lucky, this pain will distract you from what's to come."

She stood, pushed herself up, her body on fire, blood dribbling down her back, the pain intense but not as intense as it should have been, already healing.

A gift for you, Siabala murmured.

The door opened. A small home, with a quaint kitchen, a table with two chairs, and a bed.

On it, her son, pale but content, sleeping like he used to when he'd played too hard during a good day.

Last chance, Siabala said. *I can keep you safe.*

A sob caught in her throat, and she didn't care. She was human. She was not a demon, even if one currently used her for his means. Grief bubbled inside her, and she turned it to anger. Hatred. To anything that would help her take hold of her sword.

You don't need to see this.

Avarielle didn't respond, fighting with all that she was, all that she had ever been, and all that she ever would be, knowing it wasn't enough, understanding that it was no reason to stop fighting.

"Rojon," she whispered, knowing it was too late, and there was nothing she could do or say. Would it be kinder to let him sleep through the blow? To not see his mother slip Graysword through his heart?

Please, she pleaded, willing to let go of pride for him. *You can have me. All of me. I'll stop fighting you. Just let him go.*

He used to wake up with nightmares when he was a

child, and she'd sooth them away as best she could, holding him, coddling him, singing to him. Eventually he'd fall asleep in her arms, and she'd fall asleep beside him in his bed.

He was so big, now. So tall. A man, no longer a boy. But he was still, and always would be, her little boy.

This is the price, oath breaker. Claim his life, so that your soul becomes mine.

She'd told Rojon, every time he had a nightmare, that he just needed to focus on the beauty around him. On her, and his grandfather. On their home, and the hearth. On the beautiful trees regrowing in Elihor, and their friends in town. On the vast expanse of the sea. And he'd hold her hand, look at her, and her heart would melt.

"You keep me safe, Mom."

Please, she begged. *Please don't.*

You can hide. I can keep you safe here. You won't feel a thing, hear a thing. You don't need to witness this, oath breaker. Kindness is not lost on me.

Avarielle's heart shed pieces of itself, chiseled by grief, but she stood firm, watched herself walk toward her beautiful sleeping boy, her handsome son, her greatest legacy and gift.

She would not hide. Not from this. Not like this. It would kill her, but in his death Avarielle found that she had little left to live for.

Just as Siabala knew she would.

She stayed silent, tears running down her face, her struggles useless against a god, hating the power that kept her trapped, her inability to change her own future, her helplessness.

Slowly, as though Siabala enjoyed the moment, her arm reached for Graysword, even its magic muted, as unable to understand what was about to happen as Avarielle.

Rojon opened his eyes, groggy. They grew wide quickly, and he pushed himself up, voice small and so lost as he said, "Mom?"

Avarielle felt herself slip, grief overtaking anger, and she sobbed.

"I'm sorry, Rojon. I love you so much."

Graysword found its mark.

<h1 style="text-align:center">4 2</h1>

Threads of peaceful dreams slipped away as Rojon pushed himself against the wall by his bed, looking up as his mother—or something that looked like his mother—walked toward him. She was bloody, and pale, dry and fresh blood on her chin, tears streaking down her face. Her left arm moved oddly, like it had been broken.

"I'm sorry, Rojon," her voice was hoarse, like all she could do was push it out. "I love you."

And Rojon knew that she'd lost. Siabala had won, and she'd lost the fight, and she'd come to claim his blood. Her hand trembled around Graysword's pommel, her eyes wide with a pain he'd never seen in her, not even when his grandfather had died.

Before he could do or say anything, the blade plunged in, straight through, and his mother screamed, a sound so broken and grief-ridden that it hurt almost as much as the blade strike. Elihor's magic exploded out of him, but he felt Graysword's magic greedily absorb it, into his mother, who still screamed.

She pulled the blade out, covered in his blood, hazel eyes wild with grief, her face now locked in a scream that didn't know how to escape, the blood absorbed into her blade… and slowly, Avarielle Grayloft lowered the blade.

Rojon slumped against the wall, feeling his life slipping away from him, fighting to keep his head up, to see his mother, to tell her it was okay, that he knew she loved him, and that he always would.

He tried to speak, only coughing up blood. Then his mother held him, soothed him, telling him he would be okay, pressing on the wound, swearing at the Elder to help him.

There was so much to tell her. So much he wanted to do, still. To experience as he grew old. The magic of Elihor had abandoned him, absorbed by Graysword, and he felt hollow.

Rojon Kolder, son of Grayloft and last descendant of Elihor, let his mother's embrace lull him to sleep and carry him to the Afterfate.

*Q*varielle felt the lifeforce leave her son's body, sensed the moment she held but an empty husk, her grief so strong her body could no longer contain it, leaving her hollowed out. Empty.

No anger. No grief. Nothing.

Just emptiness, like in her son's body.

"There, there," Tally said, rubbing her back as she would a child. Even that failed to ignite Avarielle's anger. The empty space left behind refused to be filled, demanded to remain hollow. What could fill her heart now that Rojon was gone?

She felt Siabala take control of her body again, and she didn't fight him, unwilling to or unable to. What did it matter? She'd killed her son. She'd fought so hard, and had failed. And now, with Elihor's blood claimed by Graysword, his claws were so deep within her that she couldn't feel the air on her skin. The pain of her back was gone.

Her body belonged to him. Her mind was still hers, but what use was a mind that had lost all hope? And her heart… that was broken. Into a thousand pieces, never to be put back together. She stood, numb, and felt Siabala's words slip from her mouth.

"One down, one to go."

Avarielle Grayloft settled into the hollow at her core, and let the magic teleport them away, not sure she could continue to fight, not sure she knew how to stand again after such a decisive blow. And not convinced any of it mattered anymore.

44

Cassara stood on the ramparts of her palace, looking across the dark kingdom, made darker by the cloudy night, and waited for dawn to break. Her guards stayed near, all those who had returned.

The day and much of the night had been spent mustering a city of thousands—from fortifications to people. Massir would forever bear the marks of her decisions.

She hoped Altessa slept. She hoped her people managed to get some sleep. The night would not be their enemy. Siabala would never attack at night. He would want her to witness the fall of her people.

Tock, tock, tock… the soft clicking of a staff, and the fact that her guards did not stop the incoming individual, told the queen who approached. Cassara's breath shuddered at her core as she looked beyond her kingdom, toward the Bloody Mountains, and the Rage beneath them.

"You're alone," she said, not needing to turn around to see Shirina. "Avarielle…"

"Siabala was too strong," Shirina whispered, coming to stand beside the queen. "I'm so sorry."

Cassara nodded, kept looking west. Avarielle loved her land, and her people. She wondered if, once Siabala was done here, he'd attack the West, just to destroy whatever remained of the warrior.

"There's more," Shirina whispered, voice grief-stricken, as though she couldn't quite believe what she was about to tell her friend. Cassara did not turn to face Shirina, unwilling to see the grief in the sorceress's eyes, unable to face it, lest it ignite her own and consume her.

"She… I think she got Rojon. I couldn't stop her. I couldn't… I couldn't…"

Cassara finally met the sorceress's face, tear-streaked and exhausted, broken.

He will break us all.

"I have no doubt that you did everything you could," Cassara whispered, unwilling to lose herself to the tides of grief that threatened to drown her. She could not, would not, allow herself the space for that. If she lived, she would grieve for Avarielle, and her son.

Shirina sought out the truth in her eyes. Cassara had never once seen the sorceress so uncertain.

"I need you, Shirina," she said softly. "I can't do this without you, all of you, here."

"I know," Shirina said. She took a deep breath, eyes hardening again. Cassara hated doing this to her friend.

She hated not just holding her and her grief. But there was no time.

"Avarielle will come here at first light, won't she?" Cassara asked.

Shirina nodded. "Yes. I assume they'll teleport here and make sure to keep you in check to watch your city crumble."

Cassara nodded. "The two most likely points of attack were from outside the walls, and also from the city beneath us. Siabala would want to see the walls fall, to show how he used Avarielle's knowledge, and from the city below, to show how he'd always been here."

"That makes sense," Shirina said. "You've prepared for both, I assume?"

"I have," Cassara said softly. "The only things I'm unclear on are: How do I stop Tally and Siabala from simply teleporting to me, and how do I get my magic for the final combat."

"I can take care of stopping the teleportation, thanks to a trick Tally kindly showed me," Shirina said. "As for reaching for your magic... I think I have an idea."

And then, in the eyes of the sorceress, she saw the same fierce determination that had inspired her time and time again, and knew that Shirina would not fail her this day. She would fight as hard as possible, just as she had for Rojon and Avarielle.

There would be time for heartbreak, if she survived.

"This will not be easy," Shirina whispered. "If I could, I would bring you to Edoline to do this."

"I will not leave my people now," Cassara said, though her heart tugged at her to hear the surf against the cliffs one more time, to hug her youngest children and feel their warmth and hear their laughter, to share jokes with her younger brother, to just… be.

"I know," Shirina said. "Come with me," she turned, and Cassara followed. They headed down the steep, narrow stone stairs, through the corridor, and into the east wing. The queen had never fallen in love with Massir as she had Edoline, but she had brought pieces of it with her, including the apple and cherry trees in the small courtyard which held the teleportation circle.

"To find your magic again," Shirina said, coming to a stop in the middle of the marred gardens, lit by moonlight. The green flames had damaged them, but there was beauty here, still. Trees cracked but not broken, pathways burned but not destroyed, flowers clinging despite the flames and frost. "You must reconnect with it, in the way you always have, Cassara. By playing your flute. By invoking the Traveler's Song."

"I haven't… I haven't played my flute in a long time, Shirina."

"That won't matter," Shirina said. "Listen, Rojon found a way to connect with his magic again, and I think it's because he worked so closely with the ground already. You used to wander your orchards and gardens as a princess, and that might explain why your magic was so powerful."

"I can't even see my magic, and haven't managed to

pull a single strand since Avarielle… since…" Cassara stopped. She'd hoped, willed it, tried to reach it, but to no avail. Even when threatened, she couldn't wield it. She feared that even Altessa being in danger wouldn't give her the emotional boost to unleash it. Lacking the time to philosophize her way to her magic, she'd focused on things she could change with tools that proved more reliable.

"It lies beneath the Bloody Mountains. I think it would come, if you could reach for it through the earth."

"A flute relies on air," Cassara said.

"Yes, but it always brought you closer to the land. To Edoline. It may help you connect to Massir."

"The music let me release my emotions, Shirina," Cassara said, facing the sorceress. "I would break if I embraced them. All of them."

"Maybe," Shirina admitted. "But you've always managed to rebuild yourself before."

The sorceress handed the queen her old flute, the blooms of Edoline etched on its side. She had not played in a long time, but she'd kept it, and oiled it, and ensured that, should she ever wish to play again, she could easily do so.

"Connect with the ground through your emotions, Cassara, and your magic will find you. I've no doubt."

Cassara looked at the flute, numb. Her mother had helped her carve it, before passing away. A last piece of Edoline, after all the others she'd lost.

"What if I can't, Shirina? What if I don't want to step

into all the emotions threatening to engulf me? What if I don't make my way back?"

Shirina placed a hand on Cassara's shoulder. Like Avarielle used to do.

Avarielle.

"You always find your way back, Cassara. You're too stubborn to have it any other way." She turned to the east. "Dawn is rising. I'll make sure they can't teleport in."

With a possibly unintended flourish of her black cloak, Shirina vanished back into the palace, leaving Cassara alone with memories, her past, and orders to walk into the fires that had once threatened to engulf her.

45

The sun would rise, soon. Tally probably needed to rest—her magic seemed to function more like the Circle's old magic, which brought interesting questions to Shirina's mind: why was Siabala's magic trapped in the air, instead of in the ground?

There was no time to parse that information, though Shirina truly wanted to know. Right now, she needed to focus on creating a similar spell-breaking barrier to the one Tally had erected around Kosel.

Rojon.

With time, she might have figured out how to break it, but…

She dropped the thought, unwilling to follow it through. To let failure crush her now would undo them all. With any luck, she'd live to see many more failures, and victories.

"Elder Quilsam," Shirina said, turning into the study

the old man had sequestered himself into. "I have need of your assistance." She'd tried to think of a different way to do this, any way that wouldn't require his assistance, but she'd found none.

Again, time was short and she had no time with which to be precious.

He looked at her suspiciously. Of course he would. Shirina sighed.

"I have no time to play any of the usual Elder games, so if you'll forgive my forthrightness, I need you to help me block Siabala's magic so he and Tally cannot simply teleport into Massir."

"You've already lost control of the Grayloft," Quilsam scoffed.

Shirina turned on her heel, faced him. Although taller than her, he visibly backed away from her anger. "I *never* controlled the Grayloft, and neither did you," Shirina practically spat, the numbness collapsing, exploding onto the Elder. "And Siabala only has her because of his dark magic. Now we need to stop him from claiming the blood of Graydon or his hold will be complete, and his return to this world will be unstoppable."

Even Elder robes wouldn't stop her from losing her temper. Avarielle would be proud of her, and the thought calmed her. She would not grieve her friend yet. She would live on her behalf.

And her son's.

Elder Quilsam paled at her words. "But... what of Rojon Kolder?"

Shirina wished she could have avoided this, for her sake and the Elder's.

"I am not certain, Elder," she said, the knot in her heart all the confirmation she needed. "But I believe he has fallen."

Elder Quilsam grew so white she feared he would faint.

"Elihor no longer has an heir."

"Elder, I understand your grief and share it, but—"

"How could you understand the loss? How could you possibly grasp the implications, you having just turned Elder…"

He sat down, his head dropped in distress. In defeat.

"Elder—"

"No. There is nothing left to fight for, Shirina. You have failed us by not killing Avarielle Grayloft."

"Rojon Kolder would have been Siabala, then. Is that a better fate?"

"Kryde Kolder should never have fallen for someone from Graydon. His grandfather's influence, undoubtedly."

"Oh, shut up," Shirina said, losing it. "You're so stuck in your ways that you're useless. Stay here and rot. I have a city to save."

Without waiting for his approval, or rebuttal, Shirina stepped out and headed back to the small orchard, where Cassara clutched her flute, staring out at her city.

Shirina gave her a wide berth and headed toward the teleportation circle. Scarred with scorch marks from the rebel attack, the flowers surrounding the circle linked her to all her other adepts, her carefully crafted teleportation plan destroyed by the new magic.

Yet all of them had been forged into earth, with flowers, linking her to the ground the magic now courted. To the land below. The scent of roses lingered in the air, but it was the roots that made it possible.

She dismissed Elder Quilsam's treacherous attitude and cleared her mind, kneeling on the old teleportation circle, which relied on a magic that no longer existed. Or, rather, that had changed beyond the scope of what it used to be.

Gently she placed her staff down before her, fingers on it, palms on the earth.

Dawn was breaking, light growing in the land. Siabala would come, soon, to claim Cassara, and force her to watch as he destroyed her city.

Just like he'd made Avarielle watch her own blade slide into her son.

Rojon.

She couldn't lose Altessa, too. Couldn't lose Cassara. But chances were that she would, and she made peace with even that as she focused on the blue whisp, settling gently on the staff between her hands.

"Can you help me?" she asked, voice raw. Tired. Afraid. "Can you help me reach everyone again? Except this time, help them find their way to me? I doubt many know how to teleport through the ground. It's not exactly instinctive."

The whisp rolled back and forth, and Shirina chose to

believe that meant yes. No, she didn't just believe it. She could feel it, like they were linked.

Shirina focused on the blue of the magic. On the lines of power in the ground, instead of Siabala's growing mists in the air. She looked to the earth. The roots. The cities that lurked beneath, with strange lights and stranger magic, and the conduits of power that allowed her to travel through the land.

Letting her mind expand to reach all the adepts, whether from Larkhold or Ravenhold. To reach anyone knowledgeable in magic, willing to come to battle, forgiven if not, but empowered to defend themselves, wherever they may be. They needed to come now, or she would block them. Possibly kill them with her spell, as Tally's had almost done to her.

The whisp's light grew, and Shirina found herself bowing toward it, resting her forehead on the blue light. It caressed her mind, warmed her soul, reached deep within her until she no longer felt her body, but tumbled into the earth, deep below.

And stepped into a city bathed in buttery light, music playing in the streets. Tanja sat at a table again, a drink before her, smiling in a way Shirina hadn't seen her do in life.

"I don't have time for this," Shirina cut to the chase. Tanja laughed, in a very non-Tanja way.

"You always have time for learning and growing, child. That is why you always end up here, with me."

"I need to contact them."

"Who?"

"The adepts."

"The Ravenhold adepts?"

"No, the ones… all of them. Whoever is left and willing to fight."

"You know that's not how things are done, Rina."

Rina. Only Rojon called her that.

"Don't call me that."

"You want to reach everyone who can wield the power?"

"Yes," she said, "anyone who can help should help."

"The Heir of Elihor should help."

Shirina felt physically slapped by her mentor's remark.

"The Heir of Elihor is dead."

The whisp appeared before her, landing on her shoulder, as though showing allegiance.

"Oh!" Tanja said, sounding genuinely surprised. Another thing the Elder had never done in life. "You've decided to attach yourself to Shirina? You could find more fun company."

The whisp shifted sideways, as though incensed.

"I'm plenty fun," Shirina said, then shook her head. "Why are we here talking about this? Let me go from this place to contact those with power."

"I am," Tanja said, rolling her eyes. Why was she acting so… *young?*

"What do you know of Rojon?" Shirina asked, then shook her head. "I need to get to Massir. To get help to stop Tally and Avarielle. Help me."

The whisp coddled closer, as though holding her. Tanja stared at the spell, then looked to the left of Shirina.

"Just look behind you, Rina."

"Don't call me tha—"

"Rina." The familiar voice behind her. Shirina turned, slowly, breath in her throat, to see Rojon standing behind her.

"Rojon," she took him in her arms, but he felt different. *Of course, this is all some sort of image. I'm still in Massir.*

"My mother killed me with Graysword."

Shirina grabbed both his arms, forcing him to stay grounded.

"But you're here," she said, looking around the city. To all the people dancing around. To Tanja, clapping along to a song. To Rojon... "This is the Afterfate," Shirina whispered. "But... how? This is the city under Graydon..."

"You don't quite understand yet," Tanja said, "but you will. Someday, should you survive Siabala's attack."

Shirina held Rojon, intent on dragging him back to his body if possible. "I won't leave without him," Shirina said. "I won't let him die."

"What if it were him or all of Graydon?"

"No," Shirina said. "That's a false choice, and an unfair one."

"It's the only choice."

"No. I won't choose one over the other. I'll save both."

"*You*'ll save both."

Shirina looked at her mentor, holding Rojon.

"Rina?" he asked, as though confused. Shirina pulled

on the Sight, the blue whisp floating up, following the lines of magic still tethering Rojon to his body. She looked up, and gasped.

She'd never once looked up during her visions with Tanja, and this wasn't like the city beneath the West. Fed by magic, what should have been a stone roof looked like a firmament of stars. Of magic conduits and power, of power lines and magic trails, in various shades, even more than the dark and white of Graydon and Elihor. Every color of the rainbow danced above her in a sky of life and light.

Blood in the water. Rainbows in the sky.

The blue whisp gently floated back down, and Shirina held out a palm to gently catch it, refusing to release Rojon.

"Rojon," Shirina said. "I think I can get you back in your body. It'll hurt, and I don't know if you'll remember any of this, but I can get you back." He looked at her, like a little boy lost, uncomprehending the harsh world around him.

"My mother stabbed me with Graysword."

"No, Rojon. That was Siabala. Do you really think your mother would do so if she had any control over her body? Think about her, Rojon. Think of your life with her. Of every gentle moment, even the difficult ones. Did you ever think that she would ever do anything to hurt you?"

He seemed to ponder it, and then reached the conclusion she knew he would.

"I'm not ready to go."

"He's a descendant of Elihor," Tanja said casually, "so is tethered in a way that few are. If his body can be saved, his soul can be, too. This would not be possible for the likes of you or me."

"Then who are you?" Shirina asked.

Tanja smiled and returned to watching the procession. That was definitely more typical.

"Do you feel your body?" Shirina asked Rojon softly.

"I don't think so. I'm pretty sure I'm dead."

The blue whisp shifted in Shirina's palm, moved to Rojon, and gently illuminated the lines of power.

"Bring him to safety," Shirina whispered, and the whisp cooed.

"I love you, Rojon," Shirina said as he started to fade, to turn the same color as those threads holding him, afraid she would never see him again. That this was her one chance to save him, a chance maybe born of dreams, and she'd just failed him.

"I love you, Rina," he said, a grin, that quick grin, a flash of those dark eyes, and he vanished.

"Everyone is tethered in this world, but certain lines are stronger than others, that's all."

Shirina softened her eyes, focused with the Sight, seeing the firmament of lights expand above her, dots of color. A sea of misty white stayed beneath the Bloody Mountains, still tethered to a glow in Massir. *Cassara.* She just needed to remember how to call her magic back to her.

Rojon's dark magic clung near him, but the veins of

power crisscrossed the land, as did Graydon's. And then there were other colors, every color of the rainbow… those, she'd have to figure out later.

The cloaks of the Circle. Every color of the Circle was represented. Was that coincidence, or…

No time.

The trickle of time started dancing around her again, as though a moment and an eternity had passed. Shirina reached out. She needed help in Massir.

She reached out to Shala in the West, opening up the lines of power. To her witches in Lisal Gardens. To the adepts of Larkhold, unwilling to leave any stone unturned. Anyone still standing, still able and willing to fight. And everyone hiding, too, in case they simply needed a call to battle.

The lines of power expanded. Grew brighter. And Shirina looked one last time at the light that was Rojon's soul, and hoped for the best as she turned to face her mentor.

Tanja smiled.

"Until next time, Elder," Tanja said, and Shirina found herself kneeling in the garden of Massir, disoriented.

The blue whisp was gone. She blinked, stood back up, holding on to her staff. She didn't feel like she'd been kneeling for very long, and the sky hadn't changed markedly.

"Shirina," Shala said, appearing beside her, Trevon in tow.

"That was unpleasant," the old Westland Warrior

mumbled. Other adepts appeared around them, cloaks of every color, robes both white and black, and Shirina felt hope. They were coming. They were figuring out their magic, moving quickly.

"Follow my lead," she said, and adepts from both Circles nodded, the ramparts of the castle filled with colored cloaks, prepared for the final battle.

Shirina embraced her fear, her sorrow, her heartache, her love, her hope, embraced all that she was and all that she would ever be, and summoned the magic to her.

And then, drifting from further in the garden, beyond a toppled cherry tree… the Traveler's Song. Cassara had found the courage to reach for her magic, too. Just like her adepts.

The sun rose.

A net of crisscrossing black and white magic greeted the first rays of sunshine over Massir. Altessa looked up to the palace, seeing cloaks of every color unfurl in the rising sun, wearing white and black robes.

The stench was almost unbearable here, Siabala's creatures gathered just outside the city. The guards had shot quite a few arrows, but their numbers seemed endless, and so they had stopped to conserve their strength overnight.

The guards had been deployed across the city, but now none remained on the wall, where they would be slaughtered. The city had never been this quiet. Usually, the sun was greeted by merchants setting up stalls. Standing on the main road to the palace, Altessa tried to calm her speeding heart as the city held its breath.

Citizens had taken refuge or arms, and everyone had been assigned a place to try to make the biggest impact.

Hopefully most would survive the day.

Ramelia stood by Altessa, and they waited. The princess gulped in deep breaths, numb as red light exploded in the sky above. A few gasps from nearby guards, and Ramelia's hand shot to her arm, gripping it.

"Not yet," Altessa whispered. "Not yet," she repeated, more to herself this time, her feet begging her to run to safety, and never look back.

But she had a task to do, had begged her mother to trust her to do it, and she refused to fail. They didn't have long to wait, as the red flames gathered near the main gates… and it was Altessa's turn to gasp. With over a hundred fake adepts and rebels stood Avarielle Grayloft.

Siabala.

Altessa knew it wasn't her, even from this distance. She stood stiffly, awkwardly, with none of her usual grace. Her features were slack, her eyes… her eyes were looking straight at her, and a dark grin twisted the warrior's face. Not the grin Altessa had learned to love, but a terrifying one belonging to the ancient demon.

Then the warrior released a war cry that echoed across the city and resonated deep in her bones. Creatures leapt forward, the net not stopping them, only able to stop the warrior and Siabala's red-robed adepts. Shirina had suspected this would happen, if they were not creatures filled with his magic but instead enslaved or mutated by it, and Altessa's part was to lure as many as she could. The bait Siabala couldn't resist.

"Let's go." Ramelia tugged on Altessa's arm, dragging her to the right, in an alleyway.

"That wasn't her," Altessa said, shaking her head as she ran, breath ragged. "That wasn't Avarielle."

"No it wasn't," Ramelia agreed. "But she's coming to kill you regardless."

Sounds of battle erupted around Massir, the earlier peace shattered with screams and clanking metal.

A creature, like a wolf with elongated legs and fangs, skirted the roofs over them and landed in the alleyway. Ramelia hurled green flames at it, and the wolf yelped back, scrambled away. Altessa dragged Ramelia into a solid stone home, slammed the door shut as they both headed to the back, throwing themselves outside and into the next house. Up the city they would go, from house to house if necessary, each an empty husk, until they'd found their mark.

By the third home they could hear more creatures skittering across the roofs, breaking houses apart, looking for their prey. They hadn't expected the creatures to move that fast, but they'd been cautious in their calculations and were already in the right home. Ramelia had practiced every exit and access point, to ensure she could keep the princess—the *bait*—safe.

Ramelia dragged her down into the basement, pushing her into the stone passage the Builders had helped solidify. They didn't have much time.

Either the monsters would get them, or they would fall by their own traps.

4 7

Cassara played the flute, but the music felt shallow. Hollow. She refused to give herself to the music, though she tried. She couldn't. Her heart felt made of stone, too tired and unwilling to take another hit.

She imagined her magic beneath the Bloody Mountains, and part of her could feel it, or so she imagined. But she refused to break to have it return to her. She needed to be whole to lead her people, and if her magic wanted to help… Cassara sighed, stopped playing.

She doubted lecturing the magic in her mind would be helpful. Besides, her daughter was out there, running for her life as creatures ran up the city. Cassara found she had no more breath with which to play the flute.

Her guards approached, Captain Garlon standing near. On the ramparts above her, guards stood at attention, including those waiting for orders, glancing at the currently empty flag mast above the highest remaining tower in the castle.

By the time the creatures were halfway up the city, Cassara returned to Shirina's side. The sorceress stood near Shala and Trevon. The old Westland warrior nodded in respect, and she returned the gesture. Mixed with the royal guards must have been about a hundred witches, all touching the stones of her palace, some dancing, some chanting, in the oddest casting of magic she'd ever witnessed, all to maintain the giant net around her city.

"I need to focus on what I can do, Shirina, not what I hope I can do."

The sorceress gave a slight nod, though she did not seem convinced.

"The creatures can still get through," Shirina said.

Cassara nodded. "We planned for that."

Shirina looked at her skeptically, the creatures scratching into homes, hundreds of them swarming over entire neighborhoods.

Cassara waited, wringing her hands behind her. This was the part of the plan she hated the most. She'd fought against it, but her stubborn daughter had been correct: They needed the right bait, and she was it. Siabala wanted her, and she would be faster than Cassara.

She'd particularly hated hearing that last part, but it made it no less true.

The third bell tower, higher in the city, away from the Tapestry—the noble quarters where her people hid— stood silent. Cassara waited for it to ring. Altessa had planned this with the Builders, and they were ready. All she had to do was ring the bell.

Please, Altessa.

Shirina stood silently beside her, waiting.

"Your Majesty," Captain Garlon said, bowing. "The creatures are in the city walls."

Cassara nodded, and focused back on the bell.

"Prepare the signal, Captain." The Captain looked to the tower, held up three fingers long enough to be spotted.

The creatures swarmed the city walls below, looking to destroy Cassara's people who had been meant to hide in there. Especially the Tranak Quarters, who had suffered so much during the last war. She'd spent more time on those walls, ensuring they were the strongest, and could contain the citizens safely. Siabala knew this because Avarielle had devised the plan. And so Cassara had followed the warrior's advice: she'd done the unexpected.

Or would, shortly.

Shirina glanced at Cassara, but held her peace.

The creatures tore down roofs and walls, claws dreadfully sharp, growling, the stench unbearable even from this distance.

Another deep, rot-filled breath.

And the bells rang, clear and perfect.

"Now, Captain," Cassara said.

A silver flag went up the flag post. The bells signaled for the houses. The flag for the walls.

The Builders received both messages almost instantaneously, and the city shook as its foundations were undone, calculated blasts from under and above the city grounds collapsing entire sections, smoke billowing up as the Tranak Quarters crumbled below, taking creatures and monsters with it and forming a kind of moat.

She's sacrificed the places she'd swore she'd never hurt. Had destroyed the walls she'd spent two decades erecting. Massir would never be the same again.

And, as she waited for the smoke to clear so she could witness the carnage she'd inflicted on her city, she just hoped that it would buy them enough time.

4 8

old. Siabala rumbled in her mind. *Your little queen is bolder than you'd have believed her to be.*

Avarielle managed to rouse herself from her grief enough to see the damage done to Massir—damage that *Cassara,* sweet, gentle, caring Cassara, had inflicted on the city she'd vowed to protect.

The princess of Edoline had come a long way, and Avarielle couldn't help but be impressed. Altessa had been the bait for the monsters, which Avarielle would have never guessed Cassara would allow.

And then, she'd destroyed the northernmost parts of her walls, and the Tranak Quarters, plus two wealthier neighborhoods above.

Cassara isn't willing to play your games, Siabala, Avarielle said with some fire. Cassara hadn't given up, and Avarielle did her son's memory injustice by giving up, too.

I look forward to killing her, Siabala said. Avarielle

ignored him and tried not to think of what other surprises Cassara might have in store. Not to mention Shirina, with her magical net that Tally still mumbled about, working on a counterspell with her useless adepts.

Avarielle needed to fight him, still. She was under siege from Siabala, as was Cassara in Massir.

Maybe she could take inspiration from the queen and blast a few walls in her mind, too.

49

Shirina allowed herself a breath before a scream from below alerted her of another incoming attack. Looking at the destruction below, at Cassara's calm, lethal calculations, the sorceress had no doubt Avarielle would be proud of her ward.

"They're in the city beneath!" A sergeant ran to inform his queen. Cassara nodded, turned to Captain Garlon, his gray eyes focused and unafraid.

"The crimson flag, please."

The captain nodded and quickly brought the flag up, indicating to someone below what to do. The city rumbled again, and purple smoke drifted up the cracks in the city.

"Poison," Cassara offered. "I'm assured by the apothecaries that it'll work on even the most foul of demons."

Cassara actually smiled at Shirina's concerned look. "It will dissipate too quickly in the air. The only reason it'll work is because they're underground, where it can remain concentrated for longer."

"I guess we're lucky Siabala's army isn't human, then," Shirina said.

"It never is." Cassara crossed her arms, waited.

The bell rang three times, and Cassara nodded.

"That did it. How long can your net hold?" Cassara asked.

"I'm not certain," Shirina replied, "but I stole the trick from Tally, so I'm sure she'll find a way through faster than I'd like her to."

Cassara squeezed her arm, then whispered so only she could hear. "Please get Shala to take Altessa out of here, if you can spare her."

"Where is she?" Shirina asked.

"She'll be in Lord Rushil's home, by now."

Shirina turned to Shala, her mentee's dark eyes focused and unrelenting, and quickly shared Cassara's request. Trevon listened in, and Shirina saw no reason not to trust the seasoned warrior.

"I take it she's not expecting this exit?" her second said.

"I would assume not," Shirina said.

"I'll come along then," Trevon offered to Shala.

"That would be good," Shala answered, then looked with worry at Shirina. "What about the queen?"

"I'll stay here," Shirina said. "If Siabala gets either of them, we're all dead, regardless."

"We would not be if you'd protected the Heir of Elihor," Elder Quilsam said, joining them. He looked twenty years older, but Shirina found that she had no pity to give him.

"You can help or leave, Elder," she said, with little fire.

He narrowed his eyes, then turned to look at his adepts, working with Ravenhold's witches, maintaining the net over the city that stopped Siabala's magic, if not his creatures. He looked at Shirina with wonder, almost as though seeing her for the first time, and tipped his head.

Then he went to join them. Shirina turned to Shala.

"Get as far as you can with Altessa," Shirina kept talking, stopping the objection about to slip from her pupil's lips. "There is no victory with her death, Shala. I know you want to stay and fight, but right now, I need you to protect her. To protect all of Graydon."

And to rebuild the Circle, should I fall.

Shala visibly struggled with all the ways she wanted to tell Shirina off, but managed to simply nod.

"Be safe, Shala." Shala gathered Shirina in her arms and hugged her fiercely, then headed for the stairs. Trevon winked at Shirina.

"I'll keep her safe," he said. Then, more somberly, "If you can save Avarielle, one way or another…"

"I'll do everything I can," she promised.

"I know."

And he was gone, along with Shala, running to the destroyed city below, as they awaited the next wave of the attack.

Cassara met her eyes, and in them, Shirina saw the same hopelessness she felt. With only one wave of the attack, a quarter of Massir was gone.

And they hadn't even faced Siabala yet.

"I should be out there," Altessa said, sitting near a mostly boarded up window. The noble's quarters had built their own walls, turning their homes into fortresses, more so than the palace. "My mother is still out there, and my father."

"Which is why you need to stay safe," Ramelia said, then shrugged. "I mean, aren't you supposed to lead us to victory if they die?"

"I doubt that'll be the case," Altessa said, imagining the destruction of her city.

"You're right," Ramelia said. "Who'd follow you anyway?"

Altessa snapped at attention, shocked and insulted, to be faced with a playful grin.

"Welcome back to the here and now, Princess," she said, lowering her head as though in respect.

"I was just—"

"You were bemoaning what can't be changed," Ramelia said. "And there's something very important you can do here."

Altessa raised an eyebrow.

"Your people," Ramelia said, not even sounding sarcastic, which surprised Altessa. "They need a leader to look up to. And that leader is you."

"I thought no one would follow me?" Her eyebrow stayed arched.

Instead of a jest, Ramelia grew serious. The unexpected turn of emotion took Altessa by surprise, as did the rebel's next words. "I would."

She took both of Altessa's hands in her own, gently held them.

"The purple smoke is rising!" someone cried.

"I thought we'd have more time," Altessa whispered, looking into Ramelia's eyes. "But I know something else I can do, for me."

Before Ramelia could ask, Altessa leaned in, and kissed her, first gently, then fiercely. The rebel returned the kiss, a moment in time, a blaze seared in their memories.

"I would give everything for more time with you," Ramelia said, breathless.

"We will have our time, even if only in the Afterfate," Altessa answered, kissing her gently again.

Then she stood, centered herself, and headed to calm her people, a feat that would prove difficult as the hammering of her heart threatened to break her ribcage, because of the kiss, and the chance that she'd never know another.

Tally had had enough. She needed to take down the blasted net keeping her master at bay. The adepts had performed brilliantly, but tearing them down would prove easy enough, and a pleasure. One woman had united them, and it was long due for that annoying woman to die.

"I'll take the pleasure of killing that pest Shirina myself, if Lord Siabala allows," Tally said.

"Bathe in her blood," the hiss came out of the warrior's mouth, Avarielle's hands trembling at her sides. Tally frowned. She had expected the hold on her to be more solid by now, but the warrior's stubbornness was legendary. One of the many reasons her master favored her so.

"I will claim your magic again once it is safe to do so," Tally said. She centered herself and released the red magic, though it pained her. Her neck felt stiffer where stone covered it, and her bones more brittle without her master's gift. She summoned the green flames to reinforce herself, though this magic proved more fickle than her master's. But if her master's magic could not cross the blasted net, than she would even give that up to smooth his path to victory.

She had sacrificed too much to be stopped by one insolent witch.

"Yours will be an honored place at my side," Lord Siabala spoke through the Grayloft. He understood her sacrifice. She bowed to him.

"Thank you, my lord."

"Fall in a hole," the warrior answered, and Tally did not acknowledge her. Did her master allow her to speak such ill things to his loyal follower, or did the warrior still retain some measure of autonomy? The magic of Elihor which had flowed into her blade should have been enough to strengthen Siabala's soul.

No matter. Graydon's magic would seal the deal, and she wouldn't have to put up with the annoying warrior anymore.

Slowly, Tally walked through the net, the buzzing not hurting her thanks to her giving up her master's gifts.

It would be good to finally bring this sordid tale of humanity trying too hard for too little to an end. As Avarielle had killed her son, so would she kill the last remaining Elder of Ravenhold, and sever all ties to the old, treacherous covenant.

5 2

Crimson Circle Elite Klerisse had heard Shirina's message. She'd spent days of healing in Kosel, after trying to help Avarielle Grayloft save her son from treacherous Elders from her own coven, but she managed to rouse herself, throw on her black robe and crimson cloak, and head into the breaking day to do her duty: save Rojon Kolder.

She was an adept of Larkhold and, even though some of the Elders had lost their way, she had not.

The pines of Kosel sang urgently in the wind as she followed the trail of Elihor's magic, using the Sight. It spread beneath her in great waves and, even though she could not touch the magic of Elihor in the ground, she could sense its intent, its desire for her to follow. She did so, unquestioningly, as quickly as she could, to a door in a tree.

She let her eyes adjust to the darkness inside and gasped at what she saw.

Rojon Kolder, covered in blood.

Obviously dead.

She took a deep, shuddering breath, and focused her eyes. Around him, Elihor's magic still lingered. *His soul.* He hadn't left, yet, clinging to this life even as his body stopped breathing. A blue whisp of magic sat on his chest, as though tethering him in place.

"Hang on, Rojon," Klerisse went to him, uncertain what to do. Shirina had said the magic was in the ground. She could see it in the tree home, too, staying near Rojon, who was well known for his work with plants.

"Please don't go," she pushed on the wound at the core of the last descendant of Elihor, but it was too late. The heart no longer beat. But the blood dribbled, and the body still held warmth. He hadn't been gone for long.

Klerisse struck the ground. Kicked it. She could see the magic, but not feel it.

In despair, she dragged Rojon off his bed, covered in his blood, and placed him on the floor, the ground carved from the tree trunk, magic gathering beneath him. It reached out, but seemed unable to re-enter.

She needed to heal his body, first.

Healing had never been Klerisse's greatest strength, and she'd never given herself the space to heal, either. She'd been hurt, emotionally and physically, and still… she pressed her hands against the wound, closed her eyes, reached down to the earth with the ache of her heart.

Shirina had said they needed to make allies of this magic. Klerisse wished the Ravenhold witch had been clearer, and tried the only thing she could: talked to it.

"I don't know how to do this," she said, "but I'm willing to learn if you'll trust me. Please let me help him. He's important to me. To my people."

Klerisse kept her eyes closed and pushed down, feeling nothing except the body of Rojon Kolder beneath her hands... and then a heartbeat. And another. She opened her eyes, certain she'd just imagined it.

"Rojon," she croaked, feeling surprisingly awake for having used so much magic.

Her breath caught in her throat as the dark magic of Elihor floated in the ground toward him. First, a trickle. Then more, a wave of the purest magic, of Elihor's own powers, back toward him, nesting inside the last son of Elihor.

Rojon took a deep breath. The blue whisp bounced, and vanished.

And he opened his eyes.

*a*varielle felt Siabala's grip weaken, though he tried to claw onto her. The crushing weight she'd felt since Rojon's magic had crawled up Graysword had lessened.

Your son is dead, Siabala said, and she heard it, in his voice.

Uncertainty. Fear, even.

But I'm not, she answered, and managed to move her arm to Graysword's pommel, calling her magic forth, forcing Siabala back into the tattered remains of her arm.

You cannot defeat me.

Avarielle gritted her teeth, managed to take a step forward. None of Tally's adepts questioned her. Why would they? She was their lord and master. The net buzzed before her, not unlike the Wall of Loss used to.

Dark and white strands of magic formed a strong

weave tethered comfortably in the ground. Tally had released Siabala's powers to enter.

You will perish and I will grow stronger, he said, but she called his bluff.

I don't believe you. You have nowhere to go but wait for me.

I will find your son.

I thought he was dead? She allowed herself to hope.

He was. That seems to have changed. He sounded amused. *Perhaps I would appreciate his body more.*

You and I are linked, Siabala, Avarielle took another step. *He never took an oath with you.*

Siabala growled his next words. *If you die, he will become mine.*

"Do you really think," Avarielle managed to gasp out, "that I'm that easy to kill?"

Her core rumbled with Siabala's laughter.

You are worth the hunt, he said, and she pushed through, reaching the net.

Energy pulsed in her as the net fought the magic inside her. She almost toppled to her knees, but forced herself to keep moving forward. To cross the entirety of the net. To live.

Siabala tried to hold on to her, clawing and scratching within her, trying to find purchase in the magical cracks of her bones.

Rojon was still alive. She didn't know how, and she didn't care. His magic had left her body, returning to his. With his life, he had given her a fighting chance.

A reason to fight. To live.

She screamed at the pain, like fire ants devouring her skin, and then she stood on the other side, breathing hard and shaking. The net buzzed around her, but her mind was quiet.

Siabala was gone.

He would wait for her. She wasn't free, yet. She might never be.

But, for now, sword in hand, Avarielle ran like the wind up the city of Massir, her body feeling strong and swift beneath her, Graysword singing with pure magic.

I am not a product of Siabala. I am a proud daughter of the West, a warrior, a friend, a mother.

With a smile on her face, she ran, feeling for the first time in days that she could actually make a difference.

And that Graysword's blade would only be covered in the *right* blood.

5 4

*B*ells sounded to the south, and Shirina turned to Cassara.

"Attack on that wall," the queen said.

"Will you destroy more of your city?" Shirina asked.

"I would if I could, but I figured Avarielle would be coming from the Tranak Quarters, so we focused our limited time there."

"How did you know?" Shirina asked, following the queen to look over the southern portion of the city, a less populated area with more guilds and manufacturing halls.

"Because I swore I'd never let them suffer again," Cassara whispered.

"It seems you know Avarielle as well as you feared she knew you," Shirina said. The queen looked surprised. "Surely that's no revelation?"

"I guess I'd never thought of it," Cassara shrugged.

"You underestimate yourself, Your Majesty."

"I doubt that," she said. "My magic still won't come, Shirina."

"Perhaps it's more trapped than I believed," Shirina said, though she wasn't convinced.

"Perhaps I'm more broken than you believed," Cassara answered.

"Perhaps," Shirina answered. "But I don't think that part matters."

The blue whisp appeared near Shirina, tumbling onto her shoulder and bouncing.

"Is Rojon… ?" The whisp purred, gently moved to her cheek, like a kiss, and then settled on the end of her staff.

"Is Rojon what?" Cassara asked.

"I think… I don't think he's dead, Cassara."

The queen's eyes widened, and it took a second for Shirina to realize she was looking past her.

Shirina whipped around, to where Tally stood, neck crooked, face a mask of hatred.

"How did you cross my shields?" Shirina asked, then she understood. "You gave up Siabala's magic. How noble of you."

"I came with a deal," Tally said.

Captain Garlon and three guards rushed the Elder and, before Cassara could warn them, or Shirina raise a shield, the Elder threw green flames into them. Their weapons clattered to the ground, piles of burnt bones beside them.

Cassara sucked in a breath, and Shirina stepped before her. How had she gotten this powerful? With the Sight,

Shirina looked at the Elder. Her strands of magic danced across the city, linking her to… to… to everyone.

"What did you do?" Shirina asked, then gasped as Tally pulled on the strings linking her to her stomach.

"My Circle made sure the city still had water when your *Circle* failed, Shirina. Pure and fresh, and enjoyed by all."

She'd poisoned the well with magic linked to every lifeforce here, giving her access to them all. Tally pulled again, and Shirina crumpled to her knees, spitting up blood. Her death would be distressingly quick.

"Stop," Cassara said, and Tally twisted her fingers. Cassara cried out. The queen was infected, too. Could that be what kept her magic out of her?

Shirina tried to focus. The strands closer to her were strongest. She might be linked to everyone in the city, but she had to be closer to effectively use it.

Shirina held her staff more tightly, the blue whisp bright, and started casting a teleportation spell to get her and Cassara out of there.

"Oh no you don't," Tally's face turned into a maniacal smile, and Shirina felt like she'd been cut in two. She fell to the cold stone of the palace, unable to grab the staff right before her, the blue whisp sitting on her as though trying to heal her.

Tally would kill her, so easily that it angered Shirina.

"Don't hurt her," Cassara said, kneeling by Shirina, the queen's eyes impossibly wide.

"Run," she managed to gurgle, but knew Cassara wouldn't. *Please run.*

The blue whisp sensed her intention and hopped on Cassara, as though trying to get the queen to leave while she still could.

"Don't worry, I'll make it quick, and then show the adepts their dead Elder. That should stop this little net from existing, don't you think?"

Tally twisted her wrist again and Shirina cried out.

Then the air echoed with a familiar battle cry.

Strength and grace fueled each of her movements, and she felt more like herself than she had in a long time. Her mission was clear: to save her friends. Her life didn't matter. Her soul didn't matter. That Siabala would claim her again didn't even matter.

Rojon still lived. She was free.

Shirina and Cassara would live, because she refused to let them die.

Graysword sang in her hand, and that blasted, annoying Elder had been so busy torturing Shirina that she hadn't seen her coming.

This moment, this *one* moment, was perfect. And she intended to bask in it.

Her sword cut through the Elder like butter, eviscerating the annoying woman, red robes covered in her own gore.

"I'm tired of you," Avarielle said, using the momentum

of her landing to turn and cleave the woman's head off. Only to meet resistance, where stone held.

"I'm not so easy to kill," the Elder hissed, and Avarielle grimaced.

"She's pulling magic from everyone who drank water," Cassara said.

Avarielle turned to Cassara, the queen's eyes covered in tears. The warrior held out her hand, and Cassara took it.

"I'm proud of you," she said, voice rough. Cassara nodded and swallowed hard, screams erupting from the city below.

There would never be enough time in this life, she thought as she released Cassara's hand.

"Heal Shirina and get her back in the battle," Avarielle said. "I don't deal with magic, and I really want Tally dead."

"I don't have my magic," Cassara said, sounding frustrated.

A green shield erupted around Tally, keeping Avarielle at bay. Shirina looked rough, but the blue whisp healed her and the sorceress managed to push herself up.

"It's not magic," Shirina told Cassara, as though being almost eviscerated herself gave her special knowledge. "It's a soul."

Cassara looked at the sorceress, at first with disbelief, and then horror.

"I hurt it. The magic. When I brought up the Wall of Loss again, it… it screamed…"

"And it hurt you," Shirina said. "It's like you two just need to say sorry to each other."

Cassara looked to the blue ball, held her hand toward it. It leaped in it, turning Cassara's eyes a deeper blue.

"So, it's like Siabala's soul in me?" Avarielle asked, not liking the sound of that.

"Yes, and no," Shirina said. "This one can't take over Cassara, but it's linked to you through your blood and can be your best ally. I'm sorry it took me so long to realize it. I'm not sure whose soul, or even how human it still is… I suspect it may be the soul of Graydon himself, Cassara. And Rojon's is Elihor's. That would explain why they're so powerful, filled with the magic of gods. I may be wrong, but either way, you need to meet your magic on even ground, and ask for its help."

"I…" Cassara looked toward the green flames, and the dead guards. To the long, slithering creatures invading her city to the south. And she nodded. "I'll try." She closed her eyes.

"So, will this be quick, or are we all going to die?" Avarielle whispered to Shirina as she helped the sorceress up.

"I don't know," Shirina said. "But I know Tally is about to hurt me a whole lot more."

"She wants you dead, for keeping Siabala at bay."

"You crossed the net," Shirina whispered. "I thought it might be possible, hoped, but…"

"Siabala will still come for me," Avarielle said. Shirina's face twisted with grief, then her eyes widened.

"Rojon!"

"He's fine, now," Avarielle said softly. "Siabala wants me, so he won't seek Rojon. Now, how do we kill the annoying Elder before she kills everyone here and Siabala strolls back into my body?"

"We need to stop her pulling on everyone's lifeforce."

"Great," Avarielle said. "How do we do that, exactly?"

Shirina shrugged, a slight smile on her lips.

"I'll work on it. You work on taking the whole head off."

Avarielle grinned at Shirina. "Deal."

The warrior looked to Cassara, willing her to move faster, to reconnect with her magic and, maybe, to even find a way to save her.

No matter what, Avarielle was glad she could be here, to make one final stand with Cassara and Shirina.

If this was to be her last battle, she could think of no one better to fight it with.

5 6

Shala pounded the doors open with her magic. Trevon slipped in first, sword held before him. He stopped.

"What in Eli's shadows is this?"

Everyone in the room writhed, like vices twisted their insides, or horses ran over them. Most were unconscious. Others were bleeding so badly Shala doubted they could be saved.

"Some sort of spell," Shala squinted, focused on the bodies heaped on the floor. No time. They had not time to save them. "I'm not sure. I need to find Altessa and get her out. Now."

Trevon nodded, walking over a dead noble with a cane studded with emeralds.

"Here," he said, spotting the daughter of Queen Cassara. Shala rushed to her side. Her hand was gripped with that of the rebel from what felt like a lifetime ago.

"Help her," the rebel managed to croak out, spitting blood.

"We can't just abandon these people," Trevon hissed. "They're dying."

"I can only teleport a few out of here, and must wait for the net to be down, first."

"What if we ran?" he said. "I can carry the princess easily enough."

Shala looked at the princess's hand, clutching that of the rebel.

"Don't," Altessa managed to say. "I'll not leave."

Looking around, Shala saw that those closest to the palace were in worst shape. Whatever drained them was happening there. Fighting against her instincts to run back toward her mentor, Shala nodded to Trevon.

"Take her. We need to get further away from the palace. As soon as we can, I'll teleport."

Trevon nodded and gently picked up the princess who clutched the rebel, weak sobs wracking her wounded body.

"I'm sorry," Shala told the rebel. She might have been able to carry her, but she needed to be ready to use her magic, especially since Trevon carried Altessa. Saving her meant risking Altessa's life.

The rebel gave her a weak smile, then scrunched her eyes shut and moaned. Fighting against her instincts, her deep desire to help, Shala ran after Trevon, to get further away from the palace and hope Shirina would yet find a way to save Massir's quickly dwindling population. She could see them, the green threads of magic woven, tethered to everyone, not just robbing them of life and strength, but telling the monsters exactly where to go.

"Faster," Trevon whispered, as the ground trembled with incoming monsters.

They couldn't save Massir, but perhaps they could at least save its heir.

Between Shirina's own magic and the blue whisp, the sorceress managed to stand, though her midsection felt somewhat scissored. Not as much as Tally, the woman eviscerated, visible through the green shield. Pulling on green magic, she was healing quickly.

Much too quickly.

And that wasn't her only worry. The threads revealed the Builders and guards hiding in the city, ready to spring traps. And they revealed Massir's population's hiding places: In the guild halls, the palace cellars, and the Tapestry.

The monsters converged toward them. Cassara's people would be slaughtered.

She turned to Avarielle with the Sight. A slight trail of red led beyond the net. Siabala's anchor into her arm. No, not just her arm, her entire soul.

"How did you stop Siabala's magic, after escaping the cottage?" Avarielle asked, almost conversationally, though her voice held an edge. "Tally was pretty annoyed with you for stopping us from just teleporting here. What did you do?"

"I absorbed as much magic as I could into the staff Ravenhold had gifted me and turned it to stone. Tally couldn't teleport right away as the magic had to reform across Massir, the trapped magic failing to escape..." Shirina narrowed her eyes at her. The warrior could be predictable, especially with her annoying need to save others. "No. We'll find another way."

"And if we don't?" Avarielle said. Tally's shields were dimming, the Elder's eyes opened, smiling at them. "Eli, I hate that face. If things get desperate, just do what you have to do. All of his soul is in me, remember? You can trap his magic in me. Stop him. So don't hesitate, Shirina."

Before Shirina could promise ridiculous things, Tally sent a spell rippling toward Shirina. Avarielle intercepted it, caught it on Graysword, then attacked the Elder.

Flying monsters, much like the ones from the Lisal Gardens, dive-bombed her witches on the palace rampart, a tumbling of feathers and colored cloaks, a terrifying crunching of bones. Guards with spears and arrows tried to defend them, but the monsters were powerful...

"Keep Cassara safe!" Avarielle said, forcing Shirina back to *this* battle. The warrior twisted to cut the Elder, this time in the arm. But even Graysword's magic could not cause her body to break, strings of muscle and sinew reattaching as Tally doubled her magical attacks.

Shirina struck the staff down and erected a protective barrier, and then she understood why Tally was having so much fun. The net above them began to weaken as her adepts were slaughtered.

Soon, Siabala would enter Massir, and then it would fall.

Shirina turned to Cassara, the queen frozen in place, surrounded by battle and slaughter.

"Hurry, Cassara," Shirina whispered. "Hurry, or there will be nothing left to save."

5 8

Cassara did not reach out to her magic this time, nor try to beckon it to come to her. Instead, she let herself drift toward it, toward the Bloody Mountains, which she'd avoided for twenty years. Toward the light she could see in the distance, beautiful, bright. Hiding. Her body felt ephemeral, nonexistent, though she could still smell the rot of Siabala's encroaching armies and knew her body still stood in her palace, and that her life, and all she held dear, was in grave danger.

Warmth coated her as she approached, so familiar and inviting.

"Why are you not joining me?" she asked the light. "We were powerful together. We could be again."

A man, or an outline of a man, appeared before her. *Graydon.* Sort of. He had died a thousand years ago, if this was him, and only a dim resemblance of his humanity remained. She could see some of his features, but most were blurred, as if in a dream.

"You left me," he said, voice breaking. "You left me alone, with only a monster."

Cassara hadn't expected the accusation, and it took her a moment to gather a reply. "You'd held him before, had you not? Or a piece of you had, anyway."

"With Elihor. Not alone."

She'd hurt her magic, not just abandoned it.

"I didn't want to leave you," she whispered. "I just—"

"You *left* me."

"I know, but—"

"Why didn't you come back?"

He wouldn't let her speak, her people were falling, her family could be dying, and Cassara snapped. "I did what I had to do! I didn't want to leave you!" The magic waited, the man, the apparition. "I would have stayed with you, if Shirina had not come to get me," she whispered. "I was ready to give up my life to hold Siabala."

The magic rippled. The man's features became more set, chiseled. They reminded Cassara of her older sister's cheeks. His eyes, of her mother's.

Still, he did not speak.

"You were holding Siabala!" She grew impatient, and the magic sensed it.

"You left me!" He seemed hurt again, like a child. And she realized he was, partly. A child. A warrior. A hero. A great sorcerer. A martyr. All of him was wrapped in his soul, filled with magic and pain.

"You were going to die and never come back for me!" he spat out, angry, hurt, features losing definition. There could be no reasoning with him, could there? Not while he acted like this.

"Why are you acting so helpless!" she said, annoyed. "You are powerful! Why can't you see that?"

"Why can't you?" the magic asked, an echo of her own thoughts.

We are not helpless. We've never been.

"I'm tired of this," Cassara whispered, cupping his cheek with her hand, feeling the magic, *her* magic, rippling into her. "We can end this together."

"You will not be able to save them all."

"Then help me save as many as I can."

"You gave me purpose," he said, "after centuries of quiet solitude. I've been waiting here for you to give me purpose again, Queen Cassara."

In his eyes, she saw him then. The hero. The warrior.

The legend.

His features grew crisp and he wore armor, now, and a black cloak of the Circle. A different time, a familiar circle above his heart.

"Graydon," she said.

He shook his head. "No, and yes. I am more and less than what he was. But I will fight with you once again, if you'll have me."

She held out her hand. He smiled, took the offered hand, and Cassara's eyes flew open and she unleashed her magic, tears running down her face, unchecked, letting

Graydon's powers wash out of her, letting him become part of her once more.

She was powerful, as was he.

And hopefully they weren't too late to save the land named after him.

5 9

Cassara's magic pounded out of her, slamming into the Elder and severing the green ties of magic holding Massir's people captive. Her magic covered the palace, the city, the sky, exploding outward to the borders of Massir, killing all of Siabala's summoned creatures. A power long waiting to be unleashed finally free.

"Now, Avarielle!" Shirina cried out.

The warrior didn't need further encouragement, Graysword cutting from shoulder to hip, avoiding the stone in the neck, and cleaving the Elder in two.

"Finally!" the warrior exclaimed, cleaning her blade on the Elder's cloak before sheathing it again. She looked to Shirina. "Wait, is she actually dead? Should I decapitate her more?"

"She's dead," Shirina said, but set the Elder on fire, just

in case. Avarielle nodded her approval, crossed her arms, her left one seeming stiff.

Shirina looked to it, where Siabala's powers grew. She glanced at the net, weakening as the remaining adepts weakened. The only reason it had held so long was because of Elder Quilsam.

The queen stood, eyes a deep blue, looking toward Avarielle with grief.

"The net is failing."

"I can maybe create one around you," Shirina said, "to keep him out of…" she stopped, knowing it wouldn't work. Siabala would be free, even if not in Avarielle, and they needed him contained.

"The Wall of Loss?" Shirina turned to Cassara, who shook her head.

"I can't. The magic was hurt badly, and I don't think it'll allow me to." The queen looked at Avarielle, eyes wide with pain, voice a whisper almost lost in the clanking of flags turning on poles. "I'm so sorry, Avarielle."

The sky crackled, and the magical net evaporated.

"Thank you," Avarielle said, hugging Cassara fiercely. "For never giving up."

Cassara hugged her back, tears streaming down her face.

"I feel like I'm giving up on you now," she whispered.

"Accepting what you can't change is hardly giving up," Avarielle said as the sorceress struggled to find a solution. She'd tried everything, and her supposedly vast Elder knowledge proved useless.

"There has to be something—" Shirina never finished the thought. Several adepts teleported around them, and Siabala's blood-red soul swirled possessively around the warrior, its power so bright it stung Shirina's eyes.

Cassara called on her magic, forming a dome of light around them, keeping the adepts at bay, but trapping Siabala's soul with them. The monster who would take over Avarielle once again, who couldn't be killed, and that Shirina had run out of ideas to stop.

All save for one. To trap him the same way she'd trapped the magic in her staff.

Except, this time, Avarielle would be the one turned to stone.

She looked to the warrior to explain it to her, but could see that she understood. She'd already pieced it together, and now she waited, knowing Shirina would do what needed to be done, no matter how much it might hurt her.

Because her role was protecting Graydon and Elihor, and its magic, even at the cost of her own heart.

60

*A*varielle focused on Shirina, on the sorceress's resigned eyes. She thought of Rojon, and felt better knowing the sorceress would be there for him. That her son, her little boy, would have her to help him heal the scars of his body and soul. That he would still have family. *Her* family. Cassara and Shirina. Those who stood with her, again and again, no matter what.

"Promise me you'll stay in his life, Shirina. Help guide him, and make sure his magic doesn't destroy him."

"I will," Shirina said, "but there has to be another way…"

"Stop," Avarielle turned to her, the warrior's eyes hard. "You know there isn't, Shirina. Not one we can find in time. I can contain Siabala's magic. Let me do this while I still can."

She felt Siabala settling into her, his soul fighting for control. Her hands ached around the pommel of

Graysword, pumping magic into herself, gritting her teeth.

"And just leave you as stone? Avarielle, you're asking a lot of me."

"What happened to the Circle witch who would do anything to protect Ravenhold?"

"She became wiser," Shirina said, "and learned that some things weren't worth fighting for." Her voice lowered. "While others are."

"And you will fight for them," Avarielle said with a smile. "You always do."

Pain lanced her side, her mind clouding as Siabala fought against her.

Not this time.

"Shirina," she croaked out. The sorceress's eyes wide as Avarielle fell to her knees. Shirina collapsed beside her.

"Avarielle..."

"I know," Avarielle said, and smiled at her. "You won't get rid of me that easily."

She looked at Cassara. "Save Dayshon, Cassara. I know you can."

The queen bit her lip, nodded, then took the warrior's extended hand, pulled her up. Shirina stood and helped steady her. Avarielle felt the strength of her legs beneath her. The strength of her heart within her. Her grip on Graysword, as she called the magic to her. What little was left, but still so much.

"I wish I could say goodbye to Rojon," she whispered. "To let him know—"

"Let me do this one thing for you, then," Shirina said, not taking no for an answer, slight fingers reaching for Avarielle's head.

Rojon, she heard the sorceress's words in her mind. *It's Shirina. We don't have much time. Your mother is here.*

A few moments passed, the battlefield raging around them.

Rina? Mom? came the muffled reply. He sounded out of breath, like he fought, too. Siabala felt her worry and twisted it, trying to claim a bigger part of her heart.

Hurry, Avarielle, Shirina said, face strained.

Avarielle wanted to tell her off. To tell the world off. How was she supposed to think of something perfect to say to her son, maybe the final words they'd ever exchange?

There was so much she wanted to tell Rojon. So much about her past, and his father. Things she wished she'd told him more about. Not about the big stuff like cutting Siabala. He'd seen these moments. He'd known them.

She wanted to tell him about the first time a bloom grew in the garden in front of their house. Of how the sands of the West smelled at first light. Of how she'd been happy, and how she'd loved life.

But there was no time, and so she said the only thing she could, the thing that had always, and would always, be true.

"I love you, Rojon. And I'm so proud of you."

The connection severed, Shirina breathed out in exhaustion at giving Avarielle this moment, the hand dropping from her face as the sorceress took a step back, leaving coldness behind as she switched to reciting. Using old spells, no longer functional, to inspire the new spell, which would listen to her through her emotion. The blue whisp crawled on Shirina's shoulder, as though lending her strength.

Siabala screamed in her mind, blocking out the incantation the sorceress recited.

Avarielle wished her son could be here, but was glad he wasn't. Her eyes found Shirina's dark eyes and tear-stained face. The sorceress's chanting was clear, unbroken, and Avarielle knew that Shirina would not fail her.

Cassara's magic danced in the air, sparkling and beautiful, singing like the Wall of Loss, protecting her, stopping desperate green flames, keeping them safe.

Same endings. New beginnings.

Her body began to stiffen, Siabala fighting to break free. She held him in, clutching Graysword, kept focusing on her friends. On the battle she'd end.

On the strangeness of life, and its unforeseen paths.

Shirina stopped chanting, holding her staff, the spell at an end. Avarielle could feel her body harden, her breath stopping, though she did not die.

It's just you and me, now, Siabala chanted in her mind.

Sleep, Avarielle, Cassara's voice whispered in her mind, her magic warm and soothing. *I'll keep him away from you. I'll keep your mind and soul safe.*

Avarielle let the once princess of a small kingdom

coddle her to sleep, comforting her in her stone body. Keeping her safe.

How the protector had become the protected, and the protected the protector.

With her last moments of sight, she saw the queen, and the sorceress, both watching over her, both keeping her safe.

She was sorry she couldn't comfort their tears away, but was glad they were the last thing she saw.

61

Cassara saw Shirina's magic take hold of Avarielle, felt the draw of her magic. The call of Graydon, and Elihor. The need to stop their oldest enemy.

She closed her eyes, and vowed to protect her friend's heart, asking her magic to protect Avarielle's soul from Siabala.

If it took all of her magic again, she would gladly give it to save her friend.

But the magic cast to save one woman instead of holding a god prisoner proved easier and more forgiving. Sensing her friend slumbered, safe from Siabala, but out of her reach, too... seeing the once fiery warrior stand so still, so muted, having sacrificed herself to save them all... grief wracked Cassara Edoline's core. For Avarielle, for her city, for her people.

For Elihor, taken from Graydon. For her children, and

the scarred world they inherited. For the souls lost, misused, destroyed.

For Rojon, alone in the world.

Cassara Edoline turned her head to the sky and screamed her anguish, and Graydon screamed in turn. Her bubble of protective magic exploded outward, incinerating anyone casting green flames, and Siabala's monsters. The circle of magic kept going, through all of Rashim, beyond its borders, as far as Graydon would allow, destroying monsters across the two lands.

Ashes drifted in the windy day, the remains of Siabala's army.

Cassara stood atop her palace, watching Tally's surviving adepts vanish below, the ones who could teleport away. They would hunt them down. The few remaining ones would not survive long.

Silence blanketed Massir, as silent as Avarielle's heart.

Then, realizing the day had been won, that Siabala was contained, and his monsters defeated, a cheer of victory resounded, echoing in the streets below.

Cassara looked at her shattered city, took a deep breath of fresh air, felt her magic warm within her... she felt whole.

And broken. She would always be broken. But she was whole.

Rojon had heard Rina, and his mother, and he knew, even after their voices had grown silent, what had happened.

"I need to go," Rojon whispered.

"Where to?" Pakana asked, healed by the Larkhold Crimson Circle.

He looked at the trees. At her.

"I'm… I'm not sure. Massir, probably?"

She nodded, ever practical. "Let's hop on Rolly. We'll be faster that way."

"Or I can teleport," Crimson Circle Elite Klerisse offered, still fairly energetic for having healed so many.

"I think I'll walk," he said. They looked ready to protest, but then just nodded and prepared traveling supplies for him.

"We'll follow along later," Pakana said softly, understanding his need to be alone.

He left before midday, the pines of Kosel singing his passage, wishing he could feel something. A sense of urgency. A desire to go quickly. A belief that he could make a difference.

But he knew, deep down, that there was no need to hurry. Everything was already done, and nothing he could do would change its outcome.

All he could do was bear witness to it, and figure out his way in this new world. One without his mother, nor his home, nor that clear-cut path he once thought he understood.

～

Ramelia's eyes cracked open. The bed beneath her was comfortable, but her thirst choked her awake.

"Don't try to sit up." Altessa appeared at her side, gently dribbling water down her throat. "Your parents survived. I made sure to find them, for you."

You're alive, she wanted to say, but Altessa simply gently kissed her, and Ramelia, sleeping once again in the home of the royal family of Rashim, drifted away to a dreamless sleep, anchored by the warmth of the princess's hand in her own.

Cassara stood before Dayshon, the red in his eyes the only magic of Siabala's left. Too little to cause damage, too much to save one man.

"I lost Avarielle today," Cassara said, the words soft, the tears warm. "But I won't lose you."

Her magic was different, too, though it danced in the air still, instead of in the ground. Now she knew it to be a soul, and understood its kindness. Its fears. Its fierce love and gentle heart.

It had been hurt, and so had she.

Graydon had lost his beloved Elihor, and understood her pain.

My heart, she said, looking to Dayshon, and the magic went inside him, held him, cleansed him.

Dayshon gasped, blinked, his familiar eyes back, tired, but himself.

"Cassara?" he croaked out.

She laughed as she cried, Graydon settling back inside her, warm and strong as she hugged Dayshon and wished for this one moment to last forever, knowing it couldn't.

They would rebuild their city. And their people again. If her life was dedicated to eternally fixing what was broken, she could make peace with that.

No one tried to stop Rojon as he walked up the central roads of Massir, more of it seeming destroyed than saved. Yet the people seemed in good spirits, helping each other rebuild, save what possessions they could, and reclaim their city again. Soldiers did the bulk of the work. From what snippets of conversation Rojon gathered, the army had arrived too late, witnessing the explosion of light from Massir—their queen's magic—in the distance.

The battle was over, but the efforts to reclaim their city were just beginning.

Even the palace guards stepped aside to let him in, as though they knew he would be coming, even if it had taken him days of numb walking to reach the city.

Still, they waited for him. Cassara. Rina.

Even Altessa, who broke away from them to gather Rojon in his arms.

"You're okay," she said, and he held her back.

"You're okay," he repeated, and she squeezed him and

let go. Her eyes were covered with tears she could not hide.

Cassara came next, kissing his cheeks, hugging him. Then she, too, let go.

Shirina waited, dark cloak somehow not covered in the dust of her city. He wanted to congratulate her for being Elder. She'd earned this. She'd worked hard for it. But he couldn't get the words past the lump in his throat. Seeing them all, seeing his mother's absence… it made it all so much more real.

She gathered him in her arms, and he cried as she held him.

"I'll bring you to her," Shirina whispered.

Rojon followed her, feet leaden, like they wanted him to stop. To go elsewhere. To ask Rina to bring him back to Raklar, or to Keshmeer to continue his studies.

Anywhere but here. To see anything but *her*.

But still he followed, until Rina stepped aside, giving him the space she thought he needed.

His mother, standing near the ramparts of Massir, on cold granite, turned to cold stone. Her eyes were open, her lips slightly quirked up like usual, her fire extinguished but her intensity somehow captured. She held Graysword, the blade turned to stone with her.

If he saw her at night, he might think her still alive, the features so finely chiseled.

With a deep breath, he closed the gap separating them and placed a hand on her cheek. She was cold. Like ice, like winter, like a corpse… a sob escaped his lips and he took a step back, crumpling to his knees.

Rina was beside him in seconds, gathering him in her arms, holding him as grief wracked him.

"Can she hear me?" he eventually asked, both still kneeling on the ground. He had no idea how long they'd been there, but he felt spent.

"I don't think so," Rina said. "Cassara used her magic to keep her safe. To preserve as much of her sanity as the woman ever had."

The jest, made with the love of a lifetime of friendship, drew a chuckle from Rojon. The mirth evaporated almost immediately.

"Will you be able to save her, like you did me?"

Shirina's eyes softened. "You remember."

"I do. I remember you coming for me. Helping me find my way back." A blue light floated from inside Shirina's cloak before him. "I remember you, too."

The whisp rolled sideways, landing on Shirina's shoulder.

"She's not dead," Rina assured him. "She's holding Siabala in her. Think of her like the Wall of Loss. We just need to figure out how else to contain his soul, and then we'll be able to free her."

Rojon nodded, though his heart was riddled with doubts. He didn't want to know more, yet he needed to.

"How long?"

Rina looked at Avarielle, then back to him, meeting his eyes. "As long as it takes."

Maybe longer than my lifetime. But she'd have a chance again, to live, and laugh, and fight. If that was all she was given, then so be it.

All he could do to honor her was live the best life he could and hope that someday, before his soul returned to the Afterfate, his mother would return to him.

EPILOGUE

Cassara cradled a cup of hot tea, regaining a sense of normalcy she hadn't known in months. Her family was finally all under the same roof, and Dayshon had been able to retake some of his royal duties.

Today, three months after the attack, her schedule once again overflowed with meetings. The Builders, for an update on the city's rebuild, focusing on homes instead of walls. Count Lensky from the Corallite Canyons to the north of Massir, with an update on the surrounding villages. General Akhalon to report how the hunt for the traitors proceeded. And so many more. Diplomats from both Graydon and Elihor, old friends and new, everyone with their own demands and needs.

For now, Cassara sipped her tea and listened to her two youngest tell stories of their current lessons, and of their adventures in Edoline, her home.

Home. This was home. Dayshon laughed with them,

still unable to use his prosthetics after three months of healing, making travel in the crumbled city difficult. He met delegates in the palace, and she traveled where needed.

Altessa tickled Alexavier, who laughed so hard he fell off his seat, his joy echoing through their home.

Home.

An empty seat at the table bothered her. Not Shirina's —the sorceress might not even currently be in Massir, though she'd spent many weeks here helping with the rebuild, and with strengthening her Circle.

Rojon's seat remained empty. He'd stayed with her, and she didn't think he knew where to go. His grandfather and mother were both gone. Trevon had invited him to join him in the West, but Rojon had declined.

To stay near his mother. But Avarielle... Cassara sighed, looked up to find Dayshon observing her closely. He reached across the table and took her hand in his. She loved him, deeply, more now that she'd nearly lost him.

"Where did you just go?" Dayshon said, as Altessa entertained her younger siblings with tales of escaping monsters.

"It's Rojon," she whispered. Altessa turned slightly her way at her friend's name, but continued her story, sensing her parents' need for this moment.

"He's in the gardens, again," Dayshon said, looking as concerned as she was. That only made her love him more.

"I wish we could do something," she said.

"Me, too," Dayshon squeezed her hand. "It's just been so busy, with everything…"

"I know."

Her two youngest children came for kisses before starting the day's studies. It was time for all of their days to begin.

"I'm worried about Rojon, too," Altessa said. "I don't know how to help him."

"He needs to grieve," Cassara said.

"It's hard when she's not dead…" Altessa whispered.

She wasn't dead, no, but he might never see her again, should Shirina's Circle fail to find a way to contain Siabala. The thought gutted her. To distract herself, she started listing her meetings in her mind… *stop.*

With a deep breath, she realized she'd been avoiding saying goodbye to Avarielle. She'd been avoiding stepping into the fire of Rojon's grief, too busy coddling her own.

She looked over the table. "Altessa, I'd like you to meet with the Builders this morning. And Count Lensky. Not to mention the general, and a few others. I'll have Carla share the list with you."

"Me?" Altessa's eyes grew wide, panicked. Dayshon stayed quiet, simply observing.

"You can handle this, Altessa. Listen to them. Make them feel heard. Ask questions. If help is easily provided, do so. If not, tell them you'll seek answers. You know how to do this."

Her eldest nodded, reinforced herself.

"I should get ready, then." She kissed her parents and

swept out of the room, looking more regal with every step.

"What can I do?" Dayshon said, rolling his chair around the table to take her hands in his.

"Just continue being you," she said, kissing him on the lips.

Everything could wait. All matters of the court were important, but not more so than this. It had been three months, and it was time to put Avarielle Grayloft to rest, and help her son finally find some peace.

The earth shifted under Rojon's hands as he planted more flowers along Massir's Path of Roses. The rose bushes had been partly destroyed, but his care over the past few months helped revive them. He understood more of Graydon's plants than ever and found them as willing to court the magic and be molded as Elihor's, with the right time and care.

There was so much to learn, and the eagerness to return to his studies in Keshmeer warred with his heartache, which rooted him in place.

He couldn't imagine moving on like nothing had happened. Going back home, or anywhere in Raklar. Of seeing faces from before, telling them of his mother's passing. He'd been tempted to go with Trevon, but the old man had loved his mother dearly and his pain only amplified his own.

She wasn't dead. But she wasn't alive, either. It made everything worse. He wanted to dedicate his life helping her return to flesh, but he lacked the knowledge. Even Rina didn't know how, though she hunted for it, he knew. Relentlessly.

If an Elder of Ravenhold didn't know how to save his mother, than what chance did he have?

None. And so he stayed here, tending to the grounds of Massir, unwilling, maybe unable to go up the steps to where his mother's stone body still stood, unmoved since the day they'd defeated Siabala's army.

Stone on stone, the coldness of Graydon's palace held her in the harsh sun and colder nights. Snow would fall on her. Just another statue. Would she be forgotten? Would someday, centuries from now, someone find the statue and think it interesting? Or perhaps throw it in a landfill, the Grayloft name forgotten by history?

Or, even worse, what if she could only be changed safely back, Siabala's soul destroyed, centuries from now? What if she awakened and he was gone, and Cassara, and Rina, and she was all alone, in a world where no one loved her?

A sob escaped him and he troweled more vigorously, willing his pain away from him, into the earth. He grew numb again, letting the movements of his body dim those of his mind, willing his fears to be buried as deep as the roots of Kosel.

"Rojon," Cassara stood at the edge of the row of roses. A few had begun to bloom again, despite the late season.

They would be fine, he'd make sure of it. Plants were resilient, unlike human hearts.

"Yes?" he said, confused to see her here. It was almost noon, and usually she spent her days with delegates, leaving him to tend the earth and his dark thoughts. She wore simple pants and a shirt, with a light coat to ward off the day's chill.

"I need your help with the gardens, if you wouldn't mind."

"Oh, of course," he stood, stretched, and followed the queen to her gardens. She'd been kind to him, as had her family. Offering him a place to call home while he figured out his next steps, asking nothing in return. He'd already tended to the queen's garden, helping the cherry and apple trees she loved survive, those that could, and planting rows of beautiful perennials. He'd even helped reform Rina's teleportation circle. Both Circles still used them, useful for knowing where to reemerge on the grounds, and not to appear accidentally in the royal palace, to the ire, and swords, of its guards.

The gardens looked much the same as the last time he'd seen them, a few days ago. He followed her to the back, where the oldest trees provided shading, a hidden oasis on the palace grounds.

She stopped, turned to him.

"What can I help with?" he asked, confused.

"You can help me choose flowers for her," she said softly, then stepped aside. At the back of the gardens, in a perfect shady spot, her mother had been moved. Away from the hard light and weather, she would be protected here. The earth had been cleared alongside her, where he could plant beautiful blooms.

He drew in a deep breath and nodded, as though answering the queen's request, and he looked away from her and studied the bulbs and seeds she'd brought. A few he didn't know. Some reminded him of home. He chose a selection of each. Orange flowers, like her hair. Yellow, bright like her laughter. Red, like fire.

All day, Rojon and Cassara planted what would be beautiful come spring, and would weather the winter. As he worked, he began telling Cassara how to make sure the plants were kept, and how they should be encouraged to grow. How tall some should be, while others kept shorter.

She listened, asked questions. Then asked other questions, of his learnings, and studies, his work helping towns in Elihor rebuild and grow. When they were done, he sat back on his heels and looked at the tended earth, the scent of life around him.

"You know I'll make sure she'll always be taken care of, right?" Cassara said beside him, wiping sweat from her brow, her coat long abandoned. "No matter how long she stays like this. She's my family, too, Rojon. And so are you."

Rojon looked up. Followed the legs, slightly apart, like she was ready to pounce. Graysword, the blade's magic muted, held beside her almost casually. The strength of her arms. And her face, eyes open, slight grin on her face.

Like she'd looked death in the face and showed it she wasn't afraid.

"Your mother wouldn't want you to spend your days looking after her," Cassara said. "You have a life to lead. Mine is here. Shirina is near. And we will never abandon her. Or you."

When the flowers would bloom, they'd create a beautiful, wild, fiery tapestry around her. She'd look alive among them.

And, whenever she did turn back to flesh, when Siabala was finally destroyed, she would see them surround her, reminding her of who she is.

"I know," he said, smiling. Actually smiling, feeling free for the first time in months. "I think it's time I go back to Elihor."

Cassara leaned into him and hugged him.

"You'll always have a home here, Rojon."

"I know," he whispered back as he hugged her, feeling her warmth, knowing he was loved and not alone.

And, more importantly, knowing that his mother would never be alone, either. And that she would want him to live his life, even if it led him away from her.

Her black cloak unfurled behind her, caught in the breeze of Massir's small garden by the teleportation circle.

Tomorrow, she would head to Elihor. To bring Rojon back to his studies in Keshmeer, and to look at everything she could find in their old ruins, in the hopes of finding secrets not revealed to her in Graydon's ruins so far. About magic, and the magic of Siabala. About history, and the ground they walked upon.

Before her, surrounded by beautiful trees and freshly seeded earth, Avarielle Grayloft stood silently, clutching Graysword.

Shirina could feel the magic trapped in the statue. And she could feel Cassara's magic there, too. The Traveler's Song, keeping Avarielle safe from Siabala. Her mind would rest, and the one magic that had managed to keep him trapped before would hopefully keep him at bay.

So that Avarielle Grayloft might be free again one day, once Shirina had discovered enough about magic. Once she'd unraveled more of its secrets, as an Elder.

"You're too stubborn to die," Shirina told Avarielle. "I'll get you free, I promise."

She meant it. With everything she was, and everything she meant her Circle to be. She would save her and give her back the life she'd willingly sacrificed time and time again to save Graydon.

"I'll watch over her," Cassara said behind her.

"Thank you," Shirina answered. She turned to look at the queen. Since the battle, Cassara seemed at peace. Something that had been broken for so long seemed to have been fixed, and she didn't think it was due to the return of her magic.

No, not fixed. Simply accepted.

She wanted to say something to Cassara. About how

she had no intention of failing their friend. About how her Circle would never fail Graydon again, and how she appreciated her always standing up for it.

But looking into Cassara's sharp blue eyes, she knew the queen already knew it all.

"She'll owe me another one after I've saved her," Shirina said instead.

Cassara smiled, with just an edge of sadness. "I'll let you tell her that."

Shirina nodded, not trusting her voice to say more. She looked back at the warrior and the queen standing before her. At the shadows falling on Avarielle's face. She'd remember her for who she'd been. And who she would be again.

By the time Shirina crossed out of the garden to look for Rojon, she heard Cassara playing her flute, strengthening her spell, or simply her heart.

Shirina's steps faltered, but she kept walking, toward her Circle, and the buried knowledge that would save Avarielle Grayloft.

The story isn't over.

To be continued in Protectors of a Broken Land, *the third and final Broken Land trilogy!*

Sign up to my newsletter at www.mariebilodeau.com to be the first to get updates.